Frances Fleetwood was born in London and brought up in Devon. She was educated at a French school in Torquay and at the Sorbonne in Paris. In 1926 she published a book of verse, *The Threshold*, but a job as a secretary to a political journalist left her little time for more writing. She was involved in Carol of Rumania's abortive attempt to regain his throne in 1926; later she met General Umberto Nobile and translated his account of the ill-fated dirigible *Italia* into English. Returning to England in 1933 she took a job with a travel agent and during the war worked in the Royal Aeronautical Society. For the past ten years she has lived in Italy, working as an interpreter during the summer. Visits to the Adriatic aroused her interest in the towns of Romagna and the Marches; also in the Malatesta family which inspired *Concordia*.

CONCORDIA

Concordia

The story of Francesca da Rimini, told by her daughter

FRANCES FLEETWOOD

SPHERE BOOKS LIMITED
30/32 Gray's Inn Road, London WC1X 8JL

First published in Great Britain by W. H. Allen & Co Ltd 1971

Published by Sphere Books 1975

Set in Intertype Baskerville

Printed in Great Britain by
Hazell Watson & Viney Ltd,
Aylesbury, Bucks

ISBN 0 7221 3542 4

INTRODUCTION

A charged silence filled the room on the first floor of a house in fifteenth-century Rimini: each of its occupants was following a different train of thought. Drawn curtains kept out most of the summer heat and light, but the tall, slim girl who stood reading at a desk had pulled two of them slightly apart, so that a ray of sunshine slanted through and gilded her hair.

Watching her, while he pretended to concentrate on the drawings spread out on the table before him, the young Lord of Rimini wondered idly why he found her so attractive. True, that shimmering hair would make an angel's halo, and there was something angelic—or at any rate sexless—about her undeveloped body in its simple white gown. Isotta might one day be a beautiful woman, but at the moment she was just an overgrown child with too strongly marked features and no breasts. Had it been worth while to forgo an afternoon's hawking, for the sake of her company?

The third person, Madonna Orsola—a comfortable, middle-aged widow—kept fluttering a small black-lace fan; at intervals of a minute or so, she coughed—a dry, artificial cough. It was an irritating sound and she meant it to be: the fluttering fan was intended to suggest that she found the room airless; the cough was her way of indicating that, to a person of her refinement, the dust from a quantity of old books piled on the floor was intolerable.

Sigismond Malatesta's impulse was to tell her to go to hell, but it did not suit his plans to be rude to Isotta's chaperone. He had been agreeably surprised when Francesco degli Atti had agreed to let his daughter come and help sort out the books collected by Sigismond's father and grandfather, before they were housed in the splendid new castle that he intended to build. The old man may merely have wished to stand well with me, reflected Sigismond—at twenty-one already an astute judge of other men's motives—but I'm inclined to acquit him of sycophancy. Probably he genuinely thought it would be good for Isotta's education. (And so it will—but perhaps not in the way he meant. . . .) In any case, he could not have sent his motherless daughter unchaperoned.

So Sigismond made the best of it, saying with his most charming smile: 'You should take care of that cough, Madonna Orsola.'

She flushed with pleasure at having attracted his notice: 'Indeed, my lord, I trust it has not disturbed you. My throat is delicate, and the dust . . .'

May it choke you! thought Sigismond. Aloud, he said: 'The books have only just been unpacked, after many years. Before you come again I will have them cleaned. Meanwhile . . .' he rang a small handbell, 'you must meet Madonna Ginevra, my wife. She has, I know, a wonderful specific to cure any cough.' He knew nothing of the sort—he was not sufficiently interested in his wife to care what remedies she possessed—but she was an ailing little creature, always dosing herself with physic. He was prepared to bank on it that she swallowed cough-mixture by the flacon.

His keen blue eyes watched with amusement the conflict in Madonna Orsola's face. She did not want to leave her charge alone with a perilously handsome man, who already had a reputation as a lady-killer; but to meet Ginevra d'Este was too good an opportunity for a hard-up widow to miss. The matter was taken out of her hands when a servant appeared and Sigismond ordered him: 'Escort this lady to my wife's apartment and, if Madonna Ginevra is still resting, see that the ladies-in-waiting provide a cup of cordial and keep her entertained until Madonna is ready to receive her.' (And may she sleep for a good hour yet! he thought hopefully.)

That settled, he leaned comfortably back in his chair and waited for Isotta to make the next move. By all the laws of the game she should, after a decent pause of a minute or two, have stopped reading and asked him some question—no matter how silly or irrelevant—as an opening gambit. But the child didn't stir: through all the conversation she had remained absorbed in her book. Could she really be more interested in it than in him?

'Isotta!' he called, with a note of irritation in his voice. Had he used that tone to Ginevra, she would have dropped her book and looked at him like a startled rabbit. Sigismond liked to frighten people, but, illogically, did not like those people whom he could frighten.

Roused from her absorption, the girl smiled at him. 'Yes . . . Sigismond?' There was just a shade of hesitation in her voice. He had suggested—in fact, insisted—that she call him by his first name, but it did not come easily to her: she still looked at him across the gulf of years that separated them. She would be happier calling me 'Uncle' Sigismond, he thought ruefully. 'Stop reading and come here,' he ordered. 'I want to discuss these plans with you.'

It was his habit to 'discuss' the plans of his new castle with all and sundry. That is to say, he told them what he intended to do, and they said 'Yes, my love!' or 'Yes, my Lord!', in admiration, real or feigned. Only Isotta took the word seriously and made suggestions—often sensible ones, as when she had said that the library should face west: 'Not north, or it will be cold and damp in winter, when one wants to use it most; nor east, for in the morning one has little time to read; nor south, or it will be too hot in summer; but it is pleasant to sit reading in the sunset.'

With a child's vision, she saw his castle as he himself imagined it: the six tall towers, the gatehouse with inlet marble beautifying its warm red brick; the walls, so thick and strong that they would even resist the new menace of gunpowder, protecting a keep that was spacious and airy, with large windows and high frescoed rooms graced with treasures of crystal, ivory and gold, with tapestry hangings and carven furniture—all the lovely things that he possessed, or hoped to acquire. It was as real to her as the miniatures of legendary castles in her father's books—Montauban, Camelot, Joyous Gard . . .

Now, however, like all the others, she was saying 'yes' and 'yes', without really giving her mind to the subject. He was on the point of calling her sharply to order, when she anticipated him by asking unexpectedly: 'Who was Concordia Malatesta?'

He reflected a moment: 'There were two of them. I expect you mean the wife of old Malatesta of Verucchio. It was she who brought the money into our family.'

'Would she have been a child in 1290?'

'No, she was dead long before then. That must have been her granddaughter—daughter of Giovanni Malatesta and Francesca da Polenta. Why do you ask?'

For answer, she placed before him the small book that she was still holding. Its pages were yellowed and the ink had faded, but on the fly-leaf could be made out, in clear fine handwriting: *Concordia Malatesta*, and the date 1290. Below it was the chequered shield of the Malatesti, neatly coloured in scarlet and gold, and an animal, at the sight of which Sigismond burst out laughing: 'She must have meant that for the Malatesta elephant, but it looks much more like a fat white pony, with its tail where its nose should be! Whatever is this book?'

'It is difficult to read,' admitted Isotta, 'the ink is so faded. But it seems to be a kind of diary. I have made out the first page.' And, laying the book in front of Sigismond, she perched on the arm of his chair and read it over his shoulder:

'RAVENNA, 5 September 1290. Tomorrow is my fourteenth birthday . . .'

'Think of it, Sigismond!—she was the same age as me. I shall be fourteen tomorrow.'

. . . and it is nearly a year since the terrible thing happened that has changed my life. The day after, with Aunt Chiara, I shall leave my grandfather's house for the convent, and there I shall stay until I am old enough to take the vows. It is the only thing left for me to do. The family want to get rid of me, I know—and, after all, who would marry me now? When I told Aunt Chiara that I felt my life was coming to an end before it had really begun, she said it was a wicked thought: I must remember that I shall spend my time praying for my mother's soul, and perhaps our prayers—hers and mine—will save her from being damned eternally.

'What does it all mean, Sigismond? What is the terrible thing that happened, and why should the child—or the child's aunt—expect her mother to be damned eternally?'

Sigismond smiled: he liked the way Isotta described a girl of her own age as a child. He liked, too, her quick rejection of the idea of eternal damnation: this young creature had a mind of her own, he reflected.

'Oh, the poor girl couldn't face up to the scandal, and I believe she did, in fact, become a nun.'

'But what was the scandal?'

'Do you mean to say you've never heard of it? I thought the odd behaviour of the Malatesti was gossip all through Romagna. They've hardly yet stopped talking about my poor little cousin Parisina.'

'You forget,' said Isotta drily, 'I have no mother to collect a circle of gossips. My father's friends are all grave, elderly men who discuss politics and business. If by any chance one of them starts on a story that promises to be amusing, my father stops him, saying: "Not before the child!" . . .'

At that, Sigismond laughed outright: 'Well, little Isotta, you have come to me to have your education completed —and so you shall. Here is the story: Giovanni—a remote great-uncle of mine—came home one night to find his beautiful Francesca in bed with her lover, who was his own brother Paolo. In true Malatesta style, he murdered them both, married another wife within the year, and ended his days as the highly respected *podestà* of Pesaro.'

Isotta looked him straight in the eyes and said, with a shade of irony: 'You seem to admire your Great-Uncle Giovanni.'

'I do. He was rough and tough, ugly and deformed—they called him Gianciotto, Gianni the Lame. But it didn't prevent his being a fine rider and a brave captain of men. And when his wife deceived him, he didn't torture her with a mock trial, as my father-in-law Este did to Parisina. He simply ran her through with his sword. What else would you have had him do?'

'Would you have done the same?'

'I would have done the same as any one of those three. As Francesca, I would have gone to bed with the handsome Paolo; as her husband, I would have killed her for it . . .' he paused a moment, and Isotta prompted him: 'And as Paolo?'

'I wouldn't have said "no" to Francesca. But somehow I think her husband would not have caught me—and if he had, maybe our lovely Francesca would have remained alive—and a widow.'

Subtly, their relationship had changed. Sigismond was no longer a man of the world talking to a little girl: he had accepted her as someone whom he could treat on equal terms. 'I did not know tomorrow was your birthday,' he said, after a pause, 'otherwise I would have had a gift ready for you. What would your father allow you to accept from me? A pair of gloves? A gold chain? A book?'

She answered unhesitatingly: 'There is something that would give me great pleasure. May I have this book?'

'That?' His tone was scornful: 'A little old notebook, written by a child? A beggarly gift indeed!'

'No!' protested Isotta. 'I don't know why—perhaps because she was the same age as myself—but I feel I could be fond of Concordia. I want to know more about her.'

'Oh, have it by all means—and tomorrow I will give you something better.' He rose and put the book into her outstretched hands.

Isotta stood on tiptoe, bringing her eyes almost on a level with his own, and impulsively kissed his cheek—the quick, cool kiss that a child gives in gratitude for a present. It was a dangerous game to play with Sigismond: in a moment he had seized her. Expertly, he kissed her temple, barely stirring the silken hair; still more softly he touched the eyelids that she had instinctively closed; then, without warning, he fastened on to her mouth with a force and fury that would have disconcerted a professional courtesan.

He felt her shock-reaction and it reminded him of his wedding night, three years previously: how Ginevra had flinched and whimpered, and the moist reproach with which she had gazed at him next morning. (Oh, these pure virgins—how little fun one has with them!) I've made a mistake, he thought: now the child will run in tears to that fool of a governess, and her father will never let her come here again. . . . And that would be a pity. It irked his pride to be living in a rented house, like any common citizen, now that he had pulled down the old Gattolo of his ancestors and had not yet rebuilt on his site. One of the compensations had been his acquaintance with his near neighbours, learned old Francesco degli Atti and his oddly attractive daughter.

Isotta, however, stood her ground. When he released her she was pale and shaken: she licked a trickle of blood from her lip, but her eyes were shining. 'I am not ready yet,' she said at last, with grave simplicity. 'Be patient with me a little longer, and I'll not disappoint you.'

Shamefacedly he muttered: '*Galeotto fu il libro e chi lo scrisse.*' It was as near an apology as his pride would let him make.

'*What* did you say?'

'I was quoting a line from Messer Dante Alighieri, who was . . .'

'Of course I know who he was!' she interrupted impatiently: 'I am studying his *Commedia* with my father.'

'And yet you didn't recognise one of the best-known lines from the *Inferno*?'

'My father says the *Inferno* is not fit reading for a young girl. We started half-way up *Purgatorio*, and have worked our way through the first four Circles of the *Paradiso*.'

'And are you enjoying it?' His tone was casual, but it was a test question: Sigismond had no use for would-be intellectual young women who went into ecstasies over books that he knew were far above their understanding.

'My father is,' said Isotta with a shrug.

'And you . . .?'

'I must lack appreciation of great poetry, for I find it very dull.'

He gave a shout of laughter: 'Good girl! At least you're honest about it. Well, come here, and I'll read you the *Inferno*, starting with Paolo and Francesco. I promise you'll not find *that* dull.'

'And what will Madonna Orsola tell my father?'

'Madonna Orsola will *not* tell your father that she spent a delightful afternoon discussing imaginary ailments with my wife—as I hope she will often do. Somehow, I feel that those two will have a great deal in common.'

'Like us,' breathed Isotta, caressing the book. 'Your first present!' she said, contentedly.

'In a day or two I will give you a gold chain, with a medallion portrait of myself. You must wear it under your dress, and everyone will think it is your patron saint.'

She looked him up and down with a quick glance, appraising his sapphire-blue eyes and sardonic mouth; the high-bridged nose and jutting chin that formed a perfectly balanced profile under the mane of crisp auburn curls, held by a golden fillet. There was gold, too, on his crimson velvet doublet and on the broad sword-belt into which, even in the peace of his own home, a jewelled dagger was thrust. 'You are far too handsome for a saint,' she said candidly, 'and far too richly dressed. Your late brother would have better suited the part.'

'Poor Galeotto! Still, if he hadn't starved himself to death with his fasting and mortifications, he'd have lost me Rimini. As it was, I had to save it for him once, when I was just about your present age.'

Isotta was listening to him, like a child intent on hearing a fairy-tale, lost to everything else in the world; but Sigismond, even while he showed off to the girl whom he had now firmly decided to make his mistress, remained alert as a fox. He sensed Madonna Orsola's return before she lifted the door-curtain, and by the time she entered he was back in his chair, with the castle plans in his hand, saying: 'You see, I intend to have a niche over the drawbridge, with the Malatesta elephant in white marble.' Then, noticing that Isotta still looked somewhat dazed, he distracted attention from her by making himself pleasant to her governess: 'I trust that Madonna Ginevra was able to soothe your cough? Yes? That is fine. It is good for her to have company at this moment. You know, she is expecting our first child—her state of health does not permit her to enjoy many distractions, and she is often lonely. Meanwhile, your young charge has found me an interesting family document. Pray ask Messer Francesco if she may come here tomorrow.'

'Tomorrow is her birthday and she will spend it with her father. But perhaps next day . . .'

'Next day, then—and meanwhile, Isotta, will you do me the favour of starting to copy that little book? I have no time or patience to decipher the faded handwriting.'

'Indeed I will!' said Isotta eagerly. And in the peace of her room that evening she sat down to her task.

This is what she wrote . . .

Concordia Malatesta: Her Book

Ravenna, 5 September 1290

Tomorrow is my fourteenth birthday, and it is nearly a year since the terrible thing happened that has changed my life. The day after, with Aunt Chiara, I shall leave my grandfather's house for the convent, and there I shall stay until I am old enough to take the vows. It is the only thing left for me to do. The family want to get rid of me, I know—and, after all, who would marry me now? When I told Aunt Chiara that I felt my life was coming to an end before it had really begun, she said it was a wicked thought: I must remember that I shall spend my time praying for my mother's soul, and perhaps our prayers —hers and mine—will save her from being damned eternally.

I could not tell Aunt Chiara—it would have hurt and shocked her too much—that I do not care about saving my own soul, if it means separation from my mother, and my father too. For if God will condemn her, who was guilty of nothing but love, what will happen to him, who has two deaths to his charge? They will tell me I ought not to ask questions of that kind—I must just accept all they say as true. And they will try to change me, to break my pride, the pride that I have inherited from Giovanni my father—Gianciotto, who accepted that nickname and wore it as a badge of courage. Worst of all, they will take away my name, call me Suor Pia, or Angelica, or something that I am not and cannot imagine that I ever shall be. So let me write it once more in full: *I am Concordia Malatesta, daughter of Giovanni the Lame*—and in spite of all that has happened I am proud of it.

Three months ago, when I made the great decision—and I made it of my own free will, for his sake—I started to write everything down as it happened. I wanted to see *why* it happened, if it could have been prevented, if I myself had any share or guilt in the matter. So I have told everything, right from the beginning.

I

I was born, Mother told me, at Gradara, and that is certainly the first place I remember. She liked it, I think, better than the grim old Gattolo at Rimini; for at Gradara the pure, hilltop air blows in at the windows: we could stand looking down on the trees and out over the valley towards Casteldimezzo and the ridge between us and the sea; or to the right, across the drawbridge into the citadel at our feet. But towards sunset Mother used often to climb the steep wooden ladders that led from Father's bedroom to the top of the keep and look towards the north, from which she had come. Ravenna itself was too far away to see, but sometimes on very clear days there was a purplish shadow on the horizon, which she said was the outpost of the Ravenna pinewoods, somewhere beyond Cesenatico. She had been happy in her childhood home with all her brothers and sisters—nine of them altogether. Often she talked to me of Chiara, who had become a nun, and of the youngest, Samaritana, with whom she had shared a room till her marriage. I think she was sorry for me, because I was an only child.

My very first memory is of Gradara; the bedroom where, later, the tragedy happened. It must have been a Saturday afternoon, for our hair had been washed in preparation for Sunday, and it was drying in the sunshine by the open window. My mother looked very young—and in fact she was under twenty, for she had been married at sixteen and I could not then have been any older than three. Her favourite tire-woman, Monna Biancarosa, was combing out her hair. I remember how it sparkled in the sunshine, and how I came up to her and stroked it. She took me on her knee and laid her cheek against my head.

'The child has hair like yours, my lady—soft as silk,' said Biancarosa, braiding a plait for her and twisting it with pearls.

My mother sighed: 'She is too much like me. I am afraid for her.' 'Afraid, my lady?' 'The Malatesta are a hard race. I wonder if she will be able to stand up to them.'

The words impressed me, though I had no idea what they meant. 'What is Malatesta?' I asked. 'That is your name, my darling.' 'But my name is Concordia.' 'Your second name—the name of your father's family.'

Perhaps that first set me thinking about my father. I had really seen very little of him, though I often heard him as a rough voice shouting in the stables or the guardroom: a dark, twisted man with a curious shambling walk, from whom I shrank instinctively. As a rule he took no notice of me, but once—that must have been some months later, for we were back in Rimini—he caught me up and tossed me towards the ceiling. I screamed, terrified: 'Mother! Mother!' And he, in exasperation, dumped me back in her lap, saying: 'Here, take your . . .!' The last words escaped me, but probably they were 'puling brat', for that is what he often called me, later, when I annoyed him.

Somehow I knew my mother was angry, though her face did not change and her voice was very quiet as she said: 'You frightened her, Giovanni. She is only four—too small for such rough play.'

But she was loyal. If she defended me against my father, she would do the same for him against me.

One morning at Gradara, she and I were walking down the steep road that leads from the castle through the fortified enclosure below it, where our servants and their families and some of the countryfolk live. It was a saint's-day and our chaplain, Don Angelo, was to hold a service for the people in the small open square inside the gatehouse, that we, out of courtesy, were to attend. (Normally, of course, we had services read for us in the castle, or on special festivals went outside the walls to Santa Sofia.) Father, who usually rode up and down the street, had on this occasion gone ahead of us on foot, and a group of children were clustered round one larger boy who was imitating his walk. They were laughing, and it was then that I heard for the first time—without knowing its meaning—the nickname 'Gianciotto'. The imitation was a good one and I too burst out laughing. At the sound the boys looked round, saw us, and hastily scampered away.

Only three times in my life was Mother really angry with me, and this was the first. She did not slap me, but her cold voice was worse than a blow. 'Concordia,' she said, 'that was a cruel and thoughtless thing to do, and tonight, when you say your prayers, you must ask God's pardon for it.' I looked up at her, astonished, and then she explained more gently that once my father had been an active young man, but an illness had lamed him. 'You must never laugh at a person's deformity, least of all at your own father,' she said. 'Remember, he resents his condition, and that makes him bad-tempered. So try not to be frightened of him—and if you are, don't show it.'

After that lecture I do not think I loved my father any the better, but I did feel sorry for him, as I might have for a bird with a broken wing, and I tried not to make him angry. The best thing, I found, was to keep out of his way when he came to my mother's room. I sensed that he did not like me any more than I liked him, but it was not till I was eight years old that I found out the real reason.

2

That was one of the most humiliating days of my life; yet it had started so well. Uncle Paolo had come to stay with us, bringing his son Uberto. At that time I loved my uncle far better than my father: he was so handsome and so gay, and always beautifully dressed. He moved gracefully like a woman, and I could have sensed his presence with my eyes shut, by the slight rustle of silk and the perfume from his long, curled hair.

During his visits we all seemed happier and better-tempered. My pale, silent mother looked like a girl again. She had not much more colour than usual, but she seemed to glow like an alabaster vessel when the lamp within it is lit. Uncle Paolo always brought her a book, so beautifully illuminated that, even before I could read, I used to stand on a stool at the tall reading-desk and turn the pages to see the miniatures—scarlet and blue, glittering with gold-leaf.

This time he had brought a present for me too, and a most unexpected one: a boy's suit of soft blue velvet, with long hose of a deeper shade; a crimson cap with a hawk's feather, and a pair of white-leather riding-boots embroidered in gold. When I unpacked the suit and clapped my hands in delight, my mother looked astonished. Paolo explained: 'Last time I saw Gianni, he said the child was growing up and it was time we taught her to ride. So I had these things made for her—she'll be safer riding astride.'

Next morning I could hardly wait till Nannie came to help me dress. While she was fastening buttons and laces I danced with impatience. There was no mirror in the small dressing-room where I slept when Father was at home, and I could not disturb Mother so early, to look into hers. How could I see myself? The answer came in a flash: I ran down to the courtyard and climbed on to the coping of the well. Down there, deep below, in a patch of sky backed by the red brick castle wall there laughed up at me a figure like one of the page-boys in Mother's books: long, slim legs, a doublet bluer than the sky behind it, and a small, clean-cut face under a red cap. Nannie had braided my hair and tucked it under the cap, lest it should come loose as I rode.

Uberto too had got up early. He was much older than me—fourteen, which I thought almost grown-up—but he still had a boy's appetite and was not too grand to come into the kitchen with me for a cup of milk and a slice of bread, before the grown-ups were around.

The first to come was my father, who waved briefly to us as he crossed the courtyard, going towards the drilling-ground where a groom was walking his horse. Then we heard horsehoofs descending the steep, narrow street that led to the lower gate of the citadel. It was always thronged, and the horse's shoes used to slip precariously on the cobbles, but he never had an accident.

Uncle Paolo, Uberto and I went out by the postern gate and down the grassy slope, to join him in the meadow below, where other grooms were holding our horses. Mother did not come: she said she had a headache. This was odd, for she looked perfectly well, and she was never a person to fuss about small ailments. Since . . . it . . . happened, I have often wondered what the real reason was. Perhaps she was reluctant to watch me run the risk of riding for the first time? Maybe she felt nervous at being in Paolo's company, even in the presence of us children? Did she fear that my father would notice how eager she was for that company? Or was the prospect of walking with him in the fragrant meadows on that lovely May morning so alluring that, for her soul's sake, she felt obliged to refuse it?

The sunshine sparkled on dewy grass and I filled my hands with flowers as we walked. Uberto remarked rather scornfully that dressing like a boy didn't make me behave like one: boys didn't pick flowers.

'They do, when they have a pretty woman to give them to,' said my uncle, 'And Concordia, I know, is picking them for the loveliest lady in Romagna.' That was nice of him, I thought: he always seemed to understand, and went out of his way to be pleasant to me. But was it to *me*, I wonder now, or to my mother's little daughter?

We soon reached the spot where Father was waiting for us. He looked well on horseback, for there his deformity was not apparent; and as he sat at ease his face had relaxed into something that was almost a smile. His head was bare, but otherwise he was dressed as if for a foray, in leathern jerkin and cuirass. Even when he rides for pleasure he wears his cuirass, because it supports his spine and eases the strain on his weak leg; but at the time I did not know that: I simply thought how imposing and martial he looked.

Uncle Paolo, on the other hand, was very elegant. As he took off his crimson cloak, his sword-belt and velvet cap, and gave them to a groom to hold, I saw that he was all in black, except for a crimson scarf wound, bandit-fashion, to hold back his dark curls. There were some gleams of silver in the slashes of his velvet tunic, and silver buttons looped up the sleeves that otherwise would almost have swept the ground.

My father's face lit with a sardonic smile: 'Mm! . . . Lucifer!' he commented. 'Is that the latest fashion in Florence, or are you in mourning for your lost youth?'

A fleck of colour rose in my uncle's cheeks, but he answered pleasantly enough that he hadn't begun to feel himself old.

'You're nearer thirty-five than thirty, my lad,' said Father with audible satisfaction. 'And what's more, you can't conceal the fact, with a son whose head has already reached the level of your eyebrows.'

Suavely Uncle Paolo replied: 'It is good to watch one's son growing to manhood.' Uberto gave his high-pitched boyish laugh and murmured a word that I had heard from the men-at-arms when they were fencing together: '*touché!*'

'What did all that mean?' I whispered to him; but he shook his head, as if to say that he couldn't explain with the others listening.

That conversation stayed in my mind, with others that I had heard without really understanding them. Grown-ups, it seemed, were always talking in riddles, or meaning something different from what they actually said. I did, however, realise that my father and my uncle had each been trying to annoy the other, and that both had succeeded. It was the first time that I had noticed any tension between those two.

'Come!' said Father, 'we're wasting time. Get the child mounted, and let's start.'

He looked at me, I noticed, with no surprise at finding me dressed as a boy. Had he asked Uncle Paolo to bring me those clothes, and given him some idea of my size? Otherwise, how could they have fitted so well? There was something like approval in his eyes. 'With her fair hair hidden, she looks like a Malatesta,' he said. And that, from him, was a compliment.

Our visitors had their own horses. Uberto's was a neat little cob, bigger than a pony but less than a full-grown horse. Both of them looked round to see if there was a pony for me, but there was only a black stallion with a white star on his forehead.

'Nerone!' exclaimed Uncle Paolo, and whistled. 'If he bolts she'll never be able to hold him.' 'He'll not bolt,' said my father, a trifle impatiently. 'He was a good horse once, but now he's grown old and sedate. Anyway, he's on the long rein. Uberto will ride beside her and give her a hand if it is needed. We will ride behind for the moment and let the children set the pace.' (Uberto, I could see, didn't like being classed with me as a child—but tact has never been my father's strong suit.)

Uncle Paolo lifted me into the saddle, then a groom shortened the stirrups for me. Nerone twitched his ears and tossed his mane, as if surprised to find such a light weight on his back.

Then we set off, Uberto's hand resting lightly on my rein. I seemed very high up, and it was not pleasant. True, I had been on a horse several times, but always sitting in front of some grown-up. My uncles from Ravenna, my mother's brothers, had a way of breezing down upon us in Rimini and catching me up to their saddle-bows. Now I was on my own, except for any help that Uberto could give me in an emergency.

Without warning the emergency came. As we rode alongside a farmstead hedge, a large brown hen, flapping and squawking, started up between Nerone's forefeet. He whinnied, pranced, and was away like a flash. The rein whipped from Uberto's unpractised hand. I lost my stirrups at once and was flung forward on the horse's neck, where I lay with closed eyes, frantically clutching his thick mane.

In my ears sang the wind of that mad course, and through it I heard confusedly the men and the boy all shouting together: Uberto, I think, was trying to explain that it wasn't his fault; my father was cursing him and yelling to Nerone to stop, while Uncle Paolo was calling to me to lie still and dig in with my hands and knees. Then I heard horsehoofs coming up fast, overtaking me; I felt Nerone check, bucking and twisting uncertainly. (Afterwards, Uncle Paolo told me that they had ridden up on either side and then curved inwards to head him off.)

Whether I was thrown at that moment, or fainted and slipped to the ground, or was snatched down by my uncle,

I do not know. Everything went dark, and when I opened my eyes I found myself lying on the grass, with my head on Paolo's knee. He was dabbing my face and wrists with a handkerchief soaked in water that one of the grooms had fetched from the farmyard well.

'It's all right, Gianni,' I heard him say. 'She's not hurt, only frightened.'

My father had not dismounted. He sat looking down at me. 'She always *is* frightened,' he said, bitterly. 'I thought I could make a man of her.' The cold contempt of his tone brought tears welling to my eyes. 'But she's not a man, brother Gianni, nor even a boy—she's just a little girl, and you put her on an unmanageable horse.' 'When you and I were her age, we could ride anything in my father's stables.'

By this time I was crying helplessly. I had forgotten about being a boy, or behaving like a Malatesta. All I could do was to wail that I wanted my mother.

Uncle Paolo stood up with me in his arms: 'I'll take her back,' he said.

'And waste this fine morning? No, that's no treat for a guest. Take Uberto with you, and go for a gallop on the sands, from Cattolica towards Rimini. All's quiet in that direction, but just in case of trouble, you'd better buckle on your sword again and have the grooms with you for extra protection.' He edged his horse closer: 'Here, hand her up!'

A trifle reluctantly, I felt, my uncle transferred me, and I exchanged the velvet softness of his shoulder for the hard, polished surface of my father's cuirass.

Again I was puzzled by the way the grown-ups were behaving. My uncle had been a shade too eager to sacrifice his morning's pleasure; my father a shade too peremptory in preventing him. It was not from fondness for me, I felt sure: he didn't care much for me at the best of times, and now he was thoroughly disgusted at the exhibition I had made of myself. I stole a glance at him, saw that he was scowling, and choked back my tears.

Soon we had climbed the hill and reached the lower gate of the citadel. Something must have been seen from above, for the door swung open at once and the door-keeper asked anxiously: 'Was there an accident, my lord? Is the Contessina hurt?' 'Not hurt,' said my father briefly. 'She had a shock when her horse bolted, so I am taking her home.'

As we clattered up the slope I felt grateful to him: he had not given me away. Not so much for my sake, I think, as for his family pride. And I, for the same reason, controlled myself and did not cry before all the people.

Having arrived in the courtyard, he stepped off on to the mounting-block and pulled me across his shoulder, like a sack of corn. Then, limping more than usual under my weight, he carried me upstairs to my mother's room.

3

Cool and beautiful as ever, Mother was standing by the northern window at her reading-desk, absorbed in the new romance that Uncle Paolo had brought her. The two elder ladies were working at an upright tapestry frame, while the youngest, Maria Pia, was standing uncomfortably in a corner—since it was not seemly that she should sit when her mistress and the others were on their feet—inexpertly jabbing a needle into some embroidery.

Father put me down, giving me a none too gentle push that sent me reeling towards my mother: 'Here, take your whinnying filly and put her back into skirts!' Then he swore violently (or so I guessed from my mother's exclamation of protest and the shocked look of her ladies) and added: 'What's the good of a brood mare if she can't—or won't—foal one a brace of stallions?'

I was puzzled: he seemed to be talking about horses, yet his words sounded like a reproach to my mother. Then I saw that her ladies' faces had grown red, and that their eyes were turned upon her. She, ivory-pale, did not answer for a moment—just signed to the women to leave the room. 'And take the child with you,' she said aloud.

The eldest, Monna Cristina, grasped my hand and took me out. Once outside, Maria Pia began to giggle; Biancarosa slapped her face, saying that my mother was a long-suffering angel. The other woman intervened, and in the confusion they forgot all about me. I took the opportunity of slipping back into the room, between the door and the arras that veiled it. I knew it was wrong—and worse, unladylike—but I could not help it. Even at that age I had guessed that there was something wrong between my parents. Instinctively I knew that now there would be an explanation between them, and I might find out what it was.

I heard her saying with weary disgust: 'Is that all I am to you, Giovanni—a brood mare useless at stud?' 'What else? Have you even tried to be of any help or comfort to me? You find me repulsive by night and boring by day—and from the first you haven't attempted to conceal it.'

'Oh, Giovanni . . .' (her voice quivered) '. . . I was so young.'

'Do you think I have had a fair deal from life, or from you?' My father's tone was controlled and bitter. 'You mightn't believe it, to look at me now, but as a boy I was healthy enough. No beauty like young Paolo, but as sound as an oak and as agile as the squirrel in its boughs. And then, at seventeen, to have my whole life wrecked—and not even in battle. If it had been, at least men would have respected me; but that a mere fever—or, as my father believed, the ill-wishing of an old hag—should have made me a gangling cripple—a figure of fun to the village boys and of repulsion to you . . . !'

He was out of my sight, but through a hole in the tapestry I could see my mother, and she was wringing her hands: 'Giovanni, why didn't you come and woo me yourself?' 'And see you shrink from my deformity?' 'I might not have done, if I had accepted you of my own free will. In any case, I would have had to marry the man my father had chosen for me. You need not have deceived me.'

'Deceived?' He gave his short, sarcastic laugh. 'You use hard words, Francesca. You know quite well it is customary, if a man is away at the wars or on urgent business, as I was at the time, to handle his marriage contract by proxy.' 'So you sent your brother—hid behind your brother. Is that your famed Malatesta courage?'

My heart began to flutter; for, young as I was, I guessed that she had said the one thing that would most infuriate my father. And in fact, he swore one of his great oaths, took her by the shoulders and began to shake her violently. Now I could see them both. His face was convulsed with rage, and I was afraid he might try to strangle her. She thought so too, for I saw her put up both hands to shield her throat.

'No man could call me a coward—and live!' he said at last, as he released her: 'Be careful, my fine lady.'

'I am sorry, Giovanni.' She was not crying, but her breath came in little gasps. 'But you had so many chances. You could have come to meet me on the journey. You could have arranged for me to arrive in daylight. You could have come to me in a lighted bedroom. But to let me wake as I did, unsuspecting, the next morning . . .' Her voice broke and then rose in a wild cry reminding me of the seagulls that wailed round the Gattolo of Rimini in the winter storms: 'Oh, that was a terrible thing to do to a girl of sixteen.' She covered her face with her hands and sobbed.

My father's dark face was working strangely, and suddenly, unexpectedly, I felt sorry for him. But he had recovered his self-control; his voice was low and edged as he sneered: 'And so—having married, as you thought, my brother, with his smooth cheeks and his nimble legs—you found yourself tied to an ugly cripple. Beauty and the Beast!'

'Giovanni, must we go over all this? It was nine years ago—nine long years. I am older now.' She had stopped crying, but she looked forlorn, stripped of her beauty: the alabaster lamp was unlit and opaque. He shrugged his shoulders and turned from her: 'What were we quarrelling about? It started over the child, didn't it—our little Discordia!' I heard him use that nickname for the first time (though not the last), and it struck me like a whip. It was my own fault, I realised: I should not have listened. I felt guilty, and even more so when I heard my mother say, with dignity: 'Let's forget it. But next time you feel inclined to use stable language to me, please do it when we are alone, not before my ladies and the child.'

Then there came on me a burning shame lest she should guess that I was listening, and I slipped quickly away from the door.

For the second time that day I had heard a conversation that I did not understand; but as I thought it over, two things became clear: my father had never really liked me, because he was disappointed that I was a girl; and my mother had never really liked him, because she had, in some way, married him by mistake. That odd word 'proxy' might be the clue, if I could find out what it meant.

But whom could I ask? Neither of my parents, for then they would know that I had been listening. Uncle Paolo? But he was in some way mixed up in the riddle. Uberto?

He probably wouldn't know anything about it, and he might tell his father that I had been questioning him.

The only person I could think of was my old nurse. So when she was brushing my hair that evening I blurted out: 'Nannie, what does "proxy" mean?' She gave a start, and her broad face turned red: 'Oh, my duckie, where did you learn that naughty word? That comes of going riding in boy's clothes, like a little hoyden. I'll wager you heard it from one of the grooms this morning. You just forget it, my little lady.'

Often since then I have wondered what she thought it meant. Perhaps she had mixed it up with 'doxy' (a word that I heard my father use, when little Maria Pia was dismissed, a couple of years later, for various indiscretions).

That discouraged me from making any further inquiries. But when my Uncle Malatestino came to stay with us at Rimini, I thought I would risk asking him. He, at any rate, would not be shocked, for even my father considered him 'tough'.

They said that in his childhood he had been as pretty as a girl, with a wild-rose skin, blue eyes and red-gold curls. He still had the red curls, but his complexion had sallowed, and the black shade over his left eye (destroyed by a stone flung by one of his playmates during a rough game) gave him a sinister look. To tell the truth, I was slightly afraid of him, and had to pluck up courage before I spoke.

One evening towards sunset, when he was leaning on the curtain-wall of the Gattolo, peering out to sea, I asked him: 'Is "proxy" a bad word, Uncle?' 'No, of course not!' he said, surprised. 'Then what does it mean?' 'A proxy is a substitute—a man who does something, by legal form, instead of another man and in his name. Why do you want to know?'

I parried with another question: 'Could a proxy marry somebody in someone else's name?' 'He could,' said my uncle drily, 'With certain reservations, which you wouldn't be expected to understand.'

I was on his blind side, and he turned his head with a semi-circular movement to look at me. It was a trick of his that made me nervous, and I never got used to it. That one cold blue eye in its deep socket always seemed to see far too much: 'Someone has been talking to you, little Concordia—or have you been listening at keyholes?'

I felt myself blushing scarlet, and dared not put a further question: 'Then did Uncle Paolo . . .?' Somehow I could not finish the sentence, even in my own mind. It all seemed strange and complicated; but I felt that, if I only rightly understood it, I should know why my parents so often behaved towards each other like hostile strangers.

4

The next year, my tenth, brought about great changes in my life: I seemed to be growing up very fast.

At Easter I had my First Communion party. We were still at the Gattolo, and my mother's people came over from Ravenna; for my cousin Guido, Uncle Ostasio's son, was the same age as me, and it had been decided that we should make a double event of it. He was a gentle, well-mannered boy and did not disdain playing with me. How I enjoyed his company and that of my Polentani uncles, who were fair and classic-featured like my mother, and seemed always to be laughing together. If anyone had told me, then, that I would one day be afraid of my Uncle Ostasio, I would not have believed it.

The ceremony was performed by a Malatesta uncle, the Archpriest Ramberto from Santa Paolo, to whom I took an instant dislike: he was large and fat, and his face, with its beaked nose and wide, flabby cheeks, looked owlish. When he put his hand on my head in blessing, I could not help shrinking from it. Afterwards Mother reproved me, and I looked apprehensively at Father while I defended myself by saying that I didn't like fat men. For once he took my part and burst out laughing: 'Too much food and no exercise!' he commented. 'He'll not live so long as the rest of us.' And he added, with a grim satisfaction: 'If I can't walk much, at least I keep myself fit by riding. I weigh no more now than when I was twenty.'

Father had ridden over for the occasion, but he went straight back to Pesaro. They had appointed him *podestà*, so for nearly a year he had been away from home: Mother said it was not the custom for the *podestà* to have his family living with him. During the summer, when we were at Gradara, only an hour's ride away, we had seen him fairly often; but at the approach of winter we had moved into the Gattolo and he rarely came to Rimini.

My mother, as always when he was away, seemed much happier, and the presence of her family made her even gayer. Laughing with them, she seemed to become a girl again. 'We used to have wonderful games at home,' she told me, not for the first time. 'All nine of us—six boys and three girls.'

I wondered how my grandfather, Guido da Polenta, had managed to have so many children, all so nearly of an age. One day I asked Uncle Bernardino something of the sort, and he gave a great shout of laughter: 'As you say, my father is a wonderful man. He got us all, right and left—some that he should have and others that he shouldn't—and swept us all into the same nest. And my mother—who was in fact his wife (lucky for me!) welcomed the whole brood, nightingales and cuckoos alike—bless her generous heart!'

Once again I had heard something that I did not quite understand. I felt it would be indiscreet to ask for explanations, but it set me watching the group. It was the nickname 'Bastardino' given affectionately to the youngest, that furnished the clue. I knew what 'bastard' meant—it was one of the words that Father was apt to throw about when he was in a temper. After watching for a while I first guessed, and then was sure, that Ostasio, Lamberto (who had not come to Rimini), Bernardino, who had married my aunt Maddalena Malatesta, and of course my mother, were the 'nightingales'; the two other sisters, Chiara and Samaritana, Guiduccio and two other brothers whom I had never seen, were the 'cuckoos'.

Maddalena was there with her husband. I never called her 'Aunt', for she seemed like an elder sister to me: she was my father's half-sister, twenty years younger than he, and had been married to Bernardino as a child, so she was still under twenty. I thought her very pretty, for she was like Uncle Paolo; in both of them the hawk-face of the Malatesti had been softened by velvety skin, large, lustrous eyes, and a mouth that seemed always ready to smile.

Aunt Chiara was pretty, too, in a different way—quiet, neat and composed, as dark as my mother was fair. I met her then for the first time (she had a week's leave from her convent to attend my First Communion), and never guessed how good she would be to me after I had lost my home and everything else that makes life worth living. But I did not take to her as I did to Samaritana, who had a tip-tilted nose and curly red-brown hair, and laughed at the same things as I did. She was Mother's favourite sister, too, I knew.

When they left, Aunt Chiara gave me a prayer-book and a lot of good advice; Samaritana and Guiduccio gave me toys; but each of the menfolk gave me a golden Ravenna pound. Bernardino suggested humorously that I had better put the money out to interest, as a base for my marriage-portion.

Then they were gone. From the battlements I watched

the little, multi-coloured group, with their retainers sporting the red Polenta eagle on their tabards and pennants, riding northwards across the plain; when they were out of sight, I went down to a house that seemed strangely quiet and empty.

Father came back from Pesaro in April, when his year of office ended; but very soon he went on to join my grandfather at Faenza. When he finally returned home it was a cool May evening—one of those evenings when it is pleasant to have a fire.

Mother had gone to bed with a bad cold and Nannie was looking after her, so no one remembered that it was past my bedtime, and I remained curled up on the hearth like a puppy-dog, almost asleep.

Father's return was unexpected, and as Mother was unwell he was not greeted with the usual loving-cup ceremony. In fact, the first intimation I had of his presence was a delicious perfume of violets that made me open my eyes and look for Uncle Paolo.

'Where's Uncle?' I asked. 'Which uncle?' 'Paolo. Isn't he with you? I can smell his perfume.' My father gave an exclamation—of mingled surprise and annoyance, it seemed—and then I realised that the scent came from him. He drew from his pocket a handkerchief—a scrap of silk and lace that quite obviously was not his. 'Ah! I must have picked this up by mistake.'

I stretched out my hand: 'Oh, how pretty it is—may I have it?' 'You may *not*,' he said curtly, and threw it into the fire. I wanted to cry, but had learned to control myself in front of him.

'Where's your mother?' he asked. 'Gone to bed—she has a cold.' He did not seem much concerned—merely snatched a handbell from the table and rang it. Father ordered the servant who answered it to fetch his valet Riccardo: 'And tell him to bring me down a chamber-robe to change into,' and, when the man had gone, he added to me: 'Your mother doesn't like it if I go in to her travel-stained and smelling of sweat and saddle-leather.' 'But you don't,' I said, 'You smell so like a flower-garden that I thought you were Uncle Paolo.'

Father gave me a quick look and told me to go upstairs at once: 'I can't think why they let you stay up after midnight. And for goodness sake, don't . . .' he broke off short, but it seemed to me that he meant to say: 'Don't tell your mother about the scented handkerchief.' In any case, I would not have done so. I was not yet ten, but I had already learned that it was better not to talk too much.

5

That winter, something happened which changed my whole outlook on life: the wall of hostility between my father and me suddenly collapsed and we grew to love each other. It was almost accidental, for the only idea in my mind had been to save his valet from a reprimand.

Romagna was comparatively quiet that year, so Father spent more time than usual at home. By now I had realised that the Gattolo was not really our house but my grandfather's: our rooms were in one wing of it. Gradara castle, too, was his, but my father had the almost exclusive use of it. In Rimini, as at Gradara, I used to sleep in my mother's bed when Father was away; but after my tenth birthday she let me sleep by myself, in a room above the entrance. It was very small, but I loved the feeling of independence that it gave me.

One cold night, when the moon was dropping low, I was roused by the creak and rattle of the drawbridge. I sat up, wide-awake and startled. I had no idea of the time, but it was certainly very late and everyone would be asleep, except the sentinels and the men on guard. There had been no parley before the lowering of the bridge, so it was undoubtedly my father who had come. Trouble in store for Riccardo, I thought! That afternoon I had seen him whispering with Maria Pia, who at seventeen was just as silly as she had been two years earlier. At suppertime he had asked permission to retire early, saying (untruthfully, I was sure) that he felt unwell. I guessed that he had an appointment with the girl. And my father, arriving at any hour and without warning, always expected people to be on their toes to receive him. The first thing he would do, as he came in, would be to call for Riccardo to bring his slippers, and if the man were not there . . .

Already I heard him in the courtyard, ordering someone to stable his horse. I threw a shawl over my nightgown and thrust my bare feet into shoes, not quite knowing what to do. Simply, I hoped to prevent a scene by fetching the slippers myself.

Snatching them from the shelf where they were kept, I ran into the great hall, just as my father entered shouting impatiently: 'Riccardo!' He was reeling on his feet, so lame that he could hardly walk. I wondered if he was drunk, then realised that he was only dead-tired. Still fully dressed in helmet, cuirass and cloak, he dropped into the nearest chair.

I went up to him, with the slippers in my hand: 'Is this what you wanted, Messer?' (My mother had taught me this formal address, and somehow it came more easily than to call him 'Father'.)

'Concordia? What in the world are you doing, out of bed at this hour?'

'The drawbridge woke me. I guessed it was you, and I thought I had better come to tell you that Riccardo is unwell. He asked leave to go to bed early this evening.'

Father grunted but made no comment. He was sitting

huddled up, as if only his cuirass kept him upright. 'You are very tired,' I said suddenly.

'Dead beat. I've ridden all over Romagna since dawn.'

This was a father I did not know. I had never heard him confess to any weakness before, and it made me less afraid of him. 'Give me your helmet,' I said, and set it down on the table. Then I loosened his gorget, took off his sword, and knelt to draw off his riding-boots. The right one came off easily enough, but the foot of his lame leg was splayed outwards almost at a right angle and the ankle was locked rigid, so that he could not pull a boot off or on: he had to wear one that was laced as far as the toe and could be opened right down. The knot was hard and I fumbled with it. He cursed impatiently, which made me still more nervous, but at last I got it undone and took off the boot. His leg was wasted, but the ankle had swelled up until the criss-cross pattern of the lace was embedded in his flesh through the stocking. He must have been in great pain—no wonder he felt cross.

Remembering what my mother sometimes did for me if I had a bruise or a sprain, I took the foot in my hands and gently rubbed it, watching him nervously. But he made no protest, and when the puffiness had abated a little I fetched a cushion and a stool and lifted his leg upon it: 'Do you want anything to eat or drink? I will go to the pantry and see if I can find you something.'

He shook his head: 'Too tired. I'm going to bed as soon as I can face the stairs.'

I fetched another cushion and slipped it behind his head. He said nothing, but his lips parted in a smile that transformed him. Sitting on the arm of his chair I waited—not too long, for I was afraid he would fall asleep where he sat. 'Will you come upstairs now?' I said. 'Lean on me if it hurts you to walk.'

He made a movement to rise, then clapped his hand to his side and swore violently.

'What is it?' I asked, frightened.

'My hip-joint has slipped—that happens sometimes when I'm overtired. I missed the bottom step of the mounting-block and jarred myself badly—that must have set it off.' He bit on his hand, as if to stop himself from groaning. 'Now you'll have to fetch Riccardo,' he said, after a pause. 'He knows what to do.'

The moon had gone by this time and the long corridors were very dark; but the sense of urgency so filled my mind that I felt no fear.

Riccardo slept at the entrance of the servants' quarters, so as to be within call from my father's room. Standing outside his door, I heard a murmur of voices, and then—Maria Pia's inane giggle. It was a shock to me. In my innocence I hadn't realised the meaning of an appointment. I had imagined Riccardo, like a troubadour in one of Mother's books, kneeling before her in some moonlit corner of the castle grounds, to assure her of his eternal devotion. Even when I heard that sound I did not realise quite what they were doing; but I did know that it was very wrong for one of my mother's ladies to be in a man's room late at night, and that both of them would be in serious trouble if it became known. I hesitated, embarrassed, but my errand was obviously urgent; so I knocked softly, hoping not to wake my mother in the nearby bedroom.

There was a little squeak from within, and a dead pause. Then Riccardo spoke, his voice sharp with annoyance but still kept low: 'Who is it? What do you want?'

'The Contessina.' I, too, instinctively hushed my voice. 'My father has come home. Something is wrong with his hip and he wants you at once.'

'One moment!' The bed creaked, there was the scraping of a tinderbox and a rustling sound. Riccardo was evidently dressing hastily. He came out with a sidelong movement, opening the door only a few inches, so that I could not look inside—quite unnecessarily, as I could not have seen anything in the blackness. By the light of the candle he was carrying he must have read my expression, for he whispered: 'Don't tell on me, Contessina!'

'No need to say that!' (my pride was up in arms). 'A Malatesta doesn't tell tales.'

Riccardo looked at me quizzically: 'Maybe *you* don't, little Contessina—you're a good sort. But I wouldn't say the same for Messer Malatestino. He sees a good deal too much with that one eye of his, and he repeats just what suits his game.'

I was inclined to agree with him and, much later, events proved that my instinct was right.

Father was sitting just as I had left him, with his eyes closed. I thought he would have abused Riccardo for his tardiness, but he seemed merely relieved to see him.

'The old trouble, *padrone*?' asked the man, sympathetically. My father nodded.

Riccardo acted promptly and efficiently. First he took a couple of wolfskin rugs from the hearth and spread them out below the chair; then he deftly took off my father's cloak and cuirass and lowered him to the floor. He began to loosen his clothing, then looked doubtfully at me. Father intercepted the glance: 'Go into the library and wait till we call you,' he ordered. I was glad he had not sent me to bed; now that I was involved in this, I wished to see it through.

I went through the curtained archway. Soon I heard my father catch his breath in something between a gasp and a groan; there was a click of the bone sliding back into its socket, and after a while Riccardo said: 'You can come back now, Contessina.'

Father's eyes were closed and his sweat-streaked face was livid, but its purposeful look told me that he had not fainted. Taking the handkerchief from his pocket, I wiped his cheeks and stroked back his lank hair; then, softly, I kissed his forehead. It struck me that this was the first time I had ever really kissed him. True, twice a year I used to touch his rough cheek with the dutiful peck that he expected in return for the presents that he brought me for my birthday and on the Befana; but never before had my heart been behind my lips. A sudden spring of love and tenderness welled up in me, as I exclaimed: 'Oh, Father, dear Father—why do you have to suffer so?'

He opened his eyes and gave a wry smile: 'Don't make a tragedy of it, little one. It's annoying and painful, but it is my own fault. I just will not admit to myself that I can't do as much as any other man of my age—or more.'

Riccardo asked if he should lift him back on to the chair.

'No, I'll lie here resting for a while. You'll have to make me up a bed in the library—I shall not be able to face the stairs tonight. Meantime, rouse one of the kitchen staff to prepare hot drinks—mulled wine for me, and milk sweetened with honey for my daughter.'

I glowed inwardly: when he quarrelled with Mother over me, he used to talk about '*your* daughter', as though she were responsible for my shortcomings; when he was in a better humour he would say casually 'the child', but never before had he claimed me as '*my* daughter'.

Riccardo laid my father's cloak over him and left us. Now that the emergency was over, I was beginning to shiver in my nightgown and Father saw it. 'You'll catch cold,' he said. 'Come here!' I nestled down on the wolf-skin under the cloak and he took my hands in his to warm them.

There was something I felt I must say to him: 'Father—I'm sorry I wasn't a boy. I know you are disappointed—but won't you try to be fond of me?'

He held my hands closer. 'I will,' he promised. 'But you mustn't be frightened of me—it makes me cruel.'

'I'm not frightened any longer,' I replied, and meant it.

Nothing more was said. We rested quietly there together until Riccardo brought the drinks. But I knew my father felt the same as I did: we had found each other and were content.

6

So now I had a definite objective: to help my father. It seemed to me that quite a lot could be done to prevent or allay the pain that made him so bad-tempered. Watching him carefully, I noticed that his lameness increased as he grew tired: in the morning it was just a heavy limp, but by evening he began to stoop so that he looked hunchbacked.

After our midday dinner, Mother used to take a siesta, but Father had always held out against this 'effeminate habit'. The most he would do was to sprawl uncomfortably for a while in one of the hard oak arm-chairs.

I thought it over; then I measured the chair-base and asked our handyman, Pietro, to cut a board of that width, with holes at each corner and thongs for fastening it. I padded it and, next afternoon, just before Father came from the dining-hall into the library, I fixed one end to a chair and the other to a stool, so that it made a leg-rest. 'Come and stretch out here,' I suggested, 'this will be much more comfortable for you.'

He gave me a sharp glance. 'My dear child,' he said tartly, 'I may be a cripple, but I am by no means an invalid.'

I took my courage in both hands and told him straight out: 'All the same, if you rested your leg more it wouldn't hurt you so often. Then you'd feel less cross, and that would be pleasanter for us all.'

Father gave a short laugh, and there actually came a twinkle into his eye: 'You win, Concordia! I surrender to your logic. On one condition—that you stay and talk to me. If I am to lie here doing nothing, with no one to amuse me, I shall certainly be, as you term it, "cross".'

I settled him comfortably, fetched a cushion for myself and sat down on the floor beside him. There was a silence. To break it I asked, 'What shall we talk about?'

'Tell me about yourself. Do you realise that, in all these years, we have never really talked to each other. A few days ago, when you showed some common sense and initiative, I was too ill. Otherwise, you seemed like a little white mouse, scurrying for shelter every time I came to your mother's room.'

'That was silly of me,' I admitted, 'but I was only young then. When I was a baby, your rough cheeks and your loud voice frightened me, and I hadn't got over it.'

'What do you do all day long—up there, among all those women?'

It was difficult to say what I *did* do, but I made an effort, telling him about my lessons. Mother had taught me to write and I practised every day, for she said it was important, even for a woman, to write a clear and beautiful hand. She used to read to me: stories about knights and ladies riding through dark forests full of perils, from which they were always rescued by some magic intervention; and sometimes she made me read to her. Twice a week Don Angelo taught me Latin and prayers, and once a week a gentle little woman (one of Mother's protégées) came to give me a French lesson. I learned embroidery, too. When Mother and her ladies made music I used to listen, and sometimes I joined in the singing. . . . It all sounded very dull, and I was not surprised when a gentle snore told me that Father had fallen asleep.

Soon it became an accepted thing that, if no urgent business called him away, Father would rest after dinner, and that I should stay with him. He hated being idle, so I suggested that if he had any letters to write he could dictate them to me. 'And have them going out in the handwriting of a child of ten?' he retorted. Expecting this, I had brought some of my exercises to show him, and he had to admit that I wrote as good a hand as any clerk.

One afternoon he asked me to fetch the chess-set kept in one of the library cupboards. I had sometimes seen him play, but had never watched closely. When I had spilled the white and red pieces out on to the board I was fascinated: elephants, horses, soldiers, crowned and turbaned figures, all exquisitely carved. They were far prettier than any of my own toys. Father deftly set out the board and began to move them about.

'Oh!' I exclaimed. 'Can you play by yourself?' 'When I haven't an adversary.' 'Couldn't you teach me how to play?' He answered shortly that it was a war-game—a game for men, that women and children couldn't understand. But after a little coaxing he told me the names of the pieces and explained how each one moved. I made up my mind that I wanted to learn, and in the end I got my way. When Father saw that I really had some aptitude he began to play seriously, handicapping himself to make the game more interesting. If I contrived to beat him, he would reduce the handicap. When it came down to two pawns, I said I would rather play him level. He always won, of course, but he would show me where I had gone wrong, or where he, intentionally, had made some risky move that, if I had been a better player, would have lost him the game. By the end of the winter I was quite good at it. Father used to tease me, saying that I was a born cavalry-leader, since my favourite piece was the knight and I had a special gift for 'forking' two pieces with it.

These games helped to pass many cold, wet afternoons. Sometimes, too, Father helped me with my French and Latin homework, and when I made some progress in Latin he began to read me passages from his favourite book, the *Aeneid.* Instead of an ordinary reading-desk, at which one stood, he had a special board that lay across the chair, so that he could read sitting or even lying down. 'It was made for me when I was ill,' he said, when I commented on it.

That gave me the chance to ask him about his illness. It was a new idea to him, apparently, that anyone should be interested in his health and should wish to improve it. He seemed to assume that his lameness made him as repulsive to everybody as it apparently did to Mother.

There wasn't much he could tell me. He had woken, he said, after some weeks of fever, to find that the muscles of his left hip and leg were completely flaccid, and the leg itself had shrunken and the foot twisted outwards. I asked if there was anything wrong with his spine, as he often seemed to have difficulty in holding himself upright. He replied that he thought not—but his shortened leg threw his whole body out of balance, putting extra strain on the muscles that remained sound, so overtiredness always brought on a fierce backache.

In all this, there was no mention of injury to his foot, and its condition puzzled me. Father said that it had simply become fixed during the long time he had to lie in bed, and that he had not been able to move it since.

I did not stop worrying about it, and next time my grandfather, old Malatesta of Verucchio, came to the Gattolo, I asked him what was wrong with the foot and whether it could be put right.

The old man shook his head—and a magnificent head it was. I always thought of him as a fierce white eagle in his mountain eyrie. Most people were afraid of him—even my father showed him a meek deference very unlike his usual manner—but I had been fond of him since my babyhood, when I used to sit on his knee and play with his bright buttons. 'Goldilocks' he used to call me then, as though my fair hair, among the black or flaming-red Malatesta heads, somehow set me apart.

Father must have told him about my childish attempts at nursing, for he showed no surprise about my question. He muttered some word I had never heard before—I think it was 'ankylosed'—and when I asked what it meant, he explained that Father had been lying for months with his leg immobilised: 'Afterwards a surgeon told us that we should have kept moving his foot, but by that time it was too late—the joint had stiffened and the muscles wasted from disuse, like a key that has rusted in the lock and will never turn again.'

7

By February the snow had melted and there was a feeling of spring in the air. One evening towards sunset I was walking with my mother inside the outer wall of the Gattolo. She told me that, from the battlements, she had looked down into a little patch of green that had once been a garden, and it had come into her mind to have it planted again. But the door that led to it had not been opened for many years and was rusted fast; so she had asked Pietro to get it open, and now we were going to see if he had succeeded.

We found the old man working away with a rag, a supply of feathers and a little terracotta jug of oil.

'Well, Pietro?' asked my mother, with that friendly smile that made all our dependants adore her.

'No luck so far, Madonna Francesca. It will take time—the key is rusted fast in the lock.'

'Then it will never turn again,' I interposed, thinking of my grandfather's words.

'Oh yes, it will, Contessina,' said Pietro confidently. 'Patience and olive oil, that's all it needs.' And we left him, pushing a new feather into the lock and muttering: 'Patience and olive oil.'

Next day Mother grew tired of waiting and suggested having the door burst open with a battering-ram, but I begged her to let Pietro go on trying for at least a couple of days longer. I was almost crying, and she looked at me curiously: 'Why, Concordia, whatever can it matter to you how the door is opened, so long as I get it done?' I could not tell her that I had made a kind of wager with myself: if Pietro does open that door, then I shall be able to make Father's foot better.

At our next visit we found the door open and gardeners at work tearing up the brambles. Pietro nodded proudly to us: 'What did I say, Madonna Francesca? Patience and olive oil—that does the trick.'

When I joined Father for his rest-hour that afternoon, I brought a little oil-flask with me and said firmly: 'Let me rub your foot with this, Father. I am sure we can cure it if we try hard.' He shrugged his shoulders, unconvinced but acquiescent. And in the days that followed, my own faith wavered, for the foot remained rigid; then at last I felt a loosening under my fingers.

For a day or two I said nothing, till I was certain; then I told him quietly: 'It *does* move, you know.' Cautiously I pressed the foot upwards and then sideways. 'I'm not hurting you?' 'No.' So I increased the pressure, and this time there was a perceptible movement.

After that, Father began to help himself, trying to twist and bend the foot, first with his hands and then, as the muscles strengthened, by its own power. Within six weeks his ankle-joint was working almost normally, and that was a great point gained: he would be able to discard the ugly laced-up boot and wear a normal pair.

We called in the bootmaker, who proved really intelligent

and suggested building up the sole to bring the shortened leg level with the other. When my father demurred that it would be heavy and clumsy, the man said he would make a double sole—the outer one normal, the inner of soft chamois leather, and fill the interstice with cork, which would weigh next to nothing. By cunning diagonal stitching on the uppers, he made the boots, in wear, look almost identical. The result was so successful that Father ordered two or three pairs of indoor shoes and slippers on the same principle.

I had won my first battle, but a harder one lay ahead, for it meant fighting his Malatesta pride. In all those years he had refused to use a crutch or stick. One day, when he was in a specially good humour, I broached the subject. As he opened his mouth to protest, I added hastily that long canes were all the rage just now in Florence (Uncle Paolo on his last visit had been flourishing one, but I had already learned better than to quote him as an example to my father). He said he was no popinjay to follow the Florentine fashions, but it was not a very strong protest, so I decided to give him a stick for his birthday.

It needed some planning. That is the worst of being very young: you cannot go about by yourself, and the grown-ups always want to know what you are going to do, and why—and to prevent you. Instinct warned me not to discuss it with Mother, who seemed to think that my new friendship with my father was treason against herself. So I took Nannie into my confidence and asked permission to go, under her escort, to Mass at San Francesco. Mother, I knew, would be pleased, for San Francesco was her name-saint. To my dismay she said that she would come too; but fortunately an unexpected visit detained her.

So after a few minutes in the church, Nannie and I went through the narrow, twisted streets, to find a shop where the fashionable canes were sold. When he heard that it was for my father, the shopkeeper said: ah, he knew exactly the thing! He took out a fine, elegant cane with an ivory pommel and, to my astonishment, whipped out from it a slender sword, saying proudly: 'Toledo steel!' I clapped my hands, realising that this was something I could give my father without humbling his pride.

'It is grand!' I said. 'But, instead of the ivory ball, could you substitute a small Malatesta elephant?' The man looked doubtful and said that, of course, it would add to the expense. That brought me to the practical consideration: could I afford it? I found that, without the elephant it would cost two of the golden pieces given me by my uncles; with it, there would not be much left of the third. Nannie was making signs of disapproval, but I said casually: 'Oh yes, that will be all right.' And I paid him on the spot.

There was no need to make a second visit: Nannie fetched the cane for me, and I hid it until I gave it to my father on his birthday morning.

He flashed me a quizzical glance: 'Very persistent, aren't you, my little Concordia? Did you by any chance inherit your obstinacy from me?' But I could see that, at bottom, he was not displeased. I said quickly: 'It's not just a stick to walk with—look!' Then I pulled out the sword. His eyes sparkled. He weighed it in his hand, tried a few passes, bent it to test the resilience, then nodded contentedly: 'A very lovely present, my darling!'

Then he tried it out as a walking-stick, strolling up and down the terrace. He was wearing his built-up shoes and, with the extra support of the cane, his limp was scarcely noticeable—little more than the roll of an old sea-dog.

I said: 'Bravo! We must go and see Mother—she'll be so proud of you.' His lips twisted in one of those smiles that made my heart ache for him. 'She won't even notice,' he said. And he was right.

Mother remarked casually that the stick was very pretty, but she thought he didn't hold with them? 'Ah, but this is a special one.' I thought he was going to pull out the sword, but he didn't. I am sure she had no idea that it was a sword-stick, perhaps not even until that last night when . . . (But I must not think of that dreadful night.)

Then she gave him her present—a dagger in a beautifully chased and jewelled scabbard. With this, too, he was delighted. His handicap had made him develop the strength and skill of his arms. He was ambidextrous and used often to amuse himself by throwing daggers, javelin-wise, left-hand and right, at a target. So, for once, we were all three happy together.

But when Father had left us, Mother asked me how I had ordered the cane and why I hadn't consulted her about it. I said vaguely: 'Oh, Nannie arranged it for me. I didn't want to bother you.' She said I mustn't be extravagant—it must have cost much more than I could afford. I explained that I had paid for it with the money given me by my uncles, and she replied, laughing, that at this rate there would be little left of it by the time I was old enough to start laying in clothes for my wedding.

8

As the spring wore on, I became increasingly conscious that Mother was jealous of the new alliance between my father and me. She had no logical reason to object, for the hour or two that we spent together was her own siesta time; if I had not been with him, I would have stayed alone, idle or doing my homework.

One beautiful evening in June this feeling broke out in a scene which, had I been older and less unsuspecting, would have revealed to me the secret that, in fact, I never guessed until the closing moments of her life.

Father had been in Forlì during May. He returned, satisfied, saying briefly that my grandfather had concluded a pact that would be useful in the future; but he was growing increasingly restless, so that often I failed to keep him still, even for half an hour. 'I shall have to give up these invalid habits,' he said, that afternoon. 'Before long I'll be in the saddle again all day. There's trouble brewing.' 'What sort of trouble?' 'Oh, politics—you wouldn't understand.' 'I would, if you explained it clearly enough.'

So he told me that the new Rector of Romagna, Pietro, son of Stefano Colonna, was trying openly to break the power of both my grandfathers—Malatesta da Verucchio and Guido da Polenta of Ravenna. He had incited the city of Cervia to rebel against Grandfather Guido, who had sent to my father for help. Meanwhile, Grandfather Malatesta was at Forlì, where he had just concluded a pact between the city, Faenza and Rimini. 'Now he and I are going to help the Polentani recapture Cervia. I shall be starting off tomorrow to join him with fifty men, but I have asked my uncle at Sogliano to come with us, and I am waiting for him now. He should arrive or send word this evening. I feel inclined to go up to the battlements and see for myself.'

'Let me go!' I said quickly. 'Tell me—what I am to look for, or to do?'

'Find a sentinel: tell him to watch for Messer Malatesta of Sogliano—he'll see the blue-and-white chequered shields and banners.'

As I ran upstairs, I met my mother coming down. She said: 'Concordia, I want to see how the new garden is looking. Let's go together.'

'I have to give the sentinel a message for Father. I'll join you there in a few minutes.'

But it took much longer. From the main staircase I had

to pass several corridors, cross a bridge to the outer wall and walk along it to the watchtower. There I found the sentinel watching a distant patch of dust which he said was raised by horsemen. So I waited for what seemed hours (possibly only ten minutes), until at last he could distinguish their devices. No, he said, those weren't Malatesta men; it was those rascals from Montefeltro. Surely they wouldn't have the audacity to approach our castle? . . . In fact, well clear of Rimini, they turned southwards out of sight.

When I went back to tell Father there was no news, he sent me to the armourer with orders to have his cuirass, helmet and greaves well polished before next morning. So altogether, a long time passed before I joined Mother.

In a very few weeks the gardeners had turned this desolate spot into a fit setting for her own loveliness. There on a low stone seat flanked by urns cascading white and crimson roses, with the mellow red of the vine-grown castle wall behind her, she looked like a lily, pale in her white, gold-embroidered gown; from her crescent head-dress a transparent veil hardly dimmed the lustre of her hair. She sat motionless, curiously remote, looking at me in silence. Then she said icily that, as I evidently preferred my father's company to hers, I had better go back to him.

Guiltily, I tried to explain: 'I am sorry, but . . .' It was not a very convincing explanation, for I had learned never to repeat to one of my parents what I had heard from the other. If Father wished to tell her his plans, he would; and he would have confidence in me if he knew that she was hearing them for the first time. So I merely said that I had given two messages for him, and that both had taken longer than I expected.

'The plain truth of the matter is,' she said, bitterly, 'that we used to be everything to each other; but since you fell in love with your father, you have had no room in your heart for me.'

There was just enough truth in this to sting me, and it brought a quick reaction: 'One can love two people at the same time!'

'I cannot,' she said with a deep sigh.

'You love me, and you love . . .' I had meant to say 'my father', but she obviously did not and never pretended to (she was no hypocrite), so I substituted '. . . Uncle Paolo.'

Her face went ivory-white, as it always did when she was really angry. Looking back, I realise that she thought I had said it on purpose, as retaliation for that remark about being 'in love with' my father, but at the time I was quite innocent. 'Love', to me, was the affection one had (or was supposed to have) for any close relative. Besides my father and mother, I loved my Malatesta grandfather (the other I had never met), and all my uncles and aunts . . . well, perhaps not Malatestino, who always made me shiver.

So I stared in amazement at my mother, while she said that it was wicked and untrue: I must never say such a thing again, or even think it.

I reflected for a moment and then asked: 'If it was wicked, must I confess it to Don Angelo?'

That brought her up with a start, and a quick flush rose to her cheeks. She said hastily: 'No, of course not. I used the wrong word. I should have said "silly" or "thoughtless". You are old enough now to know better.' And as if I had still been the five-year-old whom she had scolded in the street of Gradara, she explained that 'a married woman must not love anybody except her husband, and of course her children'.

'Then don't you love Uncle Ostasio?' I asked.

Well, yes, she admitted, but that was different—Ostasio was her brother.

It was all very puzzling: she could love Uncle Ostasio but not Uncle Paolo . . . I gave it up. Seeing my troubled face, Mother kissed me, as if to make amends. 'I was upset at waiting for you so long,' she said. 'It hurts me terribly to feel you slipping away from me—you are all that makes my life worth living.'

It struck me that she had plenty: she was young, beautiful and healthy; she had comfortable rooms and lovely clothes; books to read, people to wait on her and make music for her; nothing to do but amuse herself all day long. Perhaps that was the trouble, for I myself had been much happier since I had filled my days looking after my father. Thinking she was going to cry, I suggested that we should pick a bunch of roses.

Before we had finished Madonna Cristina came to call her, saying that Messer Malatesta of Sogliano was riding in, and Messer Giovanni wished her to be ready to receive him.

So we hurried back to the Gattolo. I had my hair combed and was put into my best frock; Mother looked beautiful and gracious as she went into the great hall and curtsied to the dignified old man. He had brought twenty men-at-arms, ready to ride next morning with my father's fifty, to Cervia.

That morning I woke with the extraordinary sense of apprehension that has seized me once or twice, and never without cause. I felt I must see my father and warn him, though I didn't quite know of what.

He was already on foot, though it was barely dawn. I could hear him shouting orders in the courtyard; horses were stamping and bridles jingling. Leaping out of bed, I threw on my clothes. No use waiting for Nannie, so I simply ran a comb through my hair and tied it back with a ribbon; then I hurried downstairs.

Father, leaning on the parapet of the loggia that enclosed the courtyard, made a brief sign of greeting. I said: 'I must see you, alone, to say goodbye properly.'

He grunted impatiently: 'I'm busy, child—can't you

see?' But he did follow me indoors. 'I hoped to be away before anyone was astir,' he said.

'Father—be careful!' I begged him.

He disengaged my clinging hands and said, with the note of irritation in his voice that I had not heard for months: 'Concordia, I'm disappointed in you. Is that how a Malatesta woman sends her menfolk into battle?'

'But you're going into danger.'

'Of course I am. What would life be, without a spice of danger?'

Pulling myself together, I tried to explain more clearly: 'It's not that. I'm glad you're going to fight, if it makes you happy. But there *is* some definite danger—I can feel it at the back of my mind. Be careful when . . .' I tried to focus the picture that kept eluding me: 'Be careful, when the sea is on both sides of you.'

'Sea on both sides? What *are* you talking about?'

I persisted: 'It sounds silly, I know. But I can see a road, with blue water and tall reeds, to left and right of it . . . and . . . and a queer hillock, pointed and shining white . . .'

Father gave a long whistle: 'The salines of Cervia!' he exclaimed. 'Just the place for an ambush. Well, I'll watch out. Now kiss me and let me go.' I stood on tiptoe to put my arms round his neck, and he gave me one of those brief, strong hugs that always made Mother wince. Then he crossed to the mounting-block where a groom was holding his horse. My Great-Uncle, Giovanni of Sogliano, was already in the saddle. Father rode up to him, the drawbridge went down, and they cantered out into the early sunlight, with their seventy men behind them.

We spent two anxious days waiting for news. On the evening of the third, news came—and it was bad. A passing pedlar, coming to sell his wares to our staff, had heard that the Malatesta troops had been defeated near Cervia, and Messer Giovanni was a prisoner.

Mother remained calm, saying: 'Well, we shall have to

find out where he is and ransom him.' I would not let her see how upset I was, but when she had gone for her siesta, I stole into the deserted library, threw myself on the floor and sobbed uncontrollably.

Wasted emotion; for that evening our head groom Aldo, one of my father's trusted elder men, came with a letter from him: it was not he but Giovanni of Sogliano who had been taken. The letter was addressed to my mother, but there was a message in it for me: 'Tell Concordia that her premonition was right, and it saved us from being trapped. As we approached the salines of Cervia, I was on the look-out for an ambush, and I noticed that the wildfowl seemed scary of one particular spot among the reeds. It seemed to me that I could see sunlight flashing from metal. I said to my father: " 'Ware ambush!" and he gave the order to charge. We were going full tilt when men leaped at us out of the reeds—they were the Rector's militia, and they outnumbered us three to one. Our impetus carried us through almost without loss, but the Sogliano horses are no match for ours and they couldn't stand the pace. I lost sight of Uncle Giovanni, but later I heard that he and some half-dozen of the rearguard had been captured. The rest of us are safe with Messer Guido in Ravenna. He sends you his loving greetings and says, don't hold it against him if he keeps me here for some time. The Rector, they say, has fallen back on Imola, but we still have to reckon with him.' And he ended with the usual greetings.

There was a postscript that gave me pleasure: 'Send Riccardo to me, and tell him to bring my stick with him. I am used to it now and I miss it.'

Father was away for several weeks, so we stayed on at the Gattolo instead of moving to Gradara, though the weather in the plain was growing hot. My two grandfathers and he spent their time negotiating with the Rector, who wanted to call a general meeting of the City States in Imola: but they were too wary to fall into that trap.

All this news came through to us in snatches, brought sometimes by casual travellers, sometimes in letters or oral messages from Ravenna.

9

It was July when Father came home. Left to myself, I would have flown straight into his arms, but protocol demanded that the son of the Lord of Rimini should be received with due ceremony, after such a long absence. So Mother put on her best gown and had a carved chair brought out into the loggia, where she sat in the midst of her ladies, with me (also dressed up) standing beside her. Then, as the drawbridge went down and the men on guard blared a fanfare, my father came riding in, followed by half a dozen of his escort, and she made a few steps towards him. Biancarosa handed her a cup, into which Cristina poured wine.

Father remained in the saddle while Mother held up the cup, saying: 'Messer Giovanni, my husband, welcome back to Rimini! Long life and happiness to you!' Then she drank from the cup and passed it to him; and he, draining it, answered: 'Long life and happiness to you, Madonna Francesca!'

Monna Cristina gave me a little push forward: I came up, curtsied and kissed his hand, saying: 'Welcome back to Rimini, my father!' And while the retainers were shouting: 'Evviva Malatesta! Viva Messer Giovanni!' I took the empty cup and handed it to one of the ladies.

All this while my father had stayed on horseback; for it was a recurrent humiliation to him that he could not mount or dismount unassisted, except at a block. In all his properties and stables he had several of these mounting-blocks. So, having given his staff the show they expected, he rode once or twice round the courtyard and then pulled up, as if casually, at the block where Aldo was waiting to take his horse. Aldo, I noticed, unobtrusively handed him his stick as he touched ground.

Then at last we had him to ourselves, indoors. I did not kiss him, wary of rousing Mother's jealousy, but we smiled into each other's eyes. 'How well you are looking!' I said, and it was true. He was bronzed and lean, he moved more easily, and his face seemed less lined. Evidently he needed to live a soldier's life now and then.

Mother, naturally, wanted to hear about her people in Ravenna. While they were talking, a servant brought in a parcel containing a length of emerald green brocade with gold thread interwoven, and the gift gave her genuine pleasure.

There was no parcel for me. I looked expectantly at Father, and he laughed: 'Of course there's something for you, but it is too big to bring indoors. You must come out with me to see it.' 'What—now?' I looked doubtfully at Mother, and she nodded: 'Very well, provided you change out of that dress into something simpler.' I didn't need to be told twice.

Mother made some excuse not to come with us and we did not press her. 'Where are we going?' I asked. 'To the stables,' was Father's unexpected reply. I looked apprehensive: since the fright Nerone had given me, I had refused to go near a horse. Any suggestion that I should ride was enough to set me crying. On our moves to Gradara I used to travel in Mother's litter, instead of riding pillion behind one of her ladies.

Father put his arm round my shoulders: 'You have encouraged me to walk again; now I am going to teach you to ride.'

My glance must have been imploring: 'Not—not Nerone!' I pleaded.

He shook his head: 'Not Nerone. That was a mistake. I thought I could treat you as my father treated me and my brothers. He taught us to swim by throwing us into the millpond. He had to fish Paolo out once or twice, but Malatestino and I splashed and puffed our way to the bank. The same with riding: as soon as our legs could span a horse's back, on we went—on stallions from his war-stable. If they threw us we got no sympathy, so we soon learned to stick on. But with you it didn't work: we'll have to go about it more gently.'

I was disappointed when Father said that my first lessons would be with Aldo, not with him. 'He's a fine old man,' he said. 'He taught me to ride—not once but twice.' And he told me how, after his illness, it was agony to sit a horse: he had to be strapped into the saddle. Once or twice he had fainted. 'And it takes a good deal to make me faint,' he said grimly. Through it all, Aldo had encouraged him to persevere, and in the end he had come to find riding easier than walking. Aldo, over sixty, could well have been content to make a sinecure of his position as head groom. Instead, he insisted on going into battle with my father and staying beside him. 'He'll have the same devotion to you, I know. So trust yourself to him and don't be afraid.'

By this time we had arrived. Father called to Aldo: 'Is he ready?' 'Yes, Messer Giovanni,' and the old man led out a small grey pony.

'I found him in Ravenna,' said my father, 'and it was quite a job getting him here: he couldn't have kept up with our huge stallions, and I had no man light enough to ride him. So I sent a trooper here, with orders that a stableboy should come over on a palfrey and lead him home.'

I loved the pony at first sight: he was chubby and had a long curled tail. Suddenly it struck me that, if the tail had been attached to his nose he would have looked uncommonly like the Malatesta elephant on Father's stick.

So when Father asked: 'What shall we call him?' I said at once: 'Elefantino'.

He was fitted with a gay red saddle—a girl's saddle this time, and when I sat sideways on his back my feet were not far from the ground. Mounted, I was as tall as my father, and it was good to look level into his laughing dark eyes—I had so seldom seen his eyes look happy. He told Aldo to walk the pony round the field while he himself mounted and sat waiting for our return. When I came back he showed me how to hold the reins, and told me the words of command and the signals to stop and start the pony. Then he sent me out again, this time trotting, with Aldo riding beside me.

This was very different from my terrifying experience on Nerone. I began to feel quite confident and was sorry when Aldo declared that I had had enough and lifted me down.

'Now I'm going to show you something,' said Father. 'Sit on the block and watch.' Riding to the far end of the field, where the grass was short and smooth, he began to turn in a wide, sweeping circle—or rather a spiral, for at each turn it narrowed until at last the animal seemed to be pivoting around its tail. There was enchantment in the rhythm, the way that long black tail swayed to balance each turn, my father's poise and absolute stillness. Had they been moving on hard sand, I thought, the imprints would have made a perfect geometrical pattern. Having made his narrowest turn, Father broke out of it in a straight line and galloped back towards us.

Aldo and I had been watching in silence. I could see that the old man was even more deeply moved than I was. As it ended, he said, his eyes shining and moist: 'Once Messer Giovanni could do the double circle, reversing out of it. Now he can only do it clockwise, controlling with his sound foot—but it is still as perfect as ever.'

I loved Elefantino because he was my father's gift. Long

after I had ceased to ride him, he was kept at Gradara and was the joy of the citadel children. But as soon as Aldo reported that I had a safe seat, Father provided me with another mount—a black horse (they called it a gelding), small and dainty. It had been a great disappointment to him, said Father. He had picked it as a likely foal, intending it for his own use, and called it Pluto. But, no one knew why, it never grew to full size. By the time it was two years old, he realised that it would never bear a grown man's weight. So he changed its name to Plato (Aldo and the stable-boys laughed at this—I couldn't see why) and sent it to the second stable, with the palfreys and the mares. The boys loved to ride it—for it had Arab blood and was very fast—but once they failed to pass the 'jockey test' he forbade them to mount it again. This test was a balance, with a large stone in one pan, as heavy as an average boy of fourteen or fifteen. Every week the stable-boys had to step into the corresponding pan, and when they outweighed the stone their usefulness as jockeys came to an end. Either they passed into the cavalry troop, or else they were given jobs about the stables.

Now, Father said, I would be able to ride out with him. 'You must be tired of going round and round this field. On Rimini sands we can gallop for miles.'

I was thrilled; but I asked if I couldn't have boy's clothes and sit astride. To my surprise, Father agreed without argument. He didn't really like the idea of skirts and a side-saddle: if a man is thrown, he commented, he usually falls clear, but a woman riding side-saddle risks being dragged if her skirt catches on the pommel. 'I will get the suit for you,' he offered, adding conspiratorially, 'but don't tell your mother!'

That was typical of our new relationship; somehow we were in league together. There was no reason to keep it from Mother: if Father and she were at variance on a point, she would have to give way. But we both wished to avoid those painful scenes in which I became their 'little Discordia'.

10

Our ride was postponed until I had become accustomed to an ordinary saddle, but at last the great day arrived. The suit, in russet-brown, was not so pretty as Uncle Paolo's gift but far more practical. When Father saw me in it for the first time he exclaimed: 'Why, you're a real Malatesta! You remind me of Malatestino.' Seeing my horrified expression, he added hastily: 'He was handsome enough, before he lost his eye; and he was the only fair-skinned one of us three. Pity you couldn't have seen us in our teens, unspoiled.'

I was surprised to find a troop waiting in the courtyard. 'Aren't we going to ride alone—you and I and Aldo?' I said.

'Not at this moment. I've plenty of enemies who would be glad enough to catch me unawares.' And he called the Captain of the guard, giving him some brief instructions. The men leaped to horse and we cantered out—Father and I in front, and the rest of them some fifty yards behind.

We circled the town walls and then struck out over grass-flats to the sea. It was a wonderful experience for me, after the monotonous to-and-fro in the paddock. Plato moved so swiftly and smoothly that we seemed to be flying; and on the sands Father called to me to let him out. He himself dashed off along the beach on his great black stallion, but to my amazement Plato kept up with him. I had never ridden so fast before, but I felt exhilarated rather than frightened. The sea, glittering crystal, was on our right hand and the dunes on our left, as we rode northwards with the sun at our backs, and our shadows slanting inland before us. When we turned and rode back to our escort, patiently waiting in formation, I felt sorry for them. It must have been so dull just to sit there while we were enjoying our gallop.

Evidently the Captain thought so too, for he asked whether next time, while they were waiting, some of the men could swim. Father gave permission, providing that half the troop remained on duty, and that—since I was there and they would be swimming naked—the bathers should go some distance down the shore, in the opposite direction from us.

Next day, as we returned towards them, Father cast a quick, appraising look at the men in the water. 'One can tell the swimmers at a glance,' he said. 'Their bodies are brown all over. The others are piebald—sunburnt arms and legs, and pale skin where it has been hidden by clothes.'

'How they are enjoying themselves!' I exclaimed thoughtlessly; then was sorry when I heard Father's sharp, indrawn breath and saw the pain in his eyes.

Next day, while he was resting, I took his hand and said: 'It made you unhappy to see the men swimming yesterday.' It was a statement, not a question, and I wondered how he would take it. Some instinct told me that it was better for him to talk about the things that hurt him, rather than brood silently. He said nothing for a while, but I kept still, with my cheek against his hand, and at last he spoke.

Of all the deprivations his crippling caused him, swimming was the one he felt most. Before his illness he had been one of the finest swimmers in Romagna; now, on a summer afternoon, when he craved for the coolness of the sea, it was agony to watch other men enjoying a pleasure that he himself could never know again.

Why didn't he try? I asked. His arms were so strong that he could surely keep afloat, with very little help from his legs. 'Daren't risk it,' he replied shortly: 'Kicking out could easily dislocate my hip.' 'Couldn't you fix it in some way? Strap it up, so that it couldn't slip?' He took this seriously and we discussed it for some time. Eventually Father agreed to call in the shoemaker who had been so intelligent over his boots, and see if he had any ideas.

Between them, they evolved a device—a belt with a cork shield protecting the hip-joint, and a light wooden splint that would keep his left leg from bending at the knee. He would not be able to draw up his legs or make any kind of rotary movement, but he could still move his feet up and down, in a limited range, and he thought that would suffice.

I said consolingly that a fish had no legs to bend, yet it swam faster than a frog—and little knew how true my comparison would prove to be. Then with a quill and a scrap of used parchment I sketched a pair of drawers that would hide the apparatus, cut full and drawn in just below the knee. Made in black taffeta they would be light and easily dried and would not hamper his movements too much. And I sketched a smaller pair for myself.

'What's this?' he said, with raised eyebrows. 'I'm going in with you,' I said. 'I want to learn to swim.'

Father said firmly that the Contessina Malatesta could not exhibit herself half naked before his men. This seemed rather absurd, since my chest was still as flat as a boy's. However, I added an apron top and he said, dubiously, that it might pass: 'But don't . . .' 'Don't tell Mother!' I anticipated, and we both burst out laughing.

Father took the sketches, added some measurements, and said he would have the things made in Rimini town, not by my mother's seamstresses.

There remained one problem to be solved. Father would have to change on the beach, for obviously he could not ride with the splint fixed. Here, it was he who found the solution: a canvas tent with collapsible framework similar to those he used on campaign but smaller, divided by a central curtain, so that we could both use it together.

All this planning took over a week. Meanwhile, we rode out and selected a spot in the dunes where we could keep the tent in a coffer: the men would cover it with sand and dig it out each time.

Father kept watching the 'piebald' bodies of his men turning a healthy brown, but now there was no pain in his eyes, only a smouldering impatience. And at last we were ready.

Father sent four men in advance, to set up the tent by the water's edge. Experimenting, he had found that he could walk with the splint fixed, but it shortened his stride, so that it would have taken him a long time to cross the beach from the dunes. As it was, the sea-bed was flat and we waded for quite a distance before the water came to my chest. Then we stopped and Father, with no preliminaries, yanked me off my feet and slipped a hand through the canvas belt that he had fastened round my middle. It was not, perhaps, such drastic treatment as Grandfather Malatesta had given his sons, but it left me no time for thinking or panicking. Instinctively I struck out, in a whirl of splashing. 'Gently, gently!' came my father's voice. 'The water will hold you up, if only you let it.' My purposeless flurry slowed down until I achieved some kind of rhythm. Father was walking beside me: I could feel the pull on the belt. Till then I had kept my eyes screwed up; now I opened them and saw the glint of the water and—very far off, it seemed—the pale sand. I wondered what was happening to Plato, left in care of one of the men: he might grow restless and escape. The idea distracted me from the thought of swimming but my arms and legs continued to move mechanically. Then I realised that for some time there had been no pull on my waist: Father had let me go! At once I went under and swallowed water. Through my closed lids I could feel the sting of salt. I was stifling. I thought I was going to die. Then my head was pulled above water and I gave a long, gasping breath. Father, beside me, was laughing: 'Do you realise, Concordia, that you swam half a dozen strokes by yourself, at your very first lesson? It was only when you discovered that I wasn't holding you that you panicked and went under. Good girl! Now get your breath back and swim inshore.' 'Come with me!' 'No! I'll watch till you are in really shallow water, but now I want to swim, myself.'

I watched him a trifle anxiously: if, now, he found out that he could not swim, it would be a real disaster. 'Be careful, won't you?' I begged.

'I will. Good swimmers don't take risks. They know that others can get drowned, trying to rescue them. Now—back to shore, child! You're getting cold.'

He gave me a push that sent me off with a flying start. When the impulse slackened and I put my feet down, I found that the water came barely to my waist; and so, a stroke or two at a time, I half swam, half scrambled back to the beach. Then I turned to see what Father was doing.

He was being sensible, as he had said—swimming parallel to the shore, so that he could get back into his depth at any moment. He was letting his legs trail behind him, barely moving, and pulling himself along with his powerful arms. Yet it seemed to me that he was making good progress.

I dressed quickly, and in about ten minutes he came into the tent; his skin was still too white for him to stay baking in the sunshine, he said; that was a pleasure he promised himself in a few days' time.

When we reached home I asked him how he felt. Good, he said: no pain, only the slight, almost pleasant ache that comes from using unexercised muscles. And the apparatus had worked perfectly; it would be quite safe for him to keep on swimming.

From then onwards we swam every afternoon. Every day the sea grew warmer and the sand hotter. Soon I was quite at home in the water, and I knew that Father was pleased with me. He himself was beginning to move at speed, flipping his feet like a fish's tail; no longer swimming parallel to shore, but straight out to sea and back. Afterwards he would lie resting on the hot sand, and soon his chest was finely bronzed. I envied him, for I had inherited my mother's milk-white skin, that reddened at once but took a long time to brown. When I came to supper one evening with a nose that was pink and peeling, my mother made an energetic protest: 'Giovanni, I will not have the child's looks ruined. What *are* you doing to her on those afternoon rides?'

A few months earlier, that would have started up one of those quarrels which made me, the cause of them, feel so guilty. But my father's temper had improved with his health, and he simply laughed: '*Donna*,' he said—and with him it was a term of affection—'why not come and see?' He knew, I think, that she would not.

One day the Captain of our escort approached him with the request: 'Messer Giovanni, will you show us how you make that new stroke of yours? I have been watching you for some time, and you seem to be swimming faster than any of our boys farther down the shore.'

Father considered this seriously. I saw that it gave him great satisfaction. 'I wasn't sure,' he said. 'It did seem to me, too, that I was swimming as fast as when I had the full use of my legs, if not faster. My daughter was right when she said that a fish swims faster than a frog! Anyway, we'll put it to the test.'

I marvelled at the change in him. His bitterness and ill-temper were left behind, and it was with the enthusiasm of a boy that he discussed with the Captain how they could make the test. He said that next day he would try out his stroke in a race against the three best swimmers of the company. They went down together to watch the swimmers and, independently, picked the same two men. The third, taken by common consent from among those who were on duty that day, was Marco, a red-headed Venetian. The two others were a stocky, barrel-chested Romagnolo named Beppo, and a gangling youth nick-named satirically Piccino (Tiny), because he was the tallest in the company. Father said privately to me that he was not really a very good swimmer, but over a short course his long limbs would give him an initial advantage.

He told the three men that they could go off duty until next day. 'And provide yourself with drawers, so that you look decent in front of the Contessina,' he warned them.

He had a course marked off, parallel with the shore, by lashing together eight lances in pairs and driving two pairs deep into the sand at each end, connected by a cord. All the escort, except the competitors, remained on shore to watch the race.

The four men were drawn up in line behind the starting-cord, standing just within their depth in order of height. Nearest the shore was Beppo, then my father, then Marco, and farthest out was Piccino. At a whistle from the Captain they moved into swimming position, one hand on the cord; then, at a second signal, dived under it and were away.

My father shot ahead, with the young men following in leisurely fashion. They were obviously not trying—perhaps from a servile anxiety lest the *padrone* should hold it against them if they excelled him; but more, I think, because they genuinely thought it unfair to race against a crippled man old enough to be their father.

He looked over his shoulder, realised the situation, and turned on his back to float until they came up to him. Across the still water I heard his incisive voice: 'You must do better than this, my lads. Don't make me waste my strength by false starts. Go back to the rope.'

Once more they were lined up. 'I'll give you ten strokes start,' he said, 'and if I overtake you less than halfway, you'll forfeit your week's pay—if you beat me, I'll double it . . . Whistle, Captain!'

They were off again, and this time the men were really doing their best. Ahead went Piccino, in a whirl of long limbs and flying spray. Marco and Beppo were swimming side by side, but it seemed to me that Marco was making less effort than the other. I sensed that everyone thought my father had handicapped himself too generously. It did seem so, and I was very anxious, for I knew what it meant to him to win this race. So I sat on the sand with hands clasped tight round my knees, and tried to still the frantic beating of my heart.

Father seemed not to be swimming very fast. Maybe he was saving his strength; or perhaps his strokes were so clean that they caused little flurry in the water. Half-way along, the men were still ahead of him, but in a different order. Piccino had fallen back: he was splashing more than ever, but without making much progress. Marco was now definitely in the lead.

Some thirty yards from the goal, my father overhauled Piccino. The youth was finished and he realised it, turned inshore and scrambled out on to the sand, where he lay gasping like a stranded fish.

Father was keeping his head low: only once in every half-dozen strokes did he raise it slightly over one shoulder to breathe. Now he was coming up with Beppo, who swam on doggedly, neither faster nor slower than at the start.

The men on shore were beginning to lay bets. I heard murmurs of 'Messer Giovanni', and once or twice the nickname 'Gianciotto'. I knew they called him that among themselves, but they must have been excited to do it before me.

There were still about ten yards to go when my father passed Beppo and began to gain on Marco. He had indeed been husbanding his strength, for now he was swimming all-out, his powerful arms flailing like those of a windmill. A yard or two before the post he drew level with Marco. Their two heads, the red one and the black, were so close in line that from the shore they seemed to be fused; their two right arms flashed together into the air—but it was my father's hand that first closed on the cord.

It must have warmed his heart to hear the spontaneous cheer that broke from his men: '*Evviva Gianciotto!*' They used the nickname now with no reticence, sure that it would not offend, and the affection in it surprised me. I knew they admired his courage, but I had always thought they were afraid of him. They probably were, but now I realised they loved him all the same.

The impetus of that double thrust had snapped the cord and carried the two men well past the goal. They paddled back and clung to the lances, waiting to recover their breath. Meanwhile, Beppo had joined them, and all three came ashore together. As they reached shallow water my father's lameness began to show itself: the two young men made a chair for him with their hands and carried him in triumph to his tent. When he was dressed, he handed his purse to the Captain, with orders to give double pay to Marco, a present to each of the other two, and drinks all round at the first tavern they reached. And so we rode back, content, to Rimini.

II

Everyone was now eager to learn the new stroke. My remark had been passed around: so they called it the 'fish-stroke' and the old way 'the frog-stroke'. Father taught Marco in a couple of days and appointed him swimming instructor. The young man was, of course, delighted, for this meant that he was excused his turn on duty and was able to swim every day.

For a while there was great emulation, but soon many of the men dropped back into the old way. 'You'll see,' said my father, 'the crossbow-men, who have developed their arm muscles, will take to the fish-stroke; most of the cavalrymen, who have strong legs, will keep to the other.' And he was right. I myself tried to learn the fish-stroke and failed; but Father told me to wait a few years, till my arms were fully grown; meanwhile, I developed a stroke of my own—over-arm side-stroke with a scissor-kick—which was quite fast.

In the days following the race, I noticed that Father was beginning to take an interest in his personal appearance. He was making a determined effort to straighten himself up. Night and morning he had his back rubbed by Riccardo, and during his rest-hour he had taken to lying flat on a sloped wooden board made by Pietro, with a weight pulling his foot downwards. When I demurred that he would tire himself without doing any real good, he said that the shortening was due to muscular contraction, and that the swimming was loosening his muscles. Apparently he was right, for he was finding his riding-boot too heavily built-up, and when the shoemaker measured him for a new pair, he found that the inner sole could be reduced to half its thickness.

One day he reminded me how I had once said that, as a baby, I had been frightened of his rough cheeks. 'They do seem to have that effect,' he said (though what experience he had of babies I couldn't imagine). 'But what can I do about it? I have a strong growth of beard.' I remarked that Uncle Paolo who, judging by his mane of black hair, must have just as strong a beard, had cheeks like velvet. 'Oh, Paolo probably spends hours having himself shaved twice a day, and rubbing creams into his face like a woman. I've no time to waste on that sort of nonsense.'

I said it wouldn't take Riccardo long to shave him; but if he really didn't want to be bothered, why not grow a beard? A stiff, pointed beard would go well with his strong features and give him a piratical look. He acted on the suggestion, and it was astonishing how quickly the beard grew and how well it suited him.

He was ordering new clothes too, with various drapes and other devices to conceal or distract attention from his crippled leg. All this, in a man who for years had not cared how he looked, might have made me suspicious; but at the time I took it as an encouraging sign that his success in the race had given a spur to his morale. I did not connect it with the letter from Faenza.

That letter was brought by a messenger one day, just before dinner, when we were all three sitting on the terrace, in the shade of the ripening vines. Father read it, laughed, as though he had received some satisfying news, and pushed it quickly into his pocket. 'I shall have to start for Faenza this afternoon,' he said, 'Rengarda wants to see me on urgent business.' (Rengarda was his young half-sister, who had been married that year to Francesco Manfredi.)

'But . . .' I began, when a warning flicker in my father's eye stopped me. I had meant to say that the seal on the letter was neither the Malatesta elephant nor the Manfredi unicorn. However, I held my tongue: if Father wanted us to think that the letter was from Aunt Rengarda, he must have some reason.

'But what, Concordia?' asked Mother.

'But I thought we were going riding this afternoon,' I substituted hastily.

Mother said rather severely that I must realise that my father had much more important things to do than to spend his afternoons amusing me. It would be much better for me to stay quietly with her in our pretty garden and read her the French fable I was learning.

Father gave orders to have his horse ready immediately after his midday rest; and that he would need an escort of half a dozen men, with their saddlebags equipped for a stay of two or three nights.

That afternoon he did not seem inclined to talk to me. He was lying with his eyes closed; not asleep but smiling now and again, as if at some secret thought. When he opened his eyes I said: 'You are happy. Did that letter bring you good news?' 'Yes, excellent.' I didn't ask what it was, but I couldn't help saying: 'It wasn't from Aunt Rengarda.' 'No,' he admitted. 'And you were wise enough not to say so. You're growing up, Concordia!'

12

In mid-September the weather broke; the *greco-levante* sent huge rollers crashing on the beach, making swimming impossible. When it calmed down there was a slight chill in the air. Father decided not to go on swimming, saying that he did not want to add rheumatism to his other pains; and he made me stop too. Some of the hardier men obtained permission to continue, but by October only Marco and one or two others were still going into the water. However, we went on riding on the beach, and there seemed no reason why this should not go on indefinitely.

On the day that ended it all I had no premonition. I was far from imagining that this was not only my last ride of the season but the last time I should ever ride with my father.

It was one of those hard, blue-and-white days of early autumn, when clouds scud like sail-boats across the sky, and each indigo wavelet is tipped with blown spray.

Reaching the shore, we turned southwards. The troop stayed where they were, some still in the saddle, a few walking their mounts; others stretched idly on the sand. Marco and two others had obtained leave to swim.

I was riding just ahead of my father, watching a dark mass inland, quite a long way distant. It looked like a cloud—one of those summer clouds with soundless lightning-flashes flickering through them. Suddenly I heard my father's voice, like the crack of a whiplash: 'Stop, Concordia!' Startled, I reined in and wheeled round to face him. 'What's wrong?' I asked.

'Armed men, coming down from San Marino. It's too far away to see their colours, but I don't like the look of them.' And he shouted back: 'Captain, call the men!' But the Captain's whistle was already blowing.

As we galloped back, I saw Marco's red head flashing through the water, like a fox running before hounds. 'God, what a swimmer!' said my father. 'I couldn't keep up with him now.'

By the time we reached the troop, all of them were on horseback and drawn up in formation, except the three swimmers who were hurrying into their clothes. The dark cloud had resolved itself into definite shapes of men and horses, and we could see banners waving over their heads.

'Who are they, Messer Giovanni?' asked the Captain.

'By the look of their devices, a group of the Parcitadi, stiffened by some of the Rector's men. Forty or more—we're heavily outnumbered. They seem to be wheeling north, to get between us and Rimini.' His eyes—those hawk-eyes of the Malatesta—were following every movement of the group. He signed to Aldo, who was hovering near him: 'I am putting the Contessina in your care. Take her to Gradara. Leave her there and make your own way back by the inland route to Rimini. Tell Madonna Francesca and Messer Malatestino to put the Gattolo on a war footing, with the men who are left there—and not to worry if I and the rest of us don't get home tonight. I may find it better to make for Pesaro or Gradara, but I'll be back tomorrow.'

Aldo and I must both have looked at him with the same mute reproach, for he added firmly: 'Get the Contessina away! This seems a perfectly pointless attack: I suspect its object is to take her prisoner and use her as a hostage to put pressure on me. It's a compliment I'm paying you, man. You're my oldest and trustiest trooper—that's why I'm putting my daughter in your charge.'

Then he spoke to me: 'Turn Plato's head to face Segabite Mount. Sit tight. Keep your stirrups, or you'll be thrown.' And, deliberately, he whipped Plato's hindquarters with the flat of his drawn sword.

Never had my little horse known such an insult. He screamed—a high whinny of protest—and bucked, it seemed to me, with all four feet off the ground. I felt the same panic that had seized me when Nerone bolted. But this time I knew what to do; my feet were fast in the stirrups, and my hands firm on the reins. We were tearing at breakneck speed towards Segabite, but the sand was hard and smooth. Unless Plato stumbled on a piece of driftwood or put his foot in a hole, there was no danger.

Behind me—quite a long way behind—galloped Aldo. He almost ran down Marco, who was sprinting across the sands towards his tethered horse.

In the distance, I could hear my father yelling his name: 'Malatesta! Malatesta!' High and clear it rang—a clarion-call to battle. And, like a long wave rolling on the sand there came the answering roar of his men: 'Malatesta!'

Farther away, the other side were shouting too. I wanted to look round and see what was happening, but I dared not take my attention from Plato for a moment. The horsehoofs fell soft on the sand—I could only just hear those of Aldo's mount behind me—but a minute or two later I thought I could distinguish the clash of iron. It was very faint, for we had already gone a long way.

Splash, splash, through the Conca. The water was shallow, but it spurted into my face. On the farther bank Plato began to slacken; his dainty hoofs slipped on the loose, piled stones, and Aldo's heavier mount came up with me.

My cap had fallen off and my long plait was swinging on my shoulders. The wind blew deliciously through my hair. Exhilarated, I began to sing as I rode. The old man looked at me in surprise: 'Are you not afraid, Contessina?' My look must have been eloquent, for he added hastily: 'For Messer Giovanni's sake, I mean.'

'No,' I said. 'Nothing will happen to him; otherwise I should feel a presentiment. And so would you. You love him too.'

A mile or two before Segabite port we turned inland up the hill, towards the village of Cattolica, where the folk came out to stare at us. They wanted to know what was happening: one of the local fishermen had been up on the cliffs and had reported armed men clashing on Rimini sands.

'The Parcitadi are abroad!' shouted back Aldo. 'Gianciotto is fighting there, and I am taking the Contessina to Gradara.' Suddenly realising that he had used the nickname in my presence, he looked apologetically at me; but I, having heard the pride and affection in his voice, just grinned back at him.

Crossing the Tavollo bridge, we entered the wide valley between Segabite and Gradara. Ahead, on its emerald-green hill, towered the castle, its swallow-tailed battlements glowing red against the sky. The sentinels must have seen Aldo's livery, for by the time we had climbed to the lower gate, bolts and bars had been drawn; it swung open before us, and grooms were waiting to take our horses.

As we walked up the street, women came to their doors

and curtsied to me. The younger children stared, puzzled by my boy's suit; the elder ones, recognizing me, called: 'Contessina! Contessina Concordia, welcome home!' I felt in fact, that I had come home: I had always loved Gradara, and, happy as the summer in Rimini had been, I had missed it. Out of the gatehouse came the doorkeeper with his wife, Monna Elena, and their family. The eldest, Salvatore, had shot up to man's height, while the youngest —a swaddled doll when I had left—was now a sturdy little girl, walking and talking.

In the courtyard, bowing in his sober black suit, was the seneschal, Messer Rinaldo. I asked him to see that Aldo was given a quick meal before he started back to Rimini. Then I inquired what staff and garrison were in the castle when we were not in residence. He answered me, as though I were still the child I had been when I went away, that there were enough to keep one little birdie safe in her nest, adding that he would find a good, kind woman to take care of me till my nannie came.

I looked him straight in the eyes: 'Messer Rinaldo, I may be only eleven, but I am not a baby, and at the moment I am here in my father's stead. Messer Giovanni may come here tonight—alone, or with some of his men, or with the whole troop. If we have to house and feed twenty men or more, I must know how you propose to do it.'

He looked at me in surprise; then, taking me seriously this time, explained that, in time of peace, the twenty men-at-arms kept as permanent defenders lived and ate in their own houses in the citadel, except for the sentinels—two by day and four by night—who had a duty-rota and were served with meals in the guardroom.

'And what stores are there?'

He said there were supplies of salted meat and whole cheeses in the cellars; there was wine, of course, and fresh grapes, and some of last year's apples were still good. 'And bread?' I asked. Bread would be a difficulty, admitted

Messer Rinaldo; there were only three loaves, baked by Monna Elena for his own supper and that of the sentinels, and one of those would have been already cut into for Aldo. 'Could not more be baked?'

He pointed out that to light the large oven and bake in quantity, firewood would have to be chopped; the oven itself would take several hours to heat; the leavened dough would have to be raised . . . in short, it would not be practicable to bake until next day.

I was thinking fast: 'Each family in the citadel will have baked for its own needs?' He nodded, and I continued: 'Well, if the troop does come, why not send out Salvatore with two large baskets? He can go to each of the larger families and ask for one loaf, or half a loaf if they can't spare more. Say that tomorrow, when we bake, we will give them back double.'

Things were taking shape in my brain. Father would be tired: he would need a hot bath and a warmed room. It would be better to put him in Mother's bedroom, which had its bathroom-closet and was easier of access than his own room in the tower. I asked the seneschal to have a fire laid in my mother's bedroom, ready to light, and to see that water was drawn from the well and heated.

'As for your good, kind woman,' I said, 'Send for her. Not for me—I am quite independent now—but she will be useful to help in the kitchen. Tell her to bring two hens—one alive and the other freshly killed. We will stew it for broth, and if my father does not come, I will have that, with an egg broken into it, for my supper. If he does come, kill the second hen and broil it quickly on the charcoal for him.' I stopped, noting his expression of amazement. 'Why are you staring at me like that?'

He muttered, completely taken aback: 'Only eleven—and giving orders like a man. Sensible orders, too.'

All at once I was a child again, frightened at my own temerity. 'Your pardon, Messer Rinaldo!' I exclaimed, 'I did not mean to give you orders—I was only thinking what would have to be done. Don't tell my father I was interfering, or he might be angry with me.'

'On the contrary, I think he would be proud of you.' Messer Rinaldo looked me up and down: 'It's incredible, Contessina—you go away as a tiny, blonde angel, frightened of the sound of your own voice. And in less than two years you come back, looking like a handsome lad, thinking and talking like Messer Giovanni himself. What a pity you're his daughter and not his son!'

I laughed, flattered. 'I've been a great deal with him lately, and no doubt that has changed me. That reminds me—I'm still in my riding-habit and boots. I must go upstairs and put on a dress.'

In Mother's room, I knew, there was a small chest with things that I had left behind. But I had a surprise—the clothes and shoes simply would not fit me any longer. When I left Gradara I must have been small for my age; now, with the riding and swimming, I had developed very quickly. Even in the last few weeks, my breasts had begun to grow. I might as well have tried to get into doll's clothes.

Quickly making up my mind, I opened one of Mother's chests, picking out a cream-and-gold dress that I had always loved, and shoes to match it. They were loose for me, but with the toes padded they would stay on my feet. The dress, of course, was much too long, both in the skirt and the sleeves, but I found sewing materials and tacked up a frill, so that it did not trail on the ground, turned back the sleeves, and pulled the bodice strings as tightly as I could. Even so, there was too little of me inside it, so I slipped in a scarf to fill it out.

All this took time, and the low sun was shining redly across the valley before I had finished. Monna Elena came in to lay the fire, so I knew that my orders were being carried out. Then I went on to the bridge connecting my mother's room with the council chamber and the staircase that led up to the spare bedrooms. It was just above the drawbridge, and I called to the sentinel posted on the battlements, asking him to let me know if he saw my father approaching.

It was not long before I heard his voice: 'Contessina!' 'Yes—what can you see?' 'Messer Giovanni, riding fast and alone. The troop are coming up more slowly, bringing their wounded with them.'

Wounded! That was something I had not thought of. I asked how many there were. Four or five, he said—it was difficult to tell at that distance. 'One man killed—there's a riderless horse running free. No, he's been picked up—the last horse has a double load.'

I went to Messer Rinaldo and told him to send Salvatore out at once for the bread. Passing Mother's room, I saw that the fire had been lit and jars of water set to warm by it. I asked Monna Elena for the key of the linen-cupboard where Nannie kept a bag with strips of old, worn sheets cut up for use as patches: they would come in useful for bandages. Then, leaving the bag in Mother's room, I went out again on the bridge when I heard horsehoofs in the street and clatter of the drawbridge chains.

A few moments later my father rode up. I leaned over to wave to him. The sun was down by now and the bridge was in shadow. He could have seen me only as a gleam against the dark background—gold dress and pale gold hair.

'Francesca!' It was a cry of sheer surprise mingled with delight. Oh, I thought—if Mother could only have heard that, she could not fail to respond!

I ran down the stairs and into his arms. He had dismounted by the time I reached the courtyard, but he was still standing on the block as if on a pedestal. 'Father—you look splendid!'

He hugged me to him for a moment (I felt the hardness

of his cuirass against my breast), and then held me away to look at me. The joy had gone from his face and I saw that he was very tired. 'Why, it's Concordia in her mother's gown! I might have known *she'd* not throw herself into my arms and tell me I looked splendid. She'd more likely say: "Giovanni, you stink of dust and sweat and blood".' 'And so you do!' I said lightly, brushing away the sand that I could feel on my lips. 'Still, never mind—there's water heated for your bath. I've had the bed made up in Mother's room—fewer stairs to climb, both for you and for the men carrying the pitchers.'

He flung back his head and laughed: 'Bed? Bath? My dear child, I've hours of work ahead—my men to feed, the wounded to be looked after. This is war-time, Concordia—you've lost your patient now! Or at least, you've found half a dozen, if you have the pluck to help me tonight. Have you ever seen a fresh, undressed wound?' I shook my head. 'It's not pretty, but I don't think you're the type to faint or be sick. Go and get that dress off, or you'll mess it up.' He gave me a quick glance: 'Ah! there's blood on it already—off my cuirass, I suppose.'

I ran up to the bedroom, and across it to see how the fire was burning and whether the water was hot. Turning, I faced the mirror beside the wide, curtained bed. Then my heart began to flutter like a caged bird; for in the dusky, oval depths I saw my mother, all white and gold, with a dark stain on her breast. She stood there, still, anguished in the firelight. I made a quick movement towards her—and the figure moved too. Then I realised that I was looking at myself, but I did not laugh: the shock had been so intense that I felt my knees giving way and had to sit a while on the bed before I found the strength to change back into my riding-suit, merely keeping on the indoor shoes.

'You've been a long time,' said my father curtly, as I joined him in the guardroom. He gave me a piercing glance: 'White as milk—and you've seen nothing yet. That won't do, girl. Here—drink this!' 'This' was the wine in his own glass. It was straight from the vat, strong and rough: one sip of it half-choked me, made my throat burn. I blushed, embarrassed at this childish reaction, and he must have thought that the colour was due to the stimulus from the wine, for he remarked: 'That's better! Now, don't let me down.'

13

By this time the men, having stabled their horses below, were straggling in. The first to arrive were all slightly hurt, for the uninjured had stayed behind to bring up the wounded. They themselves did not count as wounded; they simply had scratches and bruises, like boys who have been playing a rough game.

Father had asked Messer Rinaldo for a bowl of pig's grease, a cake of salt and a bottle of vinegar. He told the men to rub the grease into any spot that hurt, helping each other in pairs if the place was difficult to reach. If the skin was broken they must put salt on it and wash it out with vinegar. I saw the men's expressions and I protested for them: 'But, Father, it will hurt terribly!'

'It will sting—but it stops the wound from festering. See, I'll show you how.' He pushed back his sleeve, and I saw that he had a bloodstained handkerchief tied round his wrist. 'Father—you're wounded! . . .' 'That's not a wound. Just a sword-tip graze. Untie this rag, Concordia.'

I undid the knot and looked round for water, to soak the bandage off; but Father yanked it away with a sharp pull. What he had described as a 'graze' was a nasty jagged cut, and it had started bleeding again. Imperturbable, he rubbed in the salt and held his arm out to me for a dash of vinegar. 'And that's all there is to it,' he said, smiling across at the men as I put a fresh bandage on the wound. He was pretending, of course, but only I knew it, for I was used to watching him when he was in pain. I guessed, too, that his leg was hurting him.

For the next few minutes I was kept busy tearing up linen to bandage small cuts; then came the real wounded, carried up the hill on hand-chairs by their fellows. To avoid stooping, which he always found painful, Father had them laid on the wide, sloping platform where the guard slept at night; sideways along the edge, so that he could reach them easily.

Our first patient had an arrow through his arm, which had been left in the wound. Otherwise, my father told me later, he would have bled to death, as an artery had been severed.

The water was hot by this time, and two great steaming bowls of it had been brought down. Father washed his hands and told me to do the same. Then he made me take the man's hand in both of mine and hold on with all my strength, while he himself pulled out the arrow-head. There was a yell from the patient and out it came, followed by spurting blood. Father's thumbs clamped down on the wound; he told someone to snap the shaft and give part of it to me, to be washed and wrapped in linen; then, twisting it in a bandage, he tightened it till the flow of blood stopped. His eye lighted on Beppo and he beckoned him forward. 'Stay by this man,' he said, 'Release the bolt every ten minutes or so—and see that you don't forget. If you do, the wound will mortify and he will lose his hand, maybe his arm. When you find that the blood does not spurt as you loosen the shaft, call me, and I'll fix a normal bandage.' He was a good judge of men; that stolid, reliable Beppo would, I was sure, go on tying and untying for hours, if necessary.

The next man was carried in unconscious. I thought

he was very ill, but Father, after slitting up his breeches to see the wound in his thigh, said he had simply fainted from loss of blood. It was a clean wound and not deep; probably he would be in the saddle again in less than a month.

I looked at the dagger he had used to slit the cloth. It was the beautiful jewel-hilted weapon that Mother had given him, but its blade was dull with dried blood. His glance followed mine and he exclaimed sharply: 'Hell! I forgot to clean it!' He unhooked the scabbard from his belt and handed it with the dagger to a trooper, telling him to clean both and to grease the blade so that it did not rust. I was shaking a little, for somehow I knew that the stain on it was a man's life-blood.

When we had bandaged the second man, another was waiting for us—this time with a really nasty injury, a broken bone that had pierced the skin. I must have looked sick when Father bared his arm, for he called me to order with a sharp 'Concordia!' Again he told me to hold tight on to the limb while he pulled the bone into place. This time the patient did not scream. He ground his teeth together and looked for a moment as if he had fainted, then opened his eyes and said: 'Thank you, Messer Giovanni.'

'Tough!' commented my father with his rare, wonderful smile.

He took from his pocket a small box containing an ointment that he always kept with him in case he had a sudden bout of pain. He bought it regularly, he had told me once, from a Venetian merchant who travelled in the Far East; it contained a very potent drug, distilled from crushed poppy seeds. He ordered me to rub it into the arm while he prepared a splint. 'The Contessina has magic hands,' he told the man. 'She can soothe any pain away.'

Meanwhile, the last two wounded had been carried in. One of them was apparently unhurt, but he looked dazed and was vomiting. It made me feel sick too, but I knew I must not let Father know. I sent one of the men to fetch a basin, and put another on to clearing up the mess. Then I took off the patient's helmet and held his head over the bowl. I felt a light touch on my hair and, looking up, saw Father smiling at me. He gave a cursory inspection, his fingers exploring the man's skull: 'He's been knocked on the head, but the helmet has kept off the worst of it —the skull's not broken. So we'll just leave him to sleep it off.'

Then he turned to see the last man, who had been carried in on a stretcher made of coats buttoned over two lances. It was Piccino—I recognised the sprawled look of his lanky body. A large dark patch stained his jerkin, and on his lips were streaks of blood and foam.

For the first time Father seemed to be at a loss. 'There's no surgeon nearer than Pesaro—and if I sent for him, I doubt whether he'd come so late at night,' he said thoughtfully. The Captain interposed: 'You are as good as any surgeon, Messer Giovanni.' Father shook his head: 'I can handle flesh wounds and broken bones—I've had plenty of experience. But this looks like internal bleeding—I think his lung is pierced. Can you make out what he is saying?'

A dull muttering was coming from Piccino's lips. It sounded like a series of gasps or groans: 'Ah . . . na . . . ah . . . na . . . ah . . .'

'I think he is trying to say his wife's name—Anna. They were married a few weeks ago, and she is . . . at Christmas.' I didn't grasp the word, but it must have been a vulgar one, for my father frowned and the Captain glanced apologetically at me.

'Well,' said Father with quick decision, 'see that she gets his pay until then. And when she is on her feet again, send her round to my steward at the Gattolo. We'll take her on the kitchen staff. Write me an order to that effect tomorrow and I'll sign it.'

The Captain hesitated, embarrassed: 'To tell the truth, Messer Giovanni . . .'

Father understood at once: 'You're better with your sword than with a pen, eh? Well, never mind—the Contessina will do it. She writes as well as any scribe.'

He took Piccino's hand between his own: 'Don't worry, lad: we'll look after your Anna.' A flicker passed through the young man's eyes, but he had evidently grasped the implications of that conversation. '. . . dying?' he breathed. 'I hope not. But you've a nasty wound. You won't ride again this side of Christmas—not till after the child is born.'

At an imperceptible sign from the Captain they moved a few yards away. Faintly I heard their lowered voices. 'Ought we to send for a priest?' asked the Captain. 'Not unless he asks for one. It will upset the morale of the others. For my part, I think the less a dying man is pestered about his soul, the better.' 'Then he *is* dying?' 'I'm afraid so. I've seen men live with worse wounds, but he is one of those overgrown types. No stamina.'

Only one thing penetrated my mind. Piccino was going to die—Piccino, who just a few weeks before had been competing in a race; poor simple Piccino, whose wife (I understood it now) was going to have a baby. It didn't seem fair, somehow. He looked so defenceless lying there with blood trickling from his slack mouth.

Father opened Piccino's jerkin and put a pad over the wound, which seemed to have stopped bleeding. I said so, hopefully, but Father shook his head; then he ordered two men to unroll one of the sheepskins kept for the use of the permanent guard, lay Piccino on it and cover him with another. 'Keep him warm,' he said, 'That's all we can do for him.'

14

While we had been attending to the wounded, Monna Elena had been laying the tables for supper. When Father saw the loaves he glanced approvingly at Messer Rinaldo: 'Fresh bread, so late in the day? That's good work. Where did you get it, at a moment's notice?' 'From the families in the citadel. It was the Contessina's idea.' And I had another quick smile from Father.

Men were coming and going between the courtyard and the guardroom. Among the crowd I identified Marco's red head and went up to him. By now he was one of my father's most devoted followers: I knew I could rely upon him. The hot water I had prepared for Father's bath had been used; if I asked Monna Elena to draw more, she would turn sullen. She was already working overtime.

'Marco', I said, 'can you get together a few men, draw water to fill three pitchers, and set them to warm by the hearth in Madonna Francesca's bedroom? You will need to make up the fire, too—Messer Rinaldo will tell you where to find the wood. But don't attract my father's attention, or he will say he doesn't want people fussing over him.'

Marco made me a little mock-humble bow, his sea-blue eyes twinkling: 'At your orders, Contessina! We'll be as discreet as smugglers!' I saw his red head moving to and fro among the dark ones; then for a while it disappeared.

Meanwhile, all, except the wounded and Beppo who still sat faithfully by his charge, had come to the tables. Our improvised meal smelt good. I had thought that, after all I had seen, I would have no appetite, but now I was ravenous.

Messer Rinaldo had arranged for my father and me, with the Captain, to sit at the high table and eat the broiled chicken, while the men at the other tables had boiled salt beef, but Father dismissed the idea with an impatient

Macché "high table"! We've fought together and we'll eat together. As for the chicken, give it to the wounded men. My daughter and I haven't got delicate stomachs.' So the four tables were pulled into a square and we sat around them, five to a side.

Someone had taken a plate over to Beppo. He started to wolf the food, then stopped in the middle to untie the patient's arm. Suddenly he called: 'Messer Giovanni—it's stopped bleeding!' The childlike enthusiasm of his tone raised a general laugh. Father got up and went to see (I noticed that he was limping heavily). Someone moved up to make room for Beppo, and when my father had fixed a fresh bandage we all got on with our meal.

It was my first opportunity to ask about the fight. Everyone began to talk at once, but Father was nearest, so I listened to him, as he crumbled pieces of bread to illustrate what he was saying.

So far as I could grasp it, the Parcitadi, being more numerous, had tried to encircle our group. Anticipating this, Father had drawn up his men in a double-wedge or diamond shape, with himself at the head and the Captain and Sergeant Marco in the wing positions. He, with the first wedge, had charged and broken the enemy's centre, while the second wedge, dividing in two, had unexpectedly wheeled left and right, penetrating the flanks of the groups who were trying to encircle them. By this means they had split the enemy into six small units. Without attempting to pursue the men who were escaping inland, Father had wheeled back immediately to prevent the Parcitadi from reforming. Locating their leader, he had fought his way through to him, and then . . .

'Then?' I asked, as his eyes began to sparkle.

'I got him in the throat with a flung dagger. He'd fastened his gorget carelessly and there was just a crack where the neck showed through. It needed some timing, I can tell you!'

'How did you get the dagger back?' I asked.

'Oh, his men scattered when he fell, and we chased them up the shore.'

'Almost into the Marecchia!' said someone. But Father, laughing, said there had been no time to waste on that. Once they were on the run he had come back, and by then the rest were retreating towards San Marino, taking their wounded with them but leaving the dead on the sand.

'So I told someone to dismount and pull out my dagger from the leader's throat . . .' 'It had gone right through to the spine,' interposed the man who had fetched it. '. . . then we noticed Piccino's horse running loose, and we found him lying among the Parcitadi men. And in the business of getting him picked up, I forgot all about my dagger . . . just pushed it back into the sheath unwiped. Let that be a lesson to you, my child!'

This raised a great laugh from the men. The Captain observed mildly that the Contessina was not likely to need this advice. Laughing good-humouredly, my father said he hadn't been so far mistaken: I had proved myself as good a man as any of them that night. The men cheered, raising their glasses to drink to me.

I felt a warm glow of happiness and pride. Yet at the back of my mind I couldn't help wondering about my father—this strange mixture of sensitivity and callousness. No woman could have been gentler than he while he cared for his wounded; but his only reaction to the killing of a man was satisfaction at his own skill. What really troubled his conscience was his carelessness in forgetting to clean his dagger afterwards. I thought that if I had killed someone, even in battle, I would be sorry; but evidently men look at these things differently from women.

As soon as he had finished eating, Father mixed a half cup of wine with honey and took it to Piccino. The man was lying with closed eyes and seemed unconscious. He would not drink, but Father soaked a piece of rag in the mixture and placed it between his lips. After a while he began to suck feebly at it. With infinite patience Father coaxed him to swallow part of the drink, a few drops at a time. It seemed to revive him. When his eyelids fluttered open, Father took the limp hands between his own. 'Raffaello!' he said (I heard the man's real name for the first time) 'Have you the will to live? If you add your will to mine, I can hold you.' His black eyes were fixed and hard, but Piccino shut his own to avoid the gaze. His head moved in an almost imperceptible negative gesture. 'Let me go!' he implored.

Father sighed. He did not like being beaten, but he knew when there was nothing more to be done. Gently he released Piccino's hands, crossing them on his breast. 'Go, then!' he said. 'Go, in the name of angels and of archangels, of thrones and dominations and powers.' His resonant voice filled the hall, echoed from the rafters. The men looked up, startled; some of them began to weep.

'Is he dead?' asked the Captain.

'No, but I don't think he will be conscious again. If he is, and asks for me, send someone to wake me.' Father's eyes went to the ladder that connected the guardroom with the bedroom above. 'I'll have the trapdoor set open for you,' he added.

'Can I do it?' I asked quickly, for I knew how it irked him not to be able to lift any weight from the ground.

'No. The bolts are stiff and the trap is heavy—it's a man's job.'

'I'll fetch Marco.' I wanted a private chat with Marco, and I was able to have it while Father was talking to the Captain, probably telling him what to do if Piccino died in the night.

It had struck me that Father would miss Riccardo. When he was tired it was an effort for him to undress, and I feared he would throw himself on the bed and sleep, just as he was. Normally, he would let no one but Riccardo see him naked, but I thought he might make an exception in favour of Marco. Since the swimming-match there had been a bond of comradeship between them.

I asked Marco to come up with us and open the trap-door. Then I added: 'My father is very tired and his valet is not here. Will you stay and undress him?' He answered with a quick smile: 'I would be very happy to help Messer Giovanni.' 'Good. But you mustn't use the word "help", or he will say no. Just say, taking it for granted, that I suggested you should replace Riccardo tonight. I think he will agree.' Then I handed him the box of ointment that was still in my pocket. 'When you have bathed him, get him quickly into bed and rub this into his hip, if he will let you. I know it is hurting him. If he won't let you, tell him to do it himself.' Marco looked rather alarmed at the idea of 'telling' Messer Giovanni to do anything; but I assured him that my father liked people who could stand up to him—and I knew he did like Marco.

We all went upstairs together. At the door Father kissed me and told me to go to bed. Instead, remembering the order I had to write for the Captain, I took a cresset from the wall, lit some candles in the council chamber, and found writing materials. I had just finished the order when I heard the bedroom door open, and I darted back across the bridge just as Marco came out. Before he could close the door, I had slipped into the room.

15

Father was lying very still, with the bed-curtains pulled open. The fire-glow tinged his pale face with colour. 'Not in bed yet?' he asked. 'No, I wanted to see that you were comfortable. Besides, I have been writing the order for you to sign.' One of Father's characteristics is never to waste words or time. 'Light me a candle and read what you have written,' he ordered. When I had done so he said: 'Good! Leave it on the reading-desk and I'll sign it when I get up tomorrow. Just now I don't want to move.'

He was stretched full length and his body looked very flat under the coverlet. He was not slender like Paolo nor thin like Malatestino, but in so many years of restricted exercise he had retained a solid leanness that suggested a Gothic wooden statue. I climbed up beside him on to the great bed—the bed in which I had been born and which I had so often shared with my mother. The vertical line between his eyebrows—the pain-line, as I thought of it—was still there. I smoothed it out with my finger-tips. 'Didn't the ointment work?' I asked.

'Give it time! . . . The pain is deep-seated, but it is easing. This is the type that you have to treat like an enemy in ambush—either move so fast that he can't keep up with you—and that's what I've been doing all day—or keep so still that he can't find you, as I'm doing at present.'

'What do you think brought it on?' 'Probably the twist I gave in my saddle when I threw my dagger. I must have sprained one of those weakened muscles. Still, it was worth it—I got my man.'

'Do you *like* killing people?' I couldn't help asking.

This was evidently a new thought to him. He reflected for a moment and then said: 'It's not a thing one likes or doesn't like—it's just part of a battle, as killing a stag is part of a hunt. But it does give you a sense of satisfaction when, from a galloping horse, you can cast a dagger straight into the barest crack of unprotected flesh. There's not a man in my troop who could do that—I doubt if there's anyone else in Romagna.'

'Perhaps that man had a wife, like Piccino.' 'What then?

To look after her is Parcitadi's responsibility, not mine.' 'At any rate, you were sorry for Piccino.' 'Of course. A stupid lad, but honest and brave. He will be a loss to the troop.'

'Those were splendid words you spoke for him, but do you think they really suited him?' I asked, doubtfully. 'Somehow I don't feel—even if his real name was Raffaello—that he would be happy with angels and archangels . . . he'd much rather have a little cottage with his wife.'

At that, Father laughed outright—the gay laughter that I so seldom heard from him. 'Concordia! Not for the first time you remind me of brother Tino: you see too clearly and too much. No, I didn't say that for Piccino, but for the other men. It's not pleasant to have a comrade die in the night, and I wanted to make them feel that death is something heroic and splendid. It's not, you know—it's ugly and brutal but necessary, like so many things in this life. But there's something in every man's heart that will stir at the trumpet-peal of beautiful words.'

'Where did you learn those, and what exactly do they mean?'

'The answer to both questions is—I don't really know. I think I suddenly woke up in the midst of a sermon, when some preacher was talking about the beauties of heaven and listing the hierarchies. It struck me that those words would make a good funeral for a warrior. Say them for me when you hear that I am dead.' 'When I *hear*? But . . .' 'Oh yes! You think you'll be there to close my eyes, but you won't. I shall die in battle or by treachery: a man like me doesn't die in his bed—and thank God for that!' I must have made some sound of protest, for he added: 'Promise me, then—you'll say those words for me: "Go, in the name of angels and of archangels, of thrones and dominations and powers." And you must say them, not over my dead body (God knows, I'll be glad enough to get rid of that!), but on the seashore of Rimini, where you and I have been happy together. Perhaps there'll be something of my free spirit there, ranging with the winds and the waves.'

All this disconcerted my preconceived notions. People had put into my mind precise ideas about Hell, and Purgatory, and Paradise. 'Do you think you *will* be free to roam on Rimini sea-shore?' I asked. 'Don Angelo says . . .'

'Ah yes, Don Angelo has three neat little pigeon-holes, into which he can shepherd, infallibly, any departing soul. But if he doesn't put mine straight into the one marked "Hell", that's only because he has a well-paid post as our chaplain. Well, if I do go to Hell it will be in the company of the Dark Angels, and maybe Lucifer will have a fellow-feeling for me—he's lame too.'

In the silence of the room I could hear the fire crackling. I was lying now with closed eyes, not touching him, but it seemed as though an invisible current were flowing from his mind into mine. We were no longer father and daughter, nor even brother and sister—just two disembodied spirits meeting each other in a void that was out of space and time.

After a while he spoke again: 'There is a second promise I want you to give me: if you hear that I am wounded, or ill, or a prisoner, you must not on any account try to come to me, unless you get a message in my own handwriting, brought by a man whom you know.' 'No!' I said firmly. 'No . . . what?' 'No, I won't promise; for that is exactly what I would do.' 'But, my dear, it is not for your sake I am asking this, but for mine. As I said on the sands today, I don't want to be hampered by knowing that my daughter is a hostage. Now will you promise?' 'Yes, I will. But . . .' I added, 'I would be much happier if you would take me back to Rimini with you.'

'Better here, with your mother. I shall bring or send her to you tomorrow. Then I shall be free to defend the Gattolo, or to abandon it if need be. I feel there is a lot of trouble in store for us.' 'But supposing Mother wants to stay and share it with you?' Father gave his sharp, sarcastic bark of laughter: 'Your mother, as always, will do what I tell her. In any case, I have never observed that she has any ardent desire for my company. I have had more tenderness and practical help from you tonight than from her in twelve years of marriage.'

I wanted to stretch out my hand and caress his hair; but instinct told me that the least movement on my part might break that strange contact of our minds. The quieter I kept, the more he would talk—and talking might lessen the ache at his heart.

He went on, a note of drowsiness creeping into his voice: 'I thought the gates of Heaven had opened this evening, when I saw her—as I thought for a moment—on the balcony, and she stretched out her arms and came flying to me like a homing pigeon.'

'You love her—so much?' I whispered. Perhaps I should have let him drift off to sleep; but, as once before, I felt I must know how matters stood between those two. 'So dreadfully, Concordia.' 'Then why are you unkind to her?' 'That's just why.' He did not dispute the assertion that he was unkind. I had listened to too many of those quarrels, when he used what she called 'stable language' to her, and she retaliated with her great-lady air of cool contempt. 'She maddens me, when she looks at me with that faint distaste in her beautiful eyes.'

'She is loyal,' I said, 'She never criticises you to me, or lets anyone else do so in her presence.' 'Yes, your mother is loyal. She is a virtuous woman and a proud one. Even if she does dislike and despise me, she would never deceive me. If she did . . .' He broke off and I did not prompt him, for I guessed too well what he had meant to say. I tried to comfort him by saying (not quite truthfully, I fear) that I was sure Mother was much fonder of him than he thought: 'She is a person who finds it difficult to express her feelings. Sometimes I think she is a beautiful statue carved in snow.' 'That's where you're wrong, Concordia. I'd say, rather, a volcano coated with ice. On that first night of our marriage I glimpsed the fire beneath, but I have never been able to rouse it since.'

He paused for a long while and I was wondering whether he had fallen asleep, when he began to speak again, in a much calmer voice. 'Our marriage started wrong; but of course you know nothing about that . . .' 'I do know something.' 'How?' For very shame I could not tell him that I had listened at the door like a servant, so I said only: 'I heard something about a "proxy", and later I asked Uncle Malatestino what it meant, and he told me.' 'Oh, Malatestino!' said Father with a short laugh, as though that explained everything.

There was a long pause, then he spoke again: '*She* said once that I had behaved like a coward. Do you think so too?' I hesitated: there are some wounds that cannot be touched, however gently. At last I said: 'You did make a mistake. You under-rated yourself, and her. Don't you think, if you had given her a free choice, she might have loved you for what you are—and loved you all the better for being lame?' And, trying to convince myself and him of something that I knew in my heart was not true, I added, a little breathlessly: 'After all, *I* do. If you weren't . . .' 'If I weren't, you'd still be calling me "Messer" and looking at me with those frightened-rabbit eyes that rouse all the cruelty in a man.' A whimsical note came into his voice. 'No, my dear—there are some girl-children who enjoy pulling their dolls to pieces; others who mend their sisters' dolls and their own. I don't know if your mother is one of the destroyers—though sometimes I think she might be—but she's certainly not one of the menders. You are. And I take an unfair advantage of it, to unload on to your little shoulders the burden of my pains, and my ill-temper and my anxieties; and you accept it all uncomplainingly.' I said: 'I don't feel it as a burden, Father—

I'm only sorry that you have to suffer. I wish I were older and could help you more.' 'It helps me a lot. Just to have someone who cares, someone whom I trust and can talk to.' 'You do trust me, don't you?' 'As if you were my second self.'

That gave me courage to ask him something that had been at the back of my mind for a long while: 'Then tell me something, Father—is there no one else?' 'No one else? In what way?' 'No one, besides my mother.' He was silent, and my heart began to beat faster. I wondered if he was angry. At last he said, in a curious, reluctant voice: 'There *is* someone, Concordia.' 'The woman in Faenza?' He drew in his breath sharply: 'No one but my sister knows anything about that. Has Malatestino . . .' 'No,' I reassured him, 'I just guessed. You remember, years ago, you came back from Faenza with a scented handkerchief, and when I asked for it you threw it into the fire. I thought of that, the other day, when you lied about a letter that you said was from Aunt Rengarda.'

'Well, you guessed right, my too-intelligent child. Are you shocked?' 'No—just puzzled.' And so I was: loving my mother as tragically as he did, how could he find room in his heart for anyone else? 'Do you love her?' I couldn't help asking. '*Love!*' The scorn in his voice was answer enough. 'Then why . . .?' 'Why does a starving man snatch at the bread that is offered him, without pausing to think whether it is fresh or stale?'

Such bitterness could only be dissolved in laughter or tears. The impulse was strong to gather him into my arms and let him sob himself to sleep. But to break the pride of a Malatesta and build it up again would have needed someone much older and wiser than I; so I chose the other way. 'Would she *like* being described as stale bread?' I asked. At that he did laugh—the good laughter that I liked to hear. 'She would *not*,' he agreed, 'and it wouldn't be fair, either. She's more like a ripe apricot—a dark

Romagnola, faithful and loving, a good breeder and a good mother.' 'Have you . . .?' 'Yes, two. Both of them boys. That letter was to tell me that the second one was born. Think of it! For ten years I was craving for a son—and now I have two.'

A little pang of jealousy went through me. 'Do you love them better than me?' 'No, of course not. They are only babies, and I don't like babies. I am looking forward to the time when I can teach them to ride and to swim, and can talk to them like reasonable beings.'

'What would Mother think if she found out?' A note of sardonic amusement crept into his voice. 'Behind a show of virtuous indignation, she'd be delighted, I think, at having something really to reproach me with, beyond being ugly and lame. Well, she has only herself to thank for it. At any rate, she's accustomed to the idea in her own family.'

Remembering the 'nightingales and cuckoos', I inquired whether he proposed to bring the children to live with us. The idea was evidently not new to Father. He answered slowly, as if debating it in his own mind: 'I doubt whether Ginevrasina would give them up—as I said, she's a good mother. Francesca might accept them, if I could find a way to preserve her dignity. But there's no hurry. I'll wait ten years or so, till they have grown into attractive young lads—I hope they'll inherit their mother's looks, not mine. But I do mean, sooner or later, to legitimise them. I must have a son, to carry on my name.' He waited a while, as if for some comment; then, as I said nothing, asked me: 'What are you thinking, my dear? Are you condemning me?' 'Of course not. You are just doing the same as Grandfather Guido, and it doesn't hurt Mother, so long as she doesn't know. But is it fair on the girl?' 'She's not a girl—she is a widow, and she has had an unhappy life. Her father opened the gate of Faenza to us. He was killed later, with her husband, at the battle of

Forlì, and of course the townspeople called him a traitor and ostracised Ginevra. My sister Rengarda stood by her. That's all there is to it.'

The room was very quiet; not even the fire was crackling now. Father yawned: I could tell that he was sleepy. 'You realise how confidential this is?' he warned me, 'Not a word to anyone?' 'Not a word!' 'On your honour?' 'On my honour as a Malatesta!'

Father said drowsily: 'You'll be a splendid wife for a soldier, one day. How old are you? Eleven, isn't it? Another year or two, and I shall have to set about choosing you a husband.' 'Don't you think I might choose him for myself?' I asked, and at that he laughed, saying, still more sleepily, that he would see about that when the time came. Then I kissed his forehead and left him, for I knew that the burst of confidence had done him good. The tension was gone, and the pain; now he would sleep.

16

As I went upstairs I felt the full force of my own tiredness. I did just what I had been determined my father should not do—threw myself down on the bed, fully dressed, and fell asleep. Once I half-woke, feeling cold, but did not stir. When I woke again, many hours later, a high, mid-morning sun was streaming into the room. For a moment I did not know where I was, only that I felt rested and deliciously warm. When I found that I was still in my riding-suit, everything came back to me: the ride, the fight, the chaotic evening, and that intimate talk with my father. I stirred and then realised why I was no longer cold: someone had covered me with a fur-lined cloak—one of Mother's.

Only Father could have done that. He must have found

me lying outside the bed, and made the double journey to fetch it; and stairs, I knew, were always an effort for him. And he must have come up to say good-bye, for he had meant to start at dawn.

Stopping only to wash my face and hands, I ran downstairs. In the courtyard I found two of the wounded—those with arm injuries—sitting in the sunshine. 'Where is Messer Giovanni?' I asked. 'Gone to Rimini with the troop, hours ago.' I had guessed it, but it came as a shock: somehow I felt that I had failed him. Still, there was nothing I could do about it, and I had plenty of work ahead of me.

First I went into the guardroom, to see how the other wounded were faring. They were sitting up on their sheepskins, playing some game with dice. The man with concussion said he had a splitting headache but otherwise didn't feel too bad; the other would have liked to get up, but had been ordered to keep his leg still for several days, so that the wound would heal more quickly. 'And Piccino . . .?' I asked. There was a pause, then the smothered reply: 'They've taken him away.'

This was a bad beginning to the day, but there was no time to brood. First I must find Messer Rinaldo and remind him of our promise to replace the borrowed bread. 'And remember—in double measure,' I said firmly, for I had an idea that he did not intend to do this. In fact, he replied that people would be quite satisfied to get back what they had given, half-loaves and all. I said: 'I pledged my word—and the word of a Malatesta is worth more than the price of a few loaves. What's more, I intend to be there when they are given out.'

He shrugged his shoulders resignedly, muttering something about: 'Messer Giovanni's daughter—every bit as obstinate as he.' Then he consulted me about Piccino's funeral. That gave me considerable satisfaction. Evidently, in his eyes, I was no longer a 'little birdie' but a responsible person, to whom serious matters should be referred in my father's absence.

'Ought we to wait for Madonna Francesca and bury him tomorrow?' he asked. I thought it over and replied that I saw no reason why my mother should be there. She probably hardly knew Piccino by sight, and it was not as though his wife were on the spot, to be consoled by her presence. For the sake of the other men, we had better get it over as quickly as possible. Don Angelo was at Rimini. Where was the local priest? At Pesaro, said the seneschal, but he could be fetched by the afternoon. So we settled the time for an hour after the Nones: I did not expect my mother before sundown.

Meanwhile, I had to get her dress washed before she came, and change my own blood-splashed suit for something wearable. In some distress I appealed to Monna Elena. She reassured me: it was only the little white vest that was soiled, and this was detachable. She would soak it in cold water, dry it in the sunshine, and replace it at once.

Together we looked through my own clothes. She picked out a white silk 'best' dress that had once come to my feet and was now ankle-length. 'Turn this back-to-front,' she said, 'and leave it open at the back. Then take the bodice from this green frock, cut out the sleeves, and wear it as a bolero, with a sash round your waist to hide the gap at the back.' As I said doubtfully that I wasn't very good at sewing, she offered to do it for me. In half an hour it was finished. Rather dubiously I peeped at myself in the mirror that had given me such a shock the previous evening: the effect, I decided, was unusual but quite picturesque.

Messer Rinaldo sent up to tell me that the bread was baked and would be distributed to the people in time for their dinner. So I went down to see fair play, and then ate a very late meal myself. Afterwards it was time to think about the funeral. Obviously my improvised dress was unsuitable for this occasion, so I borrowed a voluminous black shawl from Monna Elena, which covered me from head to foot.

The little cemetery was just under the towering red wall of the castle. Only the two 'walking wounded' felt strong enough to attend, but all the castle garrison turned out, taking turns to carry the light shell that did duty for a coffin.

It was not an impressive ceremony. The chaplain, hot and dusty from his ride, mumbled so indistinctly that even I, who knew Latin, could not understand him. Messer Rinaldo stood gravely by my side, trying to look as though he did, while the men stared woodenly ahead of them. I closed my eyes, trying to catch the echoes of my father's sonorous voice: 'Angels and archangels . . . thrones and dominations and powers. . . .' That had been our real farewell to poor, simple Piccino, and my tears rose as I thought of it.

Then we went back to the castle. After returning the borrowed shawl I went up to the battlements to watch with the sentries for my mother's arrival. As I had expected, the sun was sinking when I heard the call: 'Contessina! Riders coming up the valley, from the direction of Rimini.' And a few moments later: 'There are ladies in the group. It is Madonna Francesca, and Messer Malatesta is with her.' That surprised me, for they always said 'Messer Giovanni'. 'You mean my father?' 'No, the old man, Messer Malatesta of Verucchio.' And the sentinel pulled up a box for me to stand on, so that I could see out of the loophole.

Yes, it was my grandfather, riding a great black stallion. Even at a distance I recognised his tall figure and the white beard flowing beneath his helmet.

I ran down to give the news to Messer Rinaldo, who said that the head of the family must be received with due honour, and went to put on his gold chain of office. Having nothing to wear except my improvised dress, I went down just as I was, with the seneschal holding my hand and making me learn a speech of welcome. People came to their doorsteps, and some followed us to the lower gate.

We waited just outside the walls till the procession came up. First the Captain of the guard, with half a dozen picked men as an escort. Then my grandfather; then Mother in a horse-litter, with the curtains drawn back and my dear old Nannie seated beside her; then her ladies on their palfreys, bright-robed like flowers in a tapestry garden; the rest of the soldiers, protecting the servants and baggage, brought up the rear. To my delight, I saw the youngest stable-boy riding Elefantino. How good of my father, I thought! But then I reflected: he could not have sent Elefantino for me to ride, for now I had Plato. He must have wanted to put the pony and the boy into safety; that looked as if he expected an attack on the Gattolo.

With Messer Rinaldo I went forward and, when my grandfather had dismounted, I curtsied to the ground and kissed his hand. Then I took from the seneschal a red velvet cushion with a great bunch of keys upon it, and said, as I had been instructed: 'Lord of Rimini, of Verucchio, Roncofreddo, Santa Paola and Giovedia . . .' (and all these hard names came trippingly to my tongue) '. . . may it please you to receive the keys of your castle of Gradara.' And he with solemn dignity replied as he took them: 'I thank you, granddaughter; but I am happy to return the keys to the safe keeping of our trusty Messer Rinaldo.' And he gave them back to the seneschal.

Meanwhile, my mother had descended from the litter. I curtsied to her and would have kissed her hand, but she —a little impatient at all this ceremony—pulled me up and kissed me, murmuring, under cover of the clapping and '*evvivas!*' from our audience: 'What *are* you wearing, child? Luckily I brought your clothes from Rimini.'

Then we all went up the central street, with the women

curtsying, the children staring solemnly, and everyone shouting: '*Evviva* Messer Malatesta! *Evviva* Madonna Francesca!'

Once we were in our own apartments, my grandfather ungirt his sword-belt, stretched himself, and laughed: 'Well, now that you have given our retainers pleasure with your "Lord of Rimini" and all the rest of it—and very prettily you did it, my dear—come and give your old grandfather a good, honest hug.' He held out his arms and, as I came to him, swung me up in the air as if I were still a baby. He was nearly eighty, but as tall and strong as a mountain pine.

'Why in the world is the child dressed like a peasant-girl who has grown out of her clothes?' he asked, as he set me on my feet again. I explained, laughing, that that was precisely what I had done; and that, finding myself unexpectedly at Gradara in a boy's suit, I had had to make the best of it. His bright blue eyes scanned me, and I felt his experienced fingers exploring my tiny breasts. 'Yes,' he said, 'she has grown out of all recognition—we'll have to find a husband for her. My Maddalena was married when she was much younger. Whom do you suggest, Francesca? One of the Montefeltro lads? We might use her to heal that feud.'

'As Messer Guido, my father, used me,' said mother, not without bitterness.

That was the second time within twenty-four hours that someone had talked of finding me a husband. I made no comment, but fully agreed with Mother when she said: 'There's time enough to think of that—she's only eleven. She'll find out soon enough that it is none too easy to be a woman in a man's world.'

17

In the weeks that followed, I developed very quickly, physically, but a curious thing happened; at the same time I seemed to lose my precocious maturity and become a child again.

My father, once he had accepted me as an intelligent person, had treated me on equal terms. True, he ordered me about, but then he normally spoke in the imperative. My obedience to him had been something active, accepted because I wanted to please him. Or, if I particularly wished to do something different, we could discuss the question like sensible people; occasionally he even came round to my point of view.

That I had a point of view never even occurred to Mother. I was her little darling, for whom she automatically arranged everything. The first time I realised this was when, a few days later, I asked for my riding-suit. 'Oh, you won't need that again,' she said casually, 'Now you are growing up you will ride side-saddle, like any other woman.' 'But Father said . . .' 'Your father has amused himself by treating you like a boy, but now he will have no time for you. The next few months will be busy and anxious ones for him.' 'Anyway, I want my suit. Where is it?' 'We had to destroy it. Nannie said it was all bloodstained. What was your father doing, making you tend wounded men?'

Mother had a habit of asking questions to which she expected no answer; but I felt that this one deserved to be answered. I faced up to her and said: 'He was testing me, to see if I was worthy to be his daughter—and I passed the test.'

In that moment, I think, Mother and I came perilously near to hating each other. I was tempted to tell her that Father had said I helped him more in that one evening than she had done in twelve years; but I knew I must not.

If once I began to retail his confidences, there was no knowing where it would end. So I relinquished my advantage and merely said sulkily: 'It could have been washed.' 'But you would never have liked to wear it again, once it had had blood on it, would you?'

My eyes went involuntarily to the vest of the gold dress she was wearing. Monna Elena had washed it well, but it seemed to me that I could see a faint shadow on its snowy whiteness. 'Why are you smiling in that odd way?' asked Mother. 'I was just thinking that these things are very largely imagination.' Fortunately she did not ask what exactly I meant by that.

I appealed indignantly to my grandfather, but he refused to interfere, saying with truth that in my father's absence it was Mother's business to decide what I might or might not do. 'But don't worry. I'll take you both out riding together. All the young blades will envy me—the tough old soldier from Verucchio who has two such pretty young women by his side.'

When I went to the stable I found, hanging in Plato's stall, a side-saddle; and Gigino—the boy who had come over with Elefantino—told me that, on Madonna Francesca's instructions, he had been riding the horse to accustom him to it. Mother had thought of everything!

Plato and I never really reconciled ourselves to it, but nevertheless I enjoyed going out with my grandfather. Somehow he had persuaded Mother—who hadn't ridden since she was a girl—to come out with us. 'To give an old man pleasure' was his formula, when he wanted her to do anything. But I guessed that his real reason was to bring her out of that dream-world in which she seemed immersed.

He supported me strongly when I asked if I could teach some of the Gradara children to ride on Elefantino, and he made the further suggestion that Mother and I should teach some of them to read and write. Mother objected that it was quite useless—even if they could read, they would never be able to afford books. Writing, however, would be useful to some of the boys, said Grandfather: they would be able to earn their living as clerks or scribes, or (he added humorously) earn pocket-money by writing love-letters for the illiterates and reading them back to the recipients.

In the late autumn months everyone around the castle was busy, even the children. There was firewood to be cut and stored, for the castle and for their own homes; apples and late pears to be gathered and preserved; fields to be cleared of crops and ploughed before the snow came. But when, in late December, it did come, and we on the hill were cut off for days on end, looking down at the white plain that stretched to an iron-grey sea, there was a general pause in our life. Some of the young people, then, were glad to come for lessons once or twice a week; more, I think, for the pleasure of our large, beautiful rooms and warm fires than for the letters they laboriously copied on the backs of used parchment. We noticed that the boys who wanted to learn were usually the weaklings—those who, through illness or injury, would not be able to earn their living as woodmen, or ploughmen, or soldiers. The one exception was Salvatore, the doorkeeper's son, who had helped me so efficiently over collecting the loaves.

Grandfather took an interest in the classes, looking in occasionally to watch the pupils. At first, being very much in awe of him, they just stopped work, rose to their feet and bowed, and remained standing till he left; but soon they became used to his presence and, having once saluted him, went on with their work. Once he asked Salvatore why he, a strapping lad who would make a fine soldier, wanted to read and write. The boy replied, respectfully but firmly, that he did not think a man would be any the better soldier for being ignorant: 'It might make him less conscious of perils, but by learning the science of war he would be better able to avoid them.' At which my grandfather laughed heartily and clapped him on the shoulder. Salvatore then plucked up courage and asked if he might learn arithmetic. Grandfather, impressed, actually offered to give him lessons.

Although he was so paternal towards his retainers, there was another side to old Malatesta's character that I unexpectedly discovered. Once a month a Court of Justice was held in Gradara and he presided over it. Only a short corridor separated this hall from my mother's bedroom; when the Court was sitting we knew we must not pass through it but must use the bridge leading to the new part of the castle that my father had built.

One evening, just before the Court rose, I heard a piercing cry, apparently coming from the far corner of the other room. Mother, after a quick shudder, immersed herself more deeply in the book she was reading, but I was curious. I heard a murmur of voices, then silence: Grandfather must have gone downstairs to see off the councillors who had come from Pesaro. Tiptoeing into the hall I found it empty. My curiosity centred upon the narrow door in the corner by the outside wall, which was always kept locked. Now it stood ajar. I went over to investigate. The door was heavy, and to move it required my full strength. As I pulled at it I heard my grandfather's voice behind me: '*Concordia!*' a voice full of urgency, anger and fear. I turned to face him. 'Thank God I remembered that door and came back!' he exclaimed. 'Has no one told you that you must never go through it?' 'Why?' I said, surprised. 'What would happen if I did?' 'You would die.'

I looked at him doubtfully. Was this something like the fairy-tales Nannie used to tell me when I was small: the Princess who disobeys an order and falls into a death-like sleep from which only the Fairy Prince can wake her? 'No, I'm not exaggerating,' said Grandfather, reading my thoughts, 'See for yourself!' By this time he had reached me. Holding me round the waist with one arm, he swung the door open with his other hand. Instead of the stair that I had been expecting to see, there was a dark, yawning hole. 'That goes straight down to the well in the question-chamber,' he said. 'If we condemn a man to death, he passes through the door, unsuspecting, just as you would have done—and finishes up in the quicklime below.' 'Quicklime? But that burns, doesn't it? It must hurt terribly.' 'Oh, he's dead before he reaches the bottom—there are knives all the way down, you see.' Grandfather locked and bolted the door and gave me a little push: 'Run back to your mother now, and remember—keep out of mischief.'

I knew that 'question-chamber' was a polite name for what the people questioned in it called a torture-chamber. Ours was quite near the guardroom, down a few steps, but its existence had not disturbed me. Any screams that came from it were too far away to be heard in Mother's room; in fact, I did not realise that it was still in use, until one evening when I had a real fright. Mother had sent me with a message to the seneschal and I was coming back along the corridor that leads to the Court Room, when suddenly a dark, faceless figure loomed up in front of me.

When I am really afraid I do not scream and run: I freeze, like the rabbit to which my father had once compared me. Leaning back against the wall I gazed in terror; then, with unspeakable relief, heard my grandfather's voice: 'What in the world is the matter with you, child? . . . Oh, I'd forgotten that I still have this thing on.' With a jerk he swept off the tall, peaked head-dress and black veil that covered his face, and I saw his ruffled white hair, his blue eyes twinkling with amusement. 'Did I startle you?' I nodded, unable to speak. 'I didn't mean to—I've just come up from the question-chamber.'

Incredulously, I stared at him. 'Do you mean you've been *torturing* someone?' Grandfather chuckled: my shocked tone seemed to amuse him. 'Nothing so vulgar, my dear child. I have been standing on a balcony in this fancy-dress, asking a few pertinent questions, while down below, two of my men were applying—shall we say gentle persuasion?—to a young man who had been so unwary as to let us catch him.' 'That comes to the same thing,' I said, when I had unravelled the meaning of this verbiage. 'And, what's more, you sound as if you had enjoyed it.' He shrugged indifferently: 'At least it was highly satisfactory. I have full details of a plot which Montagna dei Parcitadi is making to capture the Gattolo. A messenger has already been sent to Rimini to warn your father. This night's work may well have saved his life. Don't you think that justifies it?'

I had to admit it, but I still wished he could have chosen some other way. Out of my babyhood there came back to me my mother's voice: 'The Malatesta are a hard race. I wonder if she will be able to stand up to them?' I thought now that I could; but was that because they were making me as hard as themselves?

18

Father did not come to see us for Christmas, nor even choose presents for us. He merely sent the Venetian merchant who used to call twice a year at the Gattolo to sell his fine fabrics, telling Mother to select what she wanted. He must have paid generously too, for she was able to buy materials not only for herself and me but for her three ladies as well. She said I was silly to be disappointed—it was much better to be able to choose for ourselves.

As compensation for his absence, however, Pandolfo arrived. I ought to write 'Uncle' Pandolfo, but I never thought of him as such, nor would he let me call him so. He was one of my grandfather's young second family, who seemed much more like cousins to me than uncles and aunts. At that time Pandolfo was about twenty-one—a few years older than my cousin Uberto and a much nicer person. Uberto was now seventeen, as tall as his father and giving himself the airs of a grown man. He had called in shortly before Christmas, bringing presents, ostensibly from Aunt Orabile but obviously chosen by Uncle Paolo. For Mother, a romance about a knight called Orlando, and for me a set of puppets: two knights, a king, a fair lady and a dark one, a friar, and two servants, man and woman. With these I found I could act nearly all the tales I had read with Mother. Uberto was on his way home to Ghiaggiolo, so he only stayed a few hours. I was glad of this, because he completely ignored me and was very off-hand with Pandolfo: all his conversation was addressed to Mother. He had been in Florence for a few days with his father, and on the strength of it posed as a much-travelled man of fashion.

Pandolfo, on the other hand, behaved as if he were a kind elder brother. Before starting off anywhere, he would say: 'Concordia, let's go and . . .' And we went: down to the stables, to see that the horses were keeping fit in this cold weather; out by the postern gate for a brisk walk—or even, once, a snowball fight; up to the battlements; into every nook and cranny of the castle—except that 'question-chamber' which by mutual consent we avoided.

It was he who persuaded my mother to let me sit up for the entertainment, when, at the New Year, a strolling player with his pretty wife and a son about my own age came to the castle. It was the first time I had been allowed to attend one of these shows, and Mother warned the troupe to remember my presence and not say anything unfit for me to hear. At that, Pandolfo and I exchanged a smile: during several months in the company of Father and his men I had heard many things that she would think unfit for my ears.

The entertainment was held in the Court Room. It started with a plaintive little song, in which all three players joined. They described their wandering through the snow on a weary journey; their joy at perceiving the lights of a castle, where they would find a welcome and warmth, shelter and food. This, no doubt, they sang at every castle, in the hope of softening the hearts and opening the purses of their patrons. But they really did look cold and hungry, and I made up my mind to see that they were treated well.

There followed a would-be comic scene. The girl, padded out with a cushion under her apron, and wearing a cap fringed with grey wool representing hair, portrayed a fat old peasant-woman. The boy, I gathered, was supposed to have stolen one of her hens; at any rate, she ran about at the back of the stage making clucking noises and flapping her arms, while the man chased the boy back and forth in an acrobatic dance, which ended with his being thrown high into the air, turning two somersaults and alighting on his feet. The castle servants laughed a great deal; my mother's ladies looked at her, to see if they might laugh too; but she sat, her lips half-parted in an absent smile and her lovely grey eyes fixed on vacancy, as though her thoughts were far away.

Then came the main piece of the evening—a long sad tale about a knight called Tristram, recited by the man, with occasional passages of dialogue between him and the woman. Moments of emotion were accompanied by the boy on a flute. It was all rather complicated, but I did gather that the knight had gone overseas to fetch the lady as a bride for his uncle. (So *he* was a 'proxy' too, I thought.) Several people were looking at Mother, and she, rousing herself from her abstraction, seemed to be listening rather uneasily, to find out what was going to happen next.

The lady was very beautiful, so the knight (who had swallowed a love-philtre without knowing it) fell in love with her. Mother frowned a little, and this must have reminded the entertainer of her warning; for after he had been singing for what seemed an unnecessarily long time under the picture-frame representing her window, he set one foot on a box put ready below it, evidently meaning to climb in. She stretched out a hand to help him, but he did not take it. Suddenly he shook his head and jerked his thumb, in a most unknightly gesture, towards the seat where I was sitting beside Pandolfo. The young woman looked bewildered for a moment, the comprehension dawned; she shook her head still more emphatically than he had done, pointed to the sky and crossed her hands on her breast. The knight climbed down and knelt in deep dejection.

Then Pandolfo's laughter rang out loud and clear—he still laughed like a boy. He clapped his hands vigorously. The players looked disconcerted—for the story was evidently meant to be a sad one—but his applause was so friendly, and was taken up so warmly by everyone else, that they could not feel offended. After this scene there was an interval, while sweetmeats were handed round among the audience, and the players refreshed themselves with wine brought by one of the servants.

I said quietly: 'Why did you laugh, Pandolfo? Was it because of me that he didn't climb in?' 'Yes, our good Nicola has taken seriously your mother's warning that the performance must be fit for your young mind. I wonder why people always under-rate children's intelligence? Now the whole story will make nonsense.' 'What *is* the story?' I asked. 'Do you know it?' 'Yes, I saw the same group act it in Forlì. It all turns on the jealousy—well-founded jealousy—of King Mark . . .' But I never heard the rest, for Mother—whether by chance or design—chose that moment to call me to her and offer me a candied fig.

After a few minutes the performance resumed. That virtuous refusal had not mollified the king, who arranged for the knight to be wounded by a poisoned arrow. He then went abroad to be cured by another lady, also named Isotta—and that, I thought, was really complicating matters unnecessarily, especially as the second lady was still his real-life wife, in the same dress, but looking (I thought) much prettier with her own dark hair, instead of the flaxen wig and crown she had worn in the first scene. Grandfather, who is slightly deaf, also seemed puzzled, for he said audibly to Mother: 'Why has his lady-love changed the colour of her hair?' Mother, startled out of her dream, looked vaguely at him, but Pandolfo leaned forward and said, into his ear: 'She's a different one!' 'But he's still calling her Isotta.' 'Perhaps he's absent-minded,' suggested Pandolfo cheerfully. 'He's got his two ladies mixed.' I giggled, so Mother and Grandfather looked round at me reprovingly.

Then it grew still more confusing, with something about a white sail and a black sail. In the end they both died and were buried together, and a beautiful tree grew out of their graves. (That, of course, we didn't see: the boy recited it over their prostrate bodies.)

Some of the ladies cried. Mother still looked very far away, but Pandolfo and Grandfather led a good round of applause. To finish on a lighter note, the three players performed a dance in peasant costume, with the young lad turning somersaults and capering around like a foal in spring. Then they joined hands and bowed, and the wife, curtsying, said in a rhymed couplet that she hoped their entertainment had given pleasure. Everyone clapped again, while Mother, emerging, from her dream, smiled, thanked them; then turning to Messer Rinaldo, told him to give them money and see that they were fed and lodged for the night.

But I mistrusted the seneschal, after the little streak of

meanness he had shown about the borrowed bread. So after supper I told Pandolfo quietly that I meant to see for myself if the players were really comfortable. I asked him to come with me; for, after all, he was an uncle, even though a young one, and couldn't be scolded like me.

As I suspected, the three had been put into one of the ice-cold upper rooms without a fire. We found them preparing to roll themselves up, fully dressed, in their cloaks and lie down to sleep—the two adults on a narrow bed and the boy on the floor. I noticed that the woman's hands were blue with cold.

Pandolfo, with that graceful courtesy that reminded me of Uncle Paolo, made an excuse for Messer Rinaldo, saying that he was elderly and could not mount so many stairs; otherwise he would certainly have seen to it that they were more comfortable. All three looked at him in amazement, then the man Nicola said: 'But, Messer, we expected nothing better. For us it is already a great thing to have a roof over our heads on a cold night. Please do not reproach your seneschal on our account, or he will refuse us entry next time we come to Gradara.'

'I think not,' said Pandolfo, 'Messer Rinaldo is as anxious as the rest of us to relieve the winter tedium. And, next time, the Contessina will see that you are looked after. It was she who thought that you might be cold.' Then he turned to me: 'Stay here, Concordia: I'll be back soon.'

When he had gone they all looked at me a trifle shyly. To break the ice I praised the boy's agility, asking him his name and how old he was.

'Masiello, for Tommaso,' he answered, 'and I'm thirteen. How old are you, Contessina?' 'Eleven.' We smiled at each other, and I continued: 'Next time you come, you must show me the steps of your dance. I think I could do most of it, except the somersaults.' They all laughed, and Nicola said he was sure my lady mother would not agree to that.

Then I asked the wife how, with a son of thirteen, she

contrived to look so young. He was not her son but her stepson, she explained: she herself was only nineteen.

I had unthinkingly gone upstairs in the silk dress I had been wearing in the warmed hall, and I was already beginning to shiver. Seeing it, Masiello suggested that we should start right away with a dancing-lesson—and we were both running gaily around, to a rhythmic clapping of hands from the two grown-ups, when Pandolfo came back, accompanied by four of the guard. Two of them were carrying between them a large brazier filled with glowing wood-ash from the guardroom fire; the third had a supply of fresh wood, and the fourth a sheepskin for Masiello. Pandolfo himself had a small bag in his hands.

'Good!' he said, when the men had gone and the three players were stretching their chilled hands towards the brazier. 'Now, if we may, we two will stay and roast some chestnuts on the embers—one of my boyhood pleasures that I have never outgrown.'

I realised what lay behind this apparent whim, when I found the players picking up the chestnuts and turning them in their hands, luxuriating in the warmth. My own hands were still cold, and I stretched one towards a chestnut, but Pandolfo whipped it out of the fire before I could touch it. 'Careful!' he said, 'Your little hands are very soft—you could easily burn yourself.' He turned the chestnut round several times before passing it to me. The more I saw of Pandolfo, the more I liked him. He had a quality that was rare among the Malatesti—genuine kindliness.

As we sat munching chestnuts, it was not only the atmosphere of the room that thawed but also the spirits of our guests. Before long we were talking like old friends. I asked them if their life was really as miserable as it seemed, from their first song, or if they had just wanted to make us feel sorry for them.

Nicola chuckled: 'The little one is shrewd, like her grandfather,' he commented to Pandolfo; then he answered my question: 'We wouldn't choose any other way of living, but it does have its hard moments. It killed my first wife, Masiello's mother. She had her second baby on a night like this, lying on a heap of straw in a barn. She survived the birth all right, but she caught cold and was too weak to throw it off. It went to her lungs, and a fortnight later she died.' 'And the baby . . .?' I asked. 'It never had much chance. I couldn't afford a wet-nurse, so I fed it on goat's milk and cow's milk, as best I could. Now and again a generous country wife gave it the breast. But we moved around, never more than a night or two in the same place, feeding it at odd times. And before the spring came it died too, poor little beggar.'

Then the girl interposed: 'Don't let the Contessina think our life is all hardship. It is good in the summer, with flowers, and fruit, and barns full of fresh hay. There's nothing better than supper in the Ravenna pinewoods, sitting round a wood-fire and eating baked rabbit.'

Masiello laughed: 'Esmeralda knows all about that. She bakes them in clay, you know—and hedgehogs too. She's a gipsy.' And he added, with devastating candour: 'Her father sold her to us when she was little.'

'*Sold!*' I exclaimed, shocked. The grown-ups were obviously embarrassed, but Pandolfo, with ready tact, came to their help. 'Don't look so surprised, Concordia! After all, what do our families do? The father gives his daughter, with her dowry of money and land; but he gives her to a man whom he thinks will be useful to him. The husband pays in influence, or by lending his men-at-arms when his father-in-law needs them.'

I wanted to hear the details of the sale; and Nicola, seeing that Pandolfo was taking the matter casually, overcame his reluctance and began his story: 'I had been making a long stay at the castle of Messer Guido of Montefeltro . . .' He looked at us a trifle uneasily, but neither of us reacted to this. I knew vaguely that Guido of Montefeltro was one of our chief enemies; but what interest could a strolling player take in politics? So he continued: 'While I was there I lost my horse in an accident caused by a careless groom. Messer Guido was angry with the man and gave me another from his own stable—a beautiful creature, far too good for me. All I needed was a pack-horse or mule to carry round my gear. I was afraid, too, that someone would steal him. So, instead of taking to the road alone, I joined up with a group of travellers—merchants and pilgrims.'

'And we were travelling the same road, in the opposite direction,' put in his wife. 'I remember that!' exclaimed Masiello. 'A cart with beautiful ladies in coloured silk dresses. They had gold chains round their necks and gold rings in their ears.' 'Yes,' said his father, 'But the dresses were soiled and torn, so that their brown flesh showed through. And round the cart the young men of the tribe were riding bareback, on mounts that looked roughly groomed but full of spirit. Then an older man, who seemed to be their chief, called to me: "Hi, fellow." I said: "Messer Zingaro, that is no way for one gentleman to address another." And he, looking at my horse, retorted: "Do you call it gentlemanly to treat a good horse so?" Indeed, I did not. The beautiful beast had panniers on each side, loaded with all my gear, and between them, in a basket-seat, rode little Masiello. I saw that the gipsy really loved and understood horses, and was sorry to see this one humiliated. So I replied frankly: "I do *not*—but he and I have come down in the world." "Will you sell him to me?" asked the man. "How much do you want for him?" Now, that put me in a quandary: if I asked the real value of the horse, he would be unable to pay it; and judging by the covetous gleam in his eyes, might well steal it and knife me into the bargain. But if I asked too little, he would be convinced that I had stolen it, and might make a lot of trouble for me. So I hesitated. Then something happened which decided me . . .' 'He saw *me*!'

said Esmeralda proudly. 'Yes—a skinny child with eyes like ripe chestnuts, under a mane of tangled black hair. She had scrambled down from the cart and was making friends, as children will, with little Masiello. The man told her to get back, and casually slapped her. What struck me about the blow was that it was purely instinctive —the gesture with which one pushes away an importunate kitten or puppy. She was used to it, too, for she didn't cry or protest—just stared sullenly with those wide eyes of hers. "Why did you hit the child?" I asked, "she's doing no harm." "She's a nuisance," he said impatiently. "I've too many mouths to feed, and this one is no use. Her little sister is so pretty that, when she stretches out her hand, people give her money at once; but this ugly brat gets nothing." I looked at her more closely and saw that she had the makings of a dancer. It was on the tip of my tongue to say that in five years' time she would be a beauty, but . . .' he chuckled slyly, 'it's not for the buyer to praise merchandise that the seller himself has cheapened. I said to him: "I will not sell you the horse, but I will give him to you (and how his eyes glowed!) on three conditions: that you ride him yourself, or sell him to a gentleman, so that he never again has to be a pack-horse; that you find me a good, strong donkey in exchange (he looked reflective at this— I could see he was wondering where he could steal one); and that you give me this child of yours, whom you don't seem to want. I've taken a fancy to her, and she will be useful to me, helping to look after my motherless boy." He made a great fuss, of course, saying that I was breaking a father's heart, depriving him of his little treasure . . . but neither he nor she nor I believed a word of it. By this time the convoy had moved ahead, and I would have to hurry to catch them up. I said to the gipsy: "These matters cannot be settled like this, on the open road. We are sleeping tonight at Fano, and I shall be staying there for two days . . ." (that would give him time to find the donkey). "Come to me there, with the child and the donkey, and you shall have my horse." And on that bargain we shook hands.'

'And a very good bargain, too,' said Pandolfo, smiling at Esmeralda. 'She is both beautiful and a good dancer.' Nicola nodded: 'You can't mistake them. Look at the Contessina, now . . .' (Pandolfo did: I saw new appreciation in his eyes) 'Long, slim legs, a well-poised little head on a slender neck; hands so flexible that they are almost double-jointed. I could make a first-rate dancer of her in two years.'

Pandolfo laughed: 'So now you know what to do, if ever you need to earn your living, Concordia!' They all joined in the laughter, for it was obvious that I never would. Feeling a trifle embarrassed, I turned it off by saying: 'When I am married and living in a castle of my own, you must come and dance for me, Esmeralda. You must all three come before Christmas and stay till the cold weather ends. And I will see that you have a fire in your room: and you will feed with us and entertain my guests in the long, dark evenings. Then you must come back in summer time and take me into the Ravenna woods, to eat clay-baked rabbit.'

'Will your husband let you go gipsying in the pinewoods?' asked Pandolfo with a twinkle. I had always taken it for granted that I should be married, but somehow I had never thought seriously about a husband. That he would have the right to order my doings now came to me clearly for the first time. 'Well,' I said, thinking it over, 'If we like each other, he will want to make me happy. If we don't . . .' I thought of the separate lives led by my father and mother, '. . . then I don't suppose he will be much interested in anything that I do.'

This piece of philosophy was received with more laughter, and we were all feeling friendly and happy when I heard Monna Biancarosa calling my name in a voice that meant trouble. I looked appealingly at Pandolfo. 'All right,' he said, 'Leave this to me.'

We said a quick good-bye to the players and left the room, with Pandolfo's arm protectively round my shoulders. 'You want the Contessina?' he asked briefly. 'She is with me.'

Biancarosa looked relieved, but all the same began to scold me, saying that it was long past my bedtime and my mother was upset. So Pandolfo took me straight to her and, before she too could start scolding me, put in his word: 'Concordia, like the generous little soul that she is, wanted to make sure that the players had a fire on this cold night. So we went up to see if they were comfortable . . .' (Good! he wasn't giving Messer Rinaldo away) '. . . and I kept her there, talking.'

Mother looked mollified, but made her protest all the same: 'I don't think Concordia should be brought into contact with people of that sort. One never knows what their private life may be. That so-called "wife" of his is obviously much too young to be the boy's mother.' 'She is his stepmother,' I explained. 'In any case,' declared Mother, 'I have a strong feeling that those two are not properly married.'

I could not keep myself from murmuring: 'There must have been quite a number of women whom Grandfather Guido didn't properly marry.'

Pandolfo gave a shout of laughter and my mother turned on him sharply: 'Don't encourage the child to be impertinent!' But she had the grace to blush.

19

The first months of my twelfth year, 1288, were full of change and movement.

ıe February morning when the snow was falling, co came riding up the hill with letters from Ravenna. Grandfather Guido wrote to say that my father had retaken Cervia, and that he himself was back there as its *podestà*. At the same time Father sent a few hurried lines, saying that he was well; that soon he hoped to fetch us back to Rimini. He said nothing about the capture of the city, except that: 'It was a good fight and quick. I enjoyed it.'

But Marco told us much more. Mother had invited him to sit with us in the Court Room, which we used as our winter sitting-room, when there were no trials in process, because of its splendid fireplace. It was good to feel warm and comfortable, looking at the blazing logs, while he talked of stirring deeds performed in the cold outside. 'There was snow on the ground, and eddies of it swirling in the air. The enemy were off guard, never dreaming we would move in such weather. But Messer Giovanni dressed some of his men in sheets and made them crawl across the snow, dragging scaling-ladders. When they were right under the wall, out of sight of the sentries, others came to join them, until forty men—half our troop—were ready to storm the wall.

'The rest of us, with Messer Giovanni himself, were standing by to rush in as soon as our storm-troops had opened the gate for us. He gave orders for absolute silence; no war-cry until they had been discovered. In fact, the first men reached the top, took the sentinels unawares and killed several before the alarm was raised. At last we heard shouts and clashing swords, the rattle of chains and the creak of door-hinges. Messer Giovanni raised his great cry of "Malatesta!"; then we charged the gate. A moment later we were through it and fighting our way up the street. There was very little resistance—no time to build barricades—so our impetus carried us through to the main square. And there Messer Giovanni lifted his visor and laughed . . .'

'He looked—splendid?' I asked, having seen him at Gradara after a successful battle. 'Splendid, Contessina,' agreed Marco, 'Strong, proud, noble. We were proud to be his men. We had felt chilled and miserable as we waited in the snow, but now we were glowing with warmth.

'Messer Giovanni called the *podestà* and ordered him to find us comfortable billets. The he took a roll-call. We had got off lightly. Out of eighty men we only had half a dozen wounded and three killed. But one of those was Beppo.'

'Oh, Marco! . . . Good little Beppo. What hard lines!'

'Yes. Messer Giovanni was upset. I was the one who brought him the news, and he said: "Barely half a year since our race—and of the four of us, two are dead. Take care of yourself, Marco." '

'He's fond of you, I know. Marco, *do* take care of yourself—and him.'

From that time onwards, I noticed that Father often used Marco as a messenger, perhaps to keep him out of the fighting. It was Marco whom he sent, with forty horsemen, to fetch us back to Rimini, a few weeks later. My grandfather had been chosen again for *podestà*, so it looked as if things were settling down.

How I enjoyed that return to Rimini! The March air was crisp and cool, but already there was fresh green budding in the hedges; the ditches were gay with golden celandines. Mother and Nannie travelled in the horse-litter, but I had insisted upon riding. Mounted on Plato, I easily kept pace with my grandfather. We rode slowly, not to outdistance the litter, the ladies on their palfreys, and the pack-horses. But we went by way of the shore, where the going was easier and there was less risk of encountering enemies coming down from Montefeltro or San Marino.

Suddenly Grandfather said to me: 'All's clear—let's go!' He passed the word to Marco to let us through the front ranks of the escort, and we galloped ahead. The *grecale* was blowing, cold and clear, sending long rollers to crash on the shore, and seagulls were sweeping low over their crests. I felt myself as free as they, and to complete my pleasure Grandfather said, reining in to wait for the escort: 'You ride well. It's a pity you are not a boy, Concordia.'

20

I have always remembered May 4th—our last night in the Gattolo—as 'the night my mother came alive'.

It seemed to me that I had been sleeping for a long time, but it was not yet midnight when my father roused me. He was in full armour, with his visor up, and he ordered curtly: 'Get up and dress yourself, Concordia. Tell Nannie to pack some clothes and necessities for you in a bundle—I may have to send you to Gradara.' Before I could ask any questions he had gone; but to prevent my going back to sleep, he had whisked off the bedclothes.

The urgency in his voice had thoroughly roused me. Down below in the courtyard I heard him shouting orders; heard metal clinking and men moving heavy weights around. In a very few minutes I had dressed, plaited my hair and pinned it close to my head. Then I went to find Nannie. She was scurrying around like a frightened hen. So I stayed to help her choose and pack whatever I thought would be most useful and most easily carried in saddle-bags, for I doubted whether there would be time to prepare sumpter-mules.

Mother was not in her bedroom. From Biancarosa (plain 'Bianca' would have been a more suitable name at that moment, so bleached with fear was she) I learned that she had insisted upon going on to the wall to see what was happening; and there I found her. It was a mother whom I did not know—a laughing, excited young woman, with rosy cheeks and sparkling eyes. The approach of danger had transformed her.

She was standing on a block, looking out through a loophole, while around her the defenders of the wall were preparing to throw Greek fire. When she saw me she called: 'Get back, Concordia! What are you doing up here?' I said: '*You* are here, Mother. Let me stay with you.' And she, springing from her perch, flung her arms round me and hugged me, dignity forgotten. 'Good! We'll stay together. But keep down, out of the line of arrow-shot.'

It was then that we heard the first shouts from below: '*Parcitade! Evviva Montagna dei Parcitadi! Evviva Messer Oddo Faitano!*' And our men yelled back: '*Malatesta! Evviva Malatesta!*'

One long pole, tipped with inflammable material, burst into flames. The man holding it whirled it round in a complete circle of sparking light and hurled it from the wall. Screams mingled then with the shouts below.

The noise kept growing and growing till it was like the surge of the sea. We saw one man fall, hit in the shoulder by a crossbow-bolt that shattered the bone with a sickening crunch. Then, from the angle of wall opposite us there came a hubbub and a cry for help: '*Messer Giovanni!*' Scaling-ladders had been put up, and men were fighting actually on the wall. '*Messer Giovanni!*' someone called again, and I heard my father's answering shout: 'All right—I'm coming.'

Never before had I seen my father run, but now he was doing it, using his sword-stick to give himself impetus, as a vaulter uses his pole, and covering the ground with amazing agility and speed.

'The scaling-ladders!' he yelled. 'Get together and throw down the ladders!' They took a moment to react to the order, then I saw men massing at one point of the wall. Someone shouted '*Heave!*'. There was a crash, followed by clamour from below.

Father had reached a point immediately underneath, but there were no steps and the wall was too high to climb. 'Help me up!' he ordered Marco and another man lifted him, until he was standing on their shoulders; then two of the defenders leaned over and pulled him up. Marco, with the other man's help, climbed up beside him.

Under my father's orders the second and third ladders went down, and the few men left trapped on the wall were quickly overpowered, stabbed, and thrown down on the far side. My father turned to smile at Marco, as they stood together; both gasping a little, their faces shining with sweat in the torchlight, but well content.

'That was bravely done,' said Mother, and I think that —perhaps for the first time—she was proud to be his wife. She called to him: '*Giovanni!*' blew him a kiss and stretched out her arms. Then I saw his face lighten, as it had done at Gradara, when he mistook me for her. '*Donna!*' he called, 'Keep out of danger!' But he did not tell her to get down or to go away. All at once I knew what it was that linked us three—so different and so potentially hostile each to each: we were all of us curiously indifferent to life. The menace of death, or the promise it held of an adventure greater than we had ever known, roused us to something like happiness. I thought: 'It is not too late. If they both live through tonight she may come to love him.'

It was then that we smelt the smoke. Whether it was our own Greek fire that had set alight some of the wooden sheds at the foot of the wall, or whether the enemy had deliberately fired them, we never knew—but Rimini town was burning, and the wind was blowing sparks and great clouds of smoke over our walls. The men began to cough and flap their arms, as if to drive it away. I saw Father slam his visor down; then, as smoke filtered through the slits, he pushed it up again, fumbled for his handkerchief and, unable to find it, wiped his streaming eyes with his sleeve. He began to curse impatiently.

From behind us there came a call: 'Messer Giovanni, the stable is burning!' 'The war-stable?' he asked. 'Yes. Aldo is getting the horses out.'

'Down from the wall, all of you!' ordered Father. 'There'll be no attack for the moment: the fire is between us and the enemy.'

Marco and one or two others jumped down. Father swung down at full length from the edge of the wall and dropped into their outstretched arms. Marco retrieved his stick and handed it to him. The less agile men were running towards the staircase at the end of the wall. 'Run as quickly as you can to the stables!' shouted Father, 'I will follow.' Then he called to Mother and me: 'Come down, both of you—quickly!' Mother never did anything so undignified as to run, but she made for the stairway with a swift, flowing motion, seeming to skim the ground. As for me, I called to Marco as he passed: 'Catch me!' and jumped into his arms. This brought me close beside Father. 'Are things very bad?' I asked him. 'Yes. Get ready to leave at once. I must see to the horses.' And he hurried off.

The next few minutes were turmoil. Through the courtyard, full of screaming, kicking horses and cursing men, I struggled to the staircase in the farther corner. I looked out for some servant to carry our baggage. On the first landing I found one of them skulking—a lazy, obese fellow who certainly would be no willing helper. 'Come up with me, to bring down our luggage,' I ordered him. Clasping both hands on his quaking belly, he protested that he was ruptured and could not carry any weight. I said coldly: 'My father is a cripple, but I have just seen him scale a wall more than twice his own height. You'll get no sympathy from him.' I would have sent him to fetch me two sound and willing men, but I suspected that, if I let him go, he would not come back again. So I led him to the entrance of my mother's apartment which was littered with bags, some fully packed and others still open and half-filled. Seizing my own, which were the lightest, I told him to take them down and leave them at the foot of the stairway, so that they did not hinder people running up and down. 'And come back at once, with another man, to help us,' I added. 'Otherwise, I will report you to the steward and to my father.' It was all I could do in the way of a threat, but I hoped it would suffice.

Meanwhile, where were my mother's women? I could see no sign of them anywhere. There was noise enough outside, but all around me was deadly still. Then I heard, coming from the chapel, a monotonous wailing; the sound of frightened women praying. I ran in like a whirlwind. There they all were—Nannie, Biancarosa, Cristina, and young Annabella, who had replaced the dismissed Maria Pia. When Nannie saw me, she exclaimed: 'Contessina Concordia! Thank God you are safe! Kneel down and pray with us.' I retorted (and afterwards reflected that this was a sin I ought to have confessed to Don Angelo, but he did not come with us to Gradara): 'There's no time to waste on that!' Nannie opened her mouth to reprove me, but I anticipated her: 'Get up, come with me, finish packing and bring the bags down—those are my father's orders.' I used what Nannie called my 'Malatesta voice', and they meekly obeyed me, though I could sense that Nannie wished I were five years old again, so that she could give me a good smacking.

Mother was standing under one of the arches of the loggia, away from the turmoil in the courtyard, so we made a little group behind her. A very few minutes later there came a trumpet-peal and the shout of '*Malatesta!*' from outside the walls. Mother turned so white that I thought she would faint. It struck me that perhaps she imagined

Father had made a sally and was fighting out there; but I had recognised the voice. 'It's all right, Mother,' I said reassuringly, 'It's only Uncle Paolo.' '*Only!*' echoed Mother, oddly breathless. 'Run, child—ask the steward for the loving-cup and a flask of our best wine.'

I stared at her in amazement: could she really be thinking of the loving-cup ceremony, in all this confusion? Then I thought: 'She is being brave—showing that, even during a battle, we keep up our courtesies.'

Doubting whether I could find the steward, I crossed the dining-hall, behind which he had his office and pantry. As I ran I heard my father ordering the drawbridge to be let down: 'Double crew on the chains, and crossbow-men covering the last of the riders. Hoist up, immediately the last man is across.'

Of course the steward was not there. (Later, I heard that he had been stowing valuables in a secret room.) The loving-cup was locked away, but I found a pottery beaker and a flask of wine and brought them to Mother, just as Uncle Paolo came riding in.

His visor was still down (he was running no risk of having his looks spoiled by a stray stone from a catapult); but once inside, he lifted it and looked around. My mother, standing with her ladies, immobile in the shelter of the loggia, must have made an oasis of peace amid the chaos. He rode up to her, stripped off gauntlets and helmet and handed them to the man who took his horse; then, light as a boy despite the weight of his armour, he leaped from the saddle in one graceful movement, knelt before her and kissed her hand.

I thought: 'How beautiful!' Then, catching sight of my father's face as he shouldered his way through to us, I reflected: 'But he needn't have done it in front of Father.' It was the first time I had ever, even in my mind, criticised my dharming uncle.

When Mother saw the rough beaker she exclaimed

sharply: 'But that's not . . .!' then caught herself up and, as I poured out the wine, turned to Paolo, saying clearly but very softly: 'Welcome to Rimini, Messer my brother-in-law.' She sipped the wine and passed him the cup, with hands shaking so much that its contents splashed on the ground. 'She must have been frightened during the battle, though she didn't show it,' I thought, while my uncle replied with the ritual: 'Long life and happiness to you, Madonna Francesca!' He would, I think, have drunk the wine at a draught, but seeing my father close by, he handed on the cup with a casual 'Thirsty, Gianni?'

It seemed all wrong to me that my father should drink the lees of Uncle Paolo's wine, but he himself was too truly proud to resent imagined slights, and too insensitive to trouble about omens. He *was* thirsty, he took the drink offered to him—and that was all. I was still holding the flask, so I refilled the beaker and he drank it out. Then I stood on tiptoe and wiped his sweaty face with my handkerchief: it came away black from the smoke that had coagulated on his cheeks.

'Am I in time?' asked Paolo. 'To hold the Gattolo? I fear not. We're pulling out now, once we've saved the horses and hidden our valuables; but I'm glad to have you, all the same. I want you to escort my father, Francesca and Concordia to Gradara. How many men did you bring? Thirty? That will do. The inland road by Morciano is still open?' 'I hope so: we came by Meldola and the Ronco valley to the Emilia, and got through without a fight.'

Father gave orders, and in a few minutes grooms brought a stallion for my grandfather and palfreys for the rest of us. I laughed to see Nannie hoisted, squeaking protests, behind a mounted man, and was still more amused when I saw that the man was Riccardo. He had a rueful expression, for she was clutching him round the middle, and she was no light weight. Nor was he. He was not very old—forty, perhaps—but he was putting on weight, for it was years since he had ridden with the troop. Father used to leave him at Rimini or Gradara when he was on the warpath, and send for him only when things had settled down. To be pushed into the saddle at night, with smoke and flame all around, and the possibility of being attacked outside the castle, was not at all to his taste. But the sight of him cheered me; for, if Father was sending Riccardo to Gradara, it meant that he would surely follow us there himself.

I looked at the stubby cob that had been brought for me and shook my head, 'And Plato? I want Plato!' I protested. 'The lads are busy saving the stallions—I've no one to spare for the other stable,' retorted Father. 'Never mind—I'll go and saddle him myself!' 'You will *not*!' snapped Father. (It was years since he had spoken to me so sharply.) 'You are a soldier's daughter and must obey orders. Stay here with your mother. Paolo, get the women mounted, while I see to the drawbridge.'

My uncle detailed his men in pairs, one of them leading a palfrey to the mounting-block, while the second lifted a woman into the saddle. He himself knelt down, making a step with his cupped hands, so that Mother could reach the stirrup. As she settled herself into the saddle her skirts sprayed out, showing her slender ankles, and Paolo printed a swift kiss upon one of them. No one saw it but me, for the horse's flank was between them and the courtyard. Mother turned rose-red and I thought: 'She is cross!' I felt that Uncle Paolo had done something wrong, but I told myself I was being silly; if a man may kiss a lady's hand, why not her foot?

There was no time to puzzle it out, for he had turned to me: 'Well, my independent little niece? Do you want to mount by yourself?' I shook my head: 'Last year I could have done it—but not in these silly skirts.' He laughed, caught me by the waist and swung me into the air. I was heavier than he had expected and he exclaimed, laughing, as he set me down in the saddle: 'I'll not be able to do this again—soon you'll be a grown woman. Now give me a kiss for my pains.' I bent down to him and he planted two swift kisses, one on each cheek (even after his long ride, his skin was still perfumed).

Mother's flush heightened, and there was real vexation in her voice as she exclaimed: 'Paolo!' (I noticed that she had dropped the ceremonious 'Messer my brother-in-law'). 'Do remember that Concordia is not a child any longer.' He looked at her with a flicker of laughter in his eyes and said lightly: 'Madonna, a woman may be kissed—by proxy!' Then he sprang to horse, took his helmet and slammed down the visor. The drawbridge rattled, and we cantered out into the night.

21

Father had sent a small detachment to clear the way, in case there were enemies on the landward side, but we rode through unchallenged, so they saluted and left us. We were still in drifting smoke. The women were coughing and wiping their eyes: one after another lifted her wimple to shield her face. I suffered most of all, for I had only a velvet cap over my plaited hair, and nothing round my neck. However, I narrowed my eyes, kept my mouth shut and tried to breathe normally. Uncle Paolo, choking, reluctantly pushed up his visor.

At last a turn in the road brought us into clear air, and from that point it was pleasant riding under the stars. Behind us, the smoke-curtain, lined with an orange glow, prevented us from seeing what was happening at the castle. There were scattered cries of '*Parcitade!*' and '*Malatesta!*', but the ferocity of the fighting seemed to have abated. Soon we were riding through the quiet countryside, with nothing but the sound of our own horsehoofs and the occasional call of a night-bird to break the silence.

Ahead rode six men of the escort; then my uncle, alone, followed by my grandfather, with Mother on his right and me on his left; then the rest of the troop. And so, in the dead of night, we came to Gradara.

Dawn was breaking when I was awakened by the sound of horsehoofs and drawbridge chains. That could only be my father, for no one else would have ridden up to the castle wall. Mother was fast asleep, so I slithered out of bed, wrapped her cloak round me and stole downstairs.

Father was limping heavily—a sure sign of exhaustion—and was in a very bad temper. I dared not ask him what had happened at Rimini.

'Is your mother asleep?' he asked, seeing me. 'She was, when I left her.' 'You are sharing her bed?' 'Yes, but I can go up to one of the guestrooms. You are so tired—you must come straight to bed.' 'Stop fussing!' he said curtly. 'Loosen my cuirass and let me lie down.' He signed to one of the guard to bring him a rolled sheepskin and to spread it on the outer edge of the bench, where he could swing himself on to it most easily. It was the spot where Piccino had died, I remembered with a shudder; but Father seemed to have forgotten it and I did not remind him.

The soldier beat the sheepskin on the wood, to shake off fleas, spread it out, and then helped me unbuckle Father's cuirass. As we took it off, I felt him sag and realised that his back was badly strained. He lay down at once, drawing a sigh of relief, and I covered him with his cloak. 'You ought to . . .' I began to protest, but he cut me short. 'I ought to stay here. Remember, I have forty men to fit into a room that is already overcrowded with the thirty from Ghiaggiolo. They will have to be billeted in the citadel, and that can only be done by sending them out with someone of the resident garrison. If I am not here, there will be disputes and brawls, but they'll behave themselves in front of me. Listen, they're coming in already.' And in fact we heard voices and tramping feet in the courtyard.

I ventured a question: 'And Rimini . . .?' 'I had to pull out. But I got my men and horses away without loss, and the valuables have been well hidden. There'll be looting, of course, but nothing of importance.' 'You mean —we've lost the Gattolo?' My mind tried to adjust itself to this disaster. 'We'll be back!' said my father, almost casually. 'Now kiss me and go back to bed. I've still to settle my men before I can sleep.'

The birds were singing as I went upstairs, and the double ogive of the window showed grey against a pale gold sky. In the faint light I could see Mother smiling as if at a happy dream. Usually she slept defensively, curled up at the extreme edge of the bed, although it was so wide that four people as slender as we could have slept in it without touching one another. But that night she was lying relaxed on her back, with her arms outside the coverlet. I slipped in beside her, thinking: There's no use in going to sleep again. But I did.

When I woke, the sun was high. Mother was already dressed, with Biancarosa braiding her hair. 'Your father has come,' she said, when she saw that I was awake.

I did not say that I had already seen him (the habit of secrecy was growing on me). I merely asked: 'Where is he?' 'In the council chamber, with Messer Malatesta and your Uncle Paolo. They are discussing what to do.'

About half an hour later, Father came across the gallery to our room. He wrapped Mother in one of his quick, hungry embraces, which she passively endured; then he turned to me: 'Concordia, we want you in the council room. My father has a document to prepare that he prefers not to entrust to a secretary.'

I followed him into the room where my grandfather sat, looking very imposing, in the great central arm-chair behind a long table. On his left was Uncle Paolo, less brilliantly dressed than usual, since, at my father's summons, he had ridden hastily to battle; but the soft brown leather of his jerkin, slashed to show an undervest of honey-gold silk, showed off his clear, pale olive skin. He was just as handsome now as when I first remembered him, only his face had hardened slightly and his eyes were more heavily shadowed. Father took his place on Grandfather's right. I noticed that he crossed his lame leg over the other and was pressing it as though it hurt him.

The width of the table was between Grandfather and me, so I could not kiss his hand. I dropped him a curtsy and sat down opposite him, where writing materials had been laid out.

Father burst out impatiently, banging his hand down on a document that lay open before him: 'The insolence of the man! Have you read this, Paolo? Pietro Colonna, after my capture of Cervia, writes a manifesto to all and sundry, declaring that we—*we*, the entire Malatesta family—are "stripped of our titles and honours, and of all the posts we hold", and that the people of Romagna are "released from all obligations to us". Have you ever heard a clearer incitement to our enemies, great and small, to attack us? He takes advantage of the Pope's death to act as if he himself, instead of a mere Count of Romagna, were the mouthpiece of the Papacy!' His knuckles showed white; it would have gone hard with Pietro di Stefano Colonna had he been within reach at that moment.

Paolo raised his eyebrows slightly, saying in an indifferent tone: 'Hard words won't hurt us. We'll get him out before long.' 'Indeed,' said my grandfather, 'I have heard a rumour that the new Pope has already recalled him and is sending another man, a certain . . .' (he consulted another paper) 'Ermanno Monaldeschi, in his place. That is why I intend to go direct to Forlì and lay my complaint before him.'

'Waste of time!' growled my father. 'Far better seek out Guido da Polenta at Cervia, get him to lend us a hundred men, and retake Rimini by force.'

Grandfather shook his white locks in benevolent amusement: 'Gianni, Gianni, when you've lived as long as I have—but you won't, you know; someone will have murdered you long before then—you'll know that one can't get everything by force. The fox, in the end, lives longer and fares better than the wolf.' Then he smiled across the table at me: 'You know Latin, little one?' 'Fairly well,' I said, 'Don Angelo has taught me prayers, and Father has read me the *Aeneid*.' (The mixture seemed to amuse him.) 'Well,' he said, 'this isn't exactly a prayer, but a petition or protest, which is something similar. We'll see how you manage it.' 'She writes a beautiful hand,' said my father proudly, 'and, if she finds the spelling difficult, I will help her.'

So Grandfather began to dictate: 'To Ermanno Monaldeschi di Civita Vecchia, Count and Rector of Romagna, on this day of 5 May 1288 . . .' I forget the exact wording now; but the sense of it was that he, Malatesta of Verucchio, and his sons Giovanni, Paolo and Malatestino, had always been faithful servants, followers and defenders of the Papacy, upholding the doctrines of the Church of Rome throughout Romagna . . . (my father sneered openly at this, Uncle Paolo's lips curved in a subtle smile, and the old man himself chuckled). Consequently, the behaviour of the ex-Rector was uncalled-for and unjust, and he, Malatesta, was confident that His Holiness, Nicholas IV, would defend the interests of one of his loyal supporters who, in consequence of this proclamation, had been attacked by wicked and envious persons . . . and so it went on for a long while. I had already moved the parchment twice upon the vertical leather-covered board that sustained it, before the story came to an end. I could see that Uncle Paolo was amused by this presentation of his father as an innocent lamb attacked by ravenous wolves, and I shared his amusement; but Father still scowled. Evidently the loss of the Gattolo had temporarily annulled his sense of humour.

'Finished?' asked my grandfather at last. 'That's good! I'll take it myself to Forlï, and at once.' He looked from one to the other of his sons. 'I want one of you two to escort me, while the other stays here, to protect Gradara in case of a surprise attack. Which of you would like to go?' My uncle replied smoothly: 'Gianni overtired himself yesterday. If he's not fit to ride . . .' Even before my father's fierce interruption, 'Of course I'm fit!', I had caught my breath in exasperation. It was the first time I had heard my sensitive uncle say something really tactless. Now Father will insist on going, I thought: why couldn't he have said that the main danger threatened Gradara, and that it was my father's business to protect his own wife and child?

'Well, that's settled,' said Grandfather, 'Gianni comes to Forlï and Paolo stops here, at least till the immediate danger is past.'

And so they all three seemed satisfied; but I had an uneasy feeling that Uncle Paolo had manœuvred the decision at my father's expense.

It was arranged that they should start in the late afternoon, after an early dinner and a long siesta. When Grandfather objected that this would bring them to Forlï after midnight, Father said flatly that he would not be responsible for leading tired men on nervous horses—his troopers had not slept till dawn, and their mounts were shaken by the fright of the burning stable; both must be well rested before they left. And so, I thought, must he.

As we went down to dinner I said quietly: 'We'd feel safer, Father, if you stayed to take care of us in Gradara.'

He looked at me sharply, as if he had seen through my stratagem, but all he said was: 'It has been settled now. Don't worry—I'll get through.'

He left the table after the first course, signing to Riccardo to follow him. I, of course, had to wait till my grandfather rose; then I ran quickly upstairs. Father was in his own tower-room; when I tapped on the door he told me to wait, and (having slept little the night before) I drowsed for a while on the stairs, my head on my knees; then Riccardo came out and I went in. The shutters had been closed, but in the dim light that filtered through cracks in the wood and struck glints from the row of lances against the wall (tournament lances that my father had not been able to use since his illness, but had kept burnished for over twenty years), I saw that Father was lying very still. It always surprised me, when I saw him stretched out, to find out how tall he was: his stoop detracted from his height, but otherwise he would have been little shorter than my stately grandfather.

The air was heavy with the scent of the poppy-seed ointment. It increased my drowsiness, and I knew it had the same effect on Father. Normally he would never have used it before starting out on a journey, for he said it slowed his reactions and confused his thoughts. So I guessed that he had been in real need of it.

'Can't you put off going till tomorrow?' I asked. 'No, we must get our story in first, before the Parcitadi tell theirs.' 'You know, you're just being obstinate because Uncle Paolo suggested you couldn't it.' Father did not deny this. He admitted: 'Paolo irritates me—he has so much. He's only four years younger than I am, yet by his looks he might well be my nephew, if not my son. Did you see him yesterday, leaping off his horse like a youngster, just to impress your mother?' (So he *had* noticed, I thought.) Father went on bitterly: 'Everyone loves and admires him, because he is so handsome. He has never known the humiliation of all the expedients one needs to make a wrecked body do the work of a sound one.' I said: 'If I were in your place I would not feel humiliated but very proud—with such a handicap to live so bravely and to do so much.' I gentled him for a moment, stroking his hair, then added: 'Mother was proud of you yesterday, when she saw you fighting on the wall.' His eyes lit and a sudden smile transformed him. 'So I didn't imagine it?' 'No, I saw it too. She was in love with you at that moment.'

I began to feel frightened at the turn the conversation was taking, for I had seen her lack of response to his embrace that morning, and I knew that he, with his uncanny instinct where Mother was concerned, had probably sensed it too.

So I changed the conversation, saying: 'Can you really manage the distance?' 'Yes, if we are not attacked on the way. If I have to waste my strength fighting, I may not get beyond Cesena—the long uphill pull will finish me. The rest of the way is flat and easy. A light or two on the hill to the left—that's Bertinoro; skirt around Forlimpopoli, and in less than an hour you reach Forlï. If I can still sit in the saddle there, I'll leave my father and most of the escort, and push on to Faenza. There I shall find two women only too happy to care for me.' 'Two?' I asked with surprise, and perhaps a twinge of jealousy. 'Yes, my sister Rengarda and—that other.' 'To which of them will you go?' He reflected a moment and then answered: 'If I'm really ill, to Rengarda. She, like you, is a Malatesta woman . . .' (it is good to be called a woman, when one is only twelve!) '. . . whose idea will be to make me fit for battle again. Whereas, Ginevra with all her maternal tenderness aroused would try to keep me an invalid as long as possible.'

'Do you think the ride *will* make you really ill?' I asked anxiously. 'No, I'm tough: a couple of days' rest will put me right. Don't forget to wake me, two hours after the Nones. And now I must sleep.'

As I bent down to kiss him, he caught me to him. And, in the twilight vision that comes on the borderland of sleep, he said an odd thing: 'Whatever happens, don't stop loving me, Concordia.' 'Why, what could happen?' I exclaimed. 'I don't know, but we Malatesti are a fated race. Sometimes I am afraid of the future.' He had made me afraid too, but I would not own it. 'That's just tiredness,' I said, 'Things will look brighter when you wake.' I kissed him again and said softly: 'Happy dreams!'

Only one of the guest-rooms was free, Malatestino's; so I went in there and slept for a while; then I went to see if Mother was awake. I had an idea: supposing *she* were to rouse him, instead of me? I imagined his joy, waking perhaps from a dream of her into the reality of her presence. She could not help being touched, I thought, by the light that would come into his eyes.

There was no one in the bedroom, but from the Court Room beyond it I heard voices. There I came upon them all: Mother, in one of her loveliest gowns, all green and gold, seated on the dais with her three ladies behind her; Uncle Paolo standing at the reading-desk, while a young man, who seemed to be a kind of secretary, stood beside him, turning over the pages. It was clever of my uncle, I couldn't help thinking, to choose that blond, rose-cheeked lad, dressed in sky-blue doublet and long red hose, as a foil. He himself, a harmony of brown and gold, with his pale cheeks and ebony hair, seemed like a statue carved in various kinds of wood.

Mother, absorbed in listening, made a little, friendly gesture, as if to say: 'Come and sit down by me and don't disturb me.' Annabella moved to give up her seat to me, but I shook my head and sat down on the edge of the dais.

It was the usual story of a knight undertaking adventures for love of a beautiful lady, but I could not concentrate on it. I was thinking of my father, up there alone, gathering strength for the ordeal that lay before him, and something of his own resentment invaded my mind. Obviously, Mother had no thoughts to spare for him at that moment; perhaps when the story came to an end I could have a word with her.

But when it ended, Uncle Paolo had provided a pleasant surprise: two of his troopers, one who could sing and another who played the flute, came to give us a concert. There was no sand-glass in the room, but I have a good sense of time. I watched the shadows shift across the floor, and when I judged that the hour had come, I slipped out. No one noticed me, Mother least of all.

22

Uncle Paolo stayed for about a fortnight; then, when it became obvious that there would be no attack upon Gradara, he went back to Ghiaggiolo. They were happy days, for Mother flashed and sparkled like a brook in the sunlight. Uncle arranged musical entertainments, read to us, talked to us about Florence—its beautiful churches, its fashions, its politics. Mother once asked him why he had thrown up his post as Captain of the People there. He said, watching her from under his long lashes: 'The reason I gave was that I had much private business of my own and could not afford to devote so much time to public duties. Perhaps the real reason was, that I had left my heart in Romagna.'

After the first day or two of armed watchfulness, he began to take us out for short rides near the castle and open-air meals in the meadows full of May flowers. Mother now seemed to enjoy riding, and I was happy because I had my beloved little horse again. On the third day after our arrival, Aldo—whom my father had left at Gradara

—sent a message asking me to come to the stables, and there I found Plato. He was in a pitiable state, his glossy black coat scorched away in places, his fetlocks ripped by long slashes that Aldo said were probably due to a panic flight through brambles; and he was very thin, as though he had not fed since he had left Rimini.

'A pity he can't tell us what happened,' said Aldo, fondling him. 'It's my guess that the Parcitadi, when they found that Messer Giovanni had saved the war-horses and got his men away, raided the second stable . . .' 'And Plato was too quick for them!' 'Yes, he must have broken away. By the state of his coat I'd say he went through, or close beside the burning stable and out through the postern gate—smashed in or left open—into the countryside.' 'How did he find his way here and, if he could, why was he so long about it?'

Aldo gave a whimsical chuckle: 'I've lived all my life among horses and I know how their brains work. Plato is one of the clever ones. When Messer Giovanni broke out, he took forty men with him to Gradara and sent the rest of them with Captain Marco, to Roncofreddo . . .' '*Captain* Marco!' I exclaimed. 'Yes, Messer Giovanni promoted him that night, for his good work on the wall.' Aldo sounded pleased: they all liked Marco. 'Well, maybe Plato followed the larger group and strayed for a day or two round the walls of Roncofreddo, either unnoticed or too frightened to let anyone catch him. This morning a messenger came here from Roncofreddo. Plato's sense of smell must have told him that the horse was from our stables, and he followed him here.'

I caressed the horse's muzzle and asked anxiously: 'Shall I be able to ride him again? You won't have to—kill him?' 'I hope not. Unless he has internal injuries I can't see any damage that a few weeks of grooming and good food will not put right.' And in fact, within a fortnight I was on his back again, though it was several months before he fully recovered. Only in the following spring, when he gradually shed his winter coat and grew a new one, did his glossy blackness reappear.

Meanwhile, we heard that my father and my grandfather were at Forlì, negotiating with Monaldeschi; but apparently they were getting little satisfaction.

Then Father left Forlì. He and Uncle Malatestino were somewhere in the hills, swooping down to make lightning raids on our enemies in various parts of Romagna.

From time to time Uncle Paolo spent a few days with us—officially to inspect the defences of the castle and see that the guard did not grow slack; but really, I think, to keep us company, at my grandfather's request.

Under his escort, we would ride out in the green valley below the castle, sometimes towards Pesaro but more often to Segabite Head. When I saw the long sands, stretching from Cattolica to Rimini, I craved to swim. Mother said briefly that it was out of the question: if she had realised that I was swimming with my father the previous year she would have forbidden it (I wondered secretly what use that would have been!). Anyway, she said, I was growing up and could no longer expose myself in this indecent and risky sport. But Uncle Paolo overpersuaded her—and then I was sorry that I had judged him critically. In my father's absence I was once more falling under the spell of his charm. He said he would swim with me, while Mother watched us.

It was quite a business. First a tent had to be put up on the sands—not the little camping-tent used by Father and me, but a real pavilion where, in front of the screen behind which I undressed (with Annabella to help me), Mother could sit in comfort, her feet and gown protected from the sand by a wooden platform and a carpet. Then she insisted on my wearing an absurd nightdress that came to my ankles, floated up when I entered the water, and made normal swimming impossible. However, remembering how my father contrived to swim without bending his legs, I turned on my back and began to flip my feet from the ankle—and it worked! I was able to move through the water at a fair pace . . . but oh! how I longed to be a child again; to gallop free on the sands, to ride astride, to swim with nothing hampering my legs. If these restrictions were part of growing up, I didn't like it.

One warm, still day, when a film of clouds cut off the sunrays that might have spoiled her delicate complexion, Mother decided to paddle. Her ladies, one on each side, held up her skirts to prevent their getting wet. She had the prettiest feet I have ever seen, little larger than mine at twelve years old, slender and lily-white.

Uncle Paolo, with his hair held close in a golden net and his body naked except for a loin-cloth of black silk woven with gold, was looking like a Greek god. He made a series of fancy strokes, evidently intended to impress her, and they did. She stood there on the edge of the water, looking at him with open admiration. I could have told her that he was nothing like as good a swimmer as my father, but I refrained.

Coming out of the sea, he asked Annabella to bring him his towel from the tent, and quickly dried himself. Then he said: 'Madonna Francesca, the sand will cling to your little wet feet. Allow me . . .' Without waiting for an answer he picked her up and carried her up the shore. She was certainly a light weight, but the sand above the water-line was soft and powdery and his feet sank into it. I expected, almost hoped, that he would have to make himself look slightly ridiculous by putting her down, but somehow he achieved the distance. When he reached the tent he was flushed and gasping, but she looked lovelier than I had ever seen her.

23

Summer passed into autumn, and with September came my birthday. I had not expected that Father would remember it, but to my joy he came to Gradara, bringing me an exquisitely-wrought casket that contained a dainty gold bracelet. 'As a start towards collecting jewels for your dowry,' he said. It made me feel very grown-up and important; but Mother, as always when there was talk of marrying me, sighed deeply and changed the conversation.

It was still warm, and the elm trees and oaks overhanging the deep lanes formed tunnels of russet and pale gold. We went out riding, all three together, down the steep lane and into the valley, where the peasants were harvesting their grapes. At one farm they were still cutting the bunches, at another they were treading, and we watched the crimson must pouring into the deep stone vats; at a third the casks had already been filled and we were offered a cup of the rough, new wine.

Father seemed well and good-humoured, and Mother treated him with a smiling friendliness that surprised me: it seemed as though she were so happy in herself that she had warmth to spare for all, even for him. I felt that this was going to be a really joyful day.

But I was wrong. When we came back that evening, towards sunset, we found that a messenger had brought a letter from Uncle Ostasio. Mother took it up to her bedroom to read in privacy, and I followed her. Its effect on her was immediate: she started, as if stung by a bee, flushed and then paled. For a long while she sat like a statue, still and cold, taking no notice of me.

I was on the point of asking her what bad news the letter had brought, when my father entered. She leaped to her feet and confronted him, indignation sparking from her as from the fur of an angry cat. 'So you have the brazen impudence to come to my bedroom!' she cried.

Father was taken aback. Quite genuinely, I am sure, he had no idea what he had done to provoke this outburst. With a slight shrug he remarked: 'And where, pray, have I a better right than in my wife's bedroom?' 'In that of your mistress—of Tino's mother!' she blazed at him.

I shall never forget the look of suspicion and reproach that Father cast at me. Without trying to defend myself, I indicated the open letter; when he saw the red eagle on the seal his face relaxed: betrayal from me would have been a disaster; from the Polentani it was just a nuisance.

Mother must have intercepted that quick exchange of looks between us, for she said sharply: 'Leave the room, Concordia! I have things to discuss with your father that are not fit for your ears.' As I turned to obey, I felt Father's strong hand clamp down on my shoulder. 'Stay!' he said, 'If there is to be a scene, I prefer to have a witness.' Then he added, to my mother: 'In any case, Concordia knows all about it.'

'What do you know?' she asked me. I looked up at Father, for permission to tell, and he gave an imperceptible nod. So I said, choosing my words carefully: 'I know he has two sons, Tino and Guido.' That would do: no need to tell her their mother's name, nor that she lived in Faenza—and certainly not, in this moment of discovery, that Father meant to adopt them. An approving pat from the hand on my shoulder told me that I had chosen wisely.

'I fail to understand you, Giovanni. At least you might have the decency to conceal your shame from your innocent daughter!'

Father laughed. I realised that the scene was taking a new turn. As a rule, for no valid reason, she made him feel embarrassed and guilty, and he reacted to it by losing his temper and abusing her coarsely. Now she had real cause for complaint, yet he seemed unperturbed, almost amused. 'My dear Francesca, I am not in the least ashamed. It gives me considerable satisfaction to know that, if we have remained for over ten years without a male heir, it is through no deficiency of mine.' She flushed at that and said, a trifle less arrogantly: 'How long has this affair been going on? How old is this boy, or young man, for whom (Ostasio says) you are arranging a marriage contract?' 'He is two.' 'Two?' echoed Mother incredulously. 'Anyhow,' went on Father, 'Ostasio is premature in talking about a marriage contract. The document which has—goodness knows how!—come to his knowledge is merely a preliminary approach made by my father, about a month ago, to the Pope for a dispensation from an impediment of consanguinity.' 'Who is the girl, then—and how old is she?' 'Agnese di Montefeltro, Corrado's daughter. I've no idea how old she is—something between one and five, I suppose. It doesn't matter much. In the ten years or so before there can be any actual marriage, we shall probably have made and broken three or four agreements with Montefeltro.'

Mother dropped back into her chair in a pose of utter abandonment and dejection: 'Oh, Giovanni, for a farcical pact, that may never come to anything, you are ready to humiliate your own wife in public.' Father said impatiently: 'Don't be silly, Francesca! No one is humiliating you.' 'No humiliation—for everyone to know that you have a mistress, and children by her?' 'Who does know? In that document Tino is described as the grandson of Messer Malatesta of Verucchio. No mention of my name, or of his mother's. He might equally well be the child—legitimate or illegitimate—of Paolo or Malatestino. Anyone, apart from our close relatives, who does think him mine will assume that you have at last presented me with an heir. And that, my dear, will be more to your credit than your shame.'

A great wave of despair seemed to overwhelm her at that moment. 'Oh!' she cried bitterly, 'To think that I have been faithful to you for all these years!' Something in her tone seemed to have alerted my father. His eyes glinted dangerously as he warned her: 'And you had better remain so, my fine lady!' 'While *you* . . .!' 'While I exercise a man's right to continue the family line by providing myself with a successor, and to uphold the family honour by insisting upon chastity from my wife.' 'It's not fair!' said Mother. 'Many things in this life are not fair. Is it fair that my brother should have the things denied me: agility, beauty, grace—and the power to raise a smile in your eyes? When I come home, I am given a loving-cup and a courteous speech. You smile with your lips, but your eyes are sad and cold.' 'Oh,' she said, with an impatient sigh, 'you don't mean to say that you are jealous of Paolo?' 'I am not, at the moment. But I might be—so take care.' And with that he turned and left her.

24

In October there came good news: Uncle Malatestino, with Filipuccio of Jesi and troops from the Marches, had captured the castle of Montescudolo. But that was quickly followed by bad: our enemies had retaken the castle, captured my uncle and brought him prisoner to Rimini.

Christmas would have been depressing, with my grandfather at Forlï, my father out of contact, Malatestino a prisoner and Paolo with his own family at Ghiaggiolo, had it not been enlivened by a surprise visit from Pandolfo. The players came again, and this time he saw to it that they were well lodged, and kept them with us for several days.

He himself stayed for some weeks, spending most of his time with me. By then I was almost as tall as my mother, and though I was still very slender my breasts had rounded out. In my long dresses, with my hair plaited with ribbons and held in place by pearl-tipped pins, I looked quite fourteen. And between this young uncle and myself there began a curious flirtation. He used to call me his 'little sweetheart' and vow (sometimes in front of my mother, who would look vexed and tell him not to be ridiculous) that if I really had been his cousin, he would have travelled to Rome to get a dispensation, so that he could marry me.

It was all make-believe, of course—I knew it as well as he did—but he said it was good practice for me. He would surprise me with sudden light kisses on my neck, my eyelids, my hair. Very rarely he kissed my lips, and I did not like that. But he said: 'Keep still—don't struggle. Just let your lips meet mine, and smile with your eyes.' He told me I was an apt pupil and would make a perfect bride for some lucky man.

He would write, and recite to me, verses in Italian, Latin or French, in which great play was made upon my name: Concordia — concord — harmony — pacification —peace, and all the rest of it. At first, embarrassment made me giggle. Then he showed me how to receive the homage gracefully, to smile and extend my hand for a kiss. 'Your father has made you into a gallant boy,' he said once, 'but I want to turn you into a woman as charming and gracious as your mother.'

(And to think that it has all been wasted!)

Then Pandolfo went back to his father at Forlï and the dark winter closed upon us.

From time to time my father paid us a visit, but he seemed unapproachable, wrapped in his own thoughts. The continued loss of the Gattolo was something to which he could not reconcile himself, although it was in some measure offset by the damage that his swift raids inflicted on the Parcitadi and their associates.

Curiously enough, since their quarrel on my birthday, he and Mother seemed on much friendlier terms, almost fraternal. He had stopped folding Mother in those fierce embraces from which she always shrank. Now he contented himself with kissing her hand, but she sometimes spontaneously put her arm round him and kissed his cheek.

Mother, who had been so cold and withdrawn, seemed to have affection to spare for everybody. Not only had she made splendid gifts to her ladies at Christmas, but she now seemed really interested in their welfare, and she was much less critical of me. Under Pandolfo's tuition I had become less assertive and more feminine, and that satisfied her. It seemed as though she had come down from her ivory tower into the real world. She used to wait eagerly, almost impatiently, for the couriers who brought her letters. Occasionally she heard from her family in Ravenna, sometimes from my father and my grandfather—who wrote only when there was something important to say—and nearly every week from Uncle Paolo. He was a good correspondent, writing long accounts of his own doings, news about other members of the family, and all the latest gossip from Florence.

And so the weeks passed uneventfully, until one day in March the sentinels espied a lone horseman spurring up the valley from the direction of Rimini. He was unarmed and had no attire or crest to distinguish him, but he was making straight for the castle. When they told my mother, she replied: 'A single man, unarmed, can do no harm. Tell the doorkeeper to let him enter.' But she had turned very pale. 'Why, Mother!' I exclaimed, 'You look frightened.' She held me to her, and I could feel her trembling: 'I have a strange foreboding,' she said, 'as if this man is bringing us misfortune. Maybe he has news of some disaster.'

Mother received the visitor in the Court Room, telling Messer Rinaldo to bring a flask of wine and a beaker—not the loving-cup, for by his appearance he seemed to be someone of little account.

But when he was ushered in, we had a surprise. His

clothing was stained and ragged, his cadaverous cheeks were unshaven, but there was no mistaking that one bright, fierce, blue eye.

'Malatestino!' gasped my mother. He took a step towards her: 'Francesca—I escaped!' And he collapsed in a heap at her feet.

Even at the time I suspected the genuineness of that faint on the part of my 'tough' uncle; but I gave him the benefit of the doubt. After all, he had been several months in prison, badly fed if not actually starved, and must have ridden full speed to Gradara.

In the days that followed, however, it did strike me that he was overplaying his role of interesting invalid. Since, in the absence of my grandfather and my father, there could be no meetings in the council chamber, a bed had been fixed up for him there, sparing the extra flight of stairs to the guest-rooms. He stopped in bed for about ten days, during which time Mother and Nannie nursed him. There seemed to be nothing the matter with him, except general weakness; but he evidently enjoyed lying in warmth and comfort and having good meals brought to him.

Now and again I went in to see him, but never willingly, and I resented the time that Mother spent with him. It was a curious form of jealousy, not for my own sake but for my father's, and in the end it led to a violent quarrel between us.

'You don't nurse Father when he is ill!' I remarked one day, as she came out of the room. She flushed with vexation and said curtly: 'He never *is* ill: he has an iron constitution.' Then, reading my look, she added hastily: 'Occasionally he suffers with his bad leg, but he prefers to have no notice taken of that.' I said: 'Not "occasionally", but quite often. And when he does, he needs a great deal of tenderness and care.' 'Don't you think him capable of bearing a little pain?' 'It's not the pain,' I retorted scornfully, 'It's the . . .' It was difficult to explain, but after a moment I completed the sentence: '. . . it's the hurt in his mind—and *you* do nothing to help that!' 'My dear Concordia, do you think I need a twelve-year-old child to advise me on how to look after my husband?' The temptation was strong to tell her that, if she did not look after him, another woman could, and did; but I resisted it and merely said: 'I'm only twelve, I know. But I understand him better than you do, because I love him and you don't.'

Mother boxed my ears with two stinging slaps. They were probably well deserved, but never in my life had she hit me before, and it made me feel deeply ashamed, for myself and for her. Then she did another unprecedented thing: she burst into uncontrollable tears.

25

Uncle Malatestino got up in due course, but it was a long while before he showed any signs of taking up an active life. He had just sat around in an arm-chair, talking to Mother about his sufferings and privations. I was puzzled, for this was not in his character; much as I disliked him, I had always admired his courage. I felt that his invalid pose was a device to attract sympathy—and Mother's sympathy in particular. It did not succeed, for she shared my uneasy fear and suspicion of him. We both heartily wished that he would go away, but he seemed to assume that, since the Gattolo was lost, his home was Gradara.

About a month after his arrival, there came news that my father was besieging Santarcangelo di Romagna, to the north of Rimini. It was quite a while before he captured it, and I privately thought that my uncle, fully recovered, might have gone to help him. But he continued to sit about in Gradara, under the pretext that he was protecting Mother and me, who would have felt much safer without his 'protection'.

He was still with us in June, when a letter came from my mother's brother, Bernardino. She read it and her face lit up: 'He is coming to visit us for a few days!' she said joyously, and read me part of the letter:

'We met the Ghibellines at Campaldino, near Bibbiena. It was a confused and bloody fight, but in the end we won it. I was slightly wounded—nothing much, but my left arm will be out of use for a while. They took me up to the Hermitage of Camaldoli to have my wound dressed, and there I found that only a single pass—the Mandrioli—separated me from the valley that runs through Mercato Saraceno to Cesena. That is where I am at the moment. I cannot ride far in a day, because of my wound, but I have sent news to my father that I am safe and will see him in Cervia or Ravenna on the way back. It seems to me that Gradara would be a pleasant spot to rest in until my arm is healed, so I am taking the chance to come and visit you. It is years since we have seen each other . . .'

'Indeed it is!' I interposed. 'Do you remember, he came to my First Communion party and gave me a Ravenna pound. I was only nine then.'

'And now you are getting on for thirteen. Only four years, but it seems an eternity. Time passes so slowly.' She sighed and laid down the letter.

'Look, Mother—there's something written on the other side', I pointed out.

She turned the scroll: 'Yes, here's a postscript. "I am permitting myself to bring a friend with me. He is a young Florentine, very serious-minded but good company all the same—Messer Durante, of the Alighieri family. We call him Dante for short. He stood by me gallantly in the battle, and I am sure you will find him congenial. Messer Guido Cavalcanti—whose poems I admire and in whose taste I have implicit trust—says the youth has some talent for poetry, but I haven't yet induced him to read me any of his verses.'

I was eager to see Uncle Bernardino's friend, for Uberto had given me the idea that all Florentines were brilliant talkers and models of elegance. So I was disappointed when Messer Dante proved to be a plainly dressed, hatchet-faced young man, very reserved and almost silent, whether from pride or shyness it was hard to tell.

When I asked him how he had enjoyed the battle he said gravely: 'I was very much afraid.' I was taken aback, for my relatives all spoke of war as if it were a splendid game. Seeing my look of consternation and Uncle Malatestino's hardly veiled sneer, Bernardino interposed: 'That is Dante's modest way of saying that, when I was wounded and unhorsed, he rode in between me and the enemy and held two of them at bay until I was helped into the saddle again. I certainly owe him my liberty, perhaps my life.'

'Then you are doubly welcome here, Messer,' said my mother, with one of her most beautiful smiles. The young man kissed the hand she held out to him, and I could see that he was touched.

But when, later that evening, Mother asked if he would read her some of his poetry, he politely but firmly declined. 'I have circulated nothing,' he said, 'and the little that I have written does not satisfy me. Besides, it is all very intimate: it would seem to me as though I were exposing my naked soul.'

Mother said courteously: 'No doubt the verses are addressed to some beautiful lady—perhaps the one you intend to marry?'

Bernardino laughed: 'No, poor Dante has spent the last few years, with the excuse of his studies, postponing his marriage to a lady with influential connections, to whom his father contracted him at the age of twelve. His verses are all for another, whom he hardly knows. Sometimes she bows to him in the street, but lately she has cut him—he doesn't quite know why.'

The young man's cheeks flushed as scarlet as the long tunic that he wore. We could see that he was really vexed, though he made no reply. Mother said tactfully: 'No doubt the lady is short-sighted or absent-minded.' Then she turned the conversation by asking her brother to take our guest to see the sunset from the castle battlements: 'A sight to inspire any poet.'

Our visitors stayed for about ten days; no longer, for Uncle Bernardino was at that time *podestà* of Pistoia, to which he had to return as soon as the sick-leave granted for his wound had expired. Messer Dante, too, was still on military service, and had only been granted leave to accompany him through Bernardino's personal influence with his Captain, Viero dei Cerchi.

On the last day of their visit Bernardino came to me and said: 'Little niece, do you know of any farm or cottage near by that has flowers to sell?' I told him that, about twenty minutes' walk along the road to Cattolica village there was a farm where the farmer's old mother had a garden of herbs and flowers. Every time I passed, I used to see her there: watering her flowers, staking them, collecting seeds or planting out new beds. Whatever the time of year, there was always colour and fragrance. Late roses blossomed right up to the moment when the first snow fell; in January the white coverlet was pierced with snowdrops, and with the melting of the snow there came the first violets.

I told Bernardino about the garden, asking him why he wanted to know, and he answered: 'Messer Dante has had the idea of bringing a bouquet, to thank your mother for her hospitality.' I clapped my hands, saying it was a lovely thought, and the young Florentine thanked me with a smile that lit up his thin, stern face. 'Will you come with us, Contessina, to show us the way?' he asked.

I asked whether they really wanted to walk that distance in the summer heat; would they rather not ride? But Bernardino said he would prefer to walk: he had discarded the sling only that morning and did not wish to tire his arm before starting on their ride to Cervia, where they planned to sleep. As for young Dante, he always agreed to any suggestion we made. It was not, I felt sure, that he had no will of his own; rather, he seemed to be living in a different world—a world created by his own thoughts—from which he looked down indifferently on the rest of us.

He was surprisingly good company on the walk. I had expected him to ignore me and talk to my uncle on abstruse topics that I could not understand. Instead, he courteously addressed most of his conversation to me, asking me the names of the wild flowers I was picking; for the hedges were full of cow-parsley, chicory, golden bedstraw and white clematis, and soon I had a lovely little posy. In the more open sunny places there was yarrow—not only white but the rarer mauve variety. He laughed when I told him that my mother's youngest lady, Annabella, used to put it under her pillow, because our country maids say that it makes a girl dream of her true love, and perhaps even see him next day.

'And do you do that too, Contessina?' asked Messer Dante, with an unexpected twinkle in his dark eyes. 'No,' I admitted candidly, 'but then, I haven't a true love: I shall have to wait until after my father has chosen a husband for me.'

For some reason Uncle Bernardino found that very funny and he guffawed. But Messer Dante reproved him: 'One should not laugh at a child's innocence, Bernardo. The Contessina meant no more than she actually said.' I was grateful to him, though I couldn't imagine what my uncle thought I had meant to say.

Soon we came to the farm at the foot of the hill. I

thought it a beautiful house, two-storeyed and whitewashed, with deeply curved brown and golden pantiles on the roof. The family lived in the upper rooms, but all the business of the farm went on in the three deep archways of the loggia. Two of them held hen-roosts, a pigsty, and cages full of rabbits; in the third there was a farm-cart, with its harness and accoutrements hanging on the walls. Around the house were circular hayricks with a central pole—*stolli*, we call them—some complete, others sliced away from the pole till they looked like cut cake bored through with a knitting-needle. These were a new idea to our guest, and Uncle Bernardino explained that this device helped to preserve the ricks from being blown to bits by strong winds coming in from the sea.

Barefoot children were scampering about, cheerfully keeping company with hens, geese, ducks, turkeys, rabbits, and one large black goat that kept straying in and out of the arched recesses. I knew the eldest boy by name, so I called: 'Toni! Go and fetch *nonna*, please.' He touched his forelock and ran off, returning with a black-clad old woman, so shrivelled with age that she was smaller than me.

To tell the truth, I was a little afraid of her, and I know I was not the only one. The women in the citadel used to call her when there was illness in the house, for she knew all the secrets of healing herbs; but in the streets they would cross themselves when they saw her pass. Yet she must have been kind-hearted, for Monna Cristina had once said in my hearing that the village girls went to her when they were in trouble. That stuck in my mind, because Nannie shook her head and frowned, as if Cristina had said something improper. So I said: 'Why shouldn't they, Nannie, if she is sympathetic?' And everybody laughed. All the same, I would not have felt inclined to take my troubles to her; but then, I am in the habit of keeping them to myself.

A vine hedge separated her garden from the rows of vegetables and cleared stubble fields that surrounded the farmhouse. In one part, bordered with rosemary and lavender, were all the herbs and simples that she used for her medicaments; in another were lilies, roses, and many humbler flowers. Messer Dante's eyes were attracted at once by the tall, white lilies. 'That is the flower which, to me, most fully represents Madonna Francesca,' he said. 'Grace, chastity and pride, united in one immaculate whole.' The old crone picked a number of them, cutting the stems with a knife at her belt. Behind us, the air was perfumed by a hedge of white roses. 'Let me complete the bouquet with those,' he suggested, but she shook her head, mumbling: 'White roses are for the dead.'

We all started at that: Bernardino crossed himself and muttered: 'Avert the omen!' Messer Dante turned rather pale and said, as if in apology: 'Anyone who makes a deep impression on me is associated in my mind with a colour: that of Madonna Francesca is white—the whiteness of a flower petal or of a mountain tipped with snow.' 'And mine . . .?' I couldn't help asking. He considered this seriously: I felt his eyes boring through me, as if to penetrate into my mind. After a few moments he answered: 'A clear gold, Contessina—the pale gold of dawn.' He hesitated and then added, as if reluctantly: 'But there are dark clouds on the horizon and they are spreading fast.'

The old woman gazed at him with a curious expression, between admiration and fear: 'You have the Vision, young man,' she said, in an unexpectedly sonorous voice, unlike her usual reedy treble. 'Let me see your hand.' She took it and turned it palm upward.

I had heard that she could tell the future by looking at the lines of a person's hand. Nannie had warned me never to let her do it for me, saying that it was 'the Devil's work', so I was anxious to see what would happen.

She peered in silence, and then went down to the ground

before him, in a curtsy deeper than any she had ever given to my mother: 'You are one of the Masters,' she asserted (and she no longer called him 'young man') 'I see great tribulation before you—sorrow and exile and wanderings —and in the end great glory, though maybe not until after you are dead.'

Bernardino, I could see, was impressed, though he laughed it off with some silly joke about becoming a student again, since he was in the company of a Master. And then, of course, I wanted to have my hand read. 'Can you tell me,' I asked, 'what sort of a husband they will give me?' 'What sort would you like, Contessina?' asked Messer Dante gravely, but I suspected that at bottom he was amused. I thought it over: 'Brave and proud like my father,' I said, 'but handsome, like Uncle Paolo, and as kind as Pandolfo.' 'Do you only take the Malatesti for your model?' asked Bernardino, pretending to be hurt. 'Oh no,' I rectified quickly, 'he must be gay and generous, like the Polentani, and have a castle as beautiful as Gradara, near the sea, so that I can go swimming.' Messer Dante shook his head: 'If you expect so much, little one, you cannot help being disappointed,' he warned me. 'Well, let us see what our oracle here will provide for you.'

The old woman took my hand. I heard her catch her breath sharply and saw her look, as if for help, at Messer Dante. It was a long time before she spoke, and then it was in her wheezy old-woman's voice: 'That's what I wish you, Contessina: a brave husband, handsome and rich, just as you imagine him.' She and Messer Dante looked each other in the eyes for a long minute, then he spoke, as if unwillingly: 'One should not jest with the Vision, grandmother. What did you see?' And she, under compulsion: 'That is the trouble. I see—nothing! Nothing beyond this year.' 'Do you mean, I'm going to *die*?' I asked, startled; for I could read disaster in their eyes.

'Of course not!' interposed Bernardino impatiently.

'Come, let's put a stop to all this nonsense. Finish choosing your flowers, Dante, and we'll go home.' So we selected the loveliest roses in the garden—not white, but every other shade, from shell-pink to deepest crimson, and returned, well content, to Gradara.

Mother was delighted with this tribute, saying that she could not have wished for anything more charming. But Bernardino teased his friend: 'Flowers from a poet, without even a line of verse? Surely my sister's beauty deserves to be celebrated, at the least in a sonnet?' Messer Dante did not laugh: he said gravely: 'When my talent equals her beauty, I hope to write something by which she may be for ever remembered; but the time has not yet come.'

26

I would like to linger over the rest of that summer, which remains in my mind as a succession of days brimming over with sunshine and happiness—the last happiness I shall ever know.

Mother and I were not left long alone. My father and grandfather were still away at Santarcangelo, which Father had captured brilliantly in March; but, soon after Bernardino left, my uncles, Paolo and Pandolfo, arrived together and stayed for several weeks. So Mother and I each had a cavalier, which meant much more liberty for me: Mother was so happy in Paolo's company that she seemed to care very little how I spent my time.

Pandolfo amused himself by teaching me to shoot. Every summer we held an archery tournament, and this time, as a surprise for our tenants, he had decided that he and I were to compete—not for prizes, of course, but just to show goodwill.

He had a light bow made specially for me, and a leather arm-guard; but I soon found that my ribbons and laces tangled in the bowstring, and my skirts made it difficult to take the proper stance. So Pandolfo took me to ask Mother if I could have a boy's suit again. She looked radiant that day and very lovely. On a white dress she was wearing an exquisitely wrought gold chain that I had never seen before. When I remarked on it she said that Bernardino had brought it from Florence: I wondered why he had not given it to her either when he arrived or when Messer Dante presented his bouquet before leaving.

To my surprise she made no difficulties. In fact I got the impression that she wasn't really listening. 'Of course!' she said, 'Do as you like!' And she smiled at Pandolfo and kissed me. So once more (but for how short a time!) I regained my freedom.

The competition was held outside the walls of the citadel, where the towering castle and the hill slope gave shelter from the wind. Besides our own men, many had come from Cattolica, Segabite and Pesaro; for everyone knew that the winners would be incorporated into the castle guard and would have a favoured position among my father's men-at-arms.

The green bank below the wall had been cut in steps like a Roman arena, to accommodate the non-competitors and their relatives. Opposite, on a raised platform, there was a tent for the castle folk: my mother and her ladies, my three uncles, Messer Rinaldo and our new chaplain, Don Benedetto.

First came the crossbow events; not individual scores, these, but teams of three competing against one another. It was fascinating to watch the men sitting, concentrated and composed, on their little seats, with the heavy bows resting on a kind of ledge before them. Our own team won easily in the first two heats, but, shooting against Pesaro in the final we were unlucky; the best of our men shot two bolts so close together that the second hit the tail of the first; both dropped off the target and were disqualified, and that lost us the match.

While the individual scores were being totalled up, Pandolfo led me out, in my page's costume—blue and white, with a chequerboard edging representing the device on the Malatesta shield. He brought me up quite near to the longbow target and stayed behind me, stooping to bring his eyes on a level with mine. He tilted my bow upwards, then lowered it and steadied my elbow as I drew back the string. 'Now!' he whispered. The arrow flew, and there was a cry from the spectators: it was a 'centre'! In the midst of the applause I said to Pandolfo: 'I didn't deserve that. It was your arrow, not mine. Leave me alone, for the rest.' So he stayed quiet, without giving me any advice, just handing the arrows to me until I had shot five in all. Naturally, I didn't get another bull's-eye; but all four hit the target, two of them in the inner rings—and that was good enough for more applause. I wanted to drop a curtsy, but suddenly realised that I couldn't do it without skirts; so I just waved my hand and ran back to Mother.

Then Pandolfo shot—straight to the centre: five arrows clustered in a tiny star. This feat aroused the wildest enthusiasm: the shouts of '*Evviva Messer Pandolfo!*' did not die away until the open competition for the longbow-men was announced. The various heats of this went on for the rest of the afternoon; when the scores were totalled there was a surprise. The highest of all was by no veteran archer but by young Salvatore, the doorkeeper's son. In the two years since I had sent him out for the loaves, he had grown from a lanky boy into a handsome, well-spoken young man. When Mother handed him his prize—a leather quiver, stamped with the Malatesta arms in colour and containing a dozen arrows, she congratulated him, saying she would recommend him to Messer Giovanni for a place among the castle guard. But he, kneeling before her, asked for something different: to be taken on as Messer Rinaldo's assistant. He said: 'My longbow will always be there, to defend the castle at need; but I feel I should be more useful planning and organising and keeping accounts.' Then I realised why he had been so eager to learn, the previous winter. Mother, I think, was secretly glad; for Messer Rinaldo, never very efficient, was getting old and lazy and would obviously have to retire before long.

Now that I again had a boy's suit, I took advantage of it—and of mother's absent-mindedness—to ride astride in Pandolfo's company. We rode without escort, for he said we were safe on the sands. No one could be ambushed on those open spaces; and, if enemies did show up in the distance, our swift horses would carry us back in time to the shelter of Gradara.

One day, when the water sparkled invitingly, the craving to enter it grew so strong that I burst out: 'Oh, Pandolfo—if only I could swim!' 'Well, let's do it!' he said, as though it were the simplest thing in the world. 'But there's no tent for undressing, and I have no robe to wear.' 'There are unlimited stretches of sand-dunes, and you have your own beautiful body.' 'What—naked?' I exclaimed, taken aback if not actually shocked. 'I couldn't . . .' 'Oh yes, you could—and you've never known the full joy of swimming until you have felt the water cool against your bare skin. Never let anyone make you ashamed of your naked body, Concordia.'

He was looking round for a place to tether the horses. At last he found a couple of stunted thorn bushes, wind-blown to the point that their boughs streamed inland like a mass of flying hair. 'That will do!' he said. 'Now, off with your clothes, little sweetheart. Let's see which of us will be first in the water.'

He handicapped himself by going some fifty yards along

the shore; so it was I, revelling in the ease with which I was able to pull off doublet and hose, who won the race.

I felt a trifle shy, so I flung myself full-length into the water as soon as it came to my knees. As Pandolfo had said, the feel of it was like a caress; this was swimming with a difference. Soon Pandolfo joined me and, self-consciousness forgotten, we frolicked in the water like a couple of dolphins.

The glorious game went on, day after day, through July into August. When the first Sunday came round, I had qualms of conscience: ought I to confess it? 'Why?' asked Pandolfo lightly. 'Has your mother forbidden you to go swimming with me?' 'No, but she would if she knew.' 'Still, the fact remains that she hasn't. So you are not guilty of disobedience. Are you doing any harm to yourself, to me, or to anyone else?' 'No,' I said, with more conviction. 'Then what is there to confess?' 'But I must confess *something*, and I can't think of anything else that I have done.' Pandolfo laughed: 'Well then, to satisfy your tender little conscience, confess that you smiled at me (you did, you know!) while he was reading morning prayers. Then he will give you a Paternoster to recite ten times over, and both of you will feel that you have done your duty.'

We were lying naked on the hot sand, drying ourselves after a swim. I wriggled round, to see his face. 'Pandolfo,' I asked, 'do you believe in it all?' 'In what?' 'In religion. It seems so silly that one should have to think up imaginary sins, just in order to confess them.'

He considered this seriously for a moment and then replied: 'The way we menfolk live now in Romagna, it is a useful and necessary institution. *Our* sins aren't imaginary: we rob and betray and murder, plotting against our enemies and even within our own families. But whatever we do, we can shift our responsibility upon Mother Church and buy ourselves out of trouble. It's a very comforting thought.' He began to play with the sand, building it up into a pile. 'If ever I inherit Gradara—which isn't likely, because it will probably go to you and your husband, or to . . .' He caught himself up, and I realised that he knew about the marriage plan but would not give my father away. So I completed the sentence: 'To Tino, my father's son.' In his surprise he let out a long whistle: 'So *you* know about that?' 'Yes, and so does Mother; but don't ever mention it to her. . . . Well, if you inherit Gradara, what will you do?' 'I'll build a chapel, in the upper storey—and that will wipe out all my sins. Will you let me, my little sweetheart, if Gradara comes to you?' 'Of course!' I said, 'It's a grand idea.'

Laughing, he sprang up. 'Get dressed quickly; there's a fishing-boat putting out from Segabite harbour.' 'Oh, what will the crew think, and what will they report?' 'Nothing—except perhaps that they have seen a young knight and his page-boy on the sands. Don't worry!'

One afternoon the weather broke. Great white clouds piled themselves on top of Monte Titano and came rushing down upon us. The wind raised swirling sand that stung our eyes. There was no shelter nearer than Cattolica village and Pandolfo decided we could not get there in time. 'We'll scrape out a hollow in the sand and lie there till the storm is past,' he said. 'Come, find a piece of driftwood and set to work. Meanwhile, I'll make certain that the horses can't slip their tether.'

Soon he joined me and his stronger hands quickly scooped out the sand from under the matted roots of bent grass, until he judged that the hole was deep enough. Then we lay down in it and he wrapped his cloak around us both. We were just in time, for the first large, scattered drops were falling. Two minutes later the dunes were blotted out by a curtain of lashing rain and hail. As we lay clasped together Pandolfo began to kiss me. At first I laughed, for the light, quick kisses pattering like raindrops upon my forehead and cheeks tickled me. But as the kisses became heavier I began to struggle, bringing my hands up to his chest to hold him off.

'Lie still, little sweetheart!' he said. 'Don't you trust me?' 'Let me get up!' And, brusquely, I wriggled from his arms, rolled out of the shelter and sprang to my feet. Pandolfo gave a sharp exclamation of annoyance: 'You crazy child! 'You'll be wet through.' But I was stripping off my suit, and I flung it, with my shoes, back into the shelter: 'I'm going into the sea. What does a little rain matter, if I am wet anyway?'

By this time the hail had stopped, leaving the dunes white as if sprinkled with snow. The rain on my bare skin felt warm and pleasant. I ran down into the sea. Pandolfo was shouting something—a warning, I think—and I realised that the storm had whipped up a heavy swell. The waves ahead, as I stood ankle-deep in foam, looked taller than I was, and a sudden fear took me. As I stood hesitating the matter was decided for me; a larger wave than the rest caught me and flung me off my feet: I felt myself being dragged out to sea, and in self-defence could do nothing but swim.

In the deeper water it was easier. I kept myself afloat, rising to meet the crest of each roller as it surged towards me. Though still frightened, I was beginning to enjoy it; the clouds were breaking and shafts of light came slanting and sparkling over the dark green water.

Meanwhile, Pandolfo had undressed and come to the water's edge—I think to help me. I had to get back, and it would not be easy. Each breaker carried me in some way; then I tried to hold my ground as it sucked me out again. Pandolfo was now waist-deep, and on the crest of the next wave I reached his outstretched hand. But in that moment the breaker turned, and with the undertow dragging at his feet and my weight on his arm he lost his balance and fell. We both went under, clasped together, and the pressure of the water was such that I felt my lungs were bursting. At last my head came above water and I gulped some air, while another long roller caught us and flung us ashore.

I was breathless and bruised, there was grit in my mouth, and my eyes smarted so badly that I had to keep them closed, but I was essentially unhurt. So was Pandolfo, yet he did not get up. I felt his weight crushing me into the sand, his hands gripping my upper arms so that I could not move them. He said, in a curious thick voice: 'You little devil—you did that on purpose.' I thought at first that his mouth, too, was full of sand and salt water. Then memory came to me—a faint submerged memory from my babyhood, when I had slept in my mother's bedroom even when Father came to her, and had heard that same tone in his voice.

I felt suddenly afraid. Some instinct made me cross my legs, locking them together at the ankles. Pandolfo, whose breath was coming even faster than mine, went on: 'You can't play this game indefinitely with a man—it is beyond human endurance.' He released one arm as his hand moved down to force my ankles apart, and in that respite I managed to twist free and run to the spot where I had left my clothes.

Crying was never encouraged in our family, but I could not help it then. I was soaked and cold, scratched and bruised from the undertow; already frightened from my narrow escape in the sea. Pandolfo's odd behaviour had been the last straw.

He by this time had come over to me and was looking down at me with an enigmatical expression. 'Are you cross with me?' I asked, sobbing—or rather, whimpering. 'What have I done?' 'It's what you haven't done, my child. I had forgotten that you really are a child. Now, stop crying, finish dressing, and let's go.' He snatched his own clothes and went away to dress.

In the brilliant sunshine that followed the storm we galloped along the beach until the River Tavollo blocked our way, then turned inland towards the bridge my grandfather had built. Here the water was deep and crystal-clear, reflecting the trees that lined both banks of the stream. I began to rein in as we approached the bridge: 'Pandolfo, I want to have a dip in the fresh water before we go home.' 'Haven't you had enough undressing for one day?' he retorted crudely. In this mood I did not recognise my courteous cavalier; his sullen temper had brought out an unsuspected likeness to my father when he was quarrelling with Mother. But I protested: 'My hair is full of sand and stiff with salt water. I can feel sand in my clothes, too. What will Nannie tell Mother, if I come back in this state?' This was a persuasive argument. He agreed to keep watch by the bridge, so that no one should disturb me.

The sun had already steamed some of the dampness from our clothes. Pandolfo spread mine on the hot brick-work of the bridge till they were really dry, and then shook the sand out of them. Climbing down to the water's edge, I looked at my reflection to see just what damage had been done. There were scratches and bruises on my right hip and thigh, and on my arms the marks of Pandolfo's fingers were turning blue. These would be hidden by my sleeves, but there was a scratch and a sand-rash below my elbow that might show when I put on my wide-sleeved dress for dinner.

As a rule I dislike freshwater bathing, but this was delicious. I seemed to be immersed in a bath of emeralds and rubies—those were the splashes of red reflected from the bridge. Swimming idly, just enough to keep afloat, I dipped my head and ran fingers through my hair until I no longer felt the gritty sand and the stickiness of salt water. Then I scrambled out and asked Pandolfo to bring my clothes. My hair was so thick and fine that it would take a long time to dry—much more than the few minutes that separated us from Gradara. So we went on sitting there in the sunshine. High above us curved the red arch of the bridge. There was no parapet and the banks were very steep, so we sat just above water level, leaning against the pile, so that we could feel the heat radiating from the brickwork.

Pandolfo remained silent, and so did I. Experience had taught me that a man in a temper is best left alone. In the end he spoke: 'I'm sorry, Concordia: I've spoiled for you the memory of our last swim together.' 'Last . . .?' I echoed in dismay. 'Yes. Messer Malatesta has summoned me to Santarcangelo.' There was a pause, then he added: 'Just as well, perhaps. It was a dangerous game that we were playing.' 'Is that why you were angry with me? Because I went into the water when it was too rough?' But in my heart I knew that this was not what he had meant.

I was still shaking, though I was no longer cold. It struck me that I ought to say something, show that I bore him no grudge for what had happened; but no words would come. Our easy comradeship was at an end. Next day, under my mother's eyes, I bade him a ceremonious farewell. I have never seen him since.

27

I missed Pandolfo less than I would otherwise have done; firstly because he had really frightened me quite badly, and secondly because the weather had broken and we could not have gone on swimming. So I was content to sit indoors, listening while Uncle Paolo read to Mother. His voice was as beautiful as his face.

How clearly I remember the afternoon when he read about Sir Lancelot, who loved Queen Guinevere but dared not tell her. Then another knight, Sir Galahault, went to the Queen to plead for the man who loved her so devotedly. I can still hear the tremor in my uncle's melodious voice as he continued: 'And Sir Galahault said to the Queen: "Have pity, my lady, for the good knight Sir Lancelot. Do you not see how, from day to day, he droopeth and perisheth, how wan is his cheek and how haggard his eye? And you, my lady, with one kind word, one smile . . ." '

The tremor in Paolo's voice had become uncontrollable. He asked for a glass of water.

While it was being fetched, Mother rose and went with a light, dancing step to the window. 'See, the rain is over!' she said. 'How good it is to be alive on these golden evenings.' She smiled at Uncle Paolo. 'I would like a garland of roses—white roses for my hair,' she said, 'But up here there are none left.' Then she turned to me: 'Concordia, you know the farm where the Wise Woman lives. Go down now, with Monna Cristina and Biancarosa, and fetch me a basket of roses—white ones.' At that I flinched, warning her: 'When Messer Dante wanted to bring you white roses, the old woman said they were unlucky.' Mother laughed: 'I have had so much ill-luck in my life that a few flowers can make no difference. Tell her—white ones.'

By this time my uncle's blond page had returned with the glass of water. 'Well, fetch the Contessina's cloak and go!' Mother ordered Biancarosa, with a touch of impatience. I asked: 'Mayn't I stay a little? I want to know what the Queen answered about Sir Lancelot.' 'No,' said Mother firmly, 'Very soon it will be sunset, and you have only just time to get back before dusk.' Then, seeing Annabella's wistful look, she added: 'You may go too, and, if Messer Paolo can spare him, this young man will be your escort.' That was kind of her, I thought, for he and

Annabella were obviously very happy in each other's company, and they thanked her eagerly, like two children unexpectedly released from school.

So we all went out together, leaving her with Uncle Paolo; and as we went I heard his soft voice beginning again: 'And Sir Galahault said to the Queen . . .'

As we walked down the lane, where the leaves were turning gold but had not yet begun to fall, I made the remark: 'What a beautiful voice my uncle has! No wonder Mother loves listening to him.' 'Much too beautiful, if you ask me,' commented Monna Cristina acidly. 'Madonna would do far better if she listened to him less often.' 'No one *did* ask you, Monna Cristina,' I replied, in what I was beginning to realise was my Malatesta voice: 'Your duty is to serve my mother, not to criticise her.'

How would she take that? I wondered. But people had stopped reminding me that I was only a child and, as such, had no right to express my opinions. Cristina bridled but said nothing; and Biancarosa—as always when she suspected any slight on my mother—rose hotly to her defence.

Annabella and the youth—whose name, we learned for the first time, was Lorenzo—had fallen a trifle behind the rest of us and were chatting contentedly together.

Down in the sheltered valley the late roses, mostly white and yellow, were still in flower. I had expected the old woman to make objections, but she only nodded, muttering something that sounded like: 'What must be, will be.' And with fingers that trembled a little—perhaps with old age—she began to fill the basket that Annabella had handed her.

The three women were whispering together and Annabella was giggling—a less irritating giggle than Maria Pia's but just as youthful. I was several years younger than she, but I would have thought it babyish to laugh like that.

It seemed that they were wanting to ask the old woman something but were too much in awe of her. At last

Annabella pulled at my sleeve and whispered: 'Contessina, would you be so kind as to ask the Wise Woman to read our hands?' Reluctantly, remembering my own experience, I passed on the request and felt relieved when it was categorically refused: 'I will not, and dare not, read the future for anyone at Gradara.' The women looked disappointed and rather huffed, but I did not press the matter.

When the basket was full I gave the Wise Woman a silver coin and a little jar of candied fruits that my mother had sent her; for, living on a farm, she had no need of the essential foods. She took the gifts with curtsyings and thanks, but I could see that her mind was elsewhere.

Then she pointed up to the castle, rose-lit by the rays of the setting sun. Behind it soared a tall black cloud fringed with gold—the type of cloud that often breaks down in a thunderstorm; but this one would evidently drift harmlessly out to sea. The Wise Woman was murmuring something—or was it merely that the words passed from her brain to mine, as sometimes happened between Father and me? . . . 'Don't you see the darkness approaching? Darkness and death over Gradara!'

No, she could not have said those words aloud, for the three women and the young man showed no signs of having heard them.

As we walked back, Biancarosa said to me: 'You are very silent, Contessina. Are you tired?' I shook my head, but I could not speak. Through my brain the warning continued to ring: '*Darkness and death over Gradara.*'

28

My fancies seemed absurd, for we had seldom spent a pleasanter evening. There were flowers enough to weave chaplets for us all—my mother, her three ladies and me. Mother looked lovely with the white blossoms in her golden hair. To match them she was wearing the white-and-gold dress, on which she had never noticed the slight shadow that remained from the blood on Father's cuirass. As she swooped, light and gay, about the room, it glittered around her like rays of sunshine. She said: 'The night is as warm as midsummer and there is a full moon. Let us have supper served on the battlements, where we can enjoy the sight of moonlight on the sea.'

'A lovely thought,' replied Uncle Paolo, 'and I have an idea to make it even lovelier.' His idea took shape when two or three of his men came to sing serenades under the castle wall—at first so far away that we were not sure whether the music was real, or an illusion born of the night and the moonlight. Gradually they approached, until we could hear every word and could see the blue-and-white chequered scarves that crossed their glinting cuirasses.

Even Malatestino, usually a mere background shadow, seemed to be enjoying himself, and in the end he and Paolo sang a duet—Paolo, in his clear tenor, declaring himself a servant of Venus rather than Mars; while Malatestino, in an unexpectedly rich bass, sang a refrain about the joy of leaping into the saddle and riding to war. It was surprising to hear the deep notes coming from his narrow chest.

When at last we descended from the battlements, Mother put her arm round my shoulders: 'I've a surprise for you, Concordia, as a finish to this lovely day.' We were passing along the corridors of the upper storey, and she stopped before the door of one of the guest-rooms: 'See what I have prepared for you!'

The little room, where I had occasionally slept when Father had wished to spend the night with Mother, had been transformed. It was now furnished with a bed—a real four-poster with curtains, such as the grown-ups use

—a *prie-Dieu*, a reading-desk, a table, a carved screen hiding the wash-stand, and a chest to hold my clothes—one that Mother had brought with her from Ravennn, with the red Polentani eagle carved and painted on a golden background, which I had always coveted.

'You are nearly grown-up now,' she said, 'I have been selfish keeping you with me for so long: I know how you liked having your own room in Rimini. So I have been preparing this for you: I meant it as a birthday present, but . . .' she hesitated, and Paolo came to her rescue with a valid reason for anticipating the gift: 'But Salvatore brought in the last bits of furniture, whilst you were out, and we all agreed that it would be fun to surprise you on your return.'

I flung my arms round Mother's neck and kissed her, saying, quite truly, that nothing could have given me more pleasure.

Moonlight lay bright over the floor, and, running to the window, I could see the dark tree-tops below the castle wall. 'Tomorrow,' I thought, 'I shall have a lovely view over Casteldimezzo and Segabite Head.' Then I saw that the bed had been made and turned down, my nightgown and slippers laid ready. 'I can sleep here tonight, then?' She nodded, saying with a smile that it was high time I went to bed.

I hugged her again, said good night to my uncles, and sat down to enjoy my new domain. Outside, I heard Mother saying good night to Malatestino; that surprised me, for she was ceremonious in her contacts with her Malatesta relatives, and he, as the younger brother, ought really to have come after Paolo. He went into his room. I heard him open the door, but my acute hearing missed the click of the latch as he closed it. I thought: as usual, he is spying—he has left the door ajar. But what was there for him to see or hear? Just two figures in the moonlit corridor, saying good night.

Then Mother spoke, very softly. When Malatestino was not present, she had taken to calling Paolo simply by his Christian name; but that night she said: '*Arrivederci, Messer Lancilotto.*' *Arrivederci*, not the customary *buona notte*. I was puzzled, but I thought they had invented some curious game, as grown-ups sometimes do, making a play of words upon the book they were reading. I was sure of it when, after a long pause, I heard my uncle murmur: 'Before the moon is down, my lovely lady Guinevere.' Then he shut his door, next to mine, and there came a faint echoing click from Malatestino's room opposite.

29

My thirteenth birthday started with a disappointment: Father did not come. He wrote, saying that he was busy arranging the sale of Santarcangelo castle to the Papal legate. With the letter came a small parcel containing a pearl necklace and the scrawled message: 'For your dowry-chest.' The necklace was pretty and no doubt valuable, but it was poor compensation for his absence.

Mother, seeing that I was unhappy, made much of me and, after giving me a small token present—a coloured quill for my writing-table—sent me out riding under Salvatore's escort. That ride in the cool September sunshine, under elm trees touched here and there with gold, is one of my last happy memories. Down in the valley the vines were heavy, but the harvesting had not yet begun.

As we passed the Wise Woman's farm, Toni ran out to meet us, holding up a bunch of early grapes. He asked if I wanted flowers, but I shook my head. I was afraid to meet the old woman, and I think she was keeping out of my way, for I glimpsed her bent, black figure behind a hayrick. And once more, as if from her mind into mine, flashed the ominous words: *Darkness and death over Gradara.*

Back in the castle, I burst into Mother's room, intending to give her the grapes and share them with her; but I stopped short when I saw she was not alone. Malatestino was bending over her, holding one of her hands, and she sat tensed as if trying to draw away from him.

I heard him say, with a tremor in his voice that sounded insincere: 'I have opened my heart to you. Tell me . . .' Catching sight of me, he broke off and said curtly: 'Go away, Concordia. I am having a private talk with your mother.'

She took advantage of the interruption to throw off his clasp and rise to her feet: 'Messer my brother-in-law, your "private talks" are not to my taste. When you asked me to send my ladies away, I imagined that you had some news of, or from, my husband that was for my ears alone. Instead . . .' she shrugged her shoulders.

I began: 'If I'm in the way, Mother . . .' 'Not at all. Come here to me, Concordia.' She put her arm round my waist and I could feel that she was trembling, whether from fear or indignation I could not determine. 'Messer Malatestino, I do not choose that you, or anyone else, should order my daughter out of my own room in my presence. I am glad she has come, for I am sure that, in front of her, you will not renew your—offensive proposals.'

My uncle had looked disconcerted, but, quickly recovering his assurance, he replied smoothly: 'That you find them offensive is perhaps the required answer. Maybe my brother Gianni, having heard certain rumours, had given me instructions to test your . . . unassailable virtue.' The sarcasm in his voice was unmistakable, even to me.

Mother looked at him incredulously: 'Giovanni asked you—to test me? I don't believe it! Such tricks are not in his nature. He is rough and quick-tempered, but neither mistrustful nor sly.'

'That's true,' I said, rising to Father's defence: 'If he were angry with Mother he would come here and quarrel with her, not ask you to make mischief.'

Mother hushed me, saying that I must not speak disrespectfully to my uncle, but I could see that she was not really displeased.

Malatestino by this time was standing at the door. His bright eye stared at us unwinkingly, cold as a hawk's, but his voice remained suave as he said: 'My brother, I know, will be interested to hear my report upon his virtuous wife.' And with that he quietly closed the door.

Mother drew a deep sigh, half of agitation, half of relief. 'Oh, Concordia, you came in just at the right moment.' 'Was he trying to make love to you?' She nodded, then said hastily: 'But what do you know about such things?'

'Quite a lot!' I replied boldly. 'And it's time I did, if I am to be married in a year or two.' 'Oh,' she sighed, 'I have tried so hard to keep you innocent.' 'Ignorant, don't you mean? It simply meant that I had to find things out for myself, and it wasn't a pleasant experience.' She looked startled, and I realised that I had said too much; that episode with Pandolfo was something that I must keep to myself. So I changed the conversation by asking: 'Why are you afraid of Uncle Malatestino?' Mother said reluctantly: 'He might say something to make your father angry with me.' 'But what could he say?'

That was one of the moments in which our fate was sealed. If Mother had been frank with me then; if she had confessed: 'I love Paolo in a way that I should not, and I think Malatestino knows or suspects it,' then I might have saved her when the crisis came. But she could not bring herself to say it, and I was still too simple to guess. She answered evasively: 'He might say that I *wanted* him to make love to me.' 'No, he wouldn't dare. If he said that, Father would kill him.' At that she turned pale: 'It's nearly dinner time,' she said, 'Let's go down.'

When we reached the dining-hall there was a vacant place at the high table. 'Where is Messer Malatestino?' asked Mother. No one knew. Out of courtesy we waited some minutes, then Uncle Paolo sent Lorenzo to call him. The young man returned saying that Messer Malatestino was not in his room, so we ate without him.

No comment was made in front of our retainers and servants, but afterwards I heard Uncle Paolo say quietly to Mother: 'Have you quarrelled with him, Francesca?' And she, blushing slightly, for she was not an expert liar, replied: 'He spoke sharply to Concordia and I resented it.' 'Be careful—he is a vindictive man and we cannot afford to be on bad terms with him.'

Later, inquiring at the stables, we found that my uncle, taking an escort of six men, had ridden out towards the sea. Certainly, he would not have dared approach Rimini town: was he going to Cervia, to Cesena, or (all three of us asked ourselves that question, I think), to Santarcangelo?

And so the three of us remained alone at Gradara, for what were to prove the last days of their lives and of my happiness. They passed like any other days, pleasantly and uneventfully. We rode in the lanes around Gradara, and in the evenings made music and finished reading the romance of Sir Lancelot. It ended badly, for after the King was dead, Lancelot became a monk and Queen Guinevere became a nun and they lived for years within sight of each other, without ever meeting again.

I said it was a pity: since Guinevere was a widow, she should have married Lancelot and lived happily ever after. Mother sighed deeply and opined that they should have died together. But Paolo threw back his head and laughed: 'No, Concordia is right—they should have lived, lived and loved, splendidly. I want to live to the full, right up to my last hour.'

On the third evening, Malatestino returned, as unobtrusively as he had gone. The sentinels reported his arrival, but, after a quick consultation with Uncle Paolo, Mother decided that, as he had left without the courtesy of informing her, no welcoming ceremony was necessary. So she kept to her own room and Uncle Paolo kept to his, merely ordering Messer Rinaldo to have an extra place laid for supper.

Malatestino, with a slight bow to Mother, took his seat, and no comment was made on his absence. When a few remarks had been made about the food and the weather, Uncle Paolo said amiably that he trusted Madonna Giacoma and young Ferrantino were well. 'I trust so too,' was the faintly ironic reply. 'No doubt I should have heard, had they not been.'

I could never think of him as a married man, nor feel that his wife Giacoma, whom I had never seen, was my aunt. He kept her always in the background, in one of the up-country castles—Tavoleto, I think it was—and it seemed that her only share in his life had been to bear his son, Ferrantino. This cousin of mine, about the same age as Uberto, had occasionally come with his father to Rimini—a sly, cruel-looking young man, but cleverer than Uberto and less vain.

It struck me that my uncle was not particularly pleased to be reminded of his family, but Paolo continued suavely: 'And Gianni . . .?' 'They say that he has completed the sale of Santarcangelo; furthermore, that there is talk of electing him *podestà* of Pesaro again next year. He will no doubt be looking up his contacts there, and on the way he will certainly stop here—so Madonna Francesca can rejoice in the prospect of seeing him before long.' The venom in his voice was unmistakable. I saw my mother exchange glances with Uncle Paolo: her eyes were startled, his were reassuring. 'And where did you hear all this?' he asked, smiling. 'Was it by any chance at Santarcangelo?'

It was the nearest he would go to asking: 'Have you seen my brother—and what did you tell him?' But he got no direct answer. Malatestino's sinister eye was slightly hooded as he answered: 'I learned many things of interest, here and there, on my journey.'

30

It was close on dinner time next day when trumpets sounded on the battlements, echoing a blast from the valley, and the sentinel called down: 'Messer Giovanni is here!'

I put on my prettiest dress and ran to Mother, begging her to let me wear the pearl necklace that Father had sent for my birthday: it was so long since I had seen him! He would find me grown.

Then I went to the look-out above the drawbridge, heard the well-remembered clatter of horsehoofs approaching up the street; but this time interrupted by an unusual commotion. Afterwards I heard that my father, riding faster than usual and carelessly, had knocked down a child and ridden on, without troubling to find out how badly it was hurt—merely flinging a gold coin to the distracted mother—and the people had resented this.

Then he came in sight. How I loved to see him in the saddle, where he looked straight and tall and dignified—no different from any other man and a better rider than most. I called to him and held out my arms. He looked up, scanned me with eyes that were cold and stern, then gave me a brief nod but no smile. It was as if a cloud had come over the sun. Quietly I crept down to the courtyard, where Mother was already offering the loving-cup. I heard her cold, clear voice: 'Long life and happiness to you, my lord,' and his reply, deviating from the ritual formula: 'May you have the happiness that you deserve, Madonna Francesca.'

He stood on the mounting-block for quite a while before

descending, cautiously, one step at a time. The thought flashed through my mind that he was trying to conceal his lameness—and that was absurd, since we all took it for granted. He was certainly in one of his worst moods, and it was with some trepidation that I came up to him, curtsied and dutifully kissed his hand.

He raised me, turned my face up and gazed intently into it for a moment; then he said over my head to Malatestino: 'She looks like a Malatesta—but then she would, in any case.' He spoke very quietly, and I do not think that anyone else heard him: Mother was talking to Uncle Paolo, and the rest of the group, the seneschal and his assistant, Mother's ladies and Paolo's secretary, were some way behind us.

While I pondered over the meaning of this odd remark, Father took off his helmet and handed it to one of the guards; then he signed to Aldo to unbuckle his cuirass. That was my privilege, and I felt that, by withdrawing it, he had excluded me from our comradeship. Like a whipped puppy I shrank back to my mother's side.

Dinner seemed endless. Father was sitting at the head of the table, with Mother on his right hand and me on his left; Paolo sat next to her and Malatestino next to me; then, two on either side, my mother's ladies and Lorenzo. At the foot of the table was Don Benedetto.

Between my silent, glowering father and my silent, watchful uncle I sat, trying to hold back my tears and choke down my food. Mother's breath was coming fast. I think she was frightened; for Father's ill-humour made it obvious that Malatestino had told him something—but what?

After the chaplain had read grace there was a long silence, broken by murmurs as the servants poured wine, offered bread, or set plates of meat before us. Father sat rolling pellets of bread between his fingers and drinking, as if absent-mindedly, long draughts of wine.

Then Uncle Paolo took the situation in hand. Somewhere

I have read the ancient saying: 'Whom the Gods wish to destroy, they first make mad.' And I think that, on this last day of his life, Paolo Malatesta must have been a trifle mad. He sparkled and laughed, kept up a continuous stream of conversation: news from Florence (received, he said, in a letter from Uberto); witty proverbs, to raise a smile from Mother and laughter from her ladies. When the fruit was brought in, he began to tell a humorous tale. Lost in my unhappy thoughts, I missed the beginning of it, but it was something like this: A rich merchant was angry with his young wife when she came back late one night, so he locked her out of the house (rather unkind of him, I thought; but he seemed to imagine she had been making love to someone else). She said she was going to drown herself, then ran to the well and dropped in a large stone. When her husband ran out to see what had happened, she slipped indoors and locked him out. He made such a noise that the neighbours came to see what the matter was; but she told them he was drunk, so they all sided with her against him.

My mother laughed—that girlish laughter which she had so recently recovered and which made her seem young again. Her ladies, who had looked uncertainly for her lead, took courage and laughed too. The chaplain cleared his throat deprecatingly; but no one was prepared for my father's reaction. Rousing himself from his sullen lethargy, he said bitingly: 'No doubt you find marital infidelity a subject for humour, Madonna Francesca—but I am surprised that you let such stories be told in front of your young daughter.'

Mother looked taken aback, but Paolo answered for her: 'Why, Gianni, are you going to turn monk? I have heard you laugh at stories in comparison with which this one would be a nursery tale.'

'Perhaps,' interposed Malatestino silkily, 'Gianni needs to visit Faenza, to recover his sense of humour.'

I caught my breath, looking at Father. Paolo also flashed a quick glance at him, interested but evidently puzzled. It struck me that maybe he had been in isolated Ghiaggiolo when there was the talk about little Tino's future marriage, and that it had not reached his ears. But Mother at once picked up the allusion. 'Faenza!' she said, 'Is that where . . .?' She caught herself up in time, remembering the presence of her ladies; but Father, I could see, knew what she had meant to say. He stopped crumbling bread and cast a furious look at Malatestino. Mother said hastily: 'Have we all finished? If so, perhaps Don Benedetto . . .?' And the chaplain obliged by thanking God in mellifluous Latin for the pleasant meal.

The three Malatesta men each gave a short, sardonic chuckle. It was strange how, with all the stresses and jealousies between them, there was a fundamental unity that drew them together.

Mother said: 'The afternoons are still warm. I am going to take my siesta.' 'And so will I,' said Father. 'Later, I will ride to Pesaro, where I have business that will take me a couple of days.'

I could sense Mother's relief. The two of them had drawn apart into a window embrasure, but I could hear them talking. 'You gave me no notice of your coming,' said Mother, 'but I have told Messer Rinaldo to air your room and prepare the bed.' 'No need,' he replied, 'Today we will take our siesta together.' I heard her sharp intake of breath, but she answered pleasantly enough: 'And your back? You always say that your own hard bed rests it better.' 'Since, for the first time in fourteen years, you are taking an interest in my health . . .' (the faint sneer in his voice made it sound like Malatestino's) '. . . you will be glad to hear that my back is in excellent condition. So I can allow myself the luxury of spending a pleasant hour or two with my wife.' And, drawing her arm through his, he led the way upstairs.

A siesta, to my mind, wastes the best hours of the day. However, on this occasion I went upstairs, took off my necklace and, knowing that I could not put it back in Mother's room for some time, slipped it into a hiding-place; then I threw myself upon the bed to cry and, crying, fell asleep. My father's voice woke me. He was above, on the battlements, talking to the sentinel, and I could tell by the slant of the sun that it was already late afternoon. Soon afterwards I heard horsehoofs going away. I ran up to the battlements, where the sentinel pointed out to me my father and Malatestino riding, unescorted, in the direction of Pesaro.

Our supper was a cheerless meal: Mother looked like a flower that has been buffeted by a heavy rainstorm; while Uncle Paolo had lost his urbanity and was evidently sulking. Afterwards we all went upstairs together, and again I overheard something which I only fully understood when it was too late. Mother put her hand into Paolo's and said: 'Don't be angry with me. I feel—defiled. But how could I help it?' And he, through gritted teeth: 'He hasn't the right . . .' 'Unfortunately, that's just what he *has* . . .' Her lovely grey eyes were imploring: 'Don't punish me! I've suffered enough today.' He bent to kiss her hand with a ceremonious 'goodnight', and ever so faintly she whispered: 'Later?' 'But is it safe?' 'Yes. Whatever Malatestino has told him, he worked off his ill-humour this afternoon—and now he has gone.' They then became aware of me standing behind them, and they quickly parted.

31

I sat up in bed, roused by some slight sound. Footfalls were creeping up the stairs towards my room. My first panic subsided as I recognised that uneven tread: yes, it was my father, but there was something about the steps that puzzled me. I thought: 'How light they are—yet he sounds more lame than usual.' Then it struck me—he was walking in his stockinged feet. Now, in the inconceivable event that I had come in after midnight, I might have taken my shoes off to avoid disturbing people; so perhaps might the considerate Pandolfo. But it was not in my father's nature. That he, the heir of Rimini and Gradara, should not come shouting and clattering into these castles—or any others, for that matter—at any hour that pleased him, would simply not have entered his head. Something must indeed be wrong.

Then, as fingers brushed my door, I told myself that I was being foolish: perhaps Father, having returned unexpectedly, had felt sorry for having been unkind to me and had come to say so. That, too, was not very likely. And in fact it was not my door that he wanted, but Paolo's. A moment later I heard him softly turn the handle, open and close the door; then he moved across the corridor and tried Malatestino's in the same way. Next, he went up to the battlements, and I heard him talking in hushed tones with the sentry. A great wave of terror swept over me, unreasoning terror. Some instinct kept prompting me: 'Danger! danger!', telling me to go to my mother. I threw a shawl round my shoulders and ran down to her room.

For nearly a year I have been asking myself: how much of what happened that night was my fault? If I had run straight to my father; if Mother had only listened to me . . . but what is the use?

At her door I was checked for a moment, hearing the murmur of her voice. I thought: Perhaps she is saying her prayers. Then I heard her laugh—a low, throbbing laugh that reminded me of the night when I had hesitated outside Riccardo's door, listening to voices and laughter within. Perhaps one of her ladies was with her?

Then the terror caught me again: I beat on the door with my bare hands, crying: 'Mother! I am frightened—let me in!' And these words, perhaps, cost two lives. If only I had said: 'There is danger, Mother—danger for you. Father has come back!' But, up to that very moment, I had not guessed her secret. I did not in any way connect my father's return with her; in fact, I had a confused idea that he might have had warning of some attack, and had come back to warn us.

Mother said, in the same tone of startled annoyance used long ago by Riccardo: 'Is that you, Concordia? What is the matter?' 'Mother, let me in!' 'I can't do that—there are reasons. If you have had a nightmare and are afraid to sleep alone, go to Nannie or to Biancarosa. Good night, my darling.'

In that moment there came a metallic clang from the opposite door of her bedroom. I heard the bed-springs creak, as if someone had jumped out. Mother's voice rang sharply: 'What was that?' The answer came in a lower, more controlled tone: 'Someone has dropped the bar across the inner door. Some treason of Malatestino, I suspect. I must dress quickly.' I recognised the voice—it was Paolo's.

In the shattering revelation of that moment I stood irresolute; then I heard those light, limping footsteps descending the stairs from the upper storey.

For a second time that night I had a chance of averting the tragedy, and once again I failed. Why did I not intercept my father, ask him what he was doing? He might, in his single-minded fury, have cursed, even struck me; but our raised voices would have warned those two, and in the momentary pause Paolo might have escaped. But my father's attitude that day had left me hurt and bewildered. For the first time in two years we had met and parted without a kiss or a smile. Perhaps, too, his own strong will was creating a current around him, warning off anyone who might have turned him from his goal.

In any case, instead of running out across the gallery, I stole up the three steps that led to the embrasure overlooking the drawbridge, and waited motionless. He could still have seen the glimmer of my white nightdress, had he looked up; but his eyes and his mind were fixed on the bedroom door. He stopped to draw on his boots. I heard him curse softly under his breath—it was a task he usually left to Riccardo, since it hurt him to stoop.

He tried the door, then hammered on it with his clenched fist: 'Francesca—open.' After quite a long pause she answered—and from the sound of her voice it seemed as if she were already leaning against the door. 'I cannot. It sounds absurd, but the bar has jammed in its socket.' 'Knock it up with a bit of firewood—and quickly!' ordered Father. Another pause. Then she began to give little taps on the door, saying things in a high-pitched, unnatural voice: 'Have you come back so quickly? Didn't you get to Pesaro? Was your business so soon over?' Futile, silly things—and my mother was no fool. It struck me that she was trying to gain time; and Father must have thought so too, for he exclaimed impatiently: 'Will you open, or must I call the guards to break in the door?'

Then came a sound I recognised—the rattle of the heavy trapdoor being raised. Father heard it and twisted the ring of the door-handle, as though he were trying to turn it by sheer force. Then, shouting incoherently, he put his shoulder to the solid oak.

'Giovanni, you will wake everyone!' exclaimed Mother—this time in her natural voice. 'Wait a moment—I think I have loosened the bar.' In fact, she lifted it, so that my father's thrust carried him right into the room. Then followed a double sound—a cry of surprise from her, and from him a roar that sounded hardly human.

Terrified but unable to restrain my curiosity, I stole down the steps and peeped in through the open door. In the uncertain light of the fire and a couple of candles that must have been hastily lit at it and left to burn by the hearth, I saw Paolo, midway through the trap and struggling like a hooked fish to free a loop of his doublet caught in the ironwork. My father had thrown down the cane of his sword-stick; the blade was glittering in his hand.

From below came Marco's voice: 'Do you need help, Messer Giovanni? Is it thieves?' 'One thief, and I can deal with him. Keep out!' replied my father grimly.

Then Mother spoke, in a controlled tone of admonition: 'Giovanni—he is unarmed.' And she threw herself between them.

I do not believe that he meant to kill her. I, the only witness of that scene, maintain that it was an accident. I wish to put this on record—for the Malatesti, for the Polentani, and for those who will come afterwards: *He did not mean to kill her.*

He said brusquely: 'Out of my way, woman!' and pushed her with his free hand, so that, normally, she would have fallen away from him. But she, gathering her feet under her like a cat, sprang sideways to recover her balance, still keeping her body as a shield between the two men.

My father's weight, as he lunged for Paolo, was on his sound right leg, and he was not nimble enough to shift it. Instinctively I closed my eyes. There was no sound from my mother. It was Paolo who screamed—a man's cry, harsh, broken short in his throat. I heard the rip of stuff as he tore himself free and sprang back into the room.

When I opened my eyes, Mother was lying with her head on his knee. I thought at first that she had fainted; then I saw the white elephant that seemed to be hovering over her breast. I thought dazedly: 'But there is no blood.'

The two men were looking at her in a stunned silence. Then Paolo said heavily: 'You should have killed *me*.' 'I intend to,' was the grim reply.

Paolo laid her on the floor. Out of my line of vision, I heard him bound across the room towards the bed; then the clang of dropped swords—he had snatched a weapon from the wall-display, loosening the rest. Recklessly, I pushed the door wider open, knowing that now the men would have eyes for nothing but each other.

I saw Father put his foot on my mother's chest, to give himself a purchase; heard him catch his breath in something between a curse and a sob as he bent to draw out his rapier. Then the horror reached its climax, for—she was not dead. The pain of the withdrawn weapon penetrated her numbed senses and she stirred, lifting her hand feebly towards the wound. Without opening her eyes she whispered: 'Paolo!' She did not speak again.

Blood welled at last from the wound—a great patch of it, black in the dim light, staining her white nightgown. As if hypnotised, my father stood in a position that was neither of attack nor defence, watching the drops fall from the point of his sword.

Then, as Paolo came at him, the instinct of self-preservation awoke. Lightning-swift, he drew his dagger and cast it, left-handed, to the throat. Haste and shock had spoiled his aim: missing the windpipe, the knife slashed the side of Paolo's neck, but it did its work. Stopped in mid-rush, my uncle clapped one hand to the wound—and in that moment of uncertainty Father ran him through.

32

How long I had been standing there, frozen into immobility, I could not tell. Something in my brain kept prompting me: this cannot be real. It is only a nightmare. Wake up! . . . But I could not wake.

Father had kept hold of his weapon as Paolo fell. He lowered it and stood leaning on the handle for a while. Then he looked around him for his dagger, flipped it into the air with the point of his rapier, and caught it as it came down. He crossed to the chest where Paolo's cloak still lay, and very deliberately wiped both weapons clean, sheathed his dagger and laid the rapier on the chest. It was not callousness—just the mechanical action of a man used to looking after his arms. Next he went to the farther door, the one that opened into the Court Room, and called in a voice that was dulled but quite steady: 'Lift the bar!' There was the clang of metal from outside, then the sound of my father turning the key and opening the door.

Then I knew that the whole tragedy had been planned; that someone within the castle must have admitted my father by the postern gate, having previously warned the sentries not to challenge anyone who entered by it, and then closed one exit from the bedroom. Malatestino? True, he had ridden with my father towards Pesaro, but he might well have returned ahead of him.

With his sound foot Father kicked the trapdoor down; then he came and stood over my mother's body, which lay beside it. I knew he was wondering how he could lift her. He solved the problem by pulling up a low stool, sitting down and drawing her up until she lay across his knees, as a child does in the lap of its nurse. In that position her hair, loose on her shoulders, hung down to the floor, gleaming in the firelight. With his dagger he cut off one shining lock and slipped it into his doublet.

For a while he sat there, holding her close in his arms, his cheek against her soft, fine hair. His face was grave and stern—the face of a judge rather than an executioner. I wondered what he was thinking—whether he was thinking at all, or just sitting with a mind blank from shock and exhaustion. The answer came when slowly he hoisted himself to his feet and began to carry her across the room. I thought he would lay her on the bed, but he went past it, through the farther door into the Court Room. Then I guessed what he intended to do, and all my soul revolted: he could not, surely he could not mean to throw her down through the knife edges to the traitors' well?

Indignation broke the spell that had immobilised me for so long. Before I knew what I was doing, I had run into the bedroom and was kneeling beside Paolo. His eyes opened and he recognised me. 'Can I do anything?' I said, 'Fetch Don Benedetto?' (There was no doctor, I knew, nearer than Pesaro.) He shook his head and whispered so faintly that I could scarcely hear him: 'No use . . . I'm finished . . .' and then, with a sigh that seemed like the breath of his escaping soul: 'I wanted to live. I love life.'

We heard my father's steps approaching, and Paolo found strength to whisper a warning: 'Hide, Concordia—under the bed!' Mechanically I obeyed him. As I ran across the room, my foot slipped upon something viscid; only later did I realise that it was blood.

Just in time I flung myself under the bed and lay there, shivering all over but too much afraid even to whimper. I heard my father's dragging steps; then the whole framework of the bed sagged as he dropped on to it.

From where I lay I could almost have touched his feet. I saw how the left one was splayed outwards, and that roused the sudden surge of love and pity that I had felt years before in Rimini, seeing his exhaustion and pain. I knew how hard he always tried to bring that foot in line with the other; if he let it twist, it showed that his reserves of strength were spent.

It was one of those crucial moments in my life. I thought: 'What am I doing, hiding here like a frightened mouse? He is my father. He has done a fearful thing; but I still love him and would stand by him.' The urge was strong to emerge from my hiding-place, put my arms round him and say: 'Father! This disaster is too much for either of us to bear alone: let us face it together.'

I was plucking up courage to move, when something stopped me. I saw—saw, not heard—another pair of feet. Slender, beautiful feet in black velvet slippers, embroidered and buckled with silver: feet that had stolen silently into the room, that could belong only to my Uncle Malatestino. Instantly, I froze, My father, I knew, would have done me no real harm; but Malatestino would have no scruples about throwing an inconvenient witness to the knives. At that moment I would have been glad to die, but not in such a horrible way.

Yes, it was Malatestino; for now he spoke and his voice held a note of sardonic amusement, almost of satisfaction: 'A bad night's work, brother Gianni. The Polentani will have your blood for this.' 'What else could I have done?' Father's voice sounded dull and dead. 'Called them before a tribunal, of course, with me as your witness.' 'And make public my shame?' 'If you want to avoid publicity, you have gone the wrong way about it.' 'At least, it will not be humiliating. I have destroyed a great deal tonight, but I have preserved my self-respect.'

Father, I thought, was talking more to convince himself than his brother. He gave a long-drawn sigh and then burst out: 'Oh, what am I to do now?' It was a cry that came from his heart, revealing all his desolation. But my uncle, whether from insensitivity or on purpose, took it literally and made the prosaic rejoinder: 'Clear up the mess and go to bed.' 'In *that* bed? Still warm . . .' 'That I doubt: your dramatic protest has lasted quite a while. However, I see your point. Go upstairs to your own room, if you prefer it. But I advise you to clear out to Pesaro—and quickly. If you skulk here in Gradara . . .' (I felt the bed quiver and thought to myself: Be careful, Malatestino!) '. . . no one will be able to touch you. But the moment you leave its shelter, you risk an arrow in the throat. In

Pesaro you have powerful friends. Go and solicit their influence to make certain of your election as *podestà*—and do it before the scandal gets known. Aldo is waiting for you outside, with your black Satan.' 'On whose orders, pray?' 'On mine. I knew that either you or Paolo would need to make a quick getaway.' My father grunted: 'Paolo astride of Satan would have made a sorry spectacle: few people can ride a lame man's horse.' 'Aldo can,' remarked Malatestino smoothly. 'In the improbable event that Paolo had been the survivor, they would, of course, have exchanged mounts.'

'You worked it out in every detail, didn't you?' There was reluctant admiration in Father's voice. 'In all but one—I did not think that Francesca would die.' 'Nor I: she threw herself on my sword.' 'Did she want to die?' 'I think not—merely to save *him*.' Then Malatestino asked an interesting question: 'What would you have done with her if she had lived? How would you have punished her?' 'As I did this afternoon—by making her do her duty as a wife, and before long she would have loved me.' 'After you had murdered her lover?' '*Because* I had—I prefer the word "executed"—her lover. He was part of the unreal world in which she had lived for years. With that destroyed, she would have had to face up to reality; and that meant—me!' His voice broke on the last word, and I felt the stifled sob that shook him. I knew then that he ought to throw himself face downwards on the bed and weep; but I knew, too, that, in front of Malatestino, he would do no such thing; and in that moment I feared for his reason.

Very soon he had his voice in control. 'Is Paolo dead?' he asked. In the pause that followed I saw the slender, black-clad feet move out of sight. Then, from beside the trapdoor, came Malatestino's voice—again with that note of satisfaction: 'If not, the knives will finish him. Or do you intend to leave him here all night?' 'Help me to lift him!' 'And why should I have to tidy up the mess that you, my impulsive brother, have made?' I felt my father's rage and humiliation, even before I heard his exhausted voice: 'I am a cripple, and I have no strength left.'

In that moment, I knew why men do murder. If I had been holding a dagger, I would gladly have plunged it into Malatestino's heart, for having forced that confession from him. It was like seeing a chained stag baited by a cur. And Malatestino was palpably enjoying his advantage as he retorted: 'My dear Gianni, I have never noticed that being slightly lame has prevented you from doing anything you really wanted to do. However, let that pass. Come here and take him from me.'

Father tried to get up and failed. A second attempt brought him, staggering, to his feet. I crawled to the outer edge of the bed, where I could see into the room. In a patch of candle-light, Paolo's face, unstained by the blood that had soaked downwards from his cut neck, was like a pearl, upon which the perfect arch of his eyebrows and the long lashes on his cheeks seemed drawn in black ink.

My father stood looking down at him in silence. I wondered if he was thinking of the three little boys who had swum together in the millpond, never dreaming what their last meeting would be. When he spoke, his voice was gentle: 'A pity to destroy anything so beautiful.' 'His beauty would not have lasted much longer,' commented Malatestino. 'He was nearly forty. Perhaps you would have done better to let him live. Live, and watch himself growing daily less attractive to women. That would have been his worst punishment.'

'That, at least, *we* shall be spared,' said my father bitterly. 'We have no graces left for Time to ruin.' And he continued, musing: 'Among the three of us—you disfigured and me deformed—was it any wonder that she chose him?' 'And where do *I* come into it?' inquired Malatestino blandly. 'That, little brother, is just what I would like to know. I mistrust your sudden access of morality. Paolo's amours,

I imagine, would merely be a source of mild amusement to you—and that the lady in question was my wife would add savour to the jest.'

Malatestino shrugged his shoulders: 'Perhaps, for the sake of the family honour, I preferred not to see my brother wearing the horns.'

I was alarmed, for I knew that this was an insult to be avenged in blood. The two men bristled at each other for a moment, like mastiffs preparing to fight; but my father was too near collapse, and my uncle—the more controlled—was evidently disinclined to provoke him too far. He said, impatiently: 'Come! we're wasting time,' and stooped to raise Paolo by the shoulders. It was as much as he could manage, for he was very slightly built; I could see that he was glad to pass the weight to my father who, once he could bring his arms into play, was by far the stronger of the two.

So they slowly crossed the room, my father carrying Paolo by the shoulders and Malatestino carrying him by the feet. His long dark hair had fallen back, and I thought that his beautiful eyes flashed open for a moment and closed again. A minute or two later I heard a piercing yell from the Court Room. Malatestino had prophesied rightly—the knives had finished him.

33

At that terrible cry I must have fainted. Consciousness returned to me with a sense of cold—cold such as I had never felt before. My hands, my feet, my whole body felt like ice. I stirred, tried to sit up, but my head struck against the hard wood above me. Then a ghastly thought came to me—was I buried alive? I began to strike with hands and feet against the unyielding wood. In that moment I might well have lost my reason, had not my struggles carried me clear of the bed. As I rolled out into the blessed daylight—a cold dawn-light just clear enough to reveal outlines of furniture around me—I saw that I was lying on the floor of Mother's bedroom. Still I did not remember how I had got there, or what had happened.

Gradually I realised that, cold as I was, the room itself was warm. The fire had been made up and many things had been burned in it. Perhaps it was the stench of charred rags that had revived me.

I cowered on the floor, gasping, as remembrance came to me. Had I dreamed it all? There were no bloodstains visible, though the floor was damp in patches; the bedclothes had been roughly straightened out; Paolo's cloak had gone, and the decoration of swords on the wall was complete. What, then, had really happened?

My head was aching so badly that I could not think clearly; but I guessed that Malatestino must have been at work, and that the burnt rags had been used in wiping the floor. I remembered the sticky patch in which I had slipped. Looking down, I saw that the hem of my nightdress was stained. I lifted each foot in turn; one was caked with dried blood and the other was splashed. That, at least, was not imagination. Had my uncle seen the track of bare feet on the floor? Surely not—for then he would have traced me to the bed and I should never have woken . . . except perhaps, like Paolo, at the first slash of the knives.

No one must know that I had been in that room. Pressing both hands on my throbbing temples, I tried to think. As well as being bloodstained, my nightdress was smudged all over with dust from under the bed; it would have to be destroyed. So I made up the fire, stepped out of the gown and burned it. The thin material flared up quickly and added little to the pile of ashes. My shawl too was dirty, and this was a more difficult problem; if I tried to burn it, there would be a great stench, and bits of wool might fly all over the room. I decided to thrust it into the bottom of one of the chests and to take one of Mother's in exchange; both were home-woven on the same loom, by the same serving-woman, so they were almost identical. Nannie might be able to tell them apart; but she, I was sure, would be too distracted to notice details at this time.

In the octagonal closet opening out of the bedroom I found the basin in which Mother had washed overnight; but the water in it had been used; maybe for cleaning the floor. There were still a few drops left in the pitcher—enough to wash my feet. I threw the blood-stained water into the fire and then, naked under Mother's shawl, went up to my room, put on a fresh nightdress and crawled into bed.

I had thought that sleep would be impossible; but I must, in fact, have slept or swooned, for I was awakened by a flood of sunshine and the sound of wailing. Nannie had just opened the window-shutters. When she saw my eyes open she let out a piercing cry: 'My poor motherless child!'

'What do you mean?' I asked, trying to speak sharply; but my voice came out as a whisper. There was a tight pain in my chest, and my head seemed to be on fire, though my hands and feet were still icy. Nannie went on, half-keening, half-scolding: 'He says—the one-eyed, lying villain—that she has fled with her lover. Thirty years I've known my lovely lady Francesca, ever since she sucked at my breast—and he thinks I'd believe that of her! No, the guards say they heard screams, and sword-play, and the fall of bodies in the night . . .' her voice rose to a piercing wail, 'Dead and murdered, my lovely lady—done to death by those two evil men. I've said it once, I've said it a hundred times — no good could come of wedding my lovely lady to a man twisted like the Devil himself—twisted in his body and in his wicked soul.'

I began weakly: 'If you mean my father . . .' but the sharp reproof died away unfinished. I doubt if she even heard my faint voice, for she went on keening: 'Gone and vanished, my lovely lady Francesca—not a trace—not even her beautiful body for me to cherish . . .' And her words burst forth afresh.

Hammers seemed to be smashing at my temples. Confusedly, I tried to think: Malatestino must not know I was there. . . . What would I have done, if this had really been news to me? Certainly, I would have gone to my mother's room to see if she had really disappeared; then I would have had the castle searched for her. With an effort I sat up and put my feet to the floor: 'I'm going to see . . .' But the room was rocking around me; my feet seemed not to belong to me. I called in terror: 'Nannie!' And everything went dark.

Darkness . . . nightmares . . . a feeling of suffocation . . . moments of conscious fear. The worst, when I saw my uncle's keen eye staring down at me. I heard myself screaming, begging him not to throw me to the knives; heard his sharp query: 'What's she saying?' and Nannie's reply: 'Something about two lives, I think . . . remembering her mother in her delirium, poor lamb!'

Darkness once more, and pain . . . pain in my head, in my chest . . . always that difficulty in breathing. . . . Then I was being carried in a man's arms. I struggled and whimpered—and heard that trusty Venetian voice: 'Don't be afraid, Contessina. It is I—Marco.'

Moving . . . moving . . . the sound of horsehoofs, of wheels whispering through crisp autumn leaves. Now and again Nannie's voice and the feeling of warm liquid poured down my throat. Then once more—darkness and nightmares.

For some time I had been conscious of white wings fluttering above my head. Vaguely, I thought of the seagulls flying round our castles in the winter months. Had one of them come to visit me? Then the blurred outlines sharpened: it was not wings but a nun's coif, and the dark-eyed, gentle face beneath it was one that I knew. I said, surprised: 'Why, Aunt Chiara—however did you come here?'

The effect was startling; her eyes lit up and she exclaimed: 'God and Santa Chiara be praised! She is awake and knows me.' Then I heard Nannie's voice: 'God be praised, indeed! If she had died or lost her mind, I would never have forgiven myself.

I tried to sit up, but the effort was too great. My aunt lifted my head and gave me a drink of milk; then she laid me back on the pillow.

To give myself time to think, I closed my eyes and pretended to be asleep. Evidently I had been—for the first time in my life—seriously ill. But where was I? I was listening for the tramp of the sentinel overhead, for bird-song coming up from the trees below; but all I could hear was the sound of passers-by walking and talking, and the rumble of a cart over the cobbles. A cart? But there was no wheeled traffic on the steep slopes of Gradara. I must be in a town. I opened my eyes and asked: 'Is this Rimini?' 'No, Ravenna. You are in your Grandfather Guido's house.' Then I remembered: of course, we had lost the Gattolo; so, if they had wanted to move me, Mother might well have taken me to stay in her old home. I said: 'Please tell Mother I am awake, and send her to me.'

Aunt Chiara is not a clever woman, but she has the self-control that comes from good breeding. Her voice did not alter as she replied: 'She isn't here.' 'And Father?' Again that quiet, controlled voice: 'At Pesaro, we think.' 'Then I would like to speak to my uncle.' 'Which uncle, dear?' I had meant to say 'Paolo', but the name sent a shock through me. At the back of my mind I knew that something dreadful had happened to Uncle Paolo. In any case, I reasoned, it was most unlikely that he was staying in Ravenna. So I substituted hastily: 'Ostasio'.

Aunt Chiara said he was busy but would come as soon as possible; meanwhile, I must be good and not ask questions—just take my food and medicine, so that I would get well quickly.

Several days went by, and still Uncle Ostasio was 'busy'. It seemed to me that his official business could not be so pressing as not to leave him a few minutes to visit a sick child. He must be purposely putting it off; or was Aunt Chiara keeping him away, for fear of what he might tell me?

During this interval, you see, my memory had come back. It centred around Paolo. Each time I whispered the name, it conjured up a fearful scream—the yell that had finally broken my resistance. Later, I heard my father's weary voice: 'Is Paolo dead?' and Malatestino's reply: 'If not, the knives will finish him.' So they had killed him between them, but why—why? Still I had not associated my mother with the matter.

The clue came when Aunt Chiara was brushing my hair. I missed the long swish that came when Nannie used to do it. Putting my hand to my head, I found it covered with little curls like a baby's; yet my hair had always been as straight as floss silk and had reached half-way to my waist. My aunt explained: 'We had to shave your head when you were delirious. But don't be unhappy about it: your hair will soon grow again, long and fair like your mother's.'

I saw it then—her long, fair hair sweeping the ground as she lay like a shot bird in my father's arms, with the bloodstain like a black rose on her nightgown. He had killed her, I knew then. Again I asked myself—why? And the shock-word beat at my brain: 'Paolo!' . . . Perhaps all these images were things dreamed in my delirium. Desperately I clung to that hope.

My aunt had not noticed my agitation: she was talking to a maidservant who had brought me some broth. I forced myself to drink it and to eat a piece of bread, for I wanted to get my strength back. Then I said quietly to my aunt: 'Why doesn't Mother come to see me?' With a deep sigh she answered: 'Because she cannot, my dear.' Looking her full in the eyes I stated, rather than asked: 'Mother is dead, is she not? You will have to tell me, sooner or later—so why not now?' 'How do you know?' whispered Aunt Chiara, making a brave effort to control her tears. 'I know she would not leave me, ill and alone . . .' I nearly said 'among strangers', but that would have hurt my kind aunt's feelings, so I changed it to '. . . even among her own people. If she is alive, she must be under duress, or even more seriously ill than I have been.'

That gave my aunt a loophole of escape. She said, avoiding my gaze: 'You yourself nearly died, but Nannie and I prayed night and day to God and Saint Francis and Santa Chiara, and they saved your life. But your poor mother . . .' and her sobs burst out uncontrollably.

I did not force her any further. She has been thinking it over, was my reflection: she wants to give me the idea that Mother and I have both been ill of the plague, and that only I have survived it. That was clever of her—too clever for my simple, pious aunt. I suspected that the idea had been given her by Uncle Ostasio, and that made me even more determined to see him. 'Tell my uncle,' I said, 'that now I know the worst, so he has no longer any need to avoid me.'

34

Next evening, Ostasio did come to see me, bringing a jar of honey and some sweet cakes. Aunt Chiara had dressed me, for the first time, and let me sit up in an arm-chair. I still felt weak, but my head was perfectly clear. By this time I had remembered the whole sequence of events, from the moment I had woken, hearing my father's footsteps, right up to that last cry from Paolo.

Uncle Ostasio was manifestly ill at ease. I would not have recognised him as the joyous young man whom I remembered from my childhood. His face had hardened to a sculptured mask, in which the long, jutting chin and wide thin-lipped mouth were the dominant features. His grey eyes no longer laughed, they were cold and still like a mountain tarn in twilight; and the hair that I recalled as waves of shining gold had somehow deadened, as if a fine film of dust clouded it.

He started to make some trivial conversation about my health, the weather . . . 'The fogs from the Po are very persistent in November.' 'November!' I exclaimed: 'In Gradara it was early September. Have I been ill so long?' 'Six weeks of delirium, and a fortnight of semi-consciousness, before you really woke.' 'And what did I say in my delirium?' I had to know that. Had I given away my father, or let them guess at the scene I had witnessed? But Uncle Ostasio said vaguely that I had kept speaking of knives and had seemed to be afraid of my Uncle Malatestino, without saying anything coherent.

'And when shall I be well enough to go home?' I asked. This disconcerted him. He said my home was now in Ravenna, and this gave me the opening I wanted. I said firmly: 'Uncle Ostasio, I am grateful for your hospitality and for Aunt Chiara's nursing, which probably saved my life. But I am a Malatesta and I ought to be with my own people.' 'My poor child, *we* are your people too, and now that you are orphaned we will gladly give you a home.'

Only one word of that sentence really struck me, and struck me with such force that I felt the room spinning round me: 'Orphaned!' I gasped.

Aunt Chiara came forward and held some cordial to my lips. It must have been strong, for it burned my throat, but it pulled me together. I heard my aunt's voice, gently reproachful: 'She is very weak still, Ostasio. Don't forget —she is fond of her father, and she doesn't know . . .' 'Know what?' I interrupted. 'Is he dead? How and where?' 'He is still on this earth, unfortunately,' replied Ostasio, 'but he is dead to you. He has committed a crime that has put him out of your life for ever.'

The relief was so overwhelming that I lay back in my chair, gasping and exhausted, as I had lain on the sand where the great wave had flung me. Now I knew that I must force him to speak: the atmosphere of concealment around me was unbearable: 'Uncle Ostasio, are you trying to tell me that he killed my mother?' Silently he bowed his head. Aunt Chiara gave a little cry of protest, as though the fact should not have been put into words. 'Why should he do such a terrible thing?' I asked. 'From jealousy,' he said shortly and my aunt interposed: 'Unfounded, of course.' I said, trying to keep my voice steady: 'Tell me what happened, so far as you know.'

Ostasio hesitated, evidently trying to attenuate the story for my benefit. There must have been irony in my glance, for he averted his eyes. At last he said without much conviction: 'Apparently he came back drunk one evening, his mind inflamed by some vile slander, and stabbed her and—and a man whom he found talking to her.' 'Who was that man?' 'That, Concordia, is one of the things it is not necessary for you to know.' Yes, I thought—and in due course you will tell me that Uncle Paolo has been killed in a duel, or in a fall from his horse, or has died of a fever. But I had read murder in my uncle's eyes, and I knew there were things to be said between us that my gentle little aunt must not hear.

How could I get rid of her? I had an inspiration: 'Aunt Chiara,' I said, 'All this is very painful for me to hear. It would help if you were to go to the chapel and pray for me.' Yes, I had touched the right note. She went without discussion and I rounded on my uncle: 'Very well, if you will not tell me, I must tell you: the man was my Uncle Paolo.'

'How do you know that?' he asked sharply.

'He was the only man in Gradara that night, apart from soldiers and servants. And my father's jealousy was *not* unfounded.' Ostasio frowned, but I went on recklessly: 'Paolo was my mother's lover—and he was sleeping with her at the time.' Then, suddenly, I was afraid, for the look of fury on that pale face was not pleasant to see. 'You listen to scandal about your own mother!' he exclaimed between his teeth: 'You defend the wild beast who murdered her!' 'I listened to nothing,' I said, 'except a voice that I recognised, coming from her room that night.'

And, as concisely as possible, I told my story: how my father's return had awakened me; how I had gone to warn my mother and had found Paolo in her room. 'He might have gone there for a perfectly innocent purpose,' said my uncle. 'Such as . . .?' 'To bring her a book, or a piece of news, or consult her about some problem of his own.' 'After midnight?' I said caustically. 'Well, I must tell you what I had hoped to avoid.' And I spoke of the bar that had been dropped on the inner door, of Paolo's startled exclamation: 'I must dress quickly!' Ostasio flinched as if at a whiplash. Until that moment, I suspect, he had been clinging to a half-belief in his sister's innocence.

I described how I had hidden in the room, and how after the fight my father had said to Malatestino: 'She threw herself on my sword.' 'So, you see, it *was* an accident,' I affirmed, though with little hope that this would make my uncle, or any of the Polentani brothers, less set upon vengeance.

One thing alone I kept to myself: the horrible secret of what had happened to the bodies. When my uncle questioned me about that, I said merely that at a certain point I had fainted and, on recovering my senses, had found the room cleaned up and the bodies gone.

When I had finished, I waited—waited a long time, while Uncle Ostasio brooded in silence. I saw that he believed me, and that the revelation had been a shock to him. Then his face changed. He patted my hand and said with commiseration: 'My poor child, you have been very ill, through the shock your old nurse gave you by telling you too suddenly of your mother's death. These fevered imaginings are all part of your delirium. As you grow stronger they will fade, and you will know that you were asleep upstairs and could have seen nothing of what happened.'

I stared at him incredulously: had I indeed lost my reason? But of one thing I was certain—I had not imagined that scream in the night, nor the sight of my father, grave and stern, rocking in his arms the woman he had loved and killed. 'Uncle,' I said, 'I have told you the truth. My brain is quite clear now, and I have spent several days thinking it over. Only three people really know what happened: my father, Uncle Malatestino and I. And for my father's sake I must speak.' 'You would be better advised not to,' said Ostasio with menacing gentleness. 'No girl in her right senses would accuse her own mother of—of adultery. So if you go around retailing these fever-dreams, the only charitable conclusion must be . . .' He did not finish the sentence, but it made my heart beat faster. To defend my mother's reputation they would say that I was mad—maybe they would even shut me up.

Afraid though I was, I faced up to my uncle: 'I am not accusing anyone—just trying to see how and why this terrible thing happened, and how much each of us is to blame for it.' '*Us?*' he queried sharply. 'Whom do you mean by that?' 'Myself, first of all. If I had warned her properly and in time, Paolo might have escaped and everything been hidden or smoothed over. Grandfather Guido, because he first made her think she was to marry Paolo.' (I saw him start at that.) 'And *you* . . .' I added, summoning up what remained to me of courage and strength. 'You, who wrote and told her about Father's second family. She had always loved Paolo, but I think she would have gone on fighting it, if she hadn't known about that.'

There was no doubt about it—Ostasio was very angry now. He got up and said curtly: 'We will discuss things when you are better. Meanwhile, I advise you to keep a guard upon your tongue.' He would have thought it undignified to slam the door, but he closed it very firmly behind him.

35

After that talk there was a subtle difference in the atmosphere. I felt myself almost a prisoner, especially after Aunt Chiara went back to her convent. She had, it appeared, been given special leave to nurse me; now that I had recovered, she had to return. My only companion was Nannie, who treated me with an exasperating fussy pity, as though I were a baby or an imbecile.

Towards the end of November, I was able to leave my room and walk in the garden—the garden that Mother had found so beautiful. It has, in fact, two brick terraces with stone balustrades, a central fountain, and flower-beds edged with box. There are fruit trees trained against the high red walls, and one or two ancient yews and oak trees. Now that I have seen the garden in summer, I appreciate that they give a pleasant shade, but just then the effect was melancholy: the fallen oak leaves, sodden by frequent mists, lay underfoot and made the paths slimy; the sombre, dripping yews looked as if they were mourning, and the fountain did not play. Of flowers, only a few white roses remained—the fragile roses that Mother had loved, but which for me remained associated with the Wise Woman's prophecy. I would have liked to tear each blossom to pieces, but I restrained myself. If Uncle Ostasio thought —or wanted other people to think—that I was mad, any action of this kind could be used as proof of it. So I just wandered miserably round, escorted by Nannie, or sometimes by a hard-faced maid named Serafina who, I was convinced, had been set to spy on me.

On Christmas Day they both accompanied me to San Francesco's church, where a requiem Mass for my mother's soul was being sung in the Polenta family chapel. It seemed quite a long walk, for the house where I was living was on the far side of Ravenna; in fact, its frontage made one side of a narrow street and the town wall made the other.

Grandfather Guido, whom I now saw for the first time, was already enthroned in his imposing pew. I took my place, with my two attendants, on the women's side of the chapel, where I recognised Samaritana and Maddalena with their children; my uncles and male cousins were sitting on the other. As I knelt, I watched my grandfather through my fingers—a large, genial man with a fringe of white hair circling his bald head. Not so handsome as my Malatesta grandfather, I thought, and far less imposing; and when we met after the service I think he was equally disappointed in me. My likeness to my mother had lain chiefly in my soft fair hair; now that it had grown again as a curly, golden-brown crop, my high Malatesta features were far more obvious. I looked boyish—a fairer edition of my cousin Uberto—and the plain black dress they had provided for me did nothing to soften my face.

Afterwards, we all went back to the Polenta palace for a Christmas dinner: a dreary feast, with everyone in mourning, no minstrels or singers to entertain us; merely a long succession of dishes for which no one had much appetite. No one except my young cousin Guido, who smiled at me now and again across the table and tucked into his food as a healthy thirteen-year-old should do.

At the end of the meal, Samaritana invited me to come up with her to the bedroom she had shared with my mother, whom she had loved so dearly. She said: 'I am sorry we are making Christmas so miserable for you. Francesca herself, I know, would be the last to want this atmosphere of hate and grief and vengeance created around her death. After all, the rest of us have to go on living, and she would much rather we lived happily and remembered her with a smile.' And she began to talk about my mother as she had known her: gay, gallant, spirited, generous—how different from the ivory statue that my father and I had found so beautiful and so remote.

When she found that I knew about the proxy marriage, she told me how thrilled they had been by their occasional glimpses of the handsome young man who had come as a suitor (they imagined) from Rimini. One day, Monna Cristina had called Francesca to the window as he passed through the courtyard, and had said: 'Look! There is the man who will be your husband.' 'And when I saw him,' said Samaritana, 'with his long black curls and his flawless oval face, it was as if Apollo had come back to the earth. Francesca glowed, and I threw my arms round her neck, saying "Oh, you lucky girl!" I wondered why her mother was so unhappy about it; but of course, she *knew*.'

I noticed that odd-sounding phrase '*her* mother', and grasped its import. Not liking to question Samaritana about her own mother, I asked her where this conversation had taken place, in this palace or the house near the wall. 'Oh, here,' she said, 'in this very room. Of course Francesca lived here. She was one of the . . .' she hesitated and I filled in the gap: 'One of the nightingales.' Samaritana laughed; evidently Bernardino's joke had become a family saying. 'Yes, and the other was the cuckoo's nest. But there was no hard-and-fast rule. I usually slept here with

Francesca; but she often stayed out there, because she loved the garden.'

When it was time for me to go back, Samaritana, on an impulse, said she would come with me: 'I hate to think of you all alone out there, where we used to be such a happy family.' 'But your children?' I asked. She assured me that they would be quite happy playing with their cousins: they were old enough to look after themselves, and Maddalena would keep an eye on them.

She stayed for several days, and while she was there I ceased to feel a prisoner. Together, escorted by two of her own servants (for she detested Serafina on sight), we went to see the lovely things about which my mother had told me: San Vitale, with its blue and gold mosaics that had given her ideas for the fabrics of her splendid dresses; the adjacent tomb of Galla Placidia, where I stood, as if in a trance, watching the white doves that seem alive as they dip their beaks into a marble basin of water; the lambs on a green field of mosaic; and above all, the rich green-and-gold ceiling with its band of dusky crimson. 'When we are out of mourning,' said Samaritana, 'I must have a dress with a border of that green and gold; and you, who are fair, must have one of deep blue, bordered in that shade of red.' And she would note every detail with a practised eye. Back in the house, we used to draw the patterns, and Samaritana coloured them with paints that she had begged from Grandfather's miniaturist.

I began to emerge from my apathy and think of the future: perhaps my father or my Malatesta grandfather would fetch me away; perhaps the Polentani would let me go to stay with Samaritana and her husband at Cunio. . . . But after the New Year she left Ravenna and the fog of misery closed down again.

Before leaving, however, Samaritana had arranged for me to go, at least once a week, to my grandfather's palace. There, I still had the feeling of being in disgrace. Young

Guido evidently wanted to make friends with me; but whenever our conversation became animated, his father or grandfather would call him away rather sharply, reminding him that it was time for his lesson in sword-play or History or Latin; or would send him out riding: 'Remember,' he would say, 'in less than two years you will go for your training as a knight; so you must take your education seriously.'

As for *my* education, Grandfather Guido decided that it had been sadly neglected. True, I could ride and swim—useless accomplishments, he thought, for a girl. I could write a fair hand (how proud my father had been of that!), sing French songs and recount the adventures of Aeneas, Sir Lancelot, Sir Hoon of Bordeaux, Sir Tristram and many other heroes of chivalry; but of the lives of the saints (on which he repeatedly questioned me), I was lamentably ignorant. So my grandfather, who oddly combined a lively piety with his cheerful immorality, decreed that I should be taken once or twice a week to the convent of the Clarisses, where Aunt Chiara was immured, for religious instruction.

36

My first day at the convent was disastrous, for I actually managed to quarrel with my sweet-tempered aunt. The walk through the snowy streets in Serafina's uncongenial company had chilled me, and I did not thaw in Aunt Chiara's unwarmed cell. She started to read me an interminable story, that seemed to me as improbable as Mother's romances and far less exciting. When the decapitated saint picked up his head and walked up a hill with it in his hand, I burst out laughing. Seeing my aunt's shocked face, I tried to apologise but only made matters worse by saying: 'I'm sorry—but I've heard that tale before. It was the Giant in "Sir Gawain and the Green Knight". I thought how silly he must have looked. Anyway, it's quite impossible.'

'It was a miracle,' said my aunt with conviction. 'Nothing is impossible to God.' 'Then why didn't He work a miracle to save my beautiful mother, or to bring her back to life?' I asked bitterly. Aunt Chiara gave a wail: 'Oh!' she cried, twisting her hands together: 'How could He, when she had died unshriven in mortal sin?'

At that my Malatesta temper flared. I rounded on her pitilessly: 'So you do *not* believe that my father's jealousy was "unfounded"? Uncle Ostasio has repeated to you what I told him, and you both know it is true—but neither of you will face up to the fact. And talking about "mortal sin" is absurd: she loved Uncle Paolo and couldn't help what she did. Her real sin was her unkindness to my father; but you can't *make* yourself love anyone.' I stopped, seeing that my aunt was on the brink of tears: 'I have wrestled so hard for your soul,' she sighed, 'but I fear the cursed Malatesta blood is too strong in you, and that we are too late to save you.'

I retorted briefly: 'I am proud of my Malatesta blood. I wish you would all leave my soul alone and send me back to Rimini, to my own people.'

After that there seemed no more to be said. My aunt retreated into a kind of gentle sulk, kneeling at her *prie-Dieu* and muttering prayers. I stood on tiptoe at the high, barred window, and looked out at the wintry garden, feeling that the whole situation was extremely silly. It was a relief to us both when dinner was announced.

Aunt Chiara said she felt ill and did not want to eat, so I went alone to the refectory, curtsied to the Mother Superior and kissed her ring. She greeted me very graciously, saying: 'I have reserved a place for you beside your aunt.' When I said that she would not be coming, the Mother Superior suggested that, in that case, I would probably prefer to sit at the other table with the novices and pupils.

It was the first time I had been among a group of young girls. As an only child, I had always mixed with grown-ups. Occasionally a boy cousin would come riding in with his father, but the girls stayed at home in their upland castles. At Gradara, too, the citadel children who had come to us for lessons or for rides on Elefantino had all been boys. So it was with some trepidation that I assented.

I looked round at a row of eyes fixed on me with not unfriendly curiosity. Since some move on my part seemed necessary, I smiled and said 'Good morning!' But I was promptly hushed: the Mother Superior was about to say grace.

When we were seated, a nun at the head of the table began to read a story—again about a saint. (I wondered if she had eaten beforehand, or would have to stay hungry until we had finished our meal.) Since we were evidently not expected to talk, I studied my table companions, wondering what had driven them to choose such a life.

All were similarly dressed: the novices in white gowns, the pupils in plain grey with white collars and cuffs; but by their hands and table-manners I soon deduced that some were of peasant stock and others were gently born. The former looked well and contented; their cheeks were rosy and their appetite was keen. The girls of my own class, on the other hand, seemed apathetic, some of them sulky and others resigned. Most were rather plain and unattractive—their relatives must have decided that they were unlikely to make good marriages. In two cases I saw stark tragedy: one had been horribly scarred by smallpox, and a pair of splendid dark eyes stared agonisedly from the ruin of what must once have been a pretty face. The other was older than the rest—at least nineteen, I thought—tall and slender, with an aureole of red-gold hair and a classic beauty that set her apart. She sat there, cold and withdrawn, as though nothing would ever interest her again, so deeply lost in thought that she hardly touched her food.

Yet the meal was delicious. It was a Friday, and Friday fare at Gradara had nearly always consisted of salt *baccalà*. Here we ate grilled sole with crisply fried bread, green peas and a slice of lemon, followed by a dessert of oranges. I was amazed to see fresh peas in January: as for oranges and lemons, these were delicacies which at Rimini we reserved for special banquets.

Afterwards, when the girls had assembled for an hour of recreation, I asked one of them about this. She said that the peas were from the convent garden, bottled in the spring and kept in store: the fruit came by ship from Naples. She took a quick look round, to see that no sister was within hearing, and added in a low voice: 'This is a rich convent. Since we must forgo so many worldly pleasures, I suppose they think there is no harm in eating well. But it is not advisable to praise the food too highly; otherwise they put you on bread-and-water for a day, for the sin of gluttony.'

I would have liked to make friends with the red-haired novice; but she had withdrawn into a window embrasure with a book, turning her back on us all. Before I had thought of a valid pretext for disturbing her, Serafina came to fetch me away.

At the price of a small piece of hypocrisy I was soon reconciled to my kind-hearted aunt. It was the third week in January, the anniversary (I was told) of my Polenta grandmother's death; so a suffrage Mass was to be sung for her in the Polenta chapel of San Francesco's, which all the family was to attend.

I could see no reason whatever why I should be there, since I had had no contact of any kind with her in her lifetime. However, what my grandfather decreed had to be done, so I started out for the church with my two escorts. Partly in reaction against the damp chill of the foggy air, partly to work off my bad temper, I walked so fast that they had difficulty in keeping up with me. The fog at the same time gave an illusion of detachment and helped to carry voices; so after a while I became conscious that they were talking in low tones. Serafina was saying that 'they' were back in Rimini; to which Nannie replied shortly: 'Bad luck to the wicked murderers!' My heart gave a great leap. Who could 'they' be, if not my own people? I slackened pace till they came up with me and asked quickly: 'Who are back in Rimini?' 'No one that need interest *you*, Contessina,' was Nannie's uncompromising reply.

My blood boiled, but then I reflected that she had been a lifelong servant of the Polenta family until my mother's marriage; so it was no wonder that she had now gone over to 'the enemy', as I could not help ungratefully considering my well-meaning relatives.

In church, I was surprised to see Aunt Chiara, who must have obtained special leave for this occasion. While my lips mechanically repeated the formulae I knew by rote, I watched hers moving in a kind of rapt ecstasy. Obviously, she was convinced of the utility of what she was doing. I began to think: was there something in it, after all? What did I exactly want? Someone who would tell me if the Malatesta were really back in Rimini. Who was my best hope? Samaritana, if only I could get in touch with her. In my heart I began really to pray: 'San Francesco, San Francesco—send Samaritana to me!' Then the cold logic inculcated by my father intervened: what possible interest could San Francesco—no doubt enjoying the beatitude of Paradise—have in me? In any case, Samaritana's movements depended upon other people; she could not leave her husband and children, just because I wanted her. So, concentrating my will-power and projecting it in the direction of Cunio, where she was living, I framed my request in another way: 'Samaritana—find some way to tell me what has happened. Tell me about my father!'

When we came out of church, Aunt Chiara was radiant. She put her arm round me and said gently: 'You look transfigured, Concordia. My own prayers have been answered: I think you have at last discovered the meaning of prayer.' I smiled at her and nodded. Yes, I had: it is just to concentrate upon something, with all your heart and mind, believing implicitly that it will come to pass.

So I settled down, patiently, to wait for some sign, and three days later it came. Aristide, Samaritana's attendant footman, arrived with various small presents for her brothers and a reticule of needles and embroidery silks for me. Some instinct warned me not to open the case until I was alone; when I did, I found a letter neatly folded into the lining.

'My dear little Concordia,' it began, 'I have been thinking of you today, almost as if you were calling to me . . .' So I had not failed! I hid the letter until Nannie and Serafina were busy preparing supper, then I read on: 'Perhaps it was the news that Bernardino (my husband, not my brother) brought back some days ago from Rimini; for I know that, in spite of everything, you still feel yourself a Malatesta. Yes! your people are back in the Gattolo, and the Parcitadi have retreated to San Marino. Bernardino said it was a splendid sight to see the three of them come storming through the broken gate, in the torchlight and the snow.' (Three! then my father was there!) 'With the old man's white hair and beard hidden under his armour, they looked like brothers. Malatesta himself in the centre, with the three Saracen's heads painted on his green shield; Malatestino, with the gold rose on an azure ground; and Giovanni, your father, with the elephant trunk swinging from his helm. Out of bravado he was carrying his chequerboard shield at his saddle-bow.' (Not out of bravado, I knew—partly because the weight of it strained his back, and partly to leave his left hand free, so that he could throw his dagger at need.) 'When the cry of "Malatesta" went ringing through the streets, the citizens fled inside and bolted their doors. There was very little fighting; their cavalry swept through and took the Gattolo by surprise. Since it was sacked and partially burned last year, the Parcitadi have patched it up for their own use (Bernardino says), so your people were able to install themselves there at once. Messer Malatesta has put it about that he has retaken the city for Stefano Colonna and the Pope, but Bernardino thinks this is just a pretext. *Colonna, the new Rector, is coming to Ravenna before long.*' (This was heavily underlined.) 'There is a rumour that he will try to bring about a reconciliation between our two families, but I cannot imagine that my brothers will agree to this.'

There was very little more—just good wishes for my health and a promise that she would come to Ravenna as soon as she had the opportunity. But she had told me the one thing that really mattered: my father had weathered the storm. Shock and remorse had not unsettled his reason or his health. He had not 'fled', as they had told me. On the contrary, he was back in Rimini.

37

About a fortnight later, there was a great coming and going between my grandfather's palace and the little house by the wall. Nannie and Serafina kept whispering together and, when I asked what it was all about, Nannie replied—as always when my own family was in question—that it was nothing to interest *me*.

Next morning she announced that we were going to the convent, and that she would fetch me in the evening. I was surprised, for, after that first unfortunate experiment, the idea of taking me regularly to the convent had been dropped. When I asked the reason, Nannie said: 'Never mind!' in the voice she had used when I was five years old. 'There's folks up at the big house, and I can't be here to look after you.' (Ah! I thought . . . So he has come.) Aloud, I said that I was quite well now and could look after myself—in fact I would be glad to have a few hours alone. She could leave a cold meal ready and, if Serafina wasn't there either, I would fetch it myself when I felt hungry. But Nannie, holding out my cloak, said that: 'Messer Ostasio would never allow it.' And she made for the door.

Aunt Chiara, this time, had chosen a story that did interest me; it was about Saint George, who was a brave soldier and fought a dragon, quite in the tradition of the heroes of chivalry. So the time passed pleasantly enough till she had to go to a service that she called the Terza; so she left me in a large room where the pupils and novices were working at various handicrafts. Some were weaving, others spinning, others working at embroidery or cross-stitch. Attracted by a shy, friendly smile, I stopped by one of the peasant girls and asked her name. 'Rosanna, Contessina,' she replied, getting up to bob me a clumsy curtsy, just as the Gradara children used to do. I said: 'You may call me Concordia,' but I could see she would never venture to do it.

From a charcoal sketch she was making a picture of a man on horseback—Saint Martin, she said. Beginning at the top, she had filled in the sky and the rider's body as far as the waist, and was now preparing to start on the horse's head. She was looking rather doubtfully at the drawing, and I was more than doubtful. 'Is it a horse or a mule?' I asked. The colour deepened in her apple cheeks: 'I know it is all wrong,' she said. 'My father is a ploughman, and his horses aren't like that.' 'Nor are ours!' (I thought of Plato and of the splendid Malatesta war-horses.) 'See here—his head is too big—that's why he looks like a mule—and his ears stick out too much. Besides, his pastern-joints curve the wrong way. Hand me that charcoal, and I'll show you.' Rosanna nodded approval, then her face fell. 'When Sister Angelica gets back from the service, she will be angry. *She* drew that horse for me.' 'Then Sister Angelica can never have really looked at a horse in her life. Never mind—I'll take the blame. So I'd better stay with you till she comes. Meanwhile, tell me about yourself. Do you like being here?'

'Oh yes!' (Her face lit with a broad smile) 'I am so lucky. Our *parroco* took notice of me, because I never missed a Mass and in the summer I used to pick wild flowers to deck the Madonna's statue; so he spoke to the Mother Superior and asked her to take me. Of course I can't be a choir-nun, because I have brought no dowry and I could never learn Latin. They are trying to teach me to read and write, but somehow the words won't make sense. Still, I can be a lay-sister.' 'What's that?' I asked. Rosanna's explanations were a bit confused, but I gathered that the lay-sisters were, in a sense, the servants of the convent: they did all the necessary work and were sent out on errands, whereas the choir-nuns spent their time in prayer and contemplation and, except in real emergency or by special permission, never went beyond the walls.

'So you are happy?' I asked. 'You don't regret all you have had to give up?' 'But I hadn't anything to give up,' she said simply. 'I used to sleep on a straw mattress on the floor, with my little sister and brother, all three together. In winter, the spring where I drew water was frozen—look at my hands.' (In fact, they were patterned with healed chilblain scars.) 'All day long I worked; indoors with the smoke in my eyes, and out of doors with the wind cutting through my clothes. Here, of course, we poorer ones have to clean the floors, and scrape the vegetables, and draw water; but one gets that easily from the cloister well. And I have a real bed, all to myself, in the dormitory, and food I never dreamed of. It's like paradise.'

'*She* doesn't seem to think so,' I said, indicating the beautiful red-haired girl, who, again sitting apart, was staring out of the window, her untouched embroidery frame lying forgotten in her lap.

'Adalgisa? Oh, hers is a very sad story. She comes from a rich Venetian family and she was twice betrothed; but each time the man was killed just before the wedding—one in battle and the second in a duel.'

'That was sad,' I agreed, 'But I don't suppose she had ever seen either of them, except perhaps at the betrothal ceremony. She couldn't have been so broken-hearted that it made her want to be a nun.'

'Oh, she doesn't want to be!' said Rosanna candidly. 'But after the second man was killed, no one else would marry her. They said she was unlucky . . .' her voice dropped to a whisper '. . . that she had the *mal occhio*. So her people sent her here, and her younger sister will be married instead. She says that she will kill herself, rather than take the vows; but of course, that's just talk. She would never do anything so silly and wicked.'

Looking at that white, set face I was not so sure. I would this time have gone to speak to Adalgisa, but I had promised to stay with Rosanna until Sister Angelica came back, and very soon she did. It was amusing to watch the expressions flit over her face: surprise, approval, puzzlement, indignation. 'But you have . . .' she began. I interrupted quickly: 'It was I who altered the drawing, Sister. I thought it was Rosanna's. Of course I would not have interfered with a teacher's work, but I wanted to make it look like a special horse—a favourite riding-horse of my own.'

Mollified, Sister Angelica gave me a sycophantic smile: 'What a good idea! Then, when you come to us later on, you will be welcomed by a nice picture of your little pet.'

I shuddered—not so much at the description of my aristocratic Plato as a 'little pet', as because light had suddenly broken upon me. Now I understood the Mother Superior's complaisance when she first saw me. I was Concordia Malatesta, the daughter of two great houses, and she was trying to capture me. The horror of that moment was such that it needed all my self-control to prevent myself from screaming and running straight out into the street. I forced myself to give a mechanical smile, and stood there trying to control my beating heart.

38

How I should have endured the rest of that day I do not know; but, while I was still emerging from the shock of that moment of revelation, there came a welcome diversion. The portress entered, telling Sister Angelica that one of the Polentani ladies had come to fetch me. I took my cloak and ran eagerly to the parlour, expecting to see Samaritana; but the tall, dark woman who rose to greet me was Maddalena. She said: 'We must go at once to Messer Guido's palace.'

That surprised me, for I had been given the distinct impression that everyone wanted me out of the way. But in front of Maddalena's attendant women and the young page who was waiting for us outside, I did not question her. We walked quickly and in a few minutes reached our destination. The courtyard was full of horses and of men in livery. When I saw the column on the emblems that decked their tabards and on the saddle-cloths of the horses, I knew my surmise was right: Stefano Colonna had come.

We went upstairs into a room in which a number of black dresses in silk, satin and velvet—mourning-clothes little worn and long discarded by ladies of the family—had been spread out on a bed. A gentlewoman said to Maddalena: 'Everything is ready, Madonna.' 'Thank you. You can leave us now. I will fasten her dress myself.'

She chose the smallest of the dresses. 'Change quickly,' she said, 'You must look nice, to do us credit.' 'I see,' I remarked, 'It doesn't matter what I wear, for my own sake—but in front of Stefano Colonna I must "look nice".'

Maddalena started: 'Stefano Colonna! What do you know about that?'

Naturally I did not give Samaritana away, but said briefly: 'I can identify a coat-of-arms bearing a column, and, I may say, the more they try to keep me in blinkers, the more alert I become.'

'Keep a guard on your tongue, Concordia,' she warned me. (I had heard that very phrase from Uncle Ostasio. So she, a Malatesta born, was acting under his influence.) 'You have already antagonised your uncle,' she continued, 'He is angry now, because the Rector insisted on seeing you. So don't make matters worse by trying to justify your father. We intend to see that your mother's murderer is punished.'

'You shouldn't use that word, Maddalena—remember, he is your brother.' 'Only my half-brother, fortunately,' she said quickly. And at that 'fortunately' I knew she would not be my ally. As she stood behind me, fastening up hooks, she must have read my expression in the mirror, for she added hastily: 'You know, I have never seen Giovanni in my life, except for an hour or two at your First Communion party.' 'Never *seen* him?' I echoed, amazed. 'No. We children of the second family lived up at Verucchio when we were small. He was always in Rimini or Gradara, when he wasn't away fighting. And when I was eight I came to Ravenna. I didn't even see him at the double wedding-ceremony, for of course Paolo was acting as his substitute.'

'You were married—at eight?' (I knew she had been very young, but only then did I realise how young.) 'Not really married, of course. I lived in the women's quarters and only saw Bernardino now and again. He didn't even play with me—he was twelve and thought himself much too grand. Sometimes he would bring me presents—sweetmeats, or coloured pebbles or shells—but more often he used just to pull my hair. At fifteen he went away for his training as a knight; then he was fighting in various places, so we didn't live together till I was nearly sixteen.'

She pulled the loose folds of my gown together with a silver girdle and said, a trifle wistfully: 'What a lovely figure you have!' I noticed then, what had escaped me at Christmas and in the chapel, when she was wearing a cloak, that she was several months pregnant. She had not grown fat, for the Malatesta women are naturally lean, but her swelling stomach went oddly with a face that, though still handsome, had hardened considerably since I had seen her years before in Rimini. I said consolingly: 'You had a lovely figure, when I saw you first—and I am sure you will, again.' She gave a short laugh: 'Having children spoils one's looks. Well, that's one thing that you will be spared. Perhaps you have chosen wisely.' 'Chosen? What do you mean?' 'They tell me you are going to be a nun.' So my intuition had been right! Since I was forewarned, the words came as less of a shock than they would otherwise have been. I whipped myself out of her hands and turned on her: 'I will *not* be a nun! I want to be married and live in a castle like Gradara, and wear beautiful dresses full of colour. I want to swim during the summer, go riding and hawking in the mid-seasons, and have minstrels to amuse me in the winter.' 'But how will you find a husband now?' asked Maddalena. 'Why ever not?' 'Where is your dowry to come from? Your uncles here have their own daughters to settle in life. Your father will be in no position to make a match for you, even if our people will let you go back to him—and they will never do that.'

I was still staring fixedly at her, but she drew my arm through hers and said: 'We're wasting time. Come now—and remember, don't talk like a lunatic.' We went downstairs, and just outside the council room she added: 'Just answer as briefly as you can; say you don't remember anything. Ostasio will help you.' 'Gag me, you mean!' I burst out, but she hushed me abruptly: 'They will hear you.'

Maddalena did not come in with me. A page lifted the heavy door-curtain and I stepped into a room far larger and more splendid than ours at Gradara. I found myself alone, facing a family group. In the centre was Grandfather Guido, flanked by Ostasio, Lamberto and Bernardino, who, alone of them all, gave me a welcoming smile. I looked with interest at Lamberto, whom I was seeing for the first time. He was a less genial edition of his father, without Ostasio's good looks or Bernardino's dashing charm. I summed him up as a quiet, prudent man with a long memory—a bad man to have as an enemy. I hoped his path would never cross my father's.

At the end of the table with a scribe beside him, who had already covered several sheets of parchment, sat Stefano Colonna.

I curtsied to my relatives and then to him, trying to sum him up. The Rector of Romagna, I knew, was usually looked upon by us as an enemy; but this man was new to the post, so perhaps he would be different. He had the dignity of my Malatesta grandfather, and less fierceness. His bearded, clear-eyed face had the confident look of one who takes his greatness for granted. I felt that he could be stern, but the glance he turned on me was kindly.

'But, Messer Ostasio,' he said, 'you spoke of her as a child. She is a tall young girl who looks quite sixteen.' 'I'm only thirteen,' I said, taking courage. 'But I have been ill, and I grew while I was lying in bed.'

'Unfortunately,' said my uncle, 'the illness did not have the same maturing effect on her brain. You will find her —retarded.'

My colour rose, but I knew I must keep my temper. There was commiseration in Colonna's eyes as he said: 'I am afraid, Contessina Concordia, that I have to question you on a very painful subject. I will try to cause you as little distress as possible.'

'If you mean my mother's death,' I answered quietly, 'I shall be glad to talk about it with someone who is outside both our families. I want to explain . . .'

Like a whiplash my uncle's voice cut in: 'We want none of your fantastic "explanations", Concordia. Answer only what you are asked.'

With great dignity the Rector interposed: 'Messer Ostasio, *I* am conducting this inquiry, and I prefer to question witnesses in my own way.' And to me: 'What is it that you wish to explain, my dear?'

'That my mother's death was an accident. My father did not mean to kill her. I heard him say: "She threw herself on my sword".'

The Polentani men reacted to this with exclamations of annoyance. All except Bernardino, who looked at me intensely. He had, I knew, been very fond of his sister, and it seemed that what I had said had been a relief to him.

Ostasio burst out: 'I tell you, the child knows nothing, can have seen or heard nothing. She was asleep in bed next morning when her old nurse gave her the news. She fell straight into a swoon and was ill for months with brain-fever. All that she will tell you will be the imaginings of her delirium.' Then a thought that had been at the back of my mind for some time found expression: 'I don't think it *was* brain-fever,' I protested. 'It was my chest that hurt. I was chilled through . . .'

Colonna stopped me with a gesture, addressing himself directly to my uncle: 'There are two possibilities you have overlooked, Messer Ostasio. Her father—who, they say, loves her dearly—may have roused her to say good-bye, and given her some sort of explanation; or more probably she was wakened by the noise and went to see what was happening.' I nodded in assent, as he went on: 'She doesn't look to me the type who falls in a swoon on hearing bad news, however terrible. But if she had, in fact, witnessed something of that scene, she would already have been suffering from severe shock.' Then he spoke to me: 'I want to make things easy for you, Concordia. Just tell me the truth, so far as you know it, and don't be afraid.'

I was grateful to him. He inspired me with the same feeling of trust and confidence that I had for my Malatesta grandfather.

'You did wake and go to see what the noise was about?' 'Yes.' 'Was your Uncle Paolo in your mother's room?' 'Yes,' I repeated, though my voice was drowned by Ostasio and Lamberto protesting that the question was inadmissible. 'Was there a discussion between him and your father, before the tragedy?' 'No. My father drew his sword at once, as he broke into the room.'

'What exactly did your father say to you afterwards?' 'Nothing—he didn't see me.' 'Then how can you assert that he said he did not mean to kill your mother?' 'I overheard him saying it to someone else.' 'To whom?' 'To a man who was helping him.' 'Who was that man?' I looked into the dark, piercing eyes, meeting their gaze steadily: 'I would rather not say. My father, if he wishes, can tell you himself.'

Stefano Colonna looked angry for a moment, then his face cleared: 'Good!' he said. 'You are loyal and brave, as befits one of your family. Now, one last question—and it will be a difficult one. Your father did a terrible thing, which you must find it almost impossible to forgive. Do you think, from what you saw and heard, that the provocation justified his action?'

I had forgotten the presence of the watching Polentani. At that moment I was alone with the Rector and my own conscience. Still looking into his eyes I said firmly: 'Yes, I do.' And I added: 'I heard him say: "What else could I have done?" '

'Thank you, Concordia. That is all I need.' He pulled out a chair for me to sit beside him. Then he said to my grandfather: 'There will be no need to bring the girl to Forlï, for I can see that you will shut her up in a convent or a madhouse rather than let her testify. I will dictate a brief statement for her to sign.'

'May I write it myself?' I asked. He looked surprised: 'Can you write, beyond signing your name?' 'Indeed I can. My father sometimes used me as a scribe. He will recognise my handwriting and know that I defended him.'

They handed me the ink-horn and a quill, and I wrote: 'My mother's death was accidental. She was stabbed while my father was attacking his brother Paolo, whom he had found in her bedroom. I heard him say: "What else could I have done?" and also "She threw herself on my sword".' And I signed it: Concordia Malatesta.

Crimson in the face, Grandfather Guido spluttered: 'I will not have my daughter's reputation defamed on the word of a demented child.' To which the Rector replied, with a courteous irony: 'I may say that the impression that Messer Giovanni had adequate provocation does not rest upon Concordia's word: it is widespread. As for the Contessina, she strikes me as anything but demented. If all witnesses were as lucid as she, my task would be easier.' He rose from his chair and signed to a page to buckle on his sword. 'When I have made arrangements with the

Malatcsti, I will summon them to meet you. Keep this in mind—you are the two strongest families in Romagna, and it is in the interests of both of you that you should work in harmony. Admittedly, you have a serious grievance; but I am sure you will find Messer Giovanni properly contrite. Just one thing I want to make clear; this young girl is not to be victimised for the evidence she has given. Have I your word for that?'

Grandfather Guido, Ostasio, Lamberto glowered at me in silence. Only Bernardino spoke: 'You have, Eccellenza. I loved my sister, and for her sake, I will see to it that Concordia does not suffer for her loyalty to her father.'

Gratefully I took refuge beside him. Now that it was all over, I was beginning to tremble. I only dimly heard the Rector saying that he must leave at once, as the winter evening was short and he wished to reach Forlï before dusk.

39

Bernardino was as good as his word. He took me straight out of the room to Maddalena, before the others could speak to me, and they both escorted me to the 'cuckoo's nest'. For some days they stayed there with me, and life seemed brighter. The wind had shifted to the south, bringing warm, showery days that seemed a presage of spring. One afternoon, when a glimpse of sun kept breaking through the clouds, Bernardino suggested riding out to the church of Santa Maria in Porto Fuori, where there were some pictures he wanted to show me.

On account of her condition Maddalena did not accompany us, so we rode alone, except for an escort of six horsemen, whom Bernardino told to keep us in sight but not to close in unless there was danger. We followed the high tow-path which protects the low-lying fields from flooding by the combined Ronco and Montone rivers. Even this slight elevation gave us a fine view over Ravenna, behind us to the north, and the sea with its fringing pine-woods ahead.

This was the first time I had ridden since my illness. My uncle had considerately provided me with a steady palfrey and was reining-in to keep pace with me. Soon I recovered my nerve and longed for a real gallop. I drew in long breaths of the cool air, rejoicing to feel the wind in my face once more and to see sunlight glittering on the waves that bordered the horizon.

Once in sight of the village, we took the track branching off to the left, stopped in front of the church door and waited till the escort overtook us. Then Bernardino handed over our horses to them and we went inside.

In the porch he checked me for a moment, saying: 'Before we go in, I had better tell you what you are going to see, in case the sudden sight of it upsets you.' Then he explained that Grandfather Guido had been a lavish patron of the church, and in return had been allowed to introduce portraits of his own family into its wall-frescoes. 'You will see your mother as a girl. It may make you a little sad; but afterwards, I think, you will be glad you came.'

We stood for a while, waiting till our eyes grew accustomed to the dimmer light; then Bernardino, pointing upwards, said: 'Look!' I gasped—for there at a window so well painted that it looked real, my mother stood watching us. Her lips half-parted in a smile, her lovely, slender fingers resting on the sill, she seemed to be alive. 'That was painted in her wedding-dress,' said my uncle. I commented: 'How young she looks!' 'She *was* young: sixteen—only three years older than you are now.' The artist had reproduced her classic features, her large, calm eyes, the wavy hair that shaded her neck and ended in a neat plait bound with pearls. Otherwise, she wore no jewels;

her white shoulders rose from a simple green dress bound with a gold ribbon. There she stood, looking out, calm and confident, at the new world awaiting her. Behind her, in her nun's habit, peeping over her shoulder, was Aunt Chiara.

Another picture showed the three sisters together: Francesca, Chiara—still a novice—and Samaritana, listening attentively to San Francesco. Most delightful of all was the earliest, with all nine of Grandfather Guido's brood—'cuckoos' and 'nightingales' alike—craning their necks, like so many small birds, out of a symbolic castle, to look at no less than three kneeling saints. In the centre was my mother—composed and dignified, even at fourteen—and beside her was Samaritana's little, laughing face, framed in its dark-red curls. As I looked at them, so animated and gay, I found myself smiling. So was Bernardino, but his hand brushed over his eyes and came away wet. My own eyes were dry. It suddenly struck me that, unhappy as I was in Ravenna, I had not cried once since my mother's death: it seemed as though my tears had been scorched away on that fearful night. The curious thing was that I could still laugh; but now my laugh often sounded, in my own ears, like an echo of my father's caustic bark.

'I remember,' said my uncle, with a tremor in his voice, 'how Francesca smiled, just as you did, when she first saw that picture. She said: "We look like birds in an overcrowded nest." And that was the origin of our family joke.'

We stayed quite a while in the empty church, sitting comfortably in the family pew. Bernardino said: 'One of my reasons for bringing you was to have a quiet, private talk. Tell me—are you very unhappy in Ravenna?' I nodded, and said quickly: 'Uncle, are you going to Forlì to meet my people?' 'I doubt it. I'm only a younger brother, you see. The others will probably go with my father. Why?' 'If you do go—please ask my father to fetch me home.' There was a long pause, then he said slowly: 'I don't think he will be there.' 'Not *there*! But he is the chief person concerned.'

Bernardino glanced up at my mother's portrait, as if to ask her advice; then he made up his mind to speak: 'Listen, Concordia: I discovered this morning that you know how to keep your own counsel. What I am telling you now is strictly confidential—not even Maddalena must know. Have I your word for that?' 'You have—for years I have kept my father's secrets. Tell me—why won't he come?' 'My brothers mean to kill him.' (I caught my breath.) 'They daren't do it in front of Colonna, but they have sworn to get him on his way to the conference, or as soon as he leaves it. When I found out, I sent a warning . . .' 'Oh, but he won't take any notice of that!' I broke in. 'He'll just bring more men with him and have his dagger handy, and come all the same. I know him.' 'So do I,' said Bernardino with a wry smile. 'I knew it was useless warning Giovanni, so I sent the letter to Messer Malatesta instead—and I think he will keep your father away. It doesn't suit his book to have a blood-feud continuing between our two families. The warning had to be anonymous, but I think he'll take it seriously.' 'But will my father listen to him?' 'Not if he talks about a murder plot. But the old man is a sly fox. He'll probably send Giovanni on some unnecessary mission that will keep him safely out of the way.' I sighed deeply: 'Well, I hope so. But that means there's no help for me. Uncle, do they really mean to send me to a convent?'

Bernardino's answer, gentle and reflective as it was, caught me like a stab: 'You might do worse, you know.' I stared at him incredulously: 'Worse, than to be a nun?' 'What's so dreadful about it?' 'To be shut up—never to swim or ride again—to lose my freedom.' 'But have you ever been free?' 'Until now, yes.' 'Have you ever walked or ridden alone, outside the walls of the Gattolo or of Gradara?' I remembered all the stratagems I had needed, just to buy a birthday present for my father. 'Well, no,' I admitted. 'But then I seldom wanted to. There's plenty to do in a castle.' 'You would find plenty to do in a convent.' 'Oh! Say prayers all day long, and listen to stories about saints.'

At that Bernardino laughed outright: 'Concordia, don't let my father hear you say that! What's your objection to saints?' 'They are such irritating people. You'd think they *wanted* to be martyred. When the Romans gave them a chance, they wouldn't take it. After all, they only had to sprinkle a few grains of incense on the altar of the gods. What did that matter? They could have gone on believing whatever they liked, in their own minds.'

'You talk the way your Malatesta grandfather acts. But, when it comes to the point, you act like the early Christians.' '*I*?' 'Yes—you! A day or two ago I heard you refusing to sprinkle incense on the Polentani altar. All that Ostasio was asking you to do was to hold your tongue—to have heard and seen nothing that night.' 'But how could I? I couldn't betray my father. I had to tell the Rector it wasn't his fault.' Bernardino nodded: 'You'll not believe it, child, but you have the stuff of a saint and martyr in you.' I laughed, and heard in my laughter the harsh note of my father's.

My uncle winced at the sound: 'I know you've had a bad time, but you'll have to put it behind you and think of the future.' 'I don't seem to have any future,' I said bitterly, 'Life imprisonment—just because they're too mean or too lazy to find me a husband.'

Then Bernardino stood up, so that he was in a dominant position: 'Can't I make you realise the situation? It's not pleasant for any of us, you know, to feel that Francesca's daughter regards us as enemies.' 'Not *you*,' I protested, 'you have been kind to me, and so has Samaritana. But the others hate me because I am a Malatesta.' ' "Hate" is an exaggeration; but your uncompromising attitude towards us is one of the difficulties in finding you a husband. Supposing my father does succeed in getting back Francesca's dowry, or part of it, for you, that is one obstacle removed. But the object in marrying a girl to someone is to secure that man's alliance; and it is obvious that, whatever the relations between our families, you would induce your husband to side with the Malatesta.'

That was true, and I could see Grandfather Guido's point of view. 'Then why not simply send me back to my father?' I said.

'Apart from the fact that he will not be able to have you with him till his tenure of office in Pesaro expires next year, have you considered what your position will be if he marries again?' 'Oh, but he couldn't, he wouldn't!' There was a pause, then Bernardino said hesitantly: 'There are . . . rumours.' 'Oh! Does everybody know about Ginevra?' 'Quite a number of people, thanks to old Malatesta's desire for the Montefeltro alliance. So, I see, do you.' I sighed impatiently: 'He's had Ginevra for years—he doesn't need to marry her.' 'But he may need, or want, to legitimise his sons.'

That hadn't occurred to me, and it startled me. I had always thought of Ginevra as something outside our family—an opiate to calm my father's starved senses, just as the Eastern drug stilled his physical pain. Now I saw with devastating clarity what might lie ahead, as Bernardino continued: 'Your life as a stepdaughter wouldn't be easy, even if you reconciled yourself to seeing another woman in your mother's place. Your father spoiled you, treated you as a boy, because he wanted a son; now he has two of his own, and maybe will have more, and daughters to provide with a dowry.'

I dropped my head on my knees, and it was some time before I could pay attention to what Bernardino was saying. Gradually I realised that he was still trying to persuade me of the advantages of a convent life. '. . . there you would be somebody, since your great-aunt was the foundress. Chiara is only a "cuckoo", but she has a privileged position: she can come out to us whenever she wants. And you, if my father gets back even a part of your dowry, will be a rich woman, with the prestige of our two families behind you.'

'Aren't nuns supposed to be poor and humble, no one better than the rest?' I said, to test him; for Rosanna had given me a contrary idea. I could not imagine the dignified Adalgisa being asked to sweep floors or prepare vegetables, much less draw water from the well.

My uncle laughed: 'Don't you believe it! Your connections will give you a fine start. I shouldn't wonder if they make you an abbess before you are thirty.' 'Thirty!' I gasped, horrified, 'I hope I shall be dead long before then.' 'How young you are, Concordia! You seem so grown-up, I keep forgetting you are only thirteen. I used to think I'd be old at thirty. Now I'm not far off it, but I feel as young as ever I did.' Indeed, he looked it: the fair-skinned, fair-haired Polentani certainly seemed to possess the gift of eternal youth. 'That's enough talk!' he said, 'It's cold in here. Let's get out into the sunshine.'

But we found ourselves in a soft, drizzling mist that had blown in from the sea. 'A pity,' commented my uncle, 'I wanted to show you our famous pinewoods.' I begged him to do it just the same; it was not very wet and our cloaks would keep out the damp. And he agreed, signing to one of the men to bring over our mounts.

Just beyond the village the pinewoods began. We rode slowly, for the track was overgrown and there was a risk that the horses might stumble on some half-hidden root. Under their hoofs the trampled pine-needles, soft as velvet, released a faint scent of resin into the air, and mingling with it there came, more and more clearly, the salt tang of the sea.

Then we were through the pines and ahead of us lay

the great waste—sand and sea merging in shades of indigo, dull ochre and green, under the grey of the tattered clouds. By tacit consent we had stopped riding and were sitting side by side in our saddles, with just enough pressure on the reins to keep our horses still. I looked down the shore in the direction of the Ronco: 'If I crossed that river and rode down the sand all day long, would I come to Rimini?' I asked. 'Yes, on a decent mount it wouldn't take you all day: three or four hours' fast riding. You'd have to cross half a dozen rivers, though, before coming to the Marecchia bridge, and in early spring most of them are in spate.' 'Such a little distance—yet it seems the end of the world!' 'Why,' replied my uncle lightly, 'Are you thinking of running away?' I nodded and then, measuring the distance with my eyes till the long shore faded out of sight, added wearily: 'But it's all so hopeless.'

Silently we turned and rode back through a world that seemed drained of sound and colour. The pale shore on our right, the dark line of pine trees on our left, horsehoofs falling silently on the loose sand; only the swish of wind in the tall bent-grass, and a faint jingle and murmur of voices from our escort, seemed to keep us company.

40

The spring days were lengthening quickly, so I was able to spend long afternoons in the garden. Now that the violets perfumed it and the dark hedges were starred with winter jasmine, it seemed less desolate, and I began to understand why Mother had loved it.

Yet the time dragged interminably, for I knew that my fate would soon be decided. At long last they sent to fetch me. This time no one troubled to dress me up, but

I myself put on the velvet gown that I had brought with me from my last visit: I intended to face my destiny looking like a daughter of the Malatesta, not like an orphan waif.

The meeting was held in my grandfather's study, which was crowded. All the legitimate males of the family were there, even young Guido, and of the women, Aunt Chiara, Samaritana and Maddalena.

After I had made my curtsies I sat down opposite my grandfather, next to Bernardino, who murmured in my ear the reassuring news: 'Your father didn't come.' (That explained the scowling faces of Ostasio and Lamberto!) My heart was beating fast, but I said nothing—just waited for them to begin. At last my grandfather spoke: 'Well, Concordia, I trust you will be glad to hear that (no thanks to you!) your mother's memory has been vindicated: Messer Malatesta has made the fullest apology for the offence to our honour.'

I nodded: it was like Grandfather Malatesta to offer excuses that cost nothing but some sacrifice of his pride. My father at least had, by his absence, been saved the humiliation of a personal apology.

'So now you are friends again?' I asked hopefully. A quick flash went through Ostasio's eyes, and a slower one burned in those of Lamberto. Those two had not forgotten or forgiven, and I knew they were still to be feared.

' "Friends" is perhaps not the right word. Let us say we have agreed to bury the past and co-operate for the good of Romagna. So far as you personally are concerned, I have been only partially successful. Messer Malatesta will not give up your mother's dowry lands, but he has agreed to pay us a yearly rental for your upbringing, and I have at least recovered her jewels.' He laid his hand on the casket in front of him, which I recognised as my own. Then he opened it and spilled its contents out on to the table: 'Can you tell me if everything is here?' 'I think I can.' Mother had seldom worn more than one ornament at a time, but she loved jewels, as she loved everything beautiful. She had often amused herself and me by spreading them out to decide which piece would best set off the gown she was wearing.

I stood up and leaned across the table, spreading out the glittering heap. Lost among the rest I saw my own tiny bracelet. I was looking for the pearl necklace that had been my father's last gift to me. Then I remembered having hidden it in my room, meaning to put it back next day; but during the night the tragedy had occurred. Should I mention it? No, let it stay hidden: one day I might be able to get it back.

A leaf-patterned gold chain caught my eye. I picked it out and showed it to Bernardino: 'You gave her that. Would you like it now, for Maddalena?' 'I?' There was genuine astonishment in his voice. 'Yes, you brought it from Florence, when you came to stay with us—you and the young man who wants to write poetry.' 'But, my dear child, I came quite unexpectedly, wounded in a battle. I certainly had had no opportunity to choose a present for my sister.' He examined the chain and agreed: 'It does come from Florence, and it is very fine workmanship. In fact, there is only one goldsmith who makes that pattern, and his shop isn't easy to find. It was Paolo Malatesta who showed me . . .' He stopped abruptly as my eyes met his. I do not think the others realised the significance of what he had said. Slipping the chain into my pocket, I took a clasp of topaz and jet, just the colour of Maddalena's eyes, and pushed it along the table to her, saying: 'I would like you to have this.' For Samaritana, to set off her red hair, I found a pair of emerald ear-rings with a matching brooch, giving her also, for her little girl, the bracelet that was now too small for me. Then I pinned a silver brooch with the Malatesta arms into the bosom of my black dress.

'What are you doing?' exclaimed my grandfather crossly.

'Those jewels are your dowry.' 'There are so many—I see no harm in giving one or two to people who loved my mother and have been kind to me. If they are mine, surely I can do what I like with them?' 'They are yours —in trust,' said Ostasio curtly. 'To offer to God,' added Aunt Chiara, in an exasperating tone of sweet rectitude.

I had to make a firm stand: now or never was my chance to protest. 'Since you have recovered part of my dowry, why talk about God? There is no longer any need to push me into a convent. These jewels will buy me a husband —not such an influential one, perhaps, as if I were able to bring him a Malatesta castle and some of the Polenta lands, but at least a gentleman.'

'These jewels are the price of your poor mother's life,' interposed my aunt, who has never been taught to think logically. 'You wouldn't want to buy a husband with tainted money?' 'I see,' I said crisply. 'God is less particular.'

My cousin gave me a quick, boyish laugh, but was frowned down by his father. Grandfather thought it over —his brain works slowly—and then slammed his hand down on the table, so that the jewels quivered and sent back flashes of coloured light. Then Lamberto cut in, his voice icy: 'What man, do you suppose, will wish to marry a murderer's daughter?'

That turned my controlled anger into a flaming rage. 'Murder? To kill a man in defence of your honour? To kill a younger, more agile man in a duel? Is there any one of you who hasn't half a dozen deaths to his score, in battle or single combat?' I looked at all the men in turn, but my eyes came to rest finally on Grandfather Guido's reddening face. 'I have never killed a helpless woman,' he said, as though excusing himself. Fury had made me reckless: 'You have never had occasion,' I retorted. 'You were far too busy in the cuckoo's nest to keep an eye on your own home.' This was a shot in the dark; no doubt my late grandmother was a paragon of virtue, and I think my grandfather really did not grasp the import of what I had said. But he did catch the allusion to the cuckoo's nest, and it deepened his colour to a dull crimson. He rose and rang a handbell: 'I have stood no insolence from my children,' he said, 'and I'll have none from you. Chiara, when she has had two days on bread and water, I'll send her to you—and if she gives any further trouble, have her exorcised.'

By this time I was frightened, though I would not show it. Bernardino said quietly to me: 'Keep your head, Concordia. And later on, when we're all calmer, apologise.'

To the footman who had answered his summons my grandfather said gruffly: 'Take the Contessina to the punishment room.'

That room was at the top of the house, under the roof-terrace, and was completely bare, except for a plank-bed covered with a blanket, and in one corner a bucket with a lid, for urgent physical needs. Washing, apparently, was not considered one of them, for no pitcher or hand-basin was provided. Closed shutters darkened the room, but the footman unbolted and opened them. He seemed embarrassed, muttering something to the effect that he had never before brought a Contessina up there—it was the boys who were punished in this way.

'I deserve it,' I said frankly, 'I was very impertinent to my grandfather; but then he had said something to make me angry.'

The man looked sympathetic. 'See here, Contessina,' he said, 'If you like, I'll go to Messer Guido in an hour's time and say that you are crying, and ask if I may let you out. His rages don't last long.'

I thanked him but declined the offer, saying that it would do me no harm to stay alone in the room for a few hours, or even overnight. When he had gone, locking the door behind him, I looked out of the window. It was barred, but not very closely; had it not been for my skirts I could have slipped through; but the courtyard was very far below. It looked an easy climb to the roof, but what could I have done up there?

So I resigned myself to the situation and, since I had nothing else to do, closed the shutters, lay down and tried to sleep. My pulses were still throbbing with the stimulus of that brush with my grandfather, but gradually the tumult subsided. . . . I was back in Gradara, sitting beside my father and watching the lines of pain smooth from his forehead. And then—he was asleep and my own eyes were heavy . . . my spirit felt light, free . . . it slipped down the stairs from his tower-room to the bridge that led to my mother's bedroom, went up again to the little room where Pandolfo and I had roasted chestnuts with the players.

In a moment, it was summer, yet I was still with Esmeralda and Masiello. They had kept their promise to give me supper in the Ravenna pinewoods—no longer damp, as I had first seen them with Bernardino—but crisp, warm and fragrant, and we were sitting round a crackling wood-fire. Esmeralda was busy about the fire. From under it, with two long sticks, she drew something that looked like a roughly shaped clay pot. But when she rapped it sharply, the clay fell apart and there rose from it a delicious scent of freshly baked rabbit.

But I never tasted that rabbit, for a tap at the window roused me with a start. There was no wind to rattle them? Was it part of my dream, or a bat, or a night-bird? No, for there came a louder rap and a cautious voice (my cousin Guido's): 'Concordia, are you awake? Let me in!'

I ran to open the shutters. Guido was clinging precariously to the bars, his feet on the narrow ledge and a sheer drop below. 'Quick!' he ordered, 'Undo my belt and take the things from my waist; then I shall be able to get through.' Fastened to his waist he had a bundle tied up in a cloth, and a small earthenware flask. When I had taken it, he slid his head and shoulders through the bars and, contorting himself violently, managed to pass them. Panting a little, he dropped into the room: 'I've grown since last year,' he commented, 'Soon I'll not be able to do it at all.'

When I told him he shouldn't have taken such a risk he laughed: 'I've done it so often in the past, for myself and my younger brothers. They don't send me up here any more—I'm too old for it. Father doesn't even beat me now, just lectures me. That's one advantage of growing up.'

I sighed: '*I* don't seem to be getting any advantages. Tell me, what happened after they took me away? Were they very angry?' 'Yes, they were—and you did deserve it. Fortunately, Grandfather missed the real point of what you said, but my father and my uncles didn't. Bernardino, I think, would have liked to laugh, but he didn't dare.' 'Bernardino is nice,' I said. 'Yes, he spoke up for you and told them not to send you to the convent tomorrow: in your present temper, he said, it would be punishing the nuns more than you.' We both laughed at that, and Guido added: 'They'll wait now until after your fourteenth birthday.'

I drew a deep sigh of relief. 'Forget it,' he said, 'and let's talk of something nicer while you have your supper.' 'Supper?' 'Yes, I have good friends in the kitchen and pantry. I said I was going hawking at dawn, and see what they gave me.' He was untying his bundle, fumbling a little in the dusk. 'It smells good,' I said, 'but I can't see what it is—I can hardly see you.' 'Wait a moment. Help me lift the planks off the bed.'

We did so, and Guido showed me that one of the trestles had been hollowed out to form a receptacle, out of which he pulled a tinder-box and a candle. 'Oh!' I said admiringly, 'Did you make that?' 'No, I found it by chance one day, when I was in a temper and threw the planks off the bed. I expect Father made it, long ago. He was great fun when he was young, you know.' 'I remember how I liked him, when he came to Rimini. He seems so different now.' 'Aunt Francesca's death has made him very bitter. He's getting like Uncle Lamberto, who was always a bit sulky.' While we talked, Guido was busy striking sparks from the flint, until the wick began to burn.

My appetite revived when I saw what he had brought me: a wing of roast chicken, a large slice of meat-pie, two apples, a handful of raisins and dried figs, with two freshly baked rolls. 'And there's white wine in the flask,' he said. 'I can't eat all that,' I protested, 'you must share it with me.' But he refused to take anything except half an apple, saying wisely that I had better keep something in reserve, in case they didn't let me out until after dinner next day. With his dagger he deftly peeled and cored the apples and jointed the chicken wing.

Having appeased my first hunger, I began to talk: 'This reminds me of an evening that Pandolfo and I spent at Gradara,' and I told him how we had roasted chestnuts with the players and how, just before he came, I had been dreaming of them. 'What fun, if only I could run away to the woods and join them! I've often thought one could escape from the cuckoo's nest. It is so near the town wall, one would only need a plank to step across. 'And how would you get down the other side?' asked Guido practically. 'With a rope, of course.' 'Fixed to what?' That was a problem: there wouldn't be anything to fix it to. I said perhaps someone would hold it for me; but that problematic 'someone' complicated the scheme. 'You'd need money to bribe him,' suggested Guido sagely.

That reminded me of the gold chain in my pocket. I took it out and asked Guido if he could sell it for me. He looked taken aback, so I explained: 'I hate being without money: I can't even buy a few handkerchiefs or a hair-ribbon.' 'My father would have things bought for you, if you asked him.' I shook my head stubbornly: I was not going to ask Uncle Ostasio for anything.

Meanwhile, my cousin was examining the chain. 'It is beautiful,' he said, 'Why not keep it for yourself?' I burst out with sudden violence: 'I hate it! I want to get rid of it!' Guido looked at me curiously: 'I didn't quite understand what you and Uncle Bernardino were saying about it: why did you think he gave it to Aunt Francesca?' 'Oh, I just made a mistake.' My tone must have rung false, and Guido is an intelligent boy: 'Oh, I *see*. She said it was from him, but it was really from Paolo Malatesta?' I nodded. 'That was the first direct lie she ever told me. So it's not surprising that I dislike the chain. But it must be valuable, and the money would be useful.'

He reflected a moment: 'It's not easy—people still treat me like a child, and they'd probably ask my father before giving me the money. Anyway, gentlemen buy jewels, they don't sell them.' Then, seeing my disappointment, he added: 'Still, I'll see what I can do. There's a man who might fix it for me.'

He put the chain into his pocket and quickly removed the traces of my meal, putting the uneaten food back into the cloth and hanging it under one of the trestles. 'You think of everything!' I said, and Guido laughed: 'I know all about this room! Once I'd discovered how to amuse myself, and to get in and out without being caught, I began almost to enjoy it.'

We smiled at each other and I said: 'We've a lot in common, Guido.' He nodded: 'I do like you, Concordia. You're brave and you're clever, and . . .' He hesitated, too honest to pay an insincere compliment, and I came to his rescue: 'You needn't say I'm pretty, because I'm not and I know it.' 'No, you're too thin,' he agreed candidly, 'But Samaritana says you'll be a handsome woman by the time you're thirty.' 'Oh dear, people will talk about what will happen when I'm thirty. I want to enjoy my life now, while I am young; and if they shut me up in a convent, what life shall I have to enjoy?' 'It's all wrong,' agreed Guido, 'they ought to find you a husband.' And then he added reflectively: 'What a pity you're my cousin! If you weren't, I could marry you myself.' I laughed at this: 'You're the second person who has said that to me, or something similar.' 'Not that conceited young popinjay Uberto?' he asked quickly, with a note in his voice that was almost jealous. I couldn't bring Pandolfo into it, so I just said vaguely: 'I've lots of relatives, you know.'

Guido was ready to go. At the window he turned and asked shyly: 'May I kiss you good night, Concordia?' Four years previously, I reflected, he would have done it without asking: we were growing up! 'Of course, dear Guido!' All at once I felt myself much more mature than he. I took his face between my hands (I was still a trifle the taller), and held my lips on his—softly, as Pandolfo had taught me. His breath came quickly and I felt his young body trembling. Gently I put him from me: 'That's enough for a first time,' I said. 'It wasn't *your* first!' he retorted, with a flash of insight. I laughed and kissed him again—in cousinly fashion on the cheek. 'No!' I agreed, 'But if they have their way with me, it may be my last.'

41

I remained in disgrace at the cuckoo's nest until Samaritana, coming to visit her brothers at Easter (Grandfather Guido had already gone to Florence as *podestà*), interceded for me; so I was invited to their Easter dinner and to share her room for the night.

Six months had passed since the tragedy, so the family mourning was less rigid. After supper, there was even an entertainment provided—a juggler, a trio of minstrels and a pair of comedians. But I was told I must go to bed before it began. I was about to protest, when I caught Guido's eye and saw that he was signalling to me to keep quiet. So I let Nannie lead me upstairs, but at the door I told her firmly that I needed no help in undressing, so she had better go back and enjoy the entertainment—an offer which she, nothing loth, accepted.

I stayed fully dressed, and before long there came a light tap on the door. Yes, it was Guido. 'I slipped out while they were watching the juggler,' he said, and held out to me a long strip of weighted canvas: 'The man who sold the chain for me had the money made up into a belt. No one will notice if you wear it under all the folds of that velvet dress.' He looked critically at it: 'Why do you wear that thing? It is much too big for you—and too hot in this weather.' 'I've nothing else,' I admitted, 'But now, thanks to you, I can have some summer dresses made to fit me.' Oh, what a wonderful feeling it was to have money!

I put the belt under my pillow, wondering how I could prevent Samaritana from noticing it when I dressed next morning. Then I decided to make her my ally; after all, I would need her help in spending the money. When she came up, I pretended to be asleep, but next morning I climbed on to her bed. She had told me once how she, the little sister, used to come and sit on my mother's bed for long, confidential talks; now it was I, the younger, who came to her.

I told her that my people had found means to send me money, and that I would like her to take me shopping. She laughed, and asked no embarrassing questions. In fact, she even agreed to tell Ostasio that she herself had been approached by a Malatesta emissary, asking her to bring me the money. I think she felt that my uncles were acting towards me like overbearing schoolmasters, and that I had every right to outwit them.

Next morning we went shopping, accompanied by her gentlewomen, with Aristide to carry the parcels. And what fun it was! Samaritana knew of a merchant living near San Vitale, who seemed to have taken the mosaics as a pattern for his wonderful brocades. Wistfully we looked at their glowing blues and greens, all interwoven with gold; but there were two barriers—price, and the mourning period. 'Anyway,' I declared, 'I won't wear black any longer.' So we compromised on two lengths of taffeta, silver-grey, one shot with violet and the other with blue. There was another with glorious reflections of orange and rose, but Samaritana regretfully shook her head. 'Supposing I had it to line a cloak?' I suggested, and she agreed that, if I kept it closed in front of my uncles, it might pass. So I chose some dark grey velvet for the outside. Then I selected enough fine white silk to make three sets of underwear, for I hated the calico with which Aunt Chiara had provided me. It was not meanness, I think, but a desire to wean me from the vanities of this world. If that was her object, it failed signally: she simply made me hanker after things that, at home, had been so much a matter of course that I had never even thought about them.

When we totalled up the cost I was startled: in less than half an hour I had spent a full third of the money raised by selling the chain; and there were so many other things I urgently wanted. When Samaritana had arranged with the merchant to have the dresses and underwear sewn by women whom he employed and brought back to the shop for us to fetch (since obviously there would be trouble if they were made up by the seamstresses in my grandfather's palace) we sat down on a stone bench in San Vitale churchyard and considered the rest. I wanted writing materials, and something to occupy my mind: a lute, some French songs, and interesting books. 'Books are very expensive,' said Samaritana gravely. This was a new idea to me: 'Mother had all the books she wanted,' I said, 'and Uncle

Paolo brought her one every time he came to stay.' 'The Malatesti are rich,' commented my aunt drily: 'Ordinary people have to think twice before buying one.' Then she had an idea: 'When Francesca married, she left quite a number of things in a chest in her room. I think there is music among them, and maybe a book or two. As for a lute, we can certainly find one in our music-room—and of course we have everything necessary for writing.' 'But I don't want to accept . . .' 'Don't be silly,' said Samaritana tartly. 'Who has a better right to your mother's things than you?' And, arm in arm, we went together into Galla Placidia's tomb, to see the doves that seem to have just alighted on the marble bowl where they have been immobilised for over seven hundred years.

Samaritana provided all the things she had promised. She even stayed on in Ravenna until my dresses were ready, and brought them herself to the cuckoo's nest, to see me through the storm of disapproval that she knew they would arouse.

After months of dragging around in heavy black clothes, what a joy it was to hear the light swish of taffeta billowing out as I walked, to feel my limbs supple and free in the warm spring air. I ran down into the garden, laughing with the sheer joy of it—and then came back to face the hostile looks of my attendants.

Serafina sniffed aggressively and muttered something about telling Messer Ostasio, which gave Samaritana her chance to say with dignity: 'That, I think is my concern, and I have already done so.' Nannie, sobbing, said that my poor mother would turn in her grave. I resisted the temptation to retort that she *had* no grave, and again Samaritana rose to my defence: 'My sister loved all beautiful things,' she said, 'She would never want Concordia to be deprived of them, just because she herself is no longer here to enjoy them.'

The summer passed, if not happily, at least pleasantly

for me. Under my supervision the neglected garden began to recover its old-time beauty, and I spent many hours under the shady yew tree, improvising an accompaniment to the songs Samaritana had found for me. Sometimes I wrote new words to them. I liked drawing, too, and making up patterns. As I grew more expert, I insisted that Nannie or Serafina should accompany me to San Vitale, where I would sit copying the fantastic designs in the vaulting and would colour them from memory when I got back.

Most of my remaining money I had hidden in a stone vase in the garden, but I kept a store of small coins with which I would make occasional purchases. They came in useful, too, for bribing Serafina, who became much less hostile. Nannie, of course, was not the type to accept bribes, but she appreciated little presents now and again.

Maddalena's baby had been born just after Easter, and she had stayed on in Ravenna, since Bernardino had gone as *podestà* to Cervia. I used sometimes to spend the afternoon with her and her children. Little Franceschina, named after my mother, was my favourite; like me, she had the fair colouring of the Polenta family, combined with the finely cut Malatesta features. 'You might be sisters,' said Maddalena once, 'But you were more like her when you still had your long fair hair.' I ran my fingers through the crop of golden-brown curls that were now thick and strong but showed no sign of growing out. I liked this new hair-style, even though Guido teased me about my boyish look.

Between my cousin and me there had developed a strange relationship; partly the joyous naughtiness of our shared secret, partly a half-serious, half-jesting flirtation. For some weeks Guido really believed himself in love with me. I used to practise on him all the airs and graces that Pandolfo had taught me. After the mixture of fascination and fright that I had experienced with my young uncle, it was strange to find myself in the stronger position; to watch

Guido, on the rare occasions when we contrived to be alone together, blushing and finding excuses to kiss me, which he did a trifle clumsily but with evident satisfaction to himself. Dear Guido! I hope they will find him a wife whom he can really love, for he is such a nice boy.

42

Some instinct told me that this was just a breathing space; that sooner or later a new crisis would come to decide the course of my life. And all unexpectedly it came—the day that seemed for a moment to open the prison gates, and then closed them on me for ever.

It was towards the end of June, the feast of St Peter and St Paul, when of course I had to go to church with my usual escort of Nannie and Serafina. In the loggia outside San Francesco's I noticed a mendicant friar—one of those dishevelled vagrants who travel round the country pestering people for alms. It struck me that, though his shoulders were hunched under his cowl, he looked young and sturdy and could be better employed than in begging. So I would have ignored his outstretched hand, but as I moved to pass him, I heard him whisper my name: 'Contessina Concordia!' Of course, the Polenta family was known by all Ravenna, so he could easily have found out who I was, yet his intonation sounded familiar. Looking more closely, I saw a pair of sea-blue eyes—no beggar's eyes, but those of a soldier, bright and laughing. I know only one pair of that brilliant sapphire. In growing excitement I looked for red hair under his cowl. None was visible, but the stubbly fringe on his chin might well have been red, had it not been darkened, perhaps by dirt, perhaps intentionally with charcoal. Marco . . .!

I had enough self-control not to speak his name aloud. Turning to Nannie—to whom I now confided my purse, with a little money for charity or minor purchases—I said: 'Let us give something to this good man.' And while she was searching for a small coin I distracted Serafina's attention by asking her to look and see whether I had just dropped my handkerchief. Then, on an impulse, I snatched the purse from Nannie and gave him the coin myself. He took it, covering my small hand with both his own. I had guessed right: the rough edge of a tiny, closely rolled scroll was being pressed into my palm. Closing my fingers on it, I slipped it at once, covered by my purse, into my pocket.

'Blessings upon you, little lady!' exclaimed Marco, his Venetian accent amusingly obvious through an assumed whine. Then he added a curious phrase: 'But you should go to confession, Madonnina—go to confession today if you wish to be saved.'

I looked keenly at him: was this a pointless remark, just a bit of his masquerade? One blue eye winked at me and I suddenly realised what he meant. The wild audacity of his scheme took me aback—but how magnificently simple it was! He held up two fingers of his left hand as if in blessing, and I thought: 'The second box, on the left side of the church—the women's side.' But how was I to avoid being taken directly into the Polenta chapel? I said to Nannie: 'The church is very full, and we are late. Don't let us try to push through the crowd. We will wait here for the moment.' And I took up my place by a pillar, where I had a good view of the confessional box. I wondered how Marco would reach it without anyone seeing him and realising that a mendicant friar had no business to be hearing confessions. Then I guessed why he had chosen that particular box: it was just by the side door, and I had not been watching for more than a couple of minutes, when I saw a brown figure flash in and slip behind the curtain. I too must act quickly, before anyone else came to confess at that box. I whispered to Nannie: 'That friar was right: my confession is long overdue. I should make it now.' It was indeed a good moment; the service was just beginning, so the music would cover our voices, while the entrance of the priest and the choir would distract everyone's attention.

I knelt down at the box and whispered: 'Marco?' 'Dear little Contessina—I wish I could kiss your hand.' But the grating made that impossible. 'The letter is from *him*?' 'From Messer Giovanni, yes.' 'I can't read it here. Do you know what it says?' 'Only that he wants you to come back, and I am to take you to him.' Then the sunshine outside flooded my heart: it seemed to me that all the birds in Ravenna were singing. 'When?' I asked eagerly. 'Now, if you like. In a second we can be through that door, and before your ladies have realised what is happening, we'll reach the street corner and be out of sight. In my mendicant's bag I have a gown and sandals for you. With the hood pulled well over your face, no one will see how young you are. Ten minutes to reach the wall, and if we pass the gate unchallenged—a friar and his acolyte on an errand of mercy—we are safe. At the first inn I have horses waiting, and a page's suit for you.'

Over and over again I have asked myself—why didn't I leap at the chance? Life was offering me what I had craved for months, and I should have grasped it with both hands, thinking neither of past nor future, but only of the wonderful moment. Yet something did hold me back, telling me that I must read my father's letter before I decided. I answered: 'Not now, Marco: I must have time to think. Tell me, how is he?'

Physically, never better, Marco told me: his woman took good care of him. (I started—that must mean Ginevra.) She had insisted on his going for a month's cure at the hot springs of Castrocaro, before taking up his duties at Pesaro.

Light dawned upon me. So that was where he had been when the Polentani went to Forlì! My grandfather must have arranged it with Ginevra, to keep him out of the way; of course they had told him nothing about the meeting till it was over. I was relieved, for I had not liked to think that a mere threat had kept him away; nor that he had made no effort to claim me.

'And it did him good?' I asked. 'So much, that he can swim now without the splint. Better still, he can dismount normally and mount with the minimum of help—just a hand on my shoulder, and every time the pressure grows less. Soon he will be able to do it by himself.' That was real satisfaction to me, for I knew how bitterly he had resented his inability to leap on and off his horse like any other man.

'You said "physically",' I reminded Marco, 'How is he—in his mind? Is he very unhappy?' Marco hesitated, then brought out the curious word 'diminished'. He said my father seemed oddly quiet, absent-minded, almost gentle. They very seldom heard him shouting now. When they had charged into Rimini, it was my grandfather's great voice that had dominated the battle-cry 'Malatesta!'. But, all in all, Messer Giovanni had weathered the storm better than one would have expected. Aldo's devotion had saved him in those first terrible days.

It was a long story that Marco murmured through the grating, quickly and concisely, for we had little time. On Malatestino's orders he had accompanied Aldo and my father to Pesaro, for if the latter had collapsed on the way, the old man could have done little to help him. To spare him effort, they avoided the hilly coast road through Casteldimezzo, risking the boggy track in the valley, which at this dry end of summer had been firm enough to take the weight of a horse and man. So, in the dead of night, they came to the closed gates of Pesaro, where the name Malatesta gained them admittance. Soon they reached the house adjoining the *podestà's* official residence, which, when his last term of office expired, my father had rented and kept open for his occasional use. By that time he was in a stupor. Marco roused the steward, and together they carried him upstairs and put him to bed. But he did not sleep—just lay there with wide-open eyes, ice-cold, for all their efforts to warm him.

Aldo said: 'He must sleep, and for a long while, or he will lose his mind.' So, before dawn, he rode back, under the hill of Gradara, to the Wise Woman's farm and bought from her a potion so strong that it would keep a man unconscious for days without doing him any permanent injury. 'He had to get it before she knew what had happened,' commented Marco, 'for she loved Madonna Francesca and, if she had known, she might well have given him poison.' Then Aldo went to the castle and arranged to have Riccardo fetched from Santarcangelo. 'Everything there was in confusion. No one knew exactly what had happened, but the guard had seen Messer Paolo on the ladder . . .' Marco stopped abruptly, but I encouraged him: 'I know all about it: that was what made me ill.' 'Ah, we all wondered when we heard that you were delirious and that your old nurse insisted on taking you to Ravenna.' 'And my uncle let me go?' 'I think he was relieved. If you had died on his hands, Messer Giovanni would never have forgiven him. At any rate, when Riccardo arrived at Pesaro and I reported back for duty at Gradara, I was told to escort you to Ravenna. So I carried you down the hill and put you and the old dame into a horse-litter, and rode, with half a dozen of the guard, till you were past the danger point of Rimini; then I left you and returned to Gradara.'

For four days and nights, he heard later, Riccardo and Aldo had taken it in turns to nurse my father. When his physical needs roused him to semi-consciousness, they had tended and washed him, fed him with broth or milk, and put him to sleep again with diminishing doses of the drug. On the fifth day he had woken, clear-headed, asking for 'real food', and had, without any ill-effects, eaten a plateful of cold meat and a hunk of bread, washed down with red wine. Then he had slept a while—a natural sleep—and had woken in a condition to give orders.

'He sent Aldo to fetch his brother from Gradara, and I accompanied them. We found Messer Giovanni sitting in a high-backed chair by the window, fully dressed even to his cuirass. (Riccardo told us later that he had asked for it because he felt too weak to sit upright without support.) Messer Malatestino's greeting was a quip that evidently he was prepared to meet the daggers of the Polentani. Then, with that sarcastic smile of his, he handed him the sword-stick that had been left at Gradara. But he got no change from Messer Giovanni, who just thanked him, drew out the blade to see if it had been properly cleaned (it had—I had done it myself), and then sat propping himself with his clasped hands upon it.' I nodded: that was just like him—curiously insensitive to things that would have upset a more imaginative man. 'And did he ask Uncle Malatestino what had happened?' 'Not in front of us. He sent us out of the room. But there was no doubt, when Messer Malatestino left, that he knew everything.' 'Oh, my poor father! How did he take it?' 'He was very grim and quiet. That night, they told me later, Aldo begged to stay with him, but he refused, saying: "Don't worry, old friend. If I didn't kill myself when I first realised that I was crippled for life, I am not likely to do it now. You have lost enough rest for my sake. Go to bed and sleep well, as I shall do.' Next morning he got up and went about his business in Pesaro, as if nothing had happened.'

That put a fresh idea into my head. By that time, the story of his deed must have been bruited abroad. 'How did people receive him?' I asked. 'In Pesaro, with sympathy and respect. In Gradara it is different. The people had loved Madonna Francesca. They resent, too, his attitude to the accident that happened in the street. The child's kneecap was broken and he will always be lame. But Messer Giovanni takes no interest in him, never inquires after him. He has simply told Messer Rinaldo to give the boy's mother money if she asks for it.' 'Probably he doesn't want to be reminded of anything that happened that day,' I suggested, and asked anxiously how the people showed their resentment. There was no open hostility, Marco told me; but now, instead of crowding the streets to greet him, they went indoors, so that he rode up to the castle amid a great silence. 'But it doesn't seem to trouble him—he has always been a solitary man.' 'And now, except for you faithful three, he is all alone.' 'Well, no,' he answered, slightly embarrassed, 'There is always his woman, who adores him.' 'Ginevra? But she isn't at Pesaro—the *podestà* can't have his wife with him.' From the depths of the box there came a little chuckle. 'But, you see, she isn't his wife—merely a young widow (very recently widowed, it would seem, since she has two small children and is pregnant with another), who happens to have rented his private house next to the *podestà's* residence.' I gasped: the Malatesta effrontery fascinated me, perhaps because the little bit of me that came from the Polentani prevented me from taking it for granted. 'Yes,' agreed Marco, hearing my exclamation. 'And he has even built a covered bridge between the two houses—in Pesaro people call it among themselves "Ginevra's bridge".' I blushed, for my father's sake, though I knew that such conduct would, in the general opinion, only add to his prestige. 'Of course,' continued Marco reflectively, 'when he marries her, he will either have to get the rules changed, or else send her away.'

Something caught at my heart: '*When* he marries her? Does he really mean to?' 'He says so.' 'To you?' It seemed to me incredible that my father should have discussed such a personal matter with a retainer, even such a trusty one as this. Marco must have caught the inflection in my voice, for he explained quickly: 'This was the way it came about . . .' And he told me that 'the woman' (somehow it pleased me that, in loyalty to my mother, he would not give her the title of 'Madonna Ginevra') was jealous. She wanted to do everything for my father herself and was especially jealous of Riccardo who, far more than a valet, cared for him like a male nurse. Ginevra expected my father to spend the siesta hour with her; but he often preferred to pass the time performing a series of movements that the doctors at Castrocaro had suggested, to restore the suppleness of his hip-joint. They were difficult and painful, and he needed Riccardo's help in carrying them out. Once, when he had been away on official business and Ginevra had not seen him for some days, she took the unprecedented step of coming across the bridge to his residence, instead of waiting for him to come to her. Having no key, she was obliged to attract attention by knocking for admittance. This in itself annoyed and embarrassed my father, so his greeting was anything but cordial. When he reproved her, Ginevra began to make an hysterical scene, telling Riccardo to leave the room, as she had things to say that were not for the ears of a hired man. A satisfied chuckle crept into Marco's voice as he continued: 'And Riccardo answered that he had been Messer Giovanni's hired man for many more years than she had been his kept woman.' Forgetting where I was, I gave a gurgle of laughter. Marco hushed me quickly, but I sensed that his own eyes were twinkling. 'Oh!' I gasped, 'Whatever did Father say to that?' 'For the first time since . . . since the tragedy, he flew into a real rage. First he ordered Riccardo out of the room, then he turned on the woman. I happened to be there that day, having brought a message from Gradara; and for nearly half an hour Aldo and I heard him storming and the woman crying. Riccardo came down to us trembling and said: "I'm for it. It's not good for any man to fall out with his master's doxy." (Excuse the word, Contessina.) But Aldo was happy: he just nodded, saying: "All these weeks I have been waiting to hear his voice raised. Now I know that he is himself again." At last Messer Giovanni rang for Riccardo to dress him, and later he called us all together in his room and told us: "I cannot do without you three. Aldo has been a second father to me, and Riccardo more devoted than any brother. As for Marco, I wish I had a son like him." (Yes, he said that of me: you can imagine how proud I felt.) "I hope you will never leave my service while I live, and after my death I will see that you need never serve another master, except of your own free choice. But in return I must insist that you treat Madonna Ginevra with the respect due to my wife." He must have seen the protest in our faces, for he continued: "Do not think that she will ever, or can ever, take the place of—of that other to whom you were devoted. But she is the mother of my sons and as such, when I have arranged the formalities, I mean to marry her".'

This was a shock. I looked round, to see if Nannie and Serafina were getting suspicious of this ultra-long confession. They were both gazing at me curiously, so I said quickly: 'Marco, I must go. Come to the house tomorrow—not the Polenta palace, but the little house by the wall. Anyone will tell you where it is. I'll say to the gardener's boy that I have promised to give you some fruit, so come to the lower garden gate. And in the basket there'll be a letter to tell you what I have decided.' 'But, Contessina, I can't read.' This was catastrophic: if Marco had to let someone read the letter for him, that person might go straight to my uncles with the news. I thought quickly. 'Then I'll put a ribbon from my dress. If it's silver, you'll know that I am coming; if it's black, no.' 'Silver!' exclaimed Marco,

'It must be silver!' 'I think so, hope so. If it is, be at the far end of the garden just before dawn next day. Climb the wall, so that you can help me over, and lie flat, then no one will see you in the dusk. Now, good-bye. Thank you, over and over again. And be careful—don't get caught.'

Swiftly I rose and went back to my followers. Nannie looked at me in amazement: 'Whatever did you find to say, in all that time?' she whispered. 'I was seeking counsel,' I replied primly, using one of Aunt Chiara's favourite phrases.

43

As it was a feast day I went to dine at my grandfather's house. I seemed to be dancing on air; my taffeta skirt swished round me like a butterfly's wings. I was walking so fast that Nannie and Serafina panted behind me.

At table, Guido and I laughed and talked together. He told me about the falcon he was training, and I told him about my garden and my songs. At first Uncle Ostasio frowned down the table at us, but as the meal progressed, something of the weight of grief and vengeance seemed to lift from his soul. I caught a glimpse of the gay young man who had, only a few years before, caught me to his saddle-bow, given me sweets and a golden coin. My grandfather was already in Florence and Lamberto was also away. Without them, the rest of the family seemed less constrained. Even Maddalena, now the strictest of the Polentani, no longer thought it her duty to look miserable. I thought: how glad Mother would be—I know she doesn't want us to go on being unhappy about her for ever.

Before we rose from table, Guido said in a low voice: 'I wonder why I ever thought you weren't pretty,

Concordia—today you look lovely.' 'You have never seen me really happy before,' I said.

Afterwards, we all went to rest. In Samaritana's absence I could have used her bedroom—my mother's room. But that was just where anyone would look for me, and I knew I must read my father's letter undisturbed. So, on an impulse, I stole upstairs to the 'punishment room', where no one would expect me to be. It was locked, of course, but the key was in the door, so I went in and, as a precaution, relocked it on the inside. Then I opened the shutters and, with trembling fingers, took out my scroll.

Father had evidently foreseen that Marco might be intercepted, for there was no name on the outside, nor was the seal stamped with the Malatesta crest, but just pinched between finger and thumb. The marks brought up a vivid remembrance of my father's hands—those fine, strong hands that were almost his only claim to beauty. Wishing to keep the seal intact, I broke the cord by rubbing it on a window-bar, then unrolled the parchment and began to read the cramped, untidy scrawl. Dear Father, how he hates writing! Not that he finds it difficult; simply, he thinks so quickly that he is impatient because his pen will not keep pace with his brain.

Every word of that letter remains stamped on my memory. It was written very cautiously, with no names mentioned, and without any introduction or signature:

They tell me you have been ill, and I fear it is my fault. They say, too, that you want to have nothing more to do with me; but that I do not believe, unless people have given you a false report about what I did. I have taught you to think for yourself and, young as you are, you are capable of forming your own judgement. So I am going to ask you four questions, and your answers to them mean a great deal to me.

Firstly, how much do you know, or what have you been told, about the action that has broken up our family life?

Secondly, can you find it in your heart to forgive me?

Thirdly, will you come back to me? And before you answer this, I want you to realise one thing: as soon as possible, I intend to marry the woman you know about. The necessary indulgences will cost a great deal, I fear; but everything in this world can be arranged—at a price. It will be hard for you, I know, to accept her; but remember, I am marrying the mother of my sons, for their sake and my family's. In all my life I have only loved, and shall only love, one woman. No one else will ever replace her in my heart. But, my darling, if one is to go on living, one must come to terms with life.

Fourthly, if you cannot decide at once, will you at least come to see me and let me tell you exactly what happened, and why? As you can well imagine, I cannot come to you, but I am not far away. You can be with me in a couple of hours, and if in the end you decide not to stay, your absence may pass unnoticed, or at most will be excused as a childish escapade.

Think very carefully, my dear. Remember, your whole future depends upon your answer. And remember, too, that I want to do my best for you, but it may be difficult. Compounding this affair has cost me a good deal: I have had to renounce some part of your mother's dowry, and the rest has passed into your grandfather's hands. He is fond of you, though, and I think that, if we found you a suitable husband, he might relinquish some part of it. Remember that you will always be welcome in my home—and, of course, to my new wife.

(These last words, from the way they were spaced, had evidently been added as an afterthought.)

That moment should have been one of absolute happiness, but it was not. I felt like a prisoner who sees the locked doors swing open: nothing stands between him and freedom except one thin strand of cobweb, yet he is powerless to lift his hand and brush it away. What was it that held me back? Fear, jealousy, conscience . . .?

For the first time in months, I saw him put his foot on

my mother's still living breast; saw him carrying her body away, to cast into the traitors' well. And I thought: if we all meet in that Hell to which the Polentani would consign us, and I am hand-in-hand with *him*, there will be reproach in her eyes.

That was foolish, I knew. Was it possible that I had not really forgiven him, fully and freely, as I had done from the first? After all, I argued with myself, he had acted entirely within his rights: if he had not killed Paolo, he would have been shamed for ever in his own eyes, and ridiculous in those of everyone else. And my mother's death, I knew, had been accidental.

Once more I read his letter, phrase by phrase, word by word, and then I realised what was wrong. If he had said: 'I want you', 'I need you', or 'I miss you'; if Marco's story had shown him as a sick and shaken man, weighed down by remorse and the memory of his dead, then I would have brushed away that spider-thread of conscience and run straight out into his arms. But I could see, even through the guarded words of his letter, that, if he wanted me back, it was for my sake rather than his own. He had evidently, as he said, 'come to terms with life'. Perhaps his own physical tragedy had struck him so young that, after it, nothing could penetrate the armour with which he defended his spirit.

And he had his Ginevra—his 'dark Romagnola, faithful and loving'—who wanted to do everything for him and was jealous even of his servants. How much more so would she be of me! That was one thing my mother's physical repulsion from him had spared me; any jealousy she showed was not of his love for me but of mine for him, and that only because she thought (perhaps rightly) that it was love drawn away from herself. Father was undoubtedly uneasy. He would not have thought it necessary to add that 'of course' Ginevra would welcome me if he had really taken it for granted.

With a dreadful clarity I saw that I must do nothing to spoil the marriage that might be a compensation for the years of torment through which he had passed. If I came home and, in pain or trouble, he turned to me, then Ginevra would be resentful. And if we two started quarrelling, he would feel bound to side with one or the other, and that would make matters worse. He was still protesting that he did not love her, but by this time she has evidently become part of his life, a necessary habit. I know now the dangers of a marriage in which only one partner loves the other. If Ginevra came to feel herself the unloved one, there might be scene after scene, like the one Marco had described to me.

If I were to marry very soon, that would solve the difficulty; but here again I could see that Father was uneasy about my dowry. Ginevra would look on it as money robbed from her own children; and Father had obviously been made to pay heavily for the necessary absolution from blood-guilt that would enable him to marry her. There would be fresh quarrels about that.

I closed the shutters and lay down with shut eyes and clenched fists, fighting a battle with myself. Gradually the dreadful thought shaped itself in my brain: *I could not, must not, go back to him.* What then remained for me? Remorselessly, I had to answer: the Polentani and the convent.

Then came a flicker of doubt. Was I destroying my own life, just because I was jealous of Ginevra? Father had taught me to be honest with myself, so I thought this over for a long while. No, if Ginevra had been a mere parasite, interested only in marrying one of the rich and powerful lords of Romagna, I would have gone home and fought her. I am certainly not the type to let myself be ousted by any stepmother. But, by all accounts, she was slavishly devoted to him, and he, even if he did not love her, at least seemed to be finding consolation in her society. What he needed now was to forget the past, to build a new life with his young family, not to see daily the grey eyes and fair hair that would remind him of what he had lost.

For months past, Aunt Chiara had been dinning into my ears the word 'sacrifice'. I saw no reason why I should sacrifice myself to God in whose name the Polentani were determined to ruin my life; but for my father, whom I loved, I could do it: I must and would do it.

There is little more to say. I would have liked to write a long letter, telling my father why I would not come. But what use would that be? It would only leave him with a sense of resentment against Ginevra, which was just what I was trying to avoid. Or he might expose Marco to the risk of coming back again, to persuade me to change my mind; and if he did that, my resolution would give way. So, before the others were astir after their siesta, I went down to the library, took ink-horn and quill, and wrote in the small space left on Father's letter the answer to his questions. Against the first: 'Everything—I watched it happen.' To the second I replied unhesitatingly: 'Yes.' Indeed I forgave him. I knew he had done right. Then, forcing the pen that seemed reluctant to move over the paper, to the last two questions I answered: 'No'. Imagining my father's reaction when he saw his own letter returned with these curt additions, I added in a tiny space left at the bottom: 'But I love you as dearly as ever, and I always shall.'

Early next morning, at the cuckoo's nest, I spoke to the gardener's boy, saying: 'A mendicant friar will be calling here. Yesterday I promised him fruit from our garden. Fill this basket with cherries and bring it to me. And let me know when the man comes—I will give it to him myself.'

The boy, I knew, was dim-witted: he would not notice or report anything. And indeed, all went smoothly. I cut off a slip of black ribbon and put it with the letter into the filled basket; then I hovered near the door until I heard the bell. As the boy opened it, I pushed the basket into Marco's hands, very slightly shaking my head. His blue eyes shot me a look of reproach and disappointment. 'Contessina . . .' he began. But I could not risk having my resolution shaken. I fled back to the house and the boy closed the door.

Later that morning I went to the convent. I said: 'Aunt Chiara, you were right. This world is not for me.'

44

The news of my 'conversion' was received with general satisfaction. Only Uncle Ostasio asked, a trifle suspiciously, what had made me change my mind so suddenly. I told him that a mendicant friar had advised me to go to confession, and that the priest had made me see the error of my ways. My uncle muttered something about giving a good present to that priest, and that alarmed me. What if he made inquiries at the church? Someone would know that the second confessional on the left was hardly ever used, and Serafina might have said that this was the one to which I had gone. However, it did not matter much: there was no means of connecting Marco with the affair, and he would already be far away. Aunt Chiara would probably declare that it was a miracle, and that the confessor had been my guardian angel.

I reflected that among the tough Malatesti I had learned to hold my tongue, but I had been essentially honest, not the liar and hypocrite that the pious Polentani were making me. My life was becoming a web of petty deceits.

Even to write this story I have had to use stratagems. I have heard there is a new substance called paper, much lighter and cheaper than parchment; but I do not know how to buy any and, if I made inquiries, it would be reported to my uncle. So I had to have a book, and an inconspicuous one. At the convent I had seen the copy-books in which the pupils learn to write and, later, copy out pious maxims and prayers. That was just what I wanted. So, calling at the convent, I asked Sister Angelica if I could have one. Then for the first time I realised that, here, I was a privileged person. They had caught me at last, but they meant to make their trap so attractive that I would not try to escape. The Sister made no difficulties, in fact she would have come with me to the storeroom, but I begged her not to disturb herself; if she would give me the key, Rosanna could show me where the books were kept. She replied that books given out had to be entered in a register, but I assured her that I would do this myself and, as she was busy with the pupils, she gladly agreed. With Rosanna I knew I could do whatever I liked. I easily distracted her attention while I took two books, wrapping them in the cloth I had brought with me for the purpose. For one of them I signed in my own name; then, in case there was any control between the register and the stores, I altered a previous entry from 5 to 6, so that the results would be correct and Rosanna would not get into trouble.

This done, I took the opportunity of asking where Adalgisa was, since I had not seen her on my last two visits. Rosanna's usually cheerful face fell. She looked round to see that there was no one near and said, dropping her voice: 'You won't tell anyone I told you?' 'Of course not—but you haven't told me anything yet.' 'It's too dreadful, Contessina.' 'Why—she's not dead?' Rosanna nodded. 'How?' I asked quickly. 'She threw herself into the well, the day before she was to take the vows.' Her voice was trembling. 'It was I who found her. I had to get up an hour earlier than the others, to draw water.' 'How is it my aunt didn't tell me? There must have been a fearful scandal.' 'No, I went straight to the Mother Superior . . .' (That was sensible of her, I thought—most girls would have run screaming all over the place.) '. . . and she and I and Anna, the portress, managed to pull her out. The Mother Superior made us carry her to the garden shed; then she locked it and made us swear not to tell anyone. She gave Anna a present and told her to go to her family, just outside the town, and not come back for three days. I was crying and upset, so she kept me in her room all day, in case the others saw me. And everything went on just as usual; the normal services, and the preparations for the vow-taking next day. That night I went back to the dormitory, but you know there is a silence rule, so no one could ask me what I had been doing. Next morning I got up early as usual, and there was a place at the foot of the garden, near the foot of the wall, where someone had been digging. The Mother Superior must have had someone brought in during the night to do it.'

I was gazing at her incredulously: 'But surely someone asked after Adalgisa?' I said. 'What did they tell them?' 'Oh, just that she had refused to take the vows and had been sent away in disgrace.' 'And her people?' Rosanna looked at me in some distress and answered hesitantly: 'I heard the Mother Superior dictating a letter to someone from outside, whose face I didn't know, saying that Adalgisa had died of a fever. But Contessina, how could she do that? It wasn't true—and holy women don't tell lies.' 'Apparently they do,' I commented: 'Or perhaps the Mother Superior isn't as holy as you think her.' And I thought bitterly to myself: 'If I were to commit suicide in here, I wonder whether my father or my Grandfather Malatesta would claim my body, or would they just leave me in a hole in the garden?' But then I reflected that, to avoid scandal, my Polentani relatives would insist upon my being buried with due formalities in the nuns' cemetery, as if I had in fact died of a fever.

Rosanna was looking at me anxiously, afraid that she had said too much. 'You won't give me away?' she asked. 'No, I've already promised not to, and you can trust my word.' '*I* promised not to tell,' said Rosanna candidly, 'And I haven't until now.' 'Why did you tell me?' She coloured up: 'You are a lady, and yet you are kind to me: you helped me with my horse.' I laughed and patted her shoulder. When the prison doors close on me, I know she will be my ally.

Since then, I have been writing diligently for over two months. Each morning I go out to an arbour in the garden that has a stone table in it, taking a prayer-book and one copybook with me. I copy out a prayer, spacing it as largely as possible; then I pull out the second copybook from a hiding place, and begin to write my story in a close, fine hand. Nannie and Serafina cannot read, of course, so when I come in I leave the copybook with the prayers about, for anyone to see. Once it disappeared, and, when I asked for it, Serafina said I must have left it in the garden. Later I found it there, in a spot where I would never have thought of searching, had she not called my attention to it. I gave her a long look, saying that I hoped my Uncle Ostasio had been content with my pious exercises. Like most women, she does not understand sarcasm, but I think she knew that I knew where that book had been. At any rate she avoided my gaze.

Now I have only a few days left. Adalgisa's death has been a blow, for she and I might have been some comfort to each other in our mutual desolation. Aunt Chiara, dear little soul, can be of no help whatever, and Samaritana is at Cunio. I have begged Uncle Ostasio to invite her to the birthday-party that he is giving for me, and to ask her to come without fail.

There will be no dancing at the party, for there are still several days to go before the anniversary of my mother's death, when the family will go out of mourning; but there will be a banquet and an entertainment. Uncle Ostasio, I suspect, will make a little speech, congratulating me upon having chosen the highest way of life. And I—I am Concordia Malatesta, Gianciotto's daughter, so I must hold up my head and smile.

That night I shall share Samaritana's room, and then I will give her this book and ask her to keep it safely. If she hears I am dead (and I hope I shall die soon, as a wild bird does if one shuts it up in a cage), then let her send it to my father. I would like him to know that I have not renounced my life through weakness, or fear, or over-persuasion, but in order not to risk ruining his own last chance of happiness.

And if he, too, by that time should be dead, let her send it to Pandolfo (but perhaps she had better tear out the pages about my last meeting with him: he might not understand that, after all, I am still very, very fond of him). Of one thing I am certain: the Malatesti must have it. I must bear witness for my father, make sure that his name goes down to future generations with no stain upon it, even though by so doing I have had to tell the truth about my mother.

I am writing these last few words in the library of the Polenta house. Now I shall go and put on the splendid gown that I have had made for this occasion—all green and gold brocade, like the mosaics of San Vitale—the gown that I shall wear only twice: tonight, and the day on which I take my vows and am stripped of everything lovely.

Oh, world—free world of mountains, restless waves and limitless sands, resin-scented pinewoods and the vast plain of Romagna . . . oh, Rimini, oh, my beautiful Gradara—places I have loved and shall see no more . . . And, dearest of all, my father. Be happy, Father—do not let me feel that I have cast away my life in vain.

EPILOGUE

Bronze head and golden head bent together over the last page of the book that Isotta had brought back with her finished copy. It was the end of a very pleasant task—a task that had furnished the excuse for her to come to Sigismond's house every afternoon and read him the pages that she had copied during the previous evening.

Today they were sitting closer than usual, his arm around her shoulders. There was no fear that they would be disturbed, for Ginevra lay in labour and the devoted Orsola would certainly not leave her until she was safely delivered.

Sigismond's fine, strong fingers played lightly over the faded page. 'Concordia said that, after her mother's death, she never wept,' he remarked with a whimsical smile, 'but she was crying when she finished her story—look at those tear-stains.'

'It was I who cried,' confessed Isotta, a little shamefacedly. 'I've grown very fond of Concordia, as though she were my sister—my twin sister, almost. You see, I'm an only daughter too, though I have a brother, and I'm very fond of my father. I know just how she felt.' 'How would your father feel, if he knew about—us?' She reflected an instant, then said shrewdly: 'But there's nothing to know, yet, is there?' At that he laughed, pulled her round and pressed his lips to hers, in one of those fierce kisses that no longer startled her. 'There will be, soon,' he said. 'Grow up quickly for me, Isotta.' She nodded gravely and answered his former question: 'He will be angry at first. But, after all, you are a great lord, and he will soon realise that you have honoured him by choosing his daughter.'

And her limpid eyes gazed at him with the innocence of a child and the courage of a woman.

Sigismond was still playing idly with the book, when suddenly he gave an exclamation: 'Look! The last page has been stuck down on the cover, perhaps with damp or perhaps intentionally. I wonder if there is anything underneath?' He unsheathed his dagger and, using its tip as delicately as a woman does her embroidery needle, gradually prised up the page. There *was* something underneath: a note written in fresher ink and with a firmer hand—a man's handwriting.

Here ends the first volume of my mother's life story. It was given me, with its companion, by my dear master Pandolfo when I came of age. I have kept the books all these years, while I worked in Messer Galeotto's library. Now he too is dead and his son Pandolfo is still too young to be troubled with this dark story of the past. Yet I feel that this is a story he and future generations should read—if only to clear my grandfather's memory. So, without telling Pandolfo the contents of these books, I have put them back on the shelves for some future Malatesta to find. All whom they mention are dead now except me, and I am an old man who cannot live much longer. God have mercy on their souls, for if they sinned they also suffered.

It was signed simply with the initials G.P.M. and bore the date 1385.

'His mother!' gasped Isotta, 'But she was a nun.' 'The two things aren't mutually exclusive,' remarked Sigismond drily. 'But, like you, I've grown fond of Concordia. I hope no canting priest fathered a bastard on that fine Malatesta girl.' 'Bastard? Perhaps she got a dispensation from her vows and married someone.' 'I think not. That "M" must stand for Malatesta—his mother's name. In fact, I seem vaguely to have heard rumours of some Malatesta bastard who was my Grandfather Galeotto's librarian. My father as a small boy was very fond of him and gave him employment after my grandfather's death. By then he was a lame old man with snow-white hair, but they said he had once been very handsome.'

Together, they considered the initials: ' "G", most certainly Giovanni, her father whom she loved so much. But "P" . . .?' 'Paolo?' suggested Isotta helpfully. 'No, she'd hardly have called her child after the man who had broken up her home and ruined her prospects in life. More likely Pandolfo. She was obviously fond of him, and he seems to have been more than fond of her.' Then an idea struck him: 'I wonder if . . .?' 'Oh, no!' protested Isotta, horrified, 'He was her uncle.' 'Only a step-uncle, and not much older than herself. Well, you must find that second book, and then we shall see. I would like to know what happened to Concordia. She made a brave fight against the entire Polenta family. It is a pity they broke her down in the end.' 'I don't think they did,' said Isotta reflectively. 'She decided of her own free will, because she thought it would help her father.' 'Yes, but she might not have done, if they hadn't kept insisting on the virtue of self-sacrifice. That's the weak point of you women—always wanting to sacrifice yourselves, from Iphigenia onwards. If not to God, it's to some man or other.' There was a twinkle in Isotta's eyes as she asked: 'Wouldn't you like me to sacrifice myself to you?' 'I would *not*.' Sigismond's flat denial took her aback, but her wounded pride was soothed when he added: 'I would like you to give me all that you have and are, but not as a sacrifice. Do it gladly, girl, gladly, because you want me as much as I want you—and I promise you, you'll enjoy it. We'll go down to history as one of the immortal pairs of lovers. I'll see to it that no one remembers me without thinking of you.'

Impetuously, he scrawled his monogram on a piece of paper—that SI that stood for the first syllable of his name. 'You see, intertwined—Sigismond and Isotta. When I chose that sign I didn't know what it was destined to mean, but now I do. Our lives are joined together as inseparably as those two letters.'

He had never spoken to her so frankly and freely of his love, and she watched him, wide-eyed, rapt. He took her in his arms—not violently, as he so often did, but very gently, almost solemnly, and kissed her softly on the lips. They stayed there entranced, and it seemed to them that time and eternity had blended in one moment of supreme revelation.

Then an interruption brought them suddenly back to earth. Sigismond had barely time to release her before Madonna Orsola, flushed and triumphant as though she herself had achieved something, burst into the room to announce: 'My lord—you have a son!'

Sigismond laughed. It was partly a reaction to her over-dramatic tone, partly the natural satisfaction of a man who has, after some years of marriage, at last achieved a legitimate heir. Of course, now and again a woman had come to him with a brat on her arm that he could not positively swear was not his, but he dealt with this very simply. If the child was male, he would give her a couple of gold coins and tell her to bring it back in seven years' time, when he would be able to see if it had Malatesta blood or not. If it was female, all the woman got was a silver coin, a meal in the kitchen, and a warning not to come back or she would be whipped.

Meanwhile, Isotta stood, embarrassed. Had they been alone, she would have kissed him spontaneously on the cheek and said: 'Oh, my dear, I'm glad!' but in front of Madonna Orsola this was impossible. At her governess's reproof: 'Come, Isotta, where are your manners?' she dropped a little curtsy and said: 'I congratulate Your Excellence most heartily,' blushing at Sigismond's satiric expression.

'Well,' he said, 'I must go and see if my dear wife has whelped me a lion-cub or a rabbit—the latter, I'm inclined to suspect.' 'But, my lord,' said Madonna Orsola, a trifle reproachfully, 'How can you tell, when he is scarcely born?' 'I can hear whether he is roaring the place down—as, I am told, I did when I first began to breathe—or whimpering like a new-born kitten. And I'll put my finger into his mouth, to feel whether he tries to bite me.'

With his leopard-like movements Sigismond crossed the room, unlocked an iron door in the wall and took out a small coffer filled with jewels. 'Madonna Ginevra deserves a present,' he said, spilling the contents out on to a table. 'Come and help me choose her something, Isotta.' He no longer troubled to conceal from Madonna Orsola his use of her first name, reflected the girl, watching him pick out a chain of rubies set in heavy gold, which had at once caught his eye. 'This?' he suggested. Isotta shook her head: 'It is very splendid but far too . . .' she hesitated for a word: 'too blatant for Madonna Ginevra. Her type of looks needs something subtler and more delicate.'

And she herself selected two pieces. One, that delighted her, was a necklet of life-size daisies, their centres made of topaz and their petals of mother-of-pearl tipped with tiny pieces of ruby. The other was a silver clasp, representing a basket of wild flowers, with leaves enamelled in delicate shades of green and gold. 'That,' she said with conviction, 'reminds me of your wife.' He nodded, a sarcastic smile curving his lips: 'Yes, poor little thing! This isn't a world in which miniature flowers can survive.' Carelessly, he picked up the clasp, threw the rest back into the coffer, and then impulsively snatched the necklet upon which Isotta's fingers had lingered. 'You liked this one,' he remarked, 'I'll take it too.' His eyes met hers, and Isotta knew that it was not for Ginevra he had kept that chain. She thought: 'I wonder how, and when, he will give it to me? Oh dear, what a pity I shan't be able to show it.' Her hand went instinctively to the spot where, hidden under her dress, she could feel the medallion he had given her on her birthday.

Meanwhile, Sigismond had raced upstairs, followed at a distance by the panting Madonna Orsola. Isotta, left alone, felt increasingly forlorn as the minutes passed. Ginevra, she felt, had given Sigismond something that she herself had not, and now would never be able to do. Even if in future years she bore him a son, it would not be his first. For the time being, he had forgotten her. His visit to his wife had been brief, and now he was racing round giving orders. Isotta could hear him in the hall, shouting something about bonfires and free wine.

Stifling an impulse to cry, she turned resolutely to the bookshelves. Not for the first time she was playing a curious game with herself, a kind of challenge to Fate. 'If I find that second book, then one day I shall be his love; if not, he will forget all about me, or my father will make me marry someone else.' It was absurd, she knew, to make so much depend upon so little; but to find the book seemed to her at that moment vital, essential, and wellnigh impossible. All summer she had worked steadily, arranging and cataloguing the motley heap of books turned out of the coffers in which they had lain so long. She knew for a fact that there was no second book of similar size and shape to the first. Every single volume had passed through her hands and had been placed by her in its appropriate category: Greek and Latin works (these were the majority); Law and Philosophy; Chronicles, Religion (a great number of these, but all, she had noticed, so beautifully clean that they had evidently seldom been read), and Romances. These last opened very easily; some had even fallen apart at a touch. They were probably the favourite literature of the ladies of the family. Though she knew it was useless, Isotta took down every book that she could not identify at first sight.

After a fruitless hour her heart was heavy and her slim

fingers were grey with dust. She was on the point of giving up, when the mishap occurred: trying impatiently to push a book back into an overcrowded shelf, she dislodged some old accounts ledgers from Verucchio, and they fell in an untidy pile at her feet. It was the last straw. Isotta stamped her foot and burst into angry, childish tears.

Then quick shame made her pull herself together. What if Sigismond were to come in and find her crying like a baby? She wiped her eyes with the back of her hand, heedless of the smudge of dirt that was left on her cheek. Then, sullenly, she picked the books up, one by one. It struck her that she had never really examined them—she ought at least to arrange them in date order. They seemed to have lasted a long time—about ten years each—and were in a variety of handwritings. The earliest dated from 1266; it must have been started by Margherita dei Paltanieri when she came as a young bride to Verucchio. The last one, dated 1307, had only a few entries, written at irregular intervals, as though no one had bothered to keep proper accounts. All but the first three or four pages were blank.

Having put the books in order, Isotta began to return them to the shelf, but she was still struggling to pack them into an inadequate space. The last three slipped out of her hands and fell hard on to the floor. With a cry of exasperation she stooped to pick them up; then her heart gave a leap. The last book had fallen open, upside-down, and she saw that it had been started again from the far end; its pages were covered with a fine handwriting—one that she knew. Yet there was something different about it. Yes, it was Concordia's writing, but larger, much less finicking. Isotta puzzled for a while over this and then guessed the reason: the writing was more mature, and the writer was no longer trying to compress a great deal into a very small compass, she was writing fast and fluently. Now it was time she lacked, not space.

Eagerly, Isotta took the book to the light and turned

to the cover. On it was written, in the same handwriting as the note signed 'G.P.M.' another entry: 'The second part of my mother's life story, written at Verucchio during the summer of 1308.'

Now Isotta no longer felt forlorn. Her weariness and ill-temper forgotten, she gathered up the book and went to fetch her cloak. Her father would scold her, of course, for having ventured to cross the road without being escorted by her governess; but the baby's birth would serve to excuse any minor breach of etiquette. She wanted to get home as quickly as possible, before Sigismond saw that book. 'I'll not tell him about it till I've finished reading it,' she said to herself. Now she was confident. Fate was on her side. One day, she knew, Sigismond would be hers, and nothing but death would divide them.